LOST ANF FOUND

RUBY JEAN JENSEN

Gayle J. Foster

BABY'S FIRST STEPS

The fear she had first felt when she woke came back and moved over her with coldness beyond anything she had known since that last night in the woods. She stood still, wishing now that she had called Daniel, that she had turned on lights, that she had dialed the emergency number for help.

Pat, pat, pat...

Soft footsteps in the kitchen, running. Across the tiled floor. Barefoot. It was like Sheena running, or Ward. Yet oddly, instead of coming to the door in the hall, they went in the opposite direction. For a moment, as Magret held her breath, there was silence.

Then she heard the thud of the back door closing.

She stood only a moment longer, before she walked boldly into the kitchen, puzzled and disturbed at the sounds she had heard.

She turned on the kitchen light.

Nothing in the kitchen looked as if it had been disturbed.

She went to the back door, the one that led out onto a terrace at the rear of the house.

The door was still locked.

First printing: June, 1990 in the United States of America

Published by: Gayle J. Foster Carrollton, Texas

Library of Congress Control Number: 2021905446

Cover art: SelfPubBookCovers.com/ Viergacht

❀ Created with Vellum

PROLOGUE

She was standing in a darkness through which no object was visible, as if the darkness came from within herself, a blindness of the soul or spirit, a black world filled with significance. Fear seemed at first to be her sole companion. But then the light began, slow, gray, a penetrating of the dark like the coming of a distant dawn, and she could see figures around her.

This world which surrounded her was filled with black, thick pillars, fluted, like ancient ruins of an Athens temple. The blackish fog curled slowly around them, and she lifted her hand to clear her eyes. Fear choked her. There was something here that was a terrible menace to her. The dark? The gray, dim light from an invisible source beyond? The pillars—?

Then she saw they were not pillars, they were the thick trunks of immense trees. She was in a forest.

She tried to scream, to run away, but she couldn't move or make a sound. She had meant never to come here again. What was she doing here?

Something at her feet was moving.

She stared downward, and saw clearly the cracking of the soil of the forest floor. It started with a bulging upward, of something buried beginning to rise.

In horror she watched the soil split open in three lines, star-shaped. The center bulge rose and a small object, pale and round, began emerging.

The head of a dead infant lifted slowly, dark soil falling away from the delicate features of its face, black soil clinging in grains to the creases of its closed eyes, outlining the tiny budlike nose, the corners of the mouth. She could see the creases in its neck, dark with the soil in which it had been buried.

As she watched, paralyzed with her horror and fear, the body rose from the ground, and she saw the bent legs, like the legs of a doll, and the tiny toes—and the hands—and the narrow chest stained from its burial. It lay with its face upward, head slightly back.

Then she saw its eyes were open and looking at her.

It was beginning to smile now, to widen the mouth, its lips parting.

The mouth was filled with pointed, needle-sharp teeth.

The widening of the mouth was not a smile.

It was rising, coming toward her, and the eyes were reptilian. The legs and arms were beginning to move.

It was rising. Pushing itself up.

She screamed, and her head exploded with sound.

Something had hold of her, pinning her arms to her sides, to something at her back.

"Magret! Maggie! Wake up."

The face of her husband became suddenly visible as her world lightened, and she blinked at her surroundings.

The bedroom, the familiar furniture, the French doors that led out onto the balcony at the back of the house, the draperies, floral, picking up the rose and gold of the bedroom colors, pulled back, letting in a pale outdoor glow from the moonlit night—it was all there, blessedly familiar and safe. Her haven.

Daniel sat up and turned on the bedside lamp, then he got out of bed and started toward the bathroom. He was a short, round, sturdy man, already balding when she'd married him seventeen years ago. She felt vastly relieved just looking at him. He had always been able to fix everything, hadn't he? Even from this—even from a nightmare such as this one—he had awakened her, brought her out of it.

"That must have been quite a dream," he said, going into the bath and turning on a light there. The door swung slowly shut behind him, not quite closing. "What were you dreaming?"

"Nothing. I—don't remember."

Magret pulled her feet out of bed onto the thick carpet and sat for a moment looking at the French doors. The room's interior was reflected there now in the small panes, and she saw the corner of the dresser, and the green leaves of the tall potted plant. She looked at everything with thankfulness, seeing the reality of her world so different from that terrible nightmare.

She stood up and went out into the hall, her pale blue nightgown whispering along the floor at her feet. One by one she checked the rooms of the children. Ward, eleven, was consumed by cars. Over his bed were posters of antique cars, a '29 Packard, a Model T Ford, others, sculptured metal to her.

She crossed the hall. Leigh, now sixteen, had wanted her own room, and had taken over the guest room. Next door to her was the bedroom she had once shared with her baby sister, Sheena.

The nine-year-old's interests were displayed on the chest and dresser and desk, not on the wall. Sheena was emphatic about her decorations, with delicate taste of her own. She tended to be nineteenth centuryish, it seemed to Magret, ladylike and proper. Obedient. A perfect daughter. Her pale hair, carefully curled that morning, was tousled on the pillow.

Magret stood in the hall. She had been a good mother, hadn't she? She had read all the books, gone to all the meetings, even taken courses at the local college on child psychology and parenting. She had been a good mother, an exemplary mother, hadn't she?

Then why in God's name had she been having the same nightmare lately, over and over, a nightmare she hadn't told anyone about, would never, could never tell anyone about?

Three times, in the last month.

Three times.

They were coming closer and closer now, deep in the night, each time the same so that even during the day she could see that tiny head rising out of the soil, and that face turning toward her, that mouth with its terrible widening.

The teeth.

Rows of sharp, pointed teeth, like the teeth of baby sharks.

She was afraid to go back to bed, to try to sleep. Even with Daniel there, her Rock of Gibraltar, she was afraid to sleep.

She was so thankful to be awake, to see that her family was well and safe, that her life was beautiful, that her bedroom doors opened out onto a second-floor balcony, and the yard below was green and lush, and beginning now to be spotted with orange and yellow leaves.

The fall ... the forest ...

... the forest floor, with its carpet of autumn leaves as winter approached.

She had meant never to go back there.

CHAPTER 1

"I CAN'T GO," Sheena said, looking into the darkness of the woods with curiosity and a little quiver of dread. Mama had always warned her, when Sheena came out to the edge of town to visit Wendy or her cousin, Peggy, never to go into the woods, and she never had, though she had always looked that way and wondered about the woods. The forest, Wendy called it, for after all, it went all the way to the mountains, she said. Which, for Sheena, made it all the more mysterious and frightening.

Wendy's face scrunched in impatience and disgust, the way it could when she was crossed. Sheena switched from looking into the shadowed trees to looking at her best friend, outside of Peggy. She knew what Wendy was going to do next. She'd sigh deeply. She always did when she was getting impatient.

Wendy sighed. "Why not, Sheena? You came home with me to gather leaves for class. Leaves of maple, oak, sassafras, hickory—" She was counting them off on her fingers.

"Three kinds of oak," Peggy said. She began hopping around in a circle on one foot, waiting to go into the woods. "Pin oak, because it turns dark red. And soft maple because it's yellow."

"Hickory is yellow," Sheena supplied, beginning to feel guilty for holding this important school project back.

She had known when Wendy asked her to come home on the bus with her and Peggy, who lived just around the bend in the road, even farther toward the hills, and closer into the forest than Wendy, that it was to gather leaves. She had wanted to come so badly she hadn't really, not really, thought about having to go into the woods.

Mrs. Whitney, their teacher, had listed nine different local species of trees whose leaves turned to brilliant colors in the fall. In her pocket, Sheena had a sheet of paper, just like all the other kids in the fourth grade, with descriptions of the leaves that were to be brought in. The neater the arrangement, the better it was displayed and cataloged, the higher the score. Besides, they were going to be displayed, with each student's name, in the hallways of the Dixieland Mall.

"You've got to come," Wendy said. "And if you don't hurry and come on, it will be getting late. And dark. And Islan has to take you home before dark. Come on, Sheena!"

Sheena stood still on the edge of the curling road of blacktop that led from the street where Wendy lived to the more desolate area where Peggy lived. On each side of the road, some of them fronting people's yards, were trees of all sizes, and now, with autumn, all colors from brown to red to green.

"Why can't we find the leaves here, on the road?" She looked at her sheet of paper, but saw only the patterns of leaves, some of them lobed many times, some of them the shape of teardrops and not lobed at all. There was no picture of individual trees.

Peggy asked, "Why *can't* you go into the woods, Sheena? I play there all the time. There's a path between my house and Wendy's. I walk it every day."

"Mama said never to go into the woods."

Wendy demanded, *"Why?"*

"I don't know," Sheena had to admit.

Wendy was getting mad, and Sheena felt rejected. Wendy could turn such a cold shoulder when she got mad. Her pale, lightly freckled face looked pink, her mouth pursed and red, almost as if she wore lipstick. She heaved another exaggerated sigh and took hold of Peggy's arm.

"I wonder why I even asked you to come home with me, Sheena. You say your mama doesn't let you go into the woods, but you don't even know why. Come on, Peggy, we'll go get leaves for ourselves. You can stay here and wait, Sheena, or you can go on back to the house and stay with my sister."

Sheena watched them go beneath the trees. Peggy glanced back at her once, and Sheena saw her cousin's reluctance to leave. But then she turned her head away and took a few running steps to catch up with Wendy. Sheena watched her dark, glossy braid, the end of a single French braid, bouncing on her back. She saw Wendy reach out, clasp Peggy's arm, and pull her out of sight behind the huge trunk of a tree.

Around Sheena leaves fell, almost like a rain, coming down with whispers and settling on the black surface of the road. Sheena looked at them with little interest. Her best friend, and her best cousin, had gone off and left her, and she had to stay here and wait, or go back to the house where Islan, Wendy's sister, would probably be on the telephone talking to other teenagers like her own sister, Leigh, now that she had a private phone in her private room. Not that Sheena begrudged Leigh her private room. That meant that she had a bedroom all to herself now, too, and that wasn't so bad. Not as bad as she had feared it would be.

She picked up a leaf. It was lobed, like the shape of the white oak leaf on her instruction sheet. But it was mottled brown, not brilliant as the leaves she had to gather.

Were the leaves in the forest fresher? More colorful? If Wendy and Peggy went into the woods without anything terrible happening to them, why couldn't she?

Her mother's voice came back to her, almost as if she spoke just over her shoulder. "Yes, you can go out to Wendy's, but don't go into the woods."

"But Mama, we're supposed to collect leaves. Nine different kinds, and some of them are forest trees."

"Forest trees grow along the sides of the roads, too, and also, we've got lots of trees in our backyard. Look there."

"Yes, Mama."

Sheena heard a car and stepped off the road and behind a tree. At home, on her street, she was used to cars. But out here—it was different. Other times, when she had stayed with Peggy, she had learned to get away from the road when a car came along. The bicycle had to be pulled over and stopped on the grassy verge or even in the ditch to let the car go by. And if the car stopped, you became very cautious. These people were often strangers, lots of them hunters, Peggy said, going into the mountains to hunt deer, or even bear, and wanted directions. But still, you never talked to strangers. And Sheena was afraid of people who killed animals. Who carried guns.

The automobile came closer and became a red pickup truck. Rifles were in a rack over the back window, and the driver wore a bright orange cap. He drove with one hand at the top of the steering wheel and his elbow out the window. She saw his profile as he roared past, but he didn't see her. She stayed safely behind the tree until she heard the sound of his truck fade to a moan around the next bend.

There was a noise behind her, and Sheena whirled. She squinted into the shadowy world of the edge of the forest. The floor seemed to be alive with green vines, and the falling of the leaves, a gentle pecking like rain.

Then suddenly a figure leaped out at her from behind a tree, making a terrible, deep-in-the-throat noise, and Sheena screamed, her hands jerking to her cheeks, cold palms pressing against her chilled face.

Wendy stood laughing at her, peeking out from behind a tree trunk. Peggy came out on the other side.

"There now, I promise you won't see a single thing in the woods that will scare you more," Wendy said, all her good humor back. "Will you come with us now?"

Sheena was trembling, but wouldn't have admitted it to them. Wendy kind of liked getting to her, it seemed, in whatever way she could. She shrugged.

"Are we going very far back?"

"No, come on. I've got my watch on, see?" It was a necklace watch that Sheena suspected belonged to her mother. "We'll leave the woods in one hour. But if you had come on in the first place, we could have looked for leaves for an hour and a half."

"I have to be home by five-thirty myself," Peggy said. "Mom's at home, so she'll know."

"What's she doing at home?" Wendy asked. "I thought your mother worked."

"She does, but she's got today off."

"I don't know what my mother will do to me when she finds out I've been in the woods," Sheena said as she followed the two girls.

"Who's going to tell her?" Peggy asked.

"You don't have to tell your mother everything, Sheena," Wendy said. "Nobody does."

Sheena said nothing. Her eyes searched the forest as they moved into it, looking, looking. The leaves were a solid canopy overhead, brown, gold, red in many shades, and some of them still green. The sky had disappeared, as if the tops of the trees had become the top of the world now. Around her the trees grew tall, but at her feet were vines and tree roots. Off to her right she heard something running, but it was invisible in the shadows and the green vines and ferns and falling leaves, and it was running away from them, its sound fading into the near silence of the forest.

Wendy and Peggy were talking, going single file ahead of her. They went on as if they were going to a certain place in the woods, something known to them, but a mystery to Sheena.

Wendy stopped, and Peggy bent over with her.

"Pin oak, this has got to be pin oak, look. It's so—so red."

"It's almost purple," Peggy said. "Come on, Sheena, there are enough for all of us. Look, there's the tree. See how tall and straight it is?"

Sheena stooped and picked up a perfect leaf. She compared it to the shape of the pin oak leaf on her instruction sheet, and found that it had exactly the number of lobes required, in exactly the right places. It was a perfect leaf.

She looked at the floor of the woods, where the ferns began to thin and the ground showed through, its carpeting of leaves colorful and soft beneath her feet. There she found a yellow leaf, small and almost round. Dogwood? No. Dogwood was red, too. Dark red.

She gathered the yellow leaf and went on, stooped, her hands separating leaf from leaf, the bag at her side beginning to bulge with the leaves she would take home and separate later to identify and classify.

She heard the soft crooning of her own voice. "Oooh, look at this one, it's so perfect. Oooh, and here, and here ..."

Her hand pushed aside the tall green fern, and the small pale body seemed at first so foreign and alien to this lovely world of leaves that it was a long moment before she recognized it. A doll. Someone had dropped a baby doll—a doll without clothes. It was oddly blemished—it had a dark mole on its left shoulder.

And then its head began slowly to turn and its eyes looked at her, and she veered back on her heels, her heart in her throat.

A baby.

A real, live baby.

She clambered backward to her feet and screamed, "Wendy! Peggy!"

"What!" Wendy answered impatiently from several trees away.

Sheena couldn't take her eyes off the baby. She saw it lying in its green fern bed, as still as if it were a doll after all, but its eyes were moving, looking up at her, following as she moved. But it wasn't waving its arms the way her cousin Amelia's baby did, or cooing, or kicking its legs. It wasn't doing anything but looking at her, and she began to back away, farther, her stare on the naked little baby in the ferns.

"Peggy—" she said, and heard her voice cracking and failing to leave her throat. She stared at the baby, and saw its mouth begin to open, as if it were going to smile or croon at her. But then the lips only parted and drew back, and Sheena saw the teeth ...

Tiny, sharp, as if they had been filed to a point, white teeth that gleamed in the still shadows of the woods.

A raw, cold fear gripped Sheena as she stared at the teeth, and the eyes that had no smile in them after all, and she felt the way she always had after one of her night terrors in which she woke screaming, but had no memory of a dream beyond a dark place in her mind, something she couldn't remember.

Then she felt something brushing against her, and she almost screamed again.

Wendy gripped her arm with digging fingers.

"A baby!" Wendy yelled in her ear, and Sheena blinked, then saw the infant as she'd first seen it, tiny, lost in the green bed of ferns, its small legs and arms still, its face composed, its smoky eyes looking up at them, now toward the girls who stood one on each side of Sheena.

"Oh, my God," Peggy cried. "Let's go get Mama!" She whirled and was already running away.

Wendy made a lunge for her and grabbed her arm and Peggy spun back, almost falling. It was like the game called Crack the Whip, Sheena thought, as she watched them, where the last one in line was jerked around in a wide circle and had to run in long lopes to keep from falling.

But Wendy was the strong one, the leader. They always listened to Wendy.

"It's too far to your house, Peg. We'll go get Islan. Come on, run. Sheena, you stay here and watch the baby."

Sheena felt terror rise in her. She followed in their wake a few feet before she stopped again. A leafy branch swiped against her head and pushed hair into her eyes. Frantic, she cried out for them to stop.

"I can't stay! I can't. Let me go, too."

"Oh, all right, come on, hurry. We'll all go."

They ran, Sheena behind the other two. She felt they were lost and just running through the untracked forest in a wild and zigzagging path, breaking new ground. Ahead of her the other two girls were carrying on a breathless conversation about the baby, even as they ran, wondering whose it was, what it was doing there.

"Maybe somebody—just dropped it—when they were—hiking—" Wendy gasped for breath between words, leading the way, her feet pounding the leafy floor of the forest, her hands pushing out of her way the flailing branches of undergrowth bushes. Behind, almost on her heels, Peggy dodged the branches and, between gasps, added words of her own. Sheena trailed by several feet, saying nothing, thinking nothing except that she shouldn't have come into the forest, seeing nothing but the leaves in front of her and flashing into her memory the teeth of the baby. She wanted to say, didn't you see it had teeth? Babies that little don't have teeth, do they? But she couldn't release her voice.

Suddenly they were in open surroundings, with the chain link fence of a backyard in front of them. Houses edged the open area, with only a few trees left in their yards. The cul-de-sac made a concrete circle in the slanting, yellow rays of the late afternoon sun, and trailed off into a street that led through the trees toward town, more houses, more streets. Sheena drew in a breath of relief.

They entered a back gate and kept running, through the mowed grass, past a garden shed, past a picnic table beneath a tree, onto a patio and into the big family kitchen beyond. Wendy led the way into her house shouting for her sister.

"Islan! Islan, where are you?"

The big sister came frowning into the kitchen. Like Sheena's own sister, she seemed really grown up. More like an aunt, or some other authority figure than a teenaged sister. Islan Parker looked more than one year older than Sheena's sister, Leigh. She was taller, bigger, heavier. She made Sheena think of a Dutch girl in an old-fashioned picture of Dutch girls who wore yellow braids and stood beside a big windmill with their arms filled with bright tulips. Her naturally pink cheeks were pinker than usual, and her bright blue eyes angrier.

"Wendy, why do you have to come into the house screaming at me when I'm on the phone?"

"You're always on the phone!" Wendy shouted, slapping her palm against her thigh in frustration, her body bent slightly forward.

Peggy stood just inside the sliding glass doors, and Sheena waited in the opening of the door with only her toes in the kitchen. She didn't know whether to enter or back out.

"A baby—" Peggy gasped. Her chest was still heaving from her run.

Peggy was kind of fat, and it cost her more breath to run than it did the thinner kids.

"Come with us," Wendy said, reaching out and grasping the tail of her sister's loose shirt. "Somebody's left a baby in the woods."

"Sheena found it," Peggy breathed. "We all saw it."

"A baby!" Islan looked from one face to the other. "Are you serious?"

"Yes, a baby. A tiny one. Like Teddy. Just a couple of months old, maybe. Come on."

"Was it—*alive?*"

It seemed to Sheena that a lot of the color in Islan's face drained away and she spoke her last word as if she were suddenly afraid. But then Wendy was yelling at her again, and the color came back.

"Of course it was alive, stupid! What'd you think? Come on, hurry."

"All right."

They were running again, this time with Islan behind Wendy and Peggy. Sheena hesitated, but then she followed.

She didn't want to be left alone, even here, where the houses made up a world that was more familiar and less scary. She thought of the baby, the way she had first seen it, so tiny, like Jason, her cousin Amelia's baby, and she was suddenly struck by the terrible truth. *Somebody had left their tiny baby in the woods to die.*

CHAPTER 2

"HOW ABOUT A WALK, CHIEF?" Sergeant Collins Stoddard said to the big, sleek, silver gray German shepherd in the back seat of the Sheriff's Department car as he pulled to the side of the quiet road.

They'd been driving through the countryside on the northwest edge of town, coming back from a visit to an old hermit up in the mountains who'd been taking shots at some hikers. Old Harry, as he was known in the Sheriff's Department, usually meaning hairy, because no other name had ever been verified, was actually harmless, it seemed to Collins, and all he'd had to do was go up and warn him not to shoot at hikers.

"They weren't hikers, Sheriff," he'd said, his long, gray whiskers bobbing, his wary eye on the dog that stood at Collins's side. "They were just nosing around too close. I fired a couple of shots over their heads, that was all. I didn't come out here for company."

Arguing with the old man was useless. It was like telling him he wasn't the sheriff, he worked for the Sheriff's Department. He was actually Sergeant Stoddard. He'd been up to see the old man a number of times over the three years he'd been with the department, mostly because of the hermit's complaints that people were after him. Whenever Harry came to town for supplies, he had a complaint. Searching had turned up nothing. Today, the hikers were safely away, and it wasn't likely others would be coming too close to the hermit's narrow little hollow, and the cabin he had built on national forest land.

The back seat of the patrol car was secured by a heavy mesh, to keep the dog from jumping into the front seat, or jumping out of the car until he was needed. It was a useless system, Collins felt. Chief was so well behaved he wouldn't have moved from his back seat except in an emergency. He took his work seriously. He knew the difference between a matter that needed his attention, and play, or leisure. The moment Collins asked him if he wanted to take a walk, the dog's long feathery tail began to wag, and he smiled, his muzzle parting, his mouth turning up as effectively as that of any human.

They went into the edge of the woods. Collins stretched his arms over his head and allowed himself the luxury of just breathing in the cool, scented fragrances of autumn.

There were moments like this, almost every day, when he and Chief got a chance to just wander around a bit. Most of their days were so routine they could be boring, depending on how a man and his dog looked at it. Then occasionally both of them were put to the test. One week ago today, they'd run across a robbery in progress, out at a convenience store at a country crossroads.

Collins got shivers down his spine just thinking of it, of how Chief could bound into action at a single command, or without a word, if he thought he should. They had driven up at the store like any customer going in to buy a candy bar, right behind a pickup with oversized tires. Just as he got out of the car, leaving Chief in his secured back seat, the door of the convenience store slammed open and two men backed out, one of them with a short-barreled, sawed-off shotgun. He pulled the trigger, and someone in the store screamed in unison with the roar of the shot, then the man whirled and aimed one at the patrol car. Collins went down onto his knees, one hand reaching for his holstered gun and the other opening the back door.

Chief leaped out, and in two bounds had the man who was trying to get into the driver's side of the pickup. The one with the shotgun pulled off a shot at Chief, which made Collins's heart stand still. Chief was his companion, his sidekick, his ... buddy. Anger sent him after the man with the gun, but before he could get around the pickup, Chief had left the one man flat on his back wailing over a bloody arm and had leaped onto the fender of the pickup, onto its hood, and from there, right onto the head of the man with the shotgun.

With the two men in handcuffs, both of them backed against the pickup and staring in terror at Chief, who stood guard with foam on his fangs and fury growling from the center of his being, people from the store gathered on the walk outside and gazed in awe at the dog.

Collins felt that shivery pride all over again. Here was a dog he had trained himself. A beauty. Swift and sure. Ninety pounds of muscle and bone and heart, and sometimes the fury that was needed to bring down a criminal. Then also, he could be a puppy again, gentle, playful.

Collins watched him nose into the drifts of leaves against a rotted stump, and then lift a leg against a tall tree. Out on the winding country road a car went by. Collins saw the man and woman look at the patrol car, but neither of them saw him and the big dog in the woods. He started walking back toward the car.

His mind picked up on last Saturday night and the blind date his married sister had set up for him. He'd tried to get out of it, but Joyce couldn't believe that he was happy not dating anyone at the present time. Last year there'd been Angie, and a broken engagement after they had decided they didn't have enough in common, and since then there had been his sister, Joyce, with her "great girls" that Collins just had to meet. After about a half dozen of those dates in which he felt pressured when he didn't want to be pressured, he had put his foot down. "No more," he had told Joyce. But she had slipped last Saturday's "great girl" in on him in her usual smooth, sneaky way, and he'd found himself at her and Bruce's house for dinner and cocktails, and found also another couple and a woman definitely not his type.

She was a nice person, he felt sure, but he wasn't even sure he remembered her name. Melissa? Patricia? She was tall and thin, with all the consistency and figure of a peeled sapling. At dinner he noticed she only nibbled at her food. He liked a woman who would eat with him, laugh with him. He liked curves. Big hips and legs didn't turn him off in the least, if there was a waistline above them. In fact, he liked the figure of a woman who filled out her slacks, or set her skirt swinging when she walked. He liked the self-confidence of a woman who liked herself the way she was.

He heard a crackle from the car radio and the voice of the dispatcher. He moved closer to answer the call and pick up the information.

"Child found in woods. Infant. Check report of infant seen in woods on northwest edge of town in the Greenbrier Addition."

He was within a few miles of the Greenbrier Addition, on the road leading up to the tree-covered hills of the Mark Twain National Forest in one direction, and out into the valley in the other. The dispatcher gave him the address of Lorna Parker, and little more information except that some children had claimed to have seen a naked infant in the woods.

Collins reached back and opened the door of the back seat, and Chief jumped in and settled down like a human, sitting quietly, his muzzle pointed straight ahead. The moment the dog's sensitive ears picked up the voice of the dispatcher he had come toward the car. It was almost as if he knew which calls would be theirs and which would not. At times he ignored the dispatcher as effectively as he could ignore the passersby who stared at him.

Collins pulled the car out onto the road and drove toward town. He passed a small settlement, a couple of stores, a street, a few houses back on side streets behind the main one. Then, past the village, he began to see houses here and there, and off to the right at times he saw open country, with patches of woodland, growing thinner now, where pioneers had cleared part of the land a hundred and fifty to two hundred years ago when the area was settled.

He came to heavier, older forest land and an old church and rectory, no longer used, in a growth of young trees. A few hundred yards beyond the church was an old two-story family home, still kept up, white and solid with front and back porches. In the backyard was a swing set, visible only for a moment as he passed by. A gray car sat between the driveway and house. This, he thought, as he eyed the old forest behind the house and church and extending perhaps one to five miles beyond where it gave way to the farms in the valley, must be the place where the infant was found. Houses came closer together as he drove the curving road and took a street to the right.

In the fairly new housing development of Greenbrier, which was just outside the city limits, he slowed and began looking for the house number of Lorna Parker.

He found it in a cul-de-sac, right at the rounded end. The houses here were all about the same size, three bedrooms, one and a half or two baths, nice ranch-style homes with well-landscaped yards and a wide sidewalk that ran around the edge of the cul-de-sac and down each side street of the development. The area was quiet, suggesting that the residents—both men and women probably—worked during the day, to keep up the payments on their houses.

Chief didn't move except to turn his head and look at the neighborhood as Collins got out of the car.

The walk passed between sprawling junipers and beneath the limbs of a maple tree that was as brilliant as flame with autumn colors. Around him, Collins heard the sounds of nature, blackbirds gathering like dark clouds in a big oak tree farther down the block, and smaller birds twittering at a feeder next door. There was no sound of traffic, or children playing. The silence was peaceful, and in discord with the report of an infant found in the woods. Dead? He wondered. The information had been sketchy, as it usually was.

He rang the doorbell, and almost immediately heard noises from inside the house, of footsteps on carpets, and voices hushed and hurried. Children's voices, he was sure, with their distinctive fineness, that musical quality that children and young chickens and small streams of water have in common, as if somewhere in the past all were one with one another, and with everything.

The door opened and a girl in her late teens looked out at him. Behind her and peeking around her were several more younger girls, how many he didn't know. He was aware of rounded eyes, of excitement, awe, maybe fear. The oldest girl was as lovely as a rose, with a pale pink and white complexion, full lips, blond hair pulled back from her face in a French braid.

"I'm Sergeant Stoddard of the Sheriff's Department, responding to a call about a baby found in the woods?"

"Oh, hello."

The tall girl pulled back, and Collins saw there were three younger girls, nine or ten years old, all about the same height. Two were thin, and the third a little chubby. They all wore jeans and cotton shirts or pullovers, and two of them looked eager to talk, while the third one stood back. In her face he thought he saw marked fear.

"There was a baby!" one of the little girls said with emphasis. "We all saw it! Honest!" With each emphasis she gave a nod of her head, her chin jutting forward as if to form the exclamation point.

The tall girl looked both embarrassed and unsure. "My sister," she explained. "And her friends. They came running to the house scared to death—"

"Not scared!" the little sister, the one who had spoken, said, putting the same emphasis to her words. "We saw it. All of us! Both Peggy and Sheena. It was Sheena who found it first." She reached back and touched the thin child who hung back, the one with fear on her face.

"I wasn't sure," the older sister said. "I went with them—but I didn't see anything—anyone. I just guessed the people who were there, with the baby, took it away again."

Oh, so this was one of those, Collins thought. A bunch of little kids scared of nothing, making a big thing out of an incident that had a simple and innocent explanation. Yet, looking at those faces, he felt a twinge of doubt. Even the older sister had that doubt. He could see it, feel it, as if he could pick up the emanations of her feelings.

He asked for their names and ages and home addresses, and learned one of them was Sheena Treacle, daughter of Magret and Daniel Treacle. Daniel Treacle was owner of several properties around town, and a big shot in one of the more prominent hospitals. He was several years older than his wife, so the rumors went. Collins knew Daniel when he saw him, not on a personal level. But he wouldn't have known Mrs. Treacle except for the pictures that occasionally ran in the local interest sections of the newspaper. She was often on various committees, things he couldn't have listed if his life had depended on it.

"Why don't we just go take a look?" Collins said. "I have a dog, Chief, who'll find the baby if it's there."

"It is there!" the little girl, Wendy, said. "I know it is. It was naked. Why would anyone lay a naked baby down in the damp ferns like that?" She had squeezed past the older sister and was edging past Collins, her face turned up toward his the whole time. The light from the sinking sun put a glow of red on her round cheeks. He saw they were lightly freckled, not milk white like her sister's.

"You just show me where you feel you saw it and we'll check it out," Collins said, going down the walk toward the car and Chief. He glanced westward. They wouldn't have much time before the woods would be too dark for human eyes. Only Chief would still be at ease there, able to find his way around.

The girls stood on the walk behind him as Collins opened the back door of the car and slipped Chief's leash on. The dog stood up, eager to get out, tail wagging. Collins saw the girls eyeing him warily, and got a closer grip on Chief's leash, although the dog wouldn't have harmed any of them.

"He's beautiful," Islan said, and Chief wagged his tail harder, as if he knew exactly what the compliment meant, and Collins had no doubt he did.

"It's this way," Wendy said, and led the way around the maple tree, into the fenced yard at the back, and through a gate at the rear into the forest.

The air in the woods was cooler by several degrees and had a dim, greenish quality. The fragrance of autumn leaves mingled with the musty smell of fallen rotted leaves and wood, of damp soil and the secret dens of small animals. They went single file onto a dim, narrow path that wound between stands of thick underbrush, of fallen and rotting logs, of ferns growing as if in some medieval landscape. Wendy, in front, was almost running. Chief followed at her heels, his nose to the path part of the time, straining against his leash. Collins held on tightly. Behind him came the teenage girl, Islan, and the two others, in what order he didn't know. Occasionally as they turned a bend in the almost invisible path he caught a glimpse of color and movement, of blond heads and flushed cheeks.

They had gone some distance into the woods when Wendy stopped abruptly. There was less underbrush here, with older, taller trees, larger trunks, more moss on the trunks, more long-leafed fern, growing at their bases. The light seemed to be leaving. It was a quiet, cool, shadowed world, and Chief pulled on his leash, his nose down, wanting to be given the freedom to explore the musty smells, that of which Collins was unaware.

"It was there," Wendy said, waving her hand vaguely toward an area of fallen leaves and green ferns. "It was just lying there looking up at us. It didn't have any clothes on."

"It was awake," said Peggy. The chubby little girl with the big eyes and nut brown braids had come forward silently to Collins's left. Her voice was hushed and tremulous, and he looked down at her to see that she was shivering. He could hear the soft chatter of her teeth at times. But it wasn't from cold. The girl was scared. "It was there," she said again, "and then when we came back, it wasn't there."

Islan said, "I thought maybe someone was picnicking or something, in the woods, and had just walked off for a while, and the kids found their baby. That's the only explanation. But... I thought I'd call the police anyway. They all swear it was without clothes or blanket or anything."

Collins said, "Let's just let Chief take a look." He released the tight hold on the dog, and let the leash slide through his hand to the loop at the end. The dog moved instantly into the ferns, going to the right, to the left, his head down.

It was an odd story, Collins thought as he moved into the fern and fallen leaves with Chief. Islan's explanation might have had some logic behind it except for a couple of points. Why would any couple, even the youngest and most careless and irresponsible, leave a baby lying on the ground while they went off to explore? And furthermore, why would the baby be without clothing, as all three witnesses claimed?

But where was the baby now?

Chief raised his head and looked back at Collins, waiting for instructions. Collins nodded toward the right, and Chief put his nose down again and moved over toward a ravine. Collins followed. The ravine was shallow, a clean little ditch, except for the colorful leaves in the bottom, down which water would run during a hard rain. Roots of trees had been exposed and washed clean. They looked in the dim light like coiled snakes with dark, smooth skin. Chief moved down into the bottom of the ravine and began to nose into a little burrow beneath an exposed root. From somewhere in the still cover of leaves and limbs and roots Collins heard the angry, warning chirp of a chipmunk.

"Come on, Chief, leave the little guy's house alone."

A timid voice behind Collins said, "It wasn't down there, it was up here."

Collins looked to see the little Treacle girl, Sheena, standing about ten feet to his right, on the bank above the ravine. It was the first time she had spoken. It was she, he'd been told, who had first found the infant.

"No it wasn't," Wendy and Peggy said in unison. "It was here, Sheena, closer to the path."

"No, it was here."

"Sheena," Wendy said in exasperation, her hands on her hips, her head tipped sideways. "You've never even been in the woods before today, and you just don't know your way around. It was back this way. Peggy says so, too."

Peggy nodded, and nodded, her head bobbing like the head of a wound-up doll. Peggy stood away from Wendy and Sheena, back closer to the path, as if she was eager to leave.

Collins moved toward the girls, choosing Wendy for the simple reason the light was gradually dying, and she was probably right about the other little girl not knowing the woods. He made a circle through the area, letting Chief search beneath the ferns. But part of the forest floor was almost bare, except for the leaves, and it was obvious there was no child there now.

They followed the path back toward the house. Both Wendy and Peggy were talking, telling the whole story all over again, their voices overlapping so at times he had problems separating the two or understanding what either of them said. But the same story kept repeating, he saw. The girls had gone into the woods to gather leaves for a school project, and Sheena had found the undressed infant lying in the leaves. Wendy and Peggy had seen the infant, which was about two months old. They guessed its age by comparing it to the baby of someone they knew, and Islan confirmed it was a two-month-old baby.

They had tried to get Sheena to stay with the baby while they went after Wendy's sister, Islan, but Sheena hadn't wanted to stay. So they all had gone. Evidently, Collins thought, it hadn't occurred to them that one of the other girls, who was more used to the woods, should stay with the baby. Nor had it occurred to them to take the baby with them.

Islan asked, as they went through the gate, as if the thought had just now come to her, "Why didn't you bring it with you?"

None of the three little girls answered, and Collins found himself thinking that the parents, whoever they were, would have been horrified to return and find the baby gone. Or, more likely, was it all imagination? Or could it have been a small section of some light material, such as a piece of broken limb from a sycamore tree? Perhaps they looked at it, cried "baby" and took off to get Islan to come look at it too, before they really knew what it was.

There was something too mythical about the story.

He kept his smile to himself as he went with Chief through the fenced backyard. He noticed Chief looking pointedly at one area near the back of the house and followed that indication to see a fluffy gray and white Persian cat sitting on an empty flower stand on the back patio. The cat's fur stood out to its extreme, no doubt, making it look larger than it was. Collins gave Chief a sharp little jerk, to get his mind off the cat. He lived with neighbor cats, with no problem, but you never knew what a strange cat, and especially a belligerent one, might bring out in a dog.

Collins said good-bye to the girls at the front gate. "I'll make a report," he said. "If anything new comes up, let me know."

The sun had gone down, and long, slanting, deep shadows crossed the pavement of the cul-de-sac. Lights were coming on in some of the other houses, and a different sound had come into the quiet neighborhood. Down the way, children's voices mingled with a dog's barking, as if all were greeting one another. A car came slowly by and pulled into the driveway next door to the Lorna Parker house, and as he pulled away, a small white Ford slowed to make a turn into the Parker driveway. He caught only a glimpse of the driver, who was staring curiously at him, his dog, the patrol car, probably wondering what on earth he was doing in her neck of the woods. He had an impression of a pretty, narrow face framed with long, curly dark hair. He watched the car pull into the Parker driveway and saw the girls go toward it. If she was the mother of the Parker girls, then they must have taken after their dad, wherever he was, whoever he was. Both Islan and her sister Wendy were pale blondes, and the woman in the car had glossy, rich brown hair. Like the wild hazelnuts he gathered along roadsides when he was a boy.

Collins was glad to give it up. His day was finished. His duty had actually ended an hour or more ago, but he still had to file a couple of reports. In the back seat, Chief settled down with a sigh, no longer sitting alert to watch out the window, as if he knew the workday had ended.

Collins drove out of the cul-de-sac and picked up speed toward town, running into the beginnings of traffic at the first signal light three blocks away.

He was tired, and he wanted just to go home, fix Chief's supper and his own, and settle down in front of his TV for the evening news. Except he was going to be late for that.

As he drove toward the Sheriff's Department, his mind went back to the woods and the rather strange story he had heard. He caught a glimpse of himself in the mirror and saw he was frowning.

CHAPTER 3

MAGRET WORKED IN THE KITCHEN, doing the last-minute things before dinner, those many little nuisances that came up all at once and always made her so nervous. The salads, the bowl of green peas that had to be warmed in the microwave, the glasses of water with the two ice cubes each, the hot water for the coffee ... Daniel didn't think he could sit down at the table without his hot coffee, his burning hot coffee. None of this after-dinner coffee stuff for Daniel, except when it was forced on him at one of the dinner parties he detested. And to make it all worse, Sheena wasn't home yet. The driveway light had come on, indicating approaching darkness. She wished now she hadn't let Sheena go out to Wendy's. One little girl alone was an angel; put her with one or two more and ...

Leigh had finished setting the table at the other end of the kitchen, the round, oak table that Daniel favored, at which the family ate most of its meals. The formal dining room was used perhaps once a month, but Magret often went into it when she was alone to admire the dark, rich paper, the large breakfront that lined most of one wall, and all the lovely china and glassware it contained. Over the years she had changed the china as her desires dictated, and Daniel had never objected. Probably, he never knew. She wished she had time to go now into that serene dining room, where so few of the family ever went, and try to calm her nerves. All day she had been on edge. At the hospital, where she had spent the afternoon doing volunteer work as a receptionist in the ICU, she had been as nervous as a cat on a hot stove, as the old saying went. Probably because of her dreams, and because Sheena was going out into that same area she had been dreaming of.

And because of other things, maybe, too, the constant diet she lived on, the pressure of volunteer work. Once they had your name, it was just like junk mail. The requests never ended. Your name kept coming up, more and more.

"Leigh, will you call the Parkers and find out if Sheena is still there?"

Leigh went around the table at her usual leisurely pace, the one that seemed to Magret was half laziness and half rebellion, without answering Magret, and Magret had an urge to scream at her and tell her to *move it* and do as she was told. But another idea came to Magret. Now that Leigh had her driver's license, and her first car, she might like to go after Sheena. That would definitely put the moody teenager in a better humor, if that was her problem. Magret wasn't sure she knew what was in Leigh's mind anymore, or if she ever had. She loved the girl, her firstborn, with as much devotion as she loved her other two, as any mother loved her child, but she was beginning to feel she was living with a household of strangers. Especially Leigh.

"If she's still there, tell them you'll come and get Sheena. It's almost time for dinner."

Leigh came alive and grabbed the car keys off the desk by the back door. "I'll go get her," she yelled, and the door slammed behind her before Magret could object.

She stood with a handful of ice cubes melting and running down her wrist and thought of all the things she'd been going to say. If they're already on the way here, you'll miss them. Get a sweater, it's getting chilly outside! Just make the phone call, Leigh!

Magret threw the ice cubes into the sink and went to the telephone on the kitchen wall and dialed Lorna Parker's number.

Lorna answered. Magret knew the voice from the many times they had talked to each other concerning the visits their two daughters made back and forth. The older two, Leigh and Islan, were separated in age by one year and had never been the friends Wendy and Sheena were. It was like her own acquaintance with Lorna. They had gone to school together, yet Magret had not been part of Lorna's group of friends, and if it hadn't been for their daughters' friendship, Magret probably wouldn't have known Lorna very well anymore.

"This is Magret Treacle, Lorna. I told Sheena to be sure to be home before dark when she asked to go out to Wendy's. We'll be glad to come after her, if she's still there. In fact, Leigh has already started."

"She should be home by now, Magret," Lorna said. "Islan took her not long after I got home from work. There was a delay, and I'm sorry. I knew she was late getting home."

"A delay?"

"Yes, the oddest thing. When I came home the sheriff was out here, just driving away. It seems the girls had been in the woods looking for leaves and came across a baby ... a very young, naked baby ... so they said, as unbelievable as it sounds ... and Islan went with them ... found nothing ... but the girls were so hysterical about it, Islan called the sheriff—"

Magret felt the coldness start in her, and then the heat in the outer layer of her skin drawing her face out of shape, tightening across her cheeks, taking her back into the horror of her nightmares. She wasn't exactly sure when she hung up, or even if she said another word to Lorna Parker.

She was standing in the middle of her kitchen, looking at white cabinets with the Pennsylvania Dutch trim, at the island with the double sink, the curtains at the wide windows, tied back with blue bows ... the smells of dinner wafting around her nauseatingly ... a roast the part-time maid, Carrie, had put into the oven before she left this afternoon, and a variety of vegetables cooking with it ... sounds of music in the upper part of the house, of a dog barking in the yard next door, indicating visitors ...

Then the back door opened and Leigh came in and the keys rattled on the desk as she dropped them, or threw them down. And behind her came Sheena, looking large-eyed and subdued, as if she knew she had done something wrong and would probably be punished for it. But Magret wasn't feeling up to dealing out discipline. She longed to go to the private master bath and lock the door against even Daniel and take a long soak in the tub. But if she did that the whole family would be asking her what was wrong.

It would be better to do as she always had, all her life, and pretend nothing was wrong.

Leigh said, "Just as I was backing the car out, they came spinning in. Honestly, did you ever see how fast Islan turns a corner? It's like she doesn't know what a brake is."

"I think it would be a good idea if Sheena didn't go out to Wendy's anymore. You were supposed to be home before dark, Sheena."

"I'm sorry." Sheena said, in that meek little voice she could assume.

Magret felt an urge to put her arms around the little girl and hold her close, protect her from whatever it was that had turned her so pale and wan looking, but she went instead to the sink and drew a glass of water and stood drinking it.

Leigh went after Ward and their father, and the dinner table became the usual noisy place with Ward and Leigh talking about basketball, football, band practice, and Daniel putting in a few words here and there, carrying on a conversation of sorts with them as if he were into every little thing that interested them.

The phone rang halfway through the meal and Leigh almost tipped her chair over in her hurry to answer it.

“It’s for me,” she said. "I’ll take it upstairs.” She gave Ward a sharp look. “And don’t you listen in. Just hang up the phone in a couple of minutes.”

Leigh left the room, her dinner only half eaten, and Magret stared at the plate of food. Into her mind came an image of herself at Leigh’s age, not supple and slender and lovely like Leigh, but overweight, shy, homely. At least in her own eyes she had been homely, ugly even, with her long, dark dishwater-blaugh hair unmanageable, and therefore not worth doing anything with, and her body sloppy fat and hidden the best she could under large shirts that she could let fall over her jeans or skirts. For that reason she never called Leigh back to finish her food. She might tell the younger children to finish eating their vegetables, but she let Leigh’s appetite handle its own needs, though at times she felt her daughter wasn’t getting the nutrients she needed.

Ward discussed the phone call for a moment, and Magret made herself listen, to keep her mind from the other thing.

“Must be a new guy. Didn’t have her personal phone number,” Daniel said, smiling just a little. He had always enjoyed teasing Leigh about her phone calls.

“Right,” Ward agreed. “He didn’t know she’d gotten her heart’s desire for her sixteenth birthday, her very own telephone in her own room, where she can gab all night long. Did you know she got a C on her math test?”

Daniel said, “C is average, Ward. As long as it doesn’t drop below C, we won’t complain. And Leigh has to go to bed at ten just like you do.”

“Then how come I have to have B’s and A’s or I don’t get to play ball? That’s discrimination,” said Ward calmly, as if he didn’t really care. He twisted in his chair and looked at Daniel, adding, “Parents get sued these days for things like that.”

"And mouthy teenage boys lose their allowances sometimes," Daniel replied with a smile.

Ordinarily, Magret enjoyed the banter that went on between Ward and his dad, and often included both girls, but tonight she felt the way Sheena acted, and only wished the dinner would end.

She got up for dessert, that sweet ending to a meal in which she never indulged. Tonight it was chocolate pudding and whipped cream, prepared by Carrie during the day and carefully poured into three small dessert dishes. Carrie knew that Magret never ate dessert, and she had wondered aloud about that. "How can you go on depriving yourself of all these things?" Comfortable, fat Carrie had wanted to know. "How can you be happy with a serving of green beans and salad?" Magret wondered too, at times, because the hunger was always there. She had thought when she was young, when she finally put herself on a stringent, low-calorie diet, that the hunger would go away eventually, but it never had, and it came back every night to plague her, from dinnertime to bedtime, as the nightmares had been plaguing her lately.

She wanted to talk to Sheena about what had happened in the woods, but she didn't get a chance until Sheena went up to bed. After bidding the others good night, Magret went up to tuck Sheena in and give her a kiss.

The little girl was waiting to say her prayers, and Magret knelt beside her and listened.

"God bless Mama and Daddy and Leigh and Ward, and all my best friends, and my not-so-best friends, too. And bless all the little children in the world, especially those that don't have food or homes or mamas, and bless all the little animals, and all the big animals and bless ... Sergeant Stoddard and his dog Chief... and thank you for another ... another nice day. Amen. I love you. And—and forgive me for ... going into the woods. And"—she lowered her voice as if it would help her mother from hearing —"—and—the baby—"

To Magret's surprise, she did not ask for it to be blessed. Her voice faltered and grew silent.

Sheena got into bed without looking at her mother. Magret saw the long, fair hair swing forward against the rounded cheek, and saw the downcast eyes, the shadow of long lashes on tawny cheeks. The light on the table was turned low, and the shadows in the room lay deep beyond the bed and around the edges of furniture. Dolls and stuffed animals on the shelves at the end of the room, among the books, loomed larger than during the day, their shadows adding bulk far out of proportion, it seemed.

Magret resisted an urge to reach out and turn the lamp higher, putting more light into the room, running the shadows back into that dark world they inhabited.

"Sheena, you were told not to go into the woods. You know that during this past year when you've been allowed to go home with Wendy, and even before that when you went with your cousin Peggy, that you were never, never to go into the woods."

Tears glistened in Sheena's big eyes and oozed over and became like pearls on her cheeks, catching the light in rainbow colors. They slid down and into the lace trim of her nightgown. Magret pressed her fingers against the damp cheeks.

"Are you not going to let me go to Wendy's anymore?" Sheena whispered.

"We'll see about that another time. I talked to Lorna—Mrs. Parker—and she told me you ... uh ... found a baby in the woods? That the sheriff came out?"

Sheena nodded, her eyes enlarging in wonder or excitement or fear. Magret watched her daughter, feeling the heavy pound of her own heart.

"Tell me about it, Sheena."

"It was there—I found it. We went to get leaves. Wendy and Peggy go into the woods all the time, Mama, and I thought it wouldn't hurt if I didn't stay very long ... just this once ... to get leaves." Her eyes brightened again with tears, and Magret pressed her hand to the child's cheek.

"It's all right. It's done now. Just tell me the other part."

A very faint frown lumped between Sheena's pale eyebrows as the child looked off across the room. Magret could feel the dampness of ferns around her own feet, and see the dark trunks of trees surrounding her. Once she had run through those ferns, wild and free as a woodland animal, her arms out to catch all the ecstasy of life, of something even beyond life, and now that green world came back to her through her daughter's eyes, but the fear had edged in, and grown to the nightmares that haunted her, and she almost put her hand out to stop Sheena from telling her. She didn't want to know anything beyond her own life, so carefully made, so carefully maintained.

"I was finding leaves," Sheena said, her voice barely above a whisper, her gaze finding something in the corner of the ceiling that caused the frown to deepen, or her memory adding a kind of fearful wisdom to her actions of that afternoon.

"Yes," Magret urged softly as the child paused, her eyes roaming the dark corners of the room.

"I didn't bring the leaves home. I forgot them. I guess I dropped them when I ran. Wendy and Peggy were going to leave me with the baby in the woods and I didn't want to stay."

"The baby—was it alive?"

Sheena giggled, to Magret's surprise, and looked at her mother. "Everybody asks that. Yes, it was alive. It smiled at me." The frown came back, and the voice lowered. "I mean—it kind of opened its mouth."

Magret felt ice cold fingers push heavily up her spine and into the back of her hair. "Sheena," she said with impatience. "Please tell me exactly what happened. Whose baby was it? How old was it?"

"It was like Cousin Amelia's baby, that size. Like Jason. It was just *little,* and when I pushed aside those ferns, I thought it was a doll that someone had left. Then Peggy and Wendy came, and even before that I saw it was a real baby because it looked at me. And then it opened its mouth."

"It moved." Magret squeezed Sheena's hand. "But you got the police and went back to the woods and looked, and did the police take the baby away?"

"We couldn't find it," Sheena said, her eyes now on Magret.

Magret steadied her face so that no emotion showed through. She could see the bewilderment in Sheena's eyes, the silent asking for reassurance, that it was all right she had disobeyed, this one time, that it was all right they couldn't find the naked infant again. While ice formed on Magret's heart and flowed through her blood to her skin, she tried to smile.

"Then maybe it really didn't happen at all, Sheena. Maybe it was too dark under the fern to see clearly what was there. Maybe it was a doll someone had dropped once, or—or—maybe a cluster of toadstools that looked like a baby. It could have been anything, even a small animal perhaps."

Magret saw Sheena's eyes change as she talked, going from that pleading puzzlement to disappointment. The child drew back onto her pillow and pulled up her blanket to cradle her chin. She drew a long breath and transferred her gaze to the ceiling again.

"Well," Magret said, feeling uncomfortable at the obvious withdrawal of her younger daughter. "Good night." She leaned down and kissed Sheena, then went quietly toward the door.

She longed to lock herself into the bathroom and soak in hot water.

She reached out to turn off the light, and Sheena said, "Can I sleep with it on, Mama?" So Magret withdrew her hand.

"Mama," Sheena said, just before Magret closed the bedroom door.

Magret looked back. Sheena's eyes were unusually dark in her lovely heart-shaped face. Light from the lamp turned her bangs gold and silver. She would go to sleep with her light turned low, as it was now, as she sometimes did, and Magret, or Daniel, would turn it out later.

"Yes?" Magret said, impatient now to hurry the night along to the point where she could be alone.

"Mama, does little Jason have teeth?"

"Amelia's baby, Jason?"

"Does he have teeth?"

"No, dear, he's only two months old. Tiny babies rarely have teeth. Why?"

"That one did. The one in the woods. It opened its mouth and I saw lots of real sharp teeth."

Magret stared at her daughter, but saw the child in her dreams, rising up from the ground, the soil cracking as it became visible, its head emerging first, as if it were being born. Born of its grave. And then the teeth, sharp, small, a mouthful of teeth, sharp and white like a shark's, row upon row ... needles built of bone ...

She wasn't sure if she ran from her child's bedroom, or if she had walked casually away as she would have any other night. But she was going down the stairs, her footsteps almost silent on the thick carpet, her hand gripping the banister. Anger rose like gall in her throat by the time she reached the bottom of the stairs. She had told Sheena never to go into the woods. Not those woods, not out there so close to the old home rectory where she had lived when she was growing up next door to where Sheena's cousin Peggy now lived with her parents, with Uncle Everett and Aunt Faith ... not there. But Sheena had gone, and somehow she had seen ... the nightmare that haunted Magret.

The anger edged away and left her trembling, as if it were the depths of night again, three or four in the morning when the house, the street outside, the neighborhood were still, wrapped in sleep, when even the summer insects had grown silent, and the dogs and cats slept, and she had awakened cold with the memory of her terrors.

The dream had started about a year ago when one night she dreamed she was in the woods again, just standing there, the fear in her and around her as palpable as the trunks of the trees, so magnified in her dreams, so huge and dark and still, yet menacing.

She had lain in the big bed that night with Daniel an arm's length away and stared at the dark ceiling. It was deeper into winter, she recalled, because there had been the silence of snow outside, of a world covered in the occasional snowfalls that occurred in this part of the state. She had stared up into the darkness of the room, seeing finally the black edges of different colors, of the white ceiling against the wallpaper, and the group of pictures on the wall above and around the mirror on the dresser, and had wondered at the strange dream. For years she had not consciously thought of the woods. Instead of going to Uncle Everett's house for Thanksgiving or Christmas or birthdays, she had insisted that he and his family come to her house, for after all, didn't the rest of the family come to her house? And why should Faith prepare for a family that really was Everett's? Of course she didn't put it in those words, to make Faith feel she was not part of the family, but she had avoided going out to her mother's old home place at the edge of the woods. And she never, never went to the rectory, or the church, both abandoned so long ago. She had even avoided thinking about it.

Then the dreams had started, taking her back into that terrible forest that once she had loved so much.

She had meant never to go back there, even in her thoughts.

But she was helpless against her dreams.

It was as if part of herself were betraying the rest of herself.

In the family room, Ward was at the game table playing something, a game that ended almost as Magret took her chair. Daniel looked up from his newspaper.

"Where's Leigh?" Magret asked, and felt surprised that her voice betrayed none of her feelings.

"She's up in her room, so far as I know." Daniel put down his paper and turned off the television with the remote control device on his table. Ward began complaining.

"And speaking of being up in her room, it's time for you to go to your room, too," he reminded Ward.

"Dad—I wanted to watch the news."

"Since when did you want to watch the news? Go to bed. It's ten o'clock."

"But I've only been finished with homework for an hour," Ward grumbled, even as he went toward the door.

Daniel folded the newspaper carefully, each page according to its number. "You shouldn't let your homework pile up so much that it takes you half the evening to get it done."

Ward went out of the room, tall for his age, a head taller than Sheena, though she was only eighteen months younger, and the two of them looking no more alike than if they had been strangers. He had been a long baby. His birth weight hadn't been above average, but his length had, and it had stayed that way. He had taken after some more distant members of Magret's family, of Great Uncle Andy and his bunch, who Magret's mother had always said were like pulled taffy, long and stringy.

Now that the paper was folded and put into the magazine rack, Daniel settled back into his chair with a sigh and turned the TV on again, low.

Magret got up.

"Aren't you going to watch the news tonight?" Daniel looked up at her. Light from a lamp in the corner glistened on the smooth, hairless top of his head. That bald spot was sometimes like glass, and she liked to tease him, in her better moments, with a rub there to bring out the gloss. Leigh had started doing the same, and Daniel always looked a little pleased. He had learned to accept the condition of baldness, although at one time he had not allowed himself to be seen without a hairpiece.

"I'm very tired this evening," Magret said. "I think I'll take a long tub bath. Are you going to stay down here very long?"

He turned off the TV and got up. "No, I can watch the news in the bedroom. If you're going up, I'll go, too."

She wanted to tell him no, that he should stay, that she wanted to be alone. But she went up the stairs with Daniel behind her, aware of his sounds, his breathing, the rustle of clothing, the soft thud of his feet on the carpet. Alone, she felt, she would be able to understand what was happening to her, what the dreams, the nightmares meant, why Sheena saw in reality, or at least in what had seemed reality, what Magret had seen in her dreams. Alone, she could understand.

With Daniel behind her, talking to her from his part of the bathroom, the door open between the tub and the area with the vanity and the stool, she ran her bath. She half listened, sometimes answering, as he told her about his day at the hospital, about the hard job of being an administrator. Nurses had quit, leaving them shorthanded. Two nurses in one day, both of them quitting because of their husbands, one because of a transfer, and the other because he wanted her to quit working. He hadn't been given sufficient notice from either one. And there had been two deaths today, one of them an elderly man who'd been ill a long time, in and out of the hospital, and the other the young leukemia patient. Five years old. Blood had been oozing from every orifice in her body these last few days, and there was nothing anyone could do. It made him mad, sometimes, most of the time, that there was nothing anyone could do. In that case, why the hell didn't God step in and do something? Couldn't death at least be easy and swift? Instead of long and lingering? But there were also four babies born, all of them healthy, apparently healthy.

"Anyone I know?" Magret asked, seeing in the wallpaper the dark trunks of trees, and the rise of ferns from a damp floor. She closed her eyes.

"I don't know. Thomas was the name of the boy. I think his dad works at the lumber yard on Walnut."

"Strickland's?"

"Yes. The others I don't remember, offhand. One was an unmarried mother. But she's going to keep her baby."

Magret heaved a great sigh of relief when Daniel finally said good night and went to bed. After that she heard the voices of the news commentators, but it was a distant murmur to the soft bursting of bubbles in her bath.

Now that she was alone and could think, her mind closed, and through her dark eyelids she saw the black trunks of trees looming closer and closer, and beneath them the dark green, many-lobed ferns ... and the black earth splitting ... three ways ... and the center rising ...

CHAPTER 4

"YOU SHOULD HAVE SEEN HIM, MOM," Islan said, her head tipped to one side and her eyes looking dreamily off into space, the way she always did when she was in the throes of a new crush. Lorna sat quietly, letting her talk, listening with only an occasional wandering of her mind. "He was absolutely exciting. Gorgeous. Really. You never saw such square shoulders in your life."

"Uniforms seem to have that effect. I think it's the way they're cut."

"Oh, it was more than the uniform, I assure you. I've seen slobs in uniforms too, and you can't hide that."

"No, maybe you're right." Lorna said carefully, not really sure what "slob" meant in Islan's vocabulary. "But it's a good idea not to fall for a uniform. And isn't he a bit old for you?"

"Old? He might be thirty, or thirty-five. But I'm seventeen. When he's forty, I'll be twenty-seven. Or he might be younger. Or even older. What difference does it make? You didn't get to see him—"

"I did see him. I drove in as he was driving out."

"Then you must have seen how handsome he was."

"Truthfully, I was looking more at the dog."

"Oh, you would." Islan made a sound that could have been a giggle or a snort.

Lorna looked down at the cat curled on her lap and gave its long fur a soft, long caress. The fur followed her hand, rising with the electricity caused by the friction. The cat purred loudly and flexed its claws, drawing them in and out against her knee. Its eyes were tightly closed. "I like animals," she said. "I have a lot of sympathy for them. And it was a marvelous-looking animal."

"Well, he took the dog along. He kept it close against him until we got to the place where the girls claimed they saw the baby, then he let out its leash. He was really great, the way he handled it."

"The dog?" Lorna asked teasingly, knowing well what her daughter meant.

"Oh, Mom. The sheriff, not the dog. Actually, he isn't the sheriff, he's a sergeant. Whatever that means."

"Don't you think you should go to bed now?" Lorna asked. She didn't like to give her older daughter orders as if she were Wendy's age, but at times a nudge was necessary. Islan's hormones seemed to have reached a new peak this past year, and hardly a month went by without both of them having to suffer through a new crush. This time was the first to involve an older man, although Lorna couldn't be sure he was very much older. It wasn't really true that she hadn't looked as carefully at the man as she had at the dog. The beautiful German shepherd actually had been the last of four things she had looked at. First she had seen the row of lights atop the brown car, none of them on. Then she had looked at the emblem on the side, which told her the car was the property of the county sheriff. Then she had gotten one glimpse of the man, just enough to see the square jaw, the high cheekbones, the dark hair, and then she had seen the dog, sitting so regally in the back seat, but behind heavy mesh as if he were a prisoner. She had driven on into her driveway with a giggle beneath her breath. The Sheriff's Department had captured one prisoner, a dog. What had he done? Did he have a lawyer to represent him?

Then something hit her. The sheriff's car, with the man in uniform and the attack dog in the back, had been at her house. *Her house.*

The girls were still in the yard, standing in a little group, Islan looking tall and lovely among the shorter, younger girls. So grown up.

They had rushed at her, all except Sheena, telling her about the baby in the woods.

The answer to that was simple. Three little girls had run across the bed of an infant that belonged to someone who was gathering nuts in the woods, or leaves, or just looking around. The parents had laid the baby down for a moment and probably were within twenty yards. She could almost visualize them standing there with their mouths open in astonishment while three little girls screamed at sight of the baby and went running as if the devil were after them.

Even as the two little ones, Wendy and Peggy, told their story, she began to smile. Islan hadn't seemed to know much. She had stood looking in the direction of the sheriff's car, and Sergeant Stoddard.

Wendy had now been in bed and, Lorna assumed, fast asleep, for a couple of hours. And it was time Islan was going, too.

"You have to go to school tomorrow." Lorna said, stretching as she got up from the soft recliner that would have been so easy to fall asleep in if Islan hadn't been in a talking mood. "And I have to go to work."

She watched Islan leave the room, and as always, she thought of Islan's daddy, Thornton. Tall and slender and so Scandinavian, he had passed his genes on to his daughters so completely it was almost as if Lorna had counted for zilch in the creation of the girls. The older Islan got, the more she looked like the Parkers. Not really Parkers, but the blond, Swedish mother of Thornton, who had married a mutt more or less like Lorna herself, whose ancestry was so mixed that nothing much stood out. In Thornton's family there were blonds, the Scandinavian blood overt, pushing aside anything else, making everything else insignificant, even though they carried the name of Parker.

Lorna went out onto the back patio, the cat going with her. She stood looking at the black wall of the forest, rising just behind her yard fence, and the paler sky above with its tiny, distant points of light. Stardust, the cat, named after those points of light on a night similar to this, one year ago when the kitten was like a soft, furry powder puff in her hands, disappeared into the shadows beneath the shrubs. Stardust would stay out only a few minutes, liking to sleep on the foot of Lorna's bed, and sometimes up on the pillow next to her head. Stardust had not needed a kitty litter pan yet—she had the whole backyard.

Lorna thought of Thornton as she looked at the stars, as she so often thought of him. Her memories picked up the feelings and the sights and smells of the first time she had seen him. His aftershave, or cologne—or whatever it was—had smelled like heaven that night in the smoky disco. She had heard a deep, soft voice, and turned to see, far above her, the most beautiful face she had ever seen on a man. His hair was so fair it was almost white, and his skin golden from the sun. Later she learned he was from the north, from a large farm family there that owned thousands of acres of land. He had come south to go to the university. And when he went back home he took a wife with him, a small, brown-haired girl who wasn't up to the kind of life that was expected of a farm wife. That they had allowed her to take the two girls when she left was still a mystery. She hadn't wanted to disrupt the lives of the girls, or Thornton's mother or father or six brothers and sisters, but it was her only chance to survive, it seemed at that time.

The hurt was still there, the edge of shock, of finding out her husband had a mistress, a married woman ten years his senior. He had never stopped seeing her. And when the woman's husband was killed in a tractor accident, Lorna knew it was over for her, too.

A few months after her divorce, Thornton married his mistress. His first love, perhaps his only love.

The hurt was there, fading, taking the anger with it.

That terrible, helpless feeling of anger.

They'd had Islan, and eight years later, Wendy.

Yet he kept going back to Justine, over and over, and lying to Lorna.

When the baby was six weeks old, when she heard about the birth of another baby to Justine, Lorna took her two children and left.

She had never told them the real truth behind her reason for leaving the security of the Parker family for the insecurity of single motherhood.

She was at peace, considering everything. The girls were fairly happy, and were in contact with their father and his second wife; and sometimes Islan went north for a couple of weeks or longer in the summer. Wendy never had, and didn't want to. She'd been only six weeks old when Lorna brought her little family back home where, for her, life was easier. Wendy knew her father only through a photograph.

Lorna had a job she didn't mind, as a secretary, and a home she'd bought with an inheritance from a childless great aunt she had loved dearly.

Sometimes she felt that life had become too routine, and her mind tended to drift to faraway places, to Alaska, to Hawaii, to Hong Kong, to the South Sea Islands made glamorous by pictures in travel magazines. To romance.

But then she told herself, weren't the lives of most people routine? Didn't most of the people in the world get up, go to work, go home, eat, sleep, get up again, and on and on until the end? The sadness she felt sometimes seemed overwhelming, and then she searched for something to add pleasure to the routineness of life. She added a video to the evening, and a different menu.

And she made herself appreciate the little things, the really important things. Her daughters, their health, their interests. Her well-fed cat. The birds the cat watched but didn't attack. Her home. Her friends and family, so few now.

She felt a ray of happiness suddenly, that uplifting of spirit that she felt must be a stroke of approval from a guardian angel.

The backyard contained patches of blackness, of the deepest of shadow behind shrubs, beneath the drooping branches of the willow tree. A small ball of lighter material moved through the darkness and out into the lighter areas of lawn, past the garden shed, on toward the bird feeder. Starlight made the scene soft and magical. A streak of light from the street lamp oozed through the fences and shrubs like a ghost. Lorna's eyes lost the movement of the cat as it passed beneath a shrub on the other side of the fenced backyard.

Lorna stepped off the patio, and felt the dampness and coldness of the grass through her thin house slippers. She walked almost as soundlessly as the cat to the center of the yard, pausing to look at the variety of shadows, of light and darkness. At times like these, she often wished she were an artist, but she wasn't, and perhaps never would be. But already she was planning to take art lessons when she retired, and perhaps earlier, maybe when both girls grew up and left home. She would love to be able to transfer the beauty of light and dark onto canvas.

The woods was a solid line of black, their treetops like jagged lace against the sky. The back of her neck ached as she looked up, the trees were so tall. She rubbed the back of her neck as she went closer to the fence at the rear of the yard. For a moment she stood at the gate, where a very faint path became visible as she searched for it. The two little girls had worn themselves a trail. A quarter-mile of interesting pathway, through a deep wood. Connecting the homes of two friends.

Something warm rubbed against her ankle and purred softly. Lorna reached down to touch the cat between the ears.

"Are you ready to go in, Stardust?"

The cat stiffened. Lorna felt the difference in its stance, and heard the rare sound of a soft growl deep in its throat. Its nose was pointed toward the fence and the woods beyond, then suddenly the cat whirled and was gone, a pale, blurry object, toward the house.

Lorna started to follow when the sound reached her, from out of the woods, not far away. A ripple of chills went up the back of her neck and stiffened her. She couldn't move as she waited, listening.

A baby's cry.

One sad wail ... one, and then silence.

Lorna stared into the darkness of the woods, the damp, the cold rising now from the forest floor, and said softly, *"oh, my God!"*

There had been a baby, and there still was a baby, lost, crying now in the darkness, one bleat like a lamb or a baby goat. One cry for help.

Lorna opened the back gate and started forward onto the path, then remembered she had no light and turned instead and ran to the house, opening the patio doors and going in. Stardust streaked through between her ankles, and Lorna stumbled, almost falling, swearing a bit under her breath as she caught herself with a hand on the corner of the kitchen cabinet. The cat ran on into the hallway.

Lorna grabbed the flashlight out of the kitchen drawer where all the stuff she needed for repairs was kept, the screwdrivers, the small hammer, three sizes of flashlights. She took the largest and tested it. Then as she left the house again she turned on the outdoor patio light, so that as she crossed the yard she had a path of dwindling brightness, ending at the gate and the path beyond.

She stood in the edge of the forest listening. There was silence again now. Except for a soft rustling in the leaves to her right that started and ended abruptly as she shined her light in that direction. She thought she saw the reflection of small eyes.

Why had the baby cried out only once? Was it ... could it be that it was impaired in some way? Mute, perhaps, except for an occasional, desperate cry?

A lump came to her throat as she thought of a helpless infant, that had no voice even to cry out for help, abandoned in the woods.

With the flashlight on and its strong beam swinging from left to right, she followed the path. Slowly, searching, listening. Something off in the dark leaped and ran, and Lorna stood still, her heart pounding. It must have been a deer, she decided as its sounds drifted away. It had sounded large as an elephant. She listened for other sounds of movements, of small legs and arms in drifted leaves, of the cry again, and heard nothing except the tinkle of leaves floating down from the treetops, the soft, rain-like patter, almost soundless.

She wished she had listened more carefully to the girls when they'd talked about the baby. Where had they found it? Her impression was only that it was close to the path.

She needed Islan. Islan at least knew where the girls had taken her.

Most of all she needed Sergeant Whomever and his dog. Did she dare go in and call him?

Had it been her imagination?

No.

She knew she had heard something, and she was sure it was a child's voice, a very young child.

She dared to call.

COLLINS'S PHONE rang at eleven-thirty, just as he was thinking about going to bed. Chief lay on the floor at the side of his chair. He had been snoring lightly for the past half hour, and when the phone rang, the snore ended abruptly, although the dog didn't lift his head. As Collins reached toward the desk for the old black dial telephone, he saw Chief's eyes follow him, swiveling round as Collins swiveled in his chair.

"Yeah, Collins." He knew who it was. The station. Every few weeks he was called on to do something or other, and he didn't feel particularly friendly.

"Sergeant Stoddard?" a soft female voice said. It sounded breathless as if the owner had been running, or fighting, or was just nervous. Ah, he thought, some guy's been beating up on his wife or girlfriend and she wants help hog-tying the bastard.

"Yeah," he said again, then, "Stoddard speaking."

Chief rose up, ears perked.

"I really hate to bother you at this time of night. I called the station and they gave me your number. It's the baby. I think I heard it." She took a long, trembling breath. Stoddard frowned, visualizing the blond girl, yet the voice didn't sound like hers. "I'm Lorna Parker, I should say. I was out in the backyard, and I heard a cry in the woods. I went out with my flashlight, but had no idea exactly where to look. I don't think my girls can help me with this. I—so I thought of your dog."

Aha, so this call was mainly for Chief, not himself. As if Chief had caught the message telepathically, he stood up, excitement in every expression of his stance.

"You say you heard a cry? A baby's cry?"

There was a slight hesitation, then she said, "I hope you won't think I've just got a wild imagination, as I'm sure you thought the girls did, but I was thinking—I was afraid—that the infant was abandoned because it was

—well—sort of impaired. What if it's mute? And can manage a cry only occasionally?"

That was all he needed to ruin this night and a good many to come. Suddenly he was feeling the terror of a helpless child being abandoned in the woods. He could feel the cold dampness on his tender, bare skin, and see nothing around him but darkness. Yet if the child had cried out ...

"If it's able to cry, it's still alive. I'll be there in fifteen minutes. Chief will, too."

The dog was ready to go. At the back door Collins snapped on the leash and then let it drag the ground as both man and dog hurried to the car. He wasn't in uniform tonight, and he started to leave the patrol car in its spot in the carport, then decided he'd better take it. He might need to call for assistance.

The small woman with the head full of dark, glossy hair stood on the front sidewalk waiting for him. She looked petite in jeans and a denim jacket that curved in beneath her hips. In the dim light of the street lamp several yards away her face looked pale, and her full lower lip trembled. He saw her look at Chief, and saw Chief's immediate response to her. He pulled against his leash enough to stick his muzzle in her hand. She cupped it for just a moment, then she turned.

"This way to the gates."

"Yes, we remember, eh, Chief?"

She hurried on without answering, and the light beams of both their flashlights crossed like beams at an airport sweeping the dark.

The house next door was far enough away that if any activity was going on Collins couldn't hear it. He saw lights on in a front room. The chain link of their fence came across the grass to join the fence that surrounded the backyard of the Parker house. There was no way through to the woods at the rear except through one of the yards.

At the back gate she stood aside to let him and Chief go first.

"I don't know where to look," she said in a low voice. "I thought of getting my two girls out of bed to help me go look, but then I thought of your dog."

"Chief," he said.

"Chief," she repeated softly. He liked the sound of her voice.

"Where were you when you heard the cry?"

"Right here. Just a few minutes before I called you."

Collins stood still, Chief on the path just in front of him. The dog's head was up, alert. There was a slight tremble in his body. Collins tried to remember just how far along the path the girls had taken him this evening. But, he thought, did it really matter? Obviously they hadn't taken him to exactly the right place.

"All right," he said. "We know it's off the path. We know it's in ferns. There are no ferns growing right here. We'll let Chief look."

He followed the path only forty to fifty yards, his light sweeping the forest floor. They came to the growth of dark green, almost reptilian-looking ferns, and he let Chief's long leash out to the end. "Go to it, boy," he said softly, and followed the dog into the undergrowth, through the ferns, deeper into the woods.

He heard the sounds of the woman behind him, of a footstep cracking a twig, of the rustle of leaves. He saw her column of light, going past him, angling to one side or another. After several minutes he looked back and was surprised to see that she had been able to keep so close.

Two hours later they returned to the gate of the backyard, slowly, and without talking. At the gate, with it closed and latched, they both stood. Collins stared into the black forest, his flashlight turned off, and thought of the helpless, mute infant Lorna had described earlier. God, he hoped not. Neither of them would be able to forget that vision in their minds, but it was, after all, he told himself, only one woman's imagination and his own readiness to pick up on it.

"Could it have been an animal?" he said, not for the first time.

He heard her let out a long, tired breath.

Chief sat down between them.

"I guess it could have, though I didn't think so."

"An owl, maybe? A bird of some kind?"

"Maybe. I don't know anymore."

"Well, you'd better go in," Collins said, wanting to ask if he could see her again, possibly in daylight or at least under the soft light of a restaurant, but his tongue lay like a piece of lead in the back of his mouth. He managed, "Well, if you need us ..."

"Would you like to come in for coffee? Or hot chocolate? I'm so keyed up ..."

He wondered if she felt, as he did, that they belonged together now, after half a night in the woods with each other. He knew he didn't want to go home, not yet.

"I'll put Chief in the car," he said.

"No, bring him in."

"Are you sure?"

"Sure I'm sure. Maybe he'd like a drink of water."

They went into the kitchen, and Collins watched her unzip her jacket, but she didn't take it off. He sat down at the kitchen table, which was covered with a floral plastic cloth and had a lazy Susan holding the sugar bowl, salt and pepper, and napkins. Chief sat beside him, watching too as Lorna got him a bowl of water. Her long, curly, glossy dark hair swung forward against her cheek as she stooped to put the water down.

Chief looked toward the door that led into a hallway, and Collins saw the fluffy cat was there, its fur expanded as it had been when he saw it earlier on the patio. It hissed at Chief. Collins got a tighter grip on Chief's collar just in case, though he wasn't really worried.

"It's okay," he assured Lorna, in case she might be concerned. "We have cats around home, and Chief never bothers them."

"Could you explain that to Stardust?" she asked in her soft voice, smiling faintly.

Looking at her, seeing the loveliness of her face and the gentleness of her eyes, Collins thought to himself that something good might have come out of this puzzling case.

MAGRET LAY in bed looking up at the ceiling. She was afraid to go to sleep again. The dream was growing, and she relived it from its inception to the horror of tonight and the question Sheena had asked her.

"Mama, does Jason have teeth?" The question was spoken, over and over in her mind.

Mama, do tiny babies have sharp, needlelike teeth in rows in their mouths?

Mama, do babies get born from the ground?

The one question—"Mama, does Jason have teeth?"—had held in its dread and fear the unspoken question of the others. Magret knew—she *knew* what her little girl had seen. She didn't know how or why.

Why? *Why?*

It was her nightmare, not Sheena's.

She was afraid to go to sleep, to turn out all the lights in the room. Even in the shadows left in the corners from the soft light at the bedside table, she saw the ferns, the tree trunks, and the black soil splitting open, and rising from it ...

Oh, Lord in heaven, where are you?

She had been reared in church. The small, old, abandoned church her father had built, a woodland church that she had both loved and feared. Her father, its preacher, had insisted on daily prayers, on obedience to the Bible and the Lord's word as it *was*. He recognized it not as his viewpoint, but the Lord's, as absolute. If the King James Version of the Bible said it, it was true. And she had believed. And been obedient. She had been a good girl, hadn't she? She had said her prayers, done her work, until ...

Hadn't her father said, your sins shall find you out?

"Oh, Lord, oh, Lord," she whispered, her hands covering her face. This was not the God she had learned to believe in these past years with Daniel. This was the hellfire her father, God bless his soul, had believed in.

She couldn't sleep. She didn't dare sleep.

Something more frightening than a nightmare was happening when she slept. And now it had reached out and touched one of her children.

She got out of bed and looked at the clock. Four-ten. Just another hour or two to go before she could sensibly be up doing her work. Yet, if she worked downstairs, and quietly, she could go now. And it was better than lying here so afraid she would go to sleep.

She put on a morning cotton duster, crisp and spring-like, and left the bedroom, closing the door softly.

In the kitchen she mixed a cup of strong coffee and drank it as she got out the mop. Carrie had always done the mopping of the tiled floors, but she probably didn't get them as clean as Magret would have liked.

She began to mop the utility room, and felt the heaviness in her eyes lift, and with it, receding to the depths of her darkest soul, part of the fear.

CHAPTER 5

"I WISH SHEENA COULD HAVE COME." Wendy said, as she met Peggy at their halfway point on the path, not far from the place where the tall sycamore tree grew on the edge of the little bank by the shallow ravine. "I asked her, but she said she had to get her leaves on her own street. She dropped hers. I dropped mine, too."

"I still had some in my pockets." Peggy looked around. "I wonder why we don't go to your house. You've got a sugar maple in your yard, and then we could go around the road to my house and get some hickory leaves from my tree, and dogwood, too, and sassafras. Even redbud. There's lots of trees in my yard."

"Is your mom home today?"

"No, she's working. Daddy has gone somewhere to a meeting and he'll be late, and Mama won't be home until after five. She told me that I could go to your house, but she won't care if you come to mine."

"Why can't we just look in the woods?" Wendy left the path, searching for the leaves she had dropped. "I already had most of my nine varieties, and they're around here somewhere. If we find them, we can take Sheena's to her, too."

"But ..." Peggy said, following a few feet behind Wendy. "But—don't you think it's a little spooky in here? It seems too dark—or something."

Wendy looked back at Peggy, then all around. She lowered her voice. "Let's look for the baby again, Peggy. I didn't think about it yesterday when Sergeant Stoddard and Chief were with us, but if we had looked for the leaves we dropped, it would have been right where we found the baby."

"My mom and dad said there was no baby."

"You know that's not true! You saw it, and I saw it, and Sheena saw it."

"But—"

"Hey!" Suddenly Wendy was seeing the light, and she smiled at her chubby friend with the round brown eyes, the tight brown braid, and the tight mouth. "You're scared. You're scared of a tiny baby that can't even turn over and crawl? You're chicken, Peg! Chicken."

"I am not!"

"All right then, prove it. Let's go look for the baby again."

"What about our leaves? We have to get our leaves. We have to turn them in on Monday."

"Well, we've got all weekend. Come on."

Wendy led the way off the path, trying to remember just exactly where they had been yesterday. All the trees looked too much alike.

"It was close to the ravine, wasn't it?"

"No, it was closer to the path. In some ferns."

"Yes, I know it was in some ferns. But don't you remember, Sheena said it was over closer to the ravine than you and I thought it was? And she found it, so maybe she was right. Come on, let's walk along the side of the ravine and when we see a lot of ferns ..."

They walked beneath a dogwood, pausing to pick a handful of dark red leaves, putting them into the plastic bags they carried. Peggy also picked the red berries, while Wendy waited a few feet on toward the ravine.

"These look like they'd be good to eat. Did you know that birds like to eat these red berries? Aren't they pretty, Wendy?"

"Come on, for gosh sakes, you've got dogwood in your own yard."

Peggy kept picking berries. "I think I'll take a whole branch and put it on the mantel for Christmas."

"Come on, Peggy."

Peggy ripped off a small limb and stuck the end into her plastic bag. It went right through, making a hole. "Oh, damn." she said, and examined the hole.

"Well, you should've known it would. Sharp objects have that tendency, you know. They do poke holes in plastic."

"Now you sound just like Miss Spencer," Peggy said, stumbling over a fallen limb as she hurried to catch up with Wendy. "Did you hear what Miss Spencer said to Terry this afternoon?"

Wendy stopped suddenly in front of Peggy. There was something standing just the other side of a tree, hidden by the tree so that Wendy had caught only a glimpse of something pale. But it had moved, she was sure, and she stopped, twisting her neck, trying to see beyond the tree without going closer. A ripple of chills had begun between her shoulder blades and was moving into her hair. She wished Peggy would shut up, just shut up, but she didn't want to risk making a sound to tell her so. Who cared what Miss Spencer said to Terry?

Peggy came closer, sounding like a bull elephant in the leaves and sticks that lay on the ground. Earlier it was Peggy who had been scared to come into the woods. Wendy had had to go almost to Peggy's house on the path, calling to her, before Peggy got the nerve to come on in. Now Wendy wished neither of them had come, not today, not with someone hiding on the other side of a big tree.

Peggy reached Wendy, still talking about some dumb thing that Terry, a boy in their class, had done, and what Miss Spencer had told him, and Wendy reached back and grabbed Peggy's arm. Her whole chest rattled when she told her, "Shhhh!"

As Peggy grew suddenly quiet, Wendy whispered, "There's someone behind that big tree over there, Peggy."

Wendy heard Peggy's breath close to her ear. It had a soft whistling sound as Peggy came closer.

"For gosh sakes be *quiet,*" Wendy hissed, thinking to herself that whoever was there might be the baby's daddy, or mother. Maybe, she wanted to tell Peggy, it was some of those homeless people who had made their home in the woods. Though today, it was almost winter cold, with no sun shining, and with the mists and fogs rising from the damp floor and the ferns and ravines where water flowed just days ago.

Peggy whispered, "Let's go!"

At that moment, before they could move, there was a rattle of leaves behind the tree, and a child—a baby girl—stepped into view.

At first glance Wendy was reminded of the New Year's child, a young, naked baby just old enough to stand on its own feet. It had its hands together in front of its rounded belly, as if they were clasped. Its hair was soft, dark brown, ringlets close against its head, and its eyes piercing blue.

It was the tiny baby, grown now to the size of a toddler.

Wendy's heart was pounding so hard it thundered in her ears, and if there was a sound from the strange, naked baby, or even from Peggy, she couldn't have heard it. She felt Peggy pulling on her, and felt herself jerked around. She hadn't known before how strong Peggy was, or why she was so afraid and so willing to run with Peggy.

With Peggy still pulling her, Wendy ran, down the path for a few yards toward Peggy's house, which was a long, long way off, it seemed. Then, as if her hands were acting out a scene that her mind hadn't grasped yet, they were turning Peggy around, fighting with her in silence over which way to run, and finally she and Peggy were running back toward Wendy's house, where, she hoped, Islan would be home now.

They both fell against the back gate, and all four hands fumbled at the latch at the same time, and finally they burst through, leaving the gate open.

They reached the patio at the same time and stumbled breathless into the kitchen yelling for Islan.

The house echoed their calls.

For a few minutes they stood panting, huffing and puffing, in the middle of the kitchen. Then Wendy led the way through the rest of the house looking for Islan. They came to a halt in Wendy's bedroom.

Peggy dropped to the floor and Wendy sat down on the bed.

Neither of them spoke.

Then Wendy began to think.

And to speak her thoughts aloud.

"It's cold out there today. The baby grew. Did you see how the baby grew?"

"Maybe it's a sister of the little baby. Little babies don't grow that fast."

"No, it was the baby. I recognized her face. Those eyes—didn't you see how blue they were? It was the same baby. She had the same mole on her shoulder. You saw it too."

"Babies don't grow that fast!" Peggy sounded angry. "Then—then maybe the baby was bigger than we thought yesterday."

Peggy said nothing for a long time. She sat looking down at her hand on the carpet. The blue fibers made her fingers look brown.

Wendy said, "We have to help her, Peggy. I'll bet she's hungry and cold."

"Yeah, I was thinking the same thing."

"What could we take?" Wendy looked around at her room, at clothes spilling out of half-opened chest and dresser drawers because she hadn't cleaned up her room lately.

Peggy reached over and pulled a heavy sweater out of a drawer. She held it up. It was Wendy's new red and white sweater. Her favorite. Wendy made a dive for it and grabbed it away.

She threw it onto the bed.

"Not that one, silly! That's my new one."

"Well, pick something else then. Your mom sure buys you a lot of stuff." Peggy was on her knees now at the chest, pulling out sweaters and tops and underwear and jeans. Wendy went down beside her and began stuffing them all back. As fast as Peggy pulled them out, Wendy stuffed them back.

"It's not Mom who buys it. Mom doesn't have that much money. My dad sends money for clothes. I bought them with what he sends."

"My mom would never let me spend this much money on clothes!" Peggy remarked disapprovingly.

"My mom doesn't either! I have to put some of it away for college. Lots of these are things Islan had."

Peggy sat back with her hands on her hips. "Well, what are you going to take to the baby?"

Wendy sighed. "This, I guess." It was a cotton flannel pullover, long and soft and warm. "And this." Socks, which would keep the baby's feet warm.

She got to her feet and started out of the room, then she turned back on sudden impulse and picked up the new sweater. With the two sweaters and the one pair of socks, she started out of the room.

At the door she noticed Peggy was not following.

"Well?" she demanded.

"I was just thinking," Peggy said in a small voice, "if we should wait for Islan."

"You scared?" Wendy said, trying to put contempt in her voice. "Scared of a little baby? That doesn't even have any clothes?"

Peggy heaved a sigh and followed.

As Wendy left the house and stepped into the chilly air, she almost admitted to Peggy that she was scared, too. Scared to leave the house and yard, scared of the woods for the first time in her life.

And maybe—even scared of the tiny baby who in one day and night had grown enough that she could stand and walk.

IF she only had an excuse to talk to him again, Islan thought as she drove home. She was late today, and she was half embarrassed to admit, even to herself, that she had hung out an hour longer than usual at the places where she thought she might see Sergeant Stoddard. She had even driven by the jail, the courthouse, and the sheriff's big building behind the courthouse. She had seen patrol cars, and Sheriff's Department cars, but none of them had a dog in the back seat as Sergeant Stoddard's car did.

Collins. Collins was his name. She had found that out by calling the sheriff's place of business, or whatever it was called, and asking the woman who answered the phone. She had tried to make it sound authentic, not just a girl wanting to know a man's name. It had been easy to get his name, but she hadn't known how to get any other information. Was he married? She wondered now, although she hadn't given it a single thought before. If he was married, she'd have to die an old maid with a broken heart, because she wasn't low enough to take any girl's husband, or boyfriend. She wouldn't want anyone to take hers.

"Hello," she had said, going over the conversation in her mind. It had been playing in her mind as she drove, over and over. "Hello, is Sergeant Stoddard there?"

"No, he isn't here at the moment. Can I help you?"

"No, I needed to talk to him about a case ..."

"Which case is that, ma'am ..."

Ma'am ... it made her feel as if she were at last an accepted member of the adult population of the world.

"It's ... uh ... the uh baby case. The found and lost baby ... uh ... you might not know about it. The sergeant—what was his name? I mean, his full name like—you know—"

There was a slight hesitation on the line, then the voice said, "Sergeant Collins Stoddard." She had emphasized the Collins. Then she said, "Yes, I'm aware of that case, miss, just as I am all of them."

Uh-oh. Now she had given herself away. The lady was calling her *miss,* which made her a child again. And Islan suspected the woman was now smiling a little.

"The thing is," Islan said with all the dignity she could muster, thankful she had called instead of actually stopping in as she had almost done, "the thing is, he told me to call if something new came up about the baby in the woods ..."

"I'll give him the message, if you'll tell me, please."

Islan spent a precious thirty seconds trying to come up with something. She hadn't anticipated this.

She finally gave in and let the child in her speak. "It's okay," she said. "It was just something I was thinking."

She trembled all over again now, as if she had just hung up the pay phone and settled back into her car, hoping no one had seen her, glad the phones didn't have little televisions connected to them yet so the woman at the Sheriff's Department could have seen her face. Her face felt hot, as if it were red as blood. Gross, *gross.* As she stopped in the driveway of her house, she put both hands to her cheeks and pressed hard.

How embarrassing.

Why had she called in the first place?

Where, she wondered as she got out of the car, did Sergeant Collins Stoddard hang out? Probably in bars and things—those places where she couldn't go yet, unless she could get a fake ID. She could pass for twenty, she felt. Certainly she could pass for eighteen. After all, in another few months she would be eighteen.

She wondered where she could get a fake ID. She had noticed a couple of bars close to the sheriff's building, on one of the back streets, just as she had noticed the stores on another street, and the little shopping center on another, all within walking distance of the courthouse. Tomorrow she would go to the shopping center ...

Wendy and Peggy came running across the yard to her car, looking as wild and excited as they had yesterday evening after they said they found the baby. She stopped, bracing herself against their assault.

She was grabbed by one on one side and the other on the other side, and all of them toppled back against the car fender.

She flung them off. "For cat's sake! What's the matter with you two?"

They were jabbering together, and from the mixture of words, she began to understand they had seen the baby again.

"What! What?" she yelled. "Just talk one at a time!"

For a second, neither girl said anything, then both started at once again. From that jumble of words, Islan picked up a story.

They had seen the baby again, but it had grown this time and was walking. They had taken clothes out to the woods for it, because it was cold, and it probably was very hungry, but mainly it was cold because it was naked. But ... they couldn't find it.

There was a moment of silence as Islan looked from face to face.

Then suddenly it struck her and she tipped her head back and laughed, and laughed. She became aware that someone—Wendy—was pounding on her arm. She tried to stop laughing, but when she looked down at her little sister, tears came to her eyes and her giggles just wouldn't stop. Through the blur of tears, she could see that Wendy was furious. Her cheeks were as red as red Delicious apples.

"It's true, it's true, it's true!" Wendy was crying over and over, and Peggy was nodding her head.

What imaginations, Islan thought. "You guys are nuts," she said aloud as she reached back for the books the girls had knocked out of her arms when they attacked her. "You are absolutely nuts. You must be eating toadstools in the woods. Psychedelic toadstools. I can't figure any other reason for such wild and ridiculous hallucinations."

She went to the house with the girls, subdued now, on each side of her. As she put her books down on the kitchen table, she looked at both faces and saw them hanging like sad clown faces, and she saw that both girls really believed what they had said, what they said they'd seen.

"I can't believe you two," she said, standing on one foot, her knee bent, her hand on her jutting hip. "Look at you. Listen to yourselves."

"What," said Wendy morosely.

"Well, listen, kids," Islan said more kindly. "Yesterday you came screaming you'd seen a tiny baby, two months old. Today you say he's grown up." She began to giggle again.

Wendy gave her a half-tearful, half-furious glare.

"Not grown up, Islan. Just bigger. Standing up now."

"Oh," Islan giggled. "Like a two-year-old maybe."

"Maybe," Wendy said seriously.

"It's true," Peggy said. "I thought maybe the baby just looked smaller yesterday when it was in the ferns. I thought maybe there were two of them, one tiny and the other bigger. I thought maybe a family had moved into the woods. You know, the homeless people."

Islan stopped giggling. She frowned. "You know you could be right about that. Peggy, that really makes sense."

"Except," Wendy said, "it's not right. It's the same baby, and it was tiny yesterday. And today it's bigger, lots bigger, and standing up, and that means it can walk around." Her eyes widened. "It can come to our yard now ... it's even tall enough to unlatch the gate."

Islan stared at Wendy. Fear? Was that fear she saw on Wendy's face?

Then suddenly something occurred to her, and she wondered why it had taken her so long to think of it. She now had an excuse to call Collins!

She reached for the wall phone. "I'll report it."

The two girls waited in silence while Islan once again called the sheriff, hoping in her heart of hearts that she wouldn't get the same woman. She hadn't liked the expression in her voice the last time.

The same woman answered.

Islan cleared the sudden frog in her throat with a small cough. "This is Islan Parker," she said clearly. "I want to report that the child in the woods has been seen again. Could I please talk to Sergeant Co—Stoddard about it?"

"Sergeant Stoddard isn't here, but I can have him dispatched."

"Yes, please, would you?" Whatever that meant, she hoped it would bring him to the house again. She gave the address and phone number again, just to be sure there would be no mistake.

When she hung up the phone she hurried to the bedroom to change her clothes. She wanted the new pink sweater, because it brought out her complexion better than any other, without overwhelming her, and the old jeans, because they were tight, so tight she had to lie down on the floor to get them on. She wouldn't wear a jacket, even though she might have if she'd been going into the outdoors with anyone else.

She changed earrings, and put on a pair that dangled almost to her shoulders. Her girlfriends had said she could wear the big earrings because she was tall. She had thought they made her look a little trashy, maybe like some hooker on Hollywood Boulevard, but she'd take a chance. They did make her look older.

Occasionally, as she heard Wendy and Peggy whispering outside her bedroom door as they waited, she burst into giggles again. Every time she thought of a two-month-old baby growing overnight to a two-year-old, she felt like she was going to crack up.

Yet, oddly, they were so serious. What was with them?

"Hey, I think he's here," Wendy yelled as she knocked on the bedroom door. "What's taking you so long? You've been in there for twenty minutes."

Islan smoothed her pale hair back on each side of her face and hurried out. Now she could hear the doorbell ringing. Collins Stoddard must have been close by to have gotten here so soon, she thought, and wondered, as her cheeks grew warm and her pulses raced, had he wanted to see her again, too? Had he been patrolling the area near her street because his heart drew him back to her?

Islan hurried, feeling self-conscious now. Would he notice that she was more made up than she was the first time he came out? Would he know she had done it for him? Maybe he'd think she had a date.

Would he feel a touch of envy, maybe jealousy?

"Oh boy," Wendy said, looking at her sharply. "What'd you do to yourself?"

"Shut up, jeezeus, shut up," Islan hissed under her breath. As she went out the door she put a smile on her face. It trembled around the edges at first, but by the time she had reached the walk where Sergeant Collins Stoddard stood, tall and handsome beside his sleek dog, the smile had become real.

CHAPTER 6

COLLINS LISTENED, his eyes taking in the surrounding lawns, houses, and the dark line of forest behind the yards at the end of the cul-de-sac. The oldest girl, Islan, kept trying to hide a case of the giggles, while the other two stood back, as solemn and silent today as if the cat had gotten both their tongues.

"They said it was still naked, and it had grown—overnight—to the size of a two-year-old." The giggles burst out, even as she tried to control them.

Collins looked at the two younger girls. Their faces were as gloomy as two small clouds, and Wendy pressed her lips tighter and tighter. He suspected she was going to explode any minute. Peggy picked almost timidly at Wendy's sleeve, trying to get her attention. She looked warily over her shoulder.

"It's true!" Wendy finally burst out. Her eyes grew larger and brighter as she blinked rapidly. "We took some clothes out to the woods, but we couldn't find her. So we brought the clothes back."

Islan shrugged, trying to suppress her giggles. "If they did see another one, there must be a family of them out there."

Collins smiled. Islan's laughter, now open, beyond giggles, was more than a little contagious. Yet the looks on the faces of the two younger girls still worried him. They didn't look like two kids playing a game. Both little girls were now looking bewildered, embarrassed, and something that concerned him more—afraid. Especially Peggy, it seemed to him, was afraid. Just as the little Treacle girl had been yesterday. He began moving on toward the gate, going ahead of the girls. "Why don't we take another look out there?"

Islan hurried ahead of him and unlocked the gate, then led the way across the backyard and through the back gate. She began asking him questions, turning her face occasionally to look back at him. Was he on another job in the area when he got the call from the Sheriff's Office? He told her he'd just been coming back from one. Had it been dangerous?

They entered the path. He remembered last night as he'd been remembering it all day, when he had walked this path with Lorna. Lorna, petite, dark-haired, and brown-eyed, with two towheads? Even though they had sat at the kitchen table until three-thirty in the morning, both of them talking as fast as they could as if they were old friends who hadn't seen each other since high school, they hadn't gotten around to her marriage. Or two marriages—or three—although he would have been surprised if there was more than one. It just didn't fit her image. He knew she was divorced. He'd had to determine that as soon as politely possible. He had asked if he could see her again, and she had looked at the floor. By that time he was standing on the patio just outside the kitchen, and he knew he should have left long ago.

She shrugged. "No," she finally said. "I don't know. I just don't think so."

It was hours before he suddenly realized she must already be serious about some other guy. And all day today he'd had Lorna on his mind, touched with sadness, as if he'd loved and lost in such a short time.

He looked back. The two little girls were following hesitantly, peering into the forest at their left. Just outside the gate Peggy stopped.

"I have to go home," she said, her round, brown eyes meeting Collins's.

"Then come on," Wendy said. "Your house is this way. And why do you have to go now? It's not dark yet."

Peggy shrugged, her plump shoulders moving up and down in her heavy sweater, her hands in the pockets of her jeans. They had all stopped now. Collins was observing the behavior of these two girls. It seemed even more important than making another search through the dwindling light of the forest.

"I just have to," Peggy said, looking at her toes.

"Okay," Wendy said. "I'll walk with you."

"I thought maybe we could go around the road."

"But that's so far." Islan said. "You girls always take the path." She added, for Collins's benefit, "They have this shortcut. Along the path it's only about half as far as around the road. Around the road they have to go down the street to the highway and then along it. It's much more dangerous that way. Our moms wouldn't let you girls visit back and forth the way they do if you didn't have this private path."

Peggy drew a long breath and looked off through the trees. Collins could see that regardless of whatever—or whomever—the girls had seen in the woods, their hide and seek game was beginning to scare Peggy. "I'll walk home with you, Peggy," he said. "I'd like to talk to your parents anyway. But first I need you to point out where you saw the child."

Wendy tugged at her. "Come on, Peg. It's okay. Sergeant Stoddard is with us, and Chief."

Collins had a feeling the presence of the dog gave Wendy a greater feeling of safety than he did. He smiled as he turned back.

They made their way to approximately the same place as yesterday. "There," Wendy said. "She was standing on the other side of that tree."

She was pointing at a tall, broad-trunked sycamore, whose white and gray trunk had large flakes of bark peeling away, leaving the smooth, white under-skin. It leaned over the ravine.

"It was there, wasn't it, Peggy? She was standing right there."

Peggy agreed. Wendy kept behind Chief, following as the dog led the way with his nose to the ground. Peggy hung back.

Collins spotted occasional signs of their presence yesterday. A footprint in soft, dark soil, a broken twig, a fern pushed aside, a frond broken. But the forest was as quiet as yesterday, with only the almost silent drifting down of leaves. As they stood quiet, Chief lifted his head and held his breath. Collins automatically held his own.

As the dog turned his head, it seemed to Collins that he seemed to be looking back toward the ravine, as if something were there, beyond the chipmunks.

But if there was any sign of a child, or two children, one of them an infant, it was gone now. Maybe, Islan suggested, there was a homeless family out here, a couple and their two children, and sometimes they were in this area.

Collins nodded, although it didn't sound consistent with the things he had heard.

"We'll walk home with you now, Peggy," he said, and pulled Chief back toward the path. As they walked, Chief kept turning his head back toward the ravine. The ditch angled, as he remembered from his and Lorna's quite thorough search last night, away from the path, off into the deeper sections of the woodland. There was a small spring at its source, Lorna had said. She and her girls had come along the ravine often in the springtime to gather wildflowers and eat a picnic lunch at the spring. The water was cold and pure, but the stream very small, so that only a pool of water lay like a basin before the small stream sank into the gravelly bottom of the ravine. In wet weather, though, it became a torrent, and made a quite respectable stream down the shallow ditch they so gloriously referred to as the ravine.

When they got to Peggy's backyard, Collins saw she lived in the big two-story house he had noticed many times. It was a typical farmhouse, on an acre or so of cleared property now grown up in young trees, or brush, over which Collins could see the spire on down the road of the small, one-room church.

"My folks aren't here," Peggy said after a peek into the kitchen. Her hand slipped along the wall, and the kitchen light came on. Collins saw bright curtains at the windows and a linoleum floor. "Mama's not home yet. She works part time at a bakery in town. My dad doesn't come home until after dark."

"So you'll be alone?" Collins asked.

"Yes, but that's all right. Mama will be here in a little while."

Collins felt reluctant to leave her. "Do you have the number of the sheriff on your telephone, in case you need to call?"

"Yes. Mama fixed it so that I only have to push a button."

"Lock your doors," he said, noticing the back door hadn't been locked. If there were people living in the woods not far from this house, there might be danger from them.

Wendy waved good-bye to Peggy. By the time Collins reached the edge of the yard again and looked back, the door was shut. Golden light filtered through the curtains at the windows.

The forest was growing dark. He let Chief go as fast as he wanted, the leash tight between them as he hurried to keep up. He motioned for the girls to wait.

At the point where Chief pulled him off the path and toward the ravine he stopped, removed Chief's leash from his collar, and let him go. The dog moved into the ferns, nose down, zigzagging back and forth as if following a trail. He was probably having one of his happy-puppy spells, and had decided he was off duty.

Collins heard a noise behind him and saw Islan had followed and was standing knee-deep in fern. He noticed for the first time she wasn't wearing a coat. Her arms were hugged tightly to her body, yet she couldn't contain the shivers that vibrated over her one after the other. Several yards behind Islan, still on the path, stood Wendy. There was no adventure left in Wendy. She had not led the way into the woods the way she had yesterday, eager to find again the infant they thought they had seen.

"You ladies go on home," he said. "It's going to be dark out here soon, and I need to be able to go at my own pace. I'll stop by when I leave."

Islan seemed reluctant but Wendy helped by edging past her on the path and reaching back to pull her along.

"We'll have coffee made," Islan said, turning her head to look back at him. "You'll need hot coffee. It's getting cold."

He felt a twinge of dismay. The look in her eyes ... *now.* She was only a kid. He was damned if he was going to be one of those men who thought every good-looking female, and some not so good-looking, was flirting with him with wedding rings in her eyes.

He removed a small flashlight from its loop. The natural light had turned gray and slanting, the sun sinking below the trees. Chief was only a silver-pale moving shape among the darker undergrowth, the vines that held their green, waxy leaves even in winter. He followed, using the flashlight to pry into the darkest growths.

Chief's tail was visible as a light plume waving vigorously in the twilight of the forest ahead of him. The waving tail meant the dog was in one spot, digging, possibly, or otherwise disturbing the nest of some little forest creature.

Then the dog whined, and his head rose above the dark line of the forest floor, searching for Collins.

The dog was at the ravine. He gave one woof at Collins, then his head disappeared again.

Collins went toward him, and shined the small flashlight beam down. Chief had been digging at the very edge of the ravine. Against the dark soil, as the dog stepped back, was part of something grayish-white, that looked, at first glance, like a part of a root, a tiny piece of light-colored tree root.

Collins leaned down and stared, his flashlight illuminating the tiny bone.

Showing through the black soil was part of a tiny skeleton, an arm and shoulder and part of the skull of a miniature creature, a human infant, it would seem.

It was the skull Chief had been unearthing, the claw marks clearly embedded in the black soil at the edge of the ravine.

"I'll be damned," Collins said in a low voice to Chief. "How long do you suppose it's been here?"

Chief whined softly close to his ear.

With his fingers, Collins nudged soil away from the skull. It became more clearly the skull of a newborn, the two halves of the skull with a separation at the top through which the dark soil of the forest showed. The sockets of the eyes looked up at him with the dark of the soil filling them. He dug the soil gently away from the twig-like right arm bone and tiny hand and fingers. Hair roots from nearby trees and undergrowth had woven and braided around the skeleton, looking, in a grisly way like a loosely woven blanket, a cocoon closing it in, holding it intact.

Past rains, one decade, or two decades of rains, had opened the grave on the side nearest the ravine, so that its arm had been exposed like the tree roots.

Judging from the depth of the soil above the infant skeleton, Collins felt the grave originally had been very shallow, as if it had been dug by desperate hands, rather than a spade or shovel.

The infant had been placed in its grave without any vestige of clothing or bedding, so far as he could see. Buried like an animal unloved.

Chief growled, a soft, deep, low sound that Collins might not have heard if the dog hadn't been right at his shoulder.

Collins sat back on his heels. Feeling a strange, electric tingle up his backbone, a sensation of nervousness across his shoulders and into his hair, Collins straightened. He noticed the direction of Chief's stare, and saw the intensity in his eyes. There was no friendliness there. It was as if the dog was warily watching an enemy, someone who might be about to make a threatening move.

Collins lifted the flashlight and shined it through the trees, toward the path. As Collins shifted the light to the left, toward the denser part of the woods, where the path angled away toward the road and the home of Peggy and her parents, something white flashed among the dark trunks. For just an instant he could have sworn he saw in the sweep of his flashlight a small, pale face staring at him with eyes that looked as dark as the eyes in the skull near his feet—eyes of soil and dampness—and a small figure that was as pale as snow and without clothing.

Collins jerked the light back. The white trunk of a sycamore tree stood among the dark trunks like one single sentry from a different army.

The flashlight trembled slightly as Collins gave a small laugh.

"A tree trunk, you brave mutt you," he said, while Chief stood staring with his brown eyes wary and steady, and the soft little growl coming again as if he didn't believe his master. Collins transferred the flashlight to his left hand and reached down to scratch the base of Chief's left ear. The dog didn't respond. He continued to stare in the direction of the sycamore tree and its gray and white bark. And to growl deep in his throat.

"Let's get out of here." Collins reached down to snap Chief's leash back on.

He marked the tree closest to the grave, and noticed it was the same big sycamore that Wendy and Peggy had pointed out as the one where they'd seen the two-year-old child.

Chief now seemed more than willing to go, pulling ahead of him on the leash.

CHAPTER 7

MAGRET FELT the pull of something on her feet as she tried to walk. It was as if she stood in something thick and viscous that was trying to draw her into itself. She was filled with a terror so deep, she was unable to scream. Gradually, she began to be less blind, and saw she was struggling through a very dark world in which she was surrounded by tall, black columns. Something on the soft, mushy floor kept her from going forward now, though she put all her strength into trying to run away from this awful fear, this terrible place.

The light was turning gray, and she could see, less blinded now, that the columns that surrounded her were trees. She looked down and saw she was embedded ankle deep in soil as black as tar and with the substance of quicksand. As she tried to move, tried to scream her fears, the dark earth at her feet began to rise. Something white was emerging from the soil as it cracked away, star-shaped.

The face of the infant looked up at her, soil in the creases of its face and in its neck. It rose and grew bigger and its mouth fell open to reveal white, sharp, saw-teeth coming toward her, its head looming larger and larger until her vision was filled with the gaping horror of the mouth.

Magret woke up trying to scream, the sound a choked gagging in her throat. She was damp but freezing cold as she sat in her bed with the blankets folded on her legs.

She forced herself to take deep breaths as her heart settled down to a hard, steady pounding.

It was almost daylight. The soft outdoor light penetrated the drawn draperies, turning the room a twilight gray. Daniel, facing away from her, was sleeping soundly. At least her nightmare cries hadn't awakened him this time.

She was so thankful to be awake, it was like being reborn. She pushed her blankets back, got out of bed, and walked barefoot across the soft carpet. Never, in her years of living with soft carpets, had she gotten over the delight of bare toes among the fibers. It was similar to the pleasure she used to feel when as a child she waded through mud puddles and felt the warm, or cold—it hadn't mattered then—squishing and oozing up between her toes.

She pulled the draperies back. The world outside her window was beginning to come alive. Today she was going to the hospital again, to be a receptionist at the desk outside the intensive care unit. A few hours of accepting flowers for patients, and monitoring the ten-minute limit for family members. It was a quiet place, where the beeping of heart monitors leaked out into the waiting room.

That would take up the morning hours from eight until twelve. Then she would have lunch in the cafeteria with other volunteers, friends, and new acquaintances. After lunch she'd come home and see how Carrie was getting along with the cleaning. Even though Carrie had been doing the housework three times a week for over ten years, Magret still liked to check on her, to make sure she didn't skip something. Daniel had suggested a few times that she might be a perfectionist, but Magret didn't consider herself that fussy. She just wanted things done right, that was all.

In the afternoon, she'd be going by the church. She had to spend a couple of hours addressing envelopes to church members, because Reverend Greystone felt requests for more money should at least be hand-addressed. The form letters might come off the computer, but the envelope must be more personal.

Thoughts of lunch depressed her, as she closed herself into the brightly lit bathroom to clean up for the day. Lunch always depressed her. For breakfast her one piece of dry toast wasn't so bad—she was seldom hungry then anyway. But at noon, with her stomach beginning to ache with hunger, and everything in her demanding real food, having to sit down with a salad made of lettuce, with only one slice of tomato, and vinegar dressing, was so depressing that sometimes she trembled thinking of it.

Still, as she stepped on the scales, she saw she hadn't lost an ounce. Her weight persisted in staying ten to fifteen pounds higher than she liked.

In front of the wide mirrors she saw the flab at her waist and around her stomach. Her breasts had grown another size, so that the bras she had worn for years now were too tight.

She tried to remember what she had eaten that had caused this bulging of her body. For her, a thousand calories a day was a feast.

She turned her back to the mirrors and pulled on underwear and a bright housecoat. Later, after breakfast, she would come back upstairs and see if there was anything in her closet that fit.

As she went downstairs, pulling the draperies open on every window she passed, she remembered the dream, and she felt again the cold terror in her heart. She'd been thinking as hard as she could, chattering within her own mind, trying to keep herself from remembering the dream.

She put her hand to her forehead in a desperate gesture. *Why is this happening to me?*

If she told Daniel he would suggest she talk to a psychiatrist—Dr. Walter, or one of the younger men or women in Walter's office.

If she talked to the Reverend, he'd want to know what was behind the nightmares.

In the kitchen she turned on the radio and began mixing bran muffins for breakfast. She switched the dial from a raucous rock station and got a preacher, whose voice irritated her so much she hurriedly turned the dial again until easy listening music flowed softly from the radio.

After she finished putting the muffins into the oven, she stood with nothing to do. It was not yet seven o'clock. She had made the muffins too early; they would be cold before Daniel and the kids came downstairs.

She stood looking toward the utility room and mudroom, and began moving in that direction without knowing why. She turned on the light in the utility room. On the other side was the door into the mudroom, standing open. That was strange. Hadn't she closed it last night?

She went forward slowly, suddenly terribly afraid of what she might find, and turned on the light above the rack of shoes and overshoes.

She bent down to examine her boots. They were clean. Thank God. Not like before—after the first time she'd had the dream—when she had come out to find her boots encrusted with soil. As if her dream had not been a dream at all, and she really had gone back, into the forest, in her sleep.

From the kitchen she heard the voice of a newscaster on the radio, and remembered the muffins.

She hurried back to the kitchen and peered through the glass on the oven door. Not done yet.

Suddenly the newscaster's words caught her attention.

"... an infant, found buried in the woods out northwest of town, near the Greenbrier Addition. It is said to be the skeleton of a newborn, buried eighteen to twenty years ago. The police are looking for—"

She lurched toward the radio and turned it off, and then drooped over it on the counter near the sink with her head down. She was going to be sick, she felt. Sick, so sick.

... they're looking for the woman who buried the baby...

Eighteen to twenty years ago.

Oh God oh God oh God.

How could she ever have thought that no one would find out?

But they didn't know yet. How could they, she asked herself as she hurried to the half-bath off the utility room and washed her face with cold water. After eighteen years, how could they find the woman—the girl—who had left her baby in the woods, to—to—

How could they?

There was nothing, nothing at all, anymore, to connect the infant, so long dead, with the person—the girl—who had given birth to it. Not even genetic testing would work now. There'd be nothing left but bones.

The skull—rising out of the earth ...

Now she knew what her dreams had meant. She had seen what was happening. She had seen it rising from the earth.

But it was dead. Only a skeleton now, although her mind had put flesh on it in her dreams.

"Maggie?" Daniel's voice called.

She dried her face and hurried back to the kitchen. He stood in the center of the room looking puzzled.

"Is something burning?"

"Oh my God!" She hurried to the oven, grabbed a mitt, and pulled out muffins that had peaked to black on the top. She shook them out onto waxed paper.

"Oh Lord. I should have set the timer."

"They'll be all right." Daniel mixed a cup of instant coffee at the counter. He was dressed in his favorite colors—dark blue suit with pale blue shirt and striped tie. How dear he was, how solid and dependable. It made her feel better just to look at him.

"I have to get dressed," she said. "I'm late."

Daniel sat down with his coffee and two of the blackened muffins. As she left the kitchen, she heard him turn the radio on. She prayed he wouldn't hear the news. But of course they all would hear it eventually, wouldn't they? Not only her family, but her friends, her acquaintances. And what would Sheena think now? What would she think about the baby she had seen in the woods? Sheena, who had dreamed her dream, shared her horror.

The terror of her nightmare and the horror of the discovery in the woods chilled her like a bleak winter wind as she moved through her day, as she forced smiles from her desk at the visitors for patients in intensive care. As she okayed or stopped flower deliveries.

Finally her time was up. Instead of going down to the cafeteria to eat, she fled the hospital, not knowing exactly where she was going, just that she wanted to be alone. She was stopped by a hand on her arm.

It was Clarice, another of the volunteers and a member of her own church. She and Clarice had been having lunch together at least twice a month for years, comparing notes on their children, on relatives, on friends, and on dieting. At any other time she would have been glad to see Clarice's very pretty, round face. At this moment she was dismayed.

"You're not leaving," Clarice said.

"Well, I really need to get home ..." Why couldn't she lie more easily? Life would be much less a burden, it seemed.

"Oh, come on, you don't really need to go home, do you? I was looking forward to having lunch with you today. It's been weeks."

"Has it been that long?"

It dawned on her why Clarice wanted to have lunch. She wanted to talk about that terrible find, that little skeleton out in the woods northwest of town. Maybe she knew that once Magret had lived there, that she had played in those woods, roamed those paths. Lots of people would remember that she had not moved away from the home in which she had been born and where she grew up until a year before she married Daniel. Seventeen years ago. She had been eighteen. They would remember that she—*she* lived there at the time of the death of the baby in the woods.

They would know it was her baby, hers. That she was the woman the police were looking for.

She felt amazed, now that she thought of it, that no one had mentioned the discovery of the newborn's grave all this morning.

Maybe they hadn't heard. Maybe Clarice hadn't heard either.

She allowed Clarice to pull her toward the elevator down to the cafeteria. She tried to respond to Clarice's chatter. Something about an old lady in a car wreck. And a speeding teenager.

In the cafeteria they got in line. Magret saw, over at a corner table, the women with whom she usually ate.

"So that's how come I was a little late. I finally backed up, when no one was watching, and went around a side street. I almost missed you."

Clarice chose the pizza, with a diet Coke and a piece of chocolate cake. "Oh, well, what the heck?" she said. "Thanksgiving is coming up one of these days, and then Christmas, and you know what that means. All those goodies and then the dark days of January and February, dark mainly because I have to go on a diet."

Magret chose the tossed salad. Then she treated herself to a packet of crackers and a dash of real French dressing.

"You have such willpower, Magret," Clarice said. "How do you do it? All the time, day after day."

"It doesn't seem to do that much good either," Magret said. Clarice glanced down over Magret's figure. "Oh, come on. You're tiny as a rail."

"I just know how to hide it well," she admitted. It was always good to have Clarice tell her she had nothing to worry about. For a moment she could almost believe it. But the reality always crept in.

They sat at the corner table with all the other volunteers who had been at the hospital during the morning, and two others who came in to work during the afternoon.

For a while the conversation was normal. There were three new babies. One of the mothers had had a hard time, even with the cesarean surgery. She'd almost bled to death and had required several units of blood.

Lunch was almost over when someone asked, "Well, ladies, did you hear the latest news? There was a grave found, of a newborn that someone buried years ago out in the woods somewhere ... they said it was buried alive ... they're looking for the mother ..."

A river made of blood and terror raged through Magret's ears, deafening her to most of all that was being said. Words reached her brain as if flung at her.

Alive ... buried alive ... not even with a blanket ...

about twenty years ago ... woman might still be here ... police looking ...

Not alive, she wanted to scream.

Not alive.

Oh, God, she hoped not alive.

She got up from the table.

"Are you all right, Magret?" Clarice asked, and Magret realized that several of the faces were looking up at her, curious, some of them concerned.

Magret forced a smile. "I'm fine. I just have to run. An errand. I have a cleaning lady in today, and I have to get home before she leaves."

She made herself walk slowly, until she reached the door. She turned and waved at Clarice, who was still watching her. Does she know? Does she know I'm the woman the police are looking for? Does Clarice remember that I once lived in the house—next door to the grave—or did I never tell her, or anyone.

Thank God, she rarely talked of the past. Since she had moved, she had put the old away, encouraging new acquaintances to talk of themselves, their interests, their pasts.

She locked herself into her car and resisted the urge to put her head down on her steering wheel.

She had to get out of here.

CHAPTER 8

As Magret drove, the rain came. Heavy, straight down, hard upon the top of her car, slanting against the front as she followed the winding strip of a two-lane highway. She remembered another time, the same time of year, with the rain pouring onto the roof of the church. Her father's voice, without benefit of a microphone, seemed muffled beneath the roar of the rain above. Magret wouldn't—couldn't—have listened to him anyway. Over the long years, her mind wandered into daydreams during her father's interminable sermons.

On this night she was cold with dread. Her father's voice was part of the furies of nature, a background for her fear. Something was happening to her body, and she wasn't sure what it was, but she was filled with terror. The stirrings within her belly, the feelings that something was fluttering there, had now changed to more definite, not to be denied sensations of movement. She'd had minor sex education in school. She'd been taught about menstruation, and the female productive organs, and a bit about the male productive organs. But she hadn't hung out with the girls to giggle over the pictures of naked men when the teacher was out of the room. She stayed pretty much to herself, knowing she was big and not pretty.

She also knew she was no fun to be with. She didn't skip school, or go on dates ... at least not real dates.

The boy she loved was a man. He sat three pews ahead of her that night in church, with his slender young wife at his side, and his two-year-old son on his lap. His wife held their baby, a six-month-old girl.

She stared at the back of his head, willing him to turn and look at her. She had to talk to him, please, Jesus, *she had to talk to him.* What was she going to do? What would her dad—even her mother—do when they found out? They must not find out. Of all things in heaven and earth, they must not find out.

If Clyde would only look at her ... meet her eyes ... so she could send him her message of desperation.

Clyde, I think I'm pregnant.

Clyde, what am I going to do?

Why wouldn't he look at her?

Last spring, and—now that she thought of it, when his wife was large and awkward with the baby she was now holding on her lap—he had looked at her. His eyes had met hers every time she glanced his way, those brown eyes that said she was beautiful, desirable, brown eyes that said he wished he had waited for her. When she looked at him he smiled, a soft and secret smile that no one but Magret saw.

It was on a picnic that they first spoke to each other beyond the ordinary greeting of one church member to another. His wife was in the hospital, and the new baby had been born. But Clyde had come to the church picnic because his wife insisted, Magret heard him say as they both moved through the line at the outdoor lunch tables with paper plates in their hands. He was only two people away from her. Then, at the dessert table, he was right beside her. She started to take a slice of chocolate cake, then drew her hand back.

"Go ahead," Clyde said, smiling, friendly, "take the cake."

"I shouldn't."

"You should," he said, and used the spatula to lift the slice of cake onto her plate. Under his breath, close to her ear, he said, "You're perfect just the way you are. All woman."

She could hardly breathe. No one had ever told her she was attractive in any way. Usually boys acted as if she weren't around. And now this grown, handsome man, with his smooth, dark brown hair and his dark eyes, his wide lips and white teeth—was telling her she was ... *all woman.*

They sat together at the edge of the church grounds, at the back, leaning against trees, with the dark, secret forest behind them. He seemed to be a little edgy, his eyes going over the crowd that milled on the church grounds, careful not to sit too close to her, it seemed.

"How old are you?" she asked.

"Twenty-two," he said. Then, "Would you like to slip into the woods for a walk?"

"Sure," she replied breathlessly. "I go there a lot. I live with my dad—he's the minister, you know—right there in the rectory. My mother grew up just down the road in a big old farmhouse. My uncle lives there now, all by himself. His wife died, you know, in a car wreck, just last year? So I go into the woods a lot. I always have ..." She stopped, hideously embarrassed, knowing she was rambling, telling him things he probably knew. She could remember seeing him at church a long time ago, before he was married. She could even remember his wedding in the church, but she hadn't really looked at him until he began looking at her.

"I tell you what," he said, getting up, pretending to bend down near her to pick up a napkin he had dropped, and an empty paper cup, "I'll meet you. Go straight back from the church about a hundred yards. That ought to be far enough not to be seen. Just wait for me. I'll be there. Don't let anyone see you leave."

She watched him walk away. He had a medium tall, slender body with square shoulders, and a swaggering walk that she hadn't noticed before. Heat rushed through her body just looking at him. Her hands trembled as she got up and took her plate to another trash can, yards away from him.

She hadn't eaten the cake after all. She had completely forgotten it.

After standing around with a group of girls her own age for a few minutes, pretending to listen to the conversation, she slipped away. She walked around the corner of the white church and along the path from church to rectory. She went into the house, just as if she were going home for a while, in case her mother or any of her relatives were watching. A couple of minutes later she went out the front door and ran into the woods on the other side of the house, circling around when she was safely hidden, to come back approximately where Clyde had suggested she meet him.

Spring flowers were blooming on the forest floor. Lady's slippers, and wild violets. The leaves overhead were young and pale, not lushly dark green as they would be in a few more weeks. But she thought, as she went more slowly among the trees and the flowers, that the woods had never been more beautiful.

A flash of white caught her eye, and then Clyde stepped out from behind a tree. There was no smile on his face now. The look in his eyes made her so weak she couldn't move.

He came to her. "A virgin," he whispered as his arms went around her and pulled in at her waistline. She felt the hard planes of his body, and had to put her hands on his shoulders to support herself. "You know," he whispered against her neck, "my wife wasn't a virgin. I didn't know it until I married her. She had told me she was. I want to know now—are you a virgin?"

"Y-yes." She didn't tell him she'd never even been kissed. She was fifteen and hadn't even been asked for a date.

He kissed her. They sank to the ground and lay on the cool floor of the forest, and she felt the cool air against her bare flesh as he removed her pantyhose.

She felt only a bare sting of pain when he came so forcefully into her, but even as he made love to her, she wondered if he would ever want to again. Hadn't she heard, even from some of the girls at school, that once a guy got in your pants, he was tired of you? But she couldn't have resisted him, even if she had wanted to. Though she knew she was doing wrong, that she was committing adultery, the same as he, was it really wrong? Wrong by her father's standards. But was he always right?

She wasn't going to think. She couldn't think.

"We have to get back," he said as he rose from her. Then he kissed her tenderly as he would have his child, and whispered, "Man, what a woman you are. I thought, looking at you lately, that you're about as ripe as a girl will ever get."

"Will I see you again?"

"You're damn right, baby. Try to keep me away."

He turned back toward her just before he hurried out of sight, and said, "Same place, Wednesday night, about seven? I have to go out on a job, or so I'll say."

She nodded.

And now, six months later, she was willing him to look at her. It had been two months or more—much more, it seemed—since he had spoken to her. And then he had only said, "I can't meet you. My wife has gotten suspicious."

Yet Magret saw no suspicion in Glorian's eyes. When the slender, blue-eyed young woman looked at Magret, it was with a gentle smile and a greeting—that was all.

She had to talk to him. She had felt the flutterings in her body even back then, and now she was terrified that she was much too far along to have an abortion.

Lord, what was she going to do?

Would he divorce his wife to marry her?

The thought had not consciously entered her mind before, and now it rose like a dying animal, one brief rise of the head, a silent cry.

He did not look at her.

But she knew where he worked, and the next week she skipped school, and went to the shop where he at times kept store, as he'd called it, and at times went out to fix somebody's appliance. When he looked up and saw her, his eyes flickered a couple of times, but not with the passion she had seen in them last spring and summer.

She stood at the counter until a customer left, then she said, "Clyde, I've got to talk to you."

Clyde's eyes looked everywhere but at her. "I can't be seen talking to you," he hissed under his breath. "Not now. Maybe another time."

She looked over her shoulder, but there were only two other customers, a man and his wife, toward the front of the store looking at a washer and dryer set. And suddenly she knew. He didn't want to talk to her. He wasn't afraid of his wife or anyone. He was simply tired of her.

She felt sick. A flash of memory came, the times late in the summer when she had to ask him to meet her. He had come, after several broken dates, and he would make love to her. But there was a difference. It wasn't love anymore, it was just sex.

She felt dirty.

"I'm pregnant, Clyde."

"What the hell is that supposed to mean?"

His voice could sound so cruel, so accusing, so filled with disgust and hate.

Before she could answer, he went on, his voice hissing like a snake's, his hands rattling papers angrily. "If you tell my wife about this, or anyone else, I'll say you lied. If you're pregnant, that's your problem. I'm a married man, I've got two kids and a wife, and you knew that when you were so fast to spread your legs out. So don't you try to get me into trouble."

She ran out, tears hot and blinding in her eyes. From that day on, she lived moment by moment, wearing heavier clothes, larger, looser clothes, thankful at last that her mother had never been very close to her, so that she didn't know that Magret hadn't had a menstrual period in months. Glad, too, that it was winter, and the clothes hid her, although she never got very large at all. In school she begged excuses from gym, saying her legs hurt, and her mother wrote her a note without questions, asking for Magret to be excused from gym.

One night in January, after a cold rain had left icicles hanging on the roof outside her window, she was suddenly bent double with pain. As she lay hugging herself, trying not to scream, she felt warm liquid between her legs.

She got out of bed, bent forward, and ran. Her pajamas were wet and clammy, clinging to her, and she knew she was bleeding.

She went out the back door, quietly, barely closing it behind her, and then she ran, awkward, pulled down by her pain, into the woods. Farther and farther, darkness around her, rough trunks of trees brushing against her, she ran from her torment, from fear and humiliation, and pain.

In the dark world of the forest she saw a pale figure, like a ghost, like a guardian angel, perhaps, and she went to it, and felt its smooth trunk where the bark had fallen away, and there by the large, leaning sycamore tree she had the baby.

She hadn't known exactly how far along she was, but as she held its warm slippery body in her hands for a moment, and felt it wriggling in the cold of the dark night, she thought it must have been premature. Eight months? Seven, even. She was no longer sure of anything. She leaned against the tree, weak and hurting, even after its birth, and held it in her hands. She felt the warmth leave its body. She sat until it stopped moving, and then she laid it on the ground, and then the afterbirth came, and she got up and followed a pinpoint of light, going to it as a moth would have. Light. Life.

She stumbled up the back porch steps of her uncle's house and collapsed against the back screen door.

She heard the door open, and Uncle Everett reached down in silence and helped her into the house.

"You need a doctor", he said.

He was talking to her as if he had known, somehow, that she was pregnant. She told him, "The baby already came. It is out by the big sycamore. The leaning sycamore."

He led her to the old leather couch in the den where a fire burned in the heating stove, where he had been reading, and told her to lie down. He covered her with a red and blue plaid blanket.

"Lie still. I'll go take care of it."

She went to sleep, and woke almost instantly trembling with anxiety.

She heard footsteps on the porch, not fast, not slow. Neither hurried, nor hesitant.

Her uncle came in, his thin face solemn, and said to her, "It's all right, I buried it."

He took her to the bathroom and helped her clean up. He gave her fresh pajamas to put on and told her he'd wash hers and slip them back to her without anyone knowing.

Then, as the icy, gray dawn broke in the east, as the forest creaked with coldness, he helped her in silence back to her own home, and left her at the back door.

The house was cold and quiet, darkness lingering like fog in every doorway, every corner. With each step she dreaded waking her parents, or her brothers, dreaded questions she wouldn't be able to answer. But she slipped unheard into her bedroom and crawled beneath her blankets, her head buried from light.

She never again talked to her uncle about that night.

No one ever knew she'd gone into the woods to have her baby, that she had laid it on the cold ground where it would freeze with the earth. No one had ever known except her uncle.

She had moved away from her father's home a little over a year later, after her mother's unexpected and fatal heart attack, and she had made a new person of herself.

She had made herself forget.

Until now ...

THAT NIGHT SHE WOKE, her heart racing. She heard Daniel snoring softly, and heard the silence in the house. It was not the dream this time that had awakened her, but something outside herself. She lay tight with fear, her ears straining for every sound.

Then it came again, a soft thud, somewhere in the house below. She heard a clink, as if something downstairs had been dropped.

She got up and hurried to the door. It was open, the way she had left it at eleven o'clock when she last checked on the children.

Someone was downstairs, in the kitchen, she thought. Was it one of the kids? Perhaps Ward had gotten hungry in the night and gone downstairs for a sandwich, although she had never known him to do such a thing before.

It couldn't be a burglar. She had left the doors locked. Breaking in would be noisier than the closing of a door.

She went down the stairs without turning on a light. A soft glow from the street light on the corner filtered through lacy panels and the stained glass on the side panels at the front doors. Light, just barely enough for her to see the dark shapes of furniture, to avoid running into anything, led her toward the kitchen.

She heard the sliding of a drawer, but there was no light on in the kitchen. Whoever was there moved in darkness.

The fear she had first felt when she woke came back and moved over her with coldness beyond anything she had known since that last night in the woods. She stood still, wishing now she had called Daniel, that she had turned on lights, that she had dialed the emergency number for help.

Pat, pat, pat ...

Soft footsteps in the kitchen, running. Across the tiled floor. Barefoot. It was like Sheena running, or Ward. Yet oddly, instead of coming to the door into the hall, they went in the opposite direction. For a moment, as Magret held her breath, there was silence.

Then she heard the thud of the back door closing.

She stood only a moment longer, before she walked boldly into the kitchen, puzzled and disturbed at the sounds she had heard.

She turned on the kitchen light.

Nothing in the kitchen looked as if it had been disturbed. She went to the back door, the one that led out onto a terrace at the rear of the house.

The door was still locked.

CHAPTER 9

EVERETT WASSON LET the newspaper fall onto his knees. He leaned his comfortable old recliner back almost as far as it would go and closed his eyes. He felt his wife's hand on his forehead. He would have recognized the feel of it anywhere, not delicate, not soft and smooth, but a firm, broad palm, thick fingers, roughened from work, and warm. Warm and comforting, always.

"You've got the look of a man who's about to go to sleep in his chair. Aren't you coming upstairs?"

"Not for a while," he said.

He heard her move away, just the soft rustle of clothing, and her soft-soled house slippers on the new carpet she'd had put down in this old den a couple of months ago. But he had a feeling that she didn't leave the room. The TV had been turned off several minutes ago. Faith didn't like the news very well to start with, always stuff about planes being shot down, she said, or planes falling without being shot down, hundreds of people killed. Or a terrible earthquake somewhere, burying thousands of people and animals alive. Who could sleep after hearing something like that?

And their young daughter, after hearing her mother go on about it, as she usually did every evening during the six o'clock news, had asked, "Does God go to sleep?"

Everett had left it for his wife to answer. He'd had preachers in his family for as long as he could remember, and the subject of religion made him a little angry.

When he was a child he'd had a preacher uncle who came around every few months. During the days Uncle Josh had stayed in the house there was nothing but gloom, and dire predictions, and having to say grace before the family could eat. Long-drawn-out prayers that went on and on while Everett's young stomach growled for food.

Later, after he was grown and his first wife, a young girl who had every right to live, had died in a car wreck at the age of twenty-five, he had lost all patience with the old "ask and ye shall receive" bit. By that time there had been his brother-in-law, who had years earlier built his own church on land that Everett's sister, Marshall's wife, had inherited. So right next door, you might say, although, thank God, he couldn't see the church and house for the trees between, he'd had another preacher. That one had later abandoned his church when he ran off with a woman twenty years younger than himself. One of his own members who, Everett supposed, got down on her knees to pray beside Reverend Singer. Of course the man was a widower by then, and if he wanted to marry again, that was his business; but he'd taken another man's bride.

The church had vines growing on it now, and boards falling off here and there, and the house wasn't much better.

It wasn't that Everett had anything against organized religion, or the concept of God. But it seemed to him there were so many missing ingredients that he felt the mystery was far greater than the Bible and religion would have it seem.

Religion ... it all came back to the past.

He opened his eyes, swiveled his chair around slightly so he could see the door. But Faith was gone, upstairs to bed, and he was alone.

He drew a long sigh.

Maybe he was wrong to blame the religion of Magret's parents, their complete devotion to something besides their daughter, yet every time he thought of that night almost twenty-one years ago, he felt sick to his heart, his stomach, his mind.

The newspaper on his knees claimed the infant had been buried in the woods, "in a shallow grave, dug by hand, with no blanket or sign of any clothing," twenty to twenty-one years ago. He wondered, as he often wondered about so-called scientific knowledge such as black holes and quasars, and antimatter, exactly how the police medical examiner had figured that out. The shallow grave, he could understand, although it hadn't seemed that shallow to him, that night, when with only his hands he had made that tiny dead creature's burial bed. But the blanket. How did they know there was no blanket? Wouldn't a blanket have deteriorated, disintegrated, in that length of time?

He wished, fervently wished, that he could have become more educated when he was young. He could have sold the old place, he supposed, the home and two acres he had inherited from his parents at his mother's death, and taken the money and gone to school. But by that time he was married, and his wife wanted a home and babies, and so did he. After her death, he hadn't had the heart to do anything but continue his job as meter man for the gas company, and come home at night to an empty house.

He had noticed that affair between the young man—he couldn't remember his name now—and Magret. He had noticed the fellow in church staring at Magret, and her barely fifteen.

Then after a while he had noticed that the guy stopped looking, and it was Magret who was doing the looking. And she kept getting fatter, and sloppier in her clothing, always covering herself with large coats, even on warmer days.

The fact that the kid was pregnant dawned on him just a few days before he heard her at his back door. *Uncle Everett.* Her voice had been as weak as a soft wind crying around the corners of the house, and it had taken him a few minutes to realize that the cry was actually Magret calling him.

He had found her slumped against the door, in her bloodied pajamas, and he had known immediately that she was having a baby. He helped her into the den, this same place where he now sat, and with the wind crying around the eaves of the house as it was doing tonight, he had made her a bed on the old leather sofa. He could remember his feelings, his anger, not at Magret, who was the one who was suffering now, but at her parents. What the holy hell was wrong with his sister that she hadn't seen what was going on?

"You need a doctor," Everett said that night, knowing that he wasn't qualified to deliver a baby. What kind of hornet's nest was this unexpected new life going to open? The thought had flashed through his mind, a brief thought that burned out in an instant. "You can stay with me," he'd said. "It's going to be all right. There's plenty of room in this big house for you and the baby—don't you worry."

Tears covered her face, and traces of blood, as if she had raised her hand to her face more than once. Her hair was tangled, and he saw bits of leaves and twigs in it. She was cold and shivering, the January night she had come out of brittle with ice. She was wearing nothing but those old flannel pajamas, and they were wet with blood. He began pulling them off her, and she didn't object.

She was weeping then, clutching at his hand. "It's too late, Uncle Everett." The tears were coming so hard it seemed they were being torn up from the bottom of her soul. "The baby—Uncle Everett—please—it was born, already."

For a moment he stood stunned, staring at her. The baby had been born. Where was it? *God, where was it?*

"At the sycamore ..." she whispered. "The old leaning sycamore ..."

He had to go to it. Magret was at least warm now, warming, with the heavy blanket over her, and the heat spreading from the stove.

"I'll be back soon," he told her, horror in his heart. A newborn infant out on this cold night? Had the girl thought to take a blanket, anything, to give it protection?

With the flashlight from the washroom, he had run, searching the woods, lost for a while, as if he were a stranger in these familiar woods. There was only one big sycamore that leaned, over the shallow little ditch down which water ran after a hard rain, or in the springtime when water more easily seeped out of the ground.

Breathless, and cold beneath his leather jacket, he had finally found the tree.

The infant was a tiny heap of bloody flesh beneath the tree, at its base, in a nest of ferns. As he had feared, there was nothing to protect it from the cold. Its body was turning blue, but as he squatted beside it, sorrow wrenching his gut, with his head bowed, he'd thought to himself, she had left it while it was still alive, left it on this cold, cold ground, a tiny, helpless thing with no chance in the world.

After a couple of minutes he looked more closely at it. Tiny, no more than four pounds, maybe five, it might have been premature. Yet it had hair like fine silk on its perfect little head, dark, like a little cap, and its nails, though incredibly tiny, were average length for a full-term baby.

It was a girl.

He wished he could wrap her in his jacket, and he thought about taking off his shirt and wrapping her in that. But then he thought, let the earth take her, without anything man-made. She deserved at least not to be defiled any further.

So he dug the grave with his hands, dug through a crust of ice at the surface, and laid the tiny creature in it, with the afterbirth beside her, and covered it all over with soft soil, patted firm by his hands, and then he pulled some ferns over the grave.

He had never forgotten it was there, and he had never told anyone. But in all his days and nights of life, he had never imagined it would be discovered.

The really odd thing was his daughter, Peggy, coming home a couple of days ago with the story of finding a little naked baby in the woods. It would have gotten funny, the next day when she said they'd seen the baby again, but it had grown a couple of years and was standing. It would have been funny, as Faith thought it was, if it hadn't been for the grave that he knew was there. Yet, there was no sense to Peggy's story, even though he knew the child had not lied. She had sat on his lap and leaned her head against his chest in a way she hadn't done since she was five years old and had the measles, and he had known by that that Peggy was disturbed.

She had seen the tiny, naked baby. "Was it a girl, Peggy?" he had asked, feeling within himself something that his deeper mind hadn't yet fully made sense of, hadn't been able to communicate to him so that he could understand, and she had nodded, yes, it was a girl. "Then today, when you saw it again and it was older and larger, it was the same child?" He was thinking ... he would have recognized that face again, anyway, after all these years. But he saw it only as a little rosebud face, round and blue-red, with a minuscule nose and puffy, closed eyes.

"It was," Peggy said, and she sat up and looked at him. "I know it was because it had a mole on its left shoulder." She put her finger on her shoulder to show him. "A brown mole."

He frowned. That wasn't what he had expected. What had he expected her to say? Never this. He remembered another little girl, who played in her sandbox when she was three years old, wearing a little sun suit. They had allowed her to wear shorts and sleeveless tops until she was seven, and after that she'd had to wear dresses. But he saw her now as clearly as he was seeing his own daughter, the mole on her shoulder like a tick there, round and dark brown against her pale, only slightly tanned skin. Magret.

It was Magret who'd had a mole on her shoulder.

The wind screamed at the house corners and under the eaves, finding every crevice on the old house. He could hear it whistle and moan through the tall pine trees outside the den window and near the back of the yard. The newspaper rustled as he moved in his chair.

What was Magret thinking tonight? She must have heard the news. It would be all over town. A town of forty thousand would not stick something like this on the back page of its newspaper. It had taken all front page headlines, giving precedence only to a new tax program the governor was trying to get through.

The police, the paper said, were investigating. Which, Everett supposed, meant they were questioning people, trying to find the woman who had left the baby in the woods to die, or who, perhaps, had buried it alive.

No, God, not alive.

He wondered if Magret was reading that article tonight and wondering if he had buried the baby alive. He wanted to go to her and tell her it was dead ... but he knew he never would. He had told no one that, in fact, the baby had probably frozen to death, left to die ... by its mother.

Yes, the police would want to talk to Magret.

He should go upstairs and go to bed, he thought as he heard the clock in the hall strike midnight. He had to get up early in the morning and go to work.

The police hadn't come to him yet, as they surely would. They would find out, in their checking, that his house had been on the edge of the woods since the early nineteen hundreds, and he had lived here all his life, first with his mother, father, and sister, and then with only his mother, and then his first wife ... that he had lived here alone during the time of the death and burial of the infant. And had lived here during the past ten years with his second wife, Faith, and their daughter, Peggy. That he was fifty-five years old, his wife fifteen years younger. They would know it all. And they would probably learn that a fifteen-year-old girl had lived in the house next to the church twenty, almost twenty-one years ago.

They might be able to trace the baby to her.

But he would lie for her as long as he could.

A tree limb was scratching against the house, a persistent sound that got to him. Finally he realized it was not a tree limb.

Someone was scratching at his door, just as Magret had that cold night a lifetime ago.

It was Magret. He knew it as certainly as if he had seen through the walls. She had come on this dark and windy night to talk to him, to be reassured by him. Perhaps he should have called her earlier, to set her mind at rest, but he hadn't talked with Magret much, ever, and it had just been easier to pretend it had never happened. He had felt sorry for the girl then, even though she had done something as cruel and inhuman as to leave the helpless infant there in the cold woods. He half blamed her parents for the whole thing. If they had paid attention to her, beyond seeing to it that she said grace at meals and attended church, if they had seen that she needed help—if they hadn't in some way made her so afraid to let them know she was going to have a baby ...

If ... If ...

He went out into the hall and stood listening. Had she been at the back door, or the front? Would Magret, now a mature and lovely woman, come to his back door on a dark night, and claw on it as she once had, rather than knock?

For a few minutes he heard only the wind. Then he heard it again, at the back door, on the screen porch, or on the step outside the screen porch. A rhythmic scratch, scratch, a fumbling at the latch of the screen door.

He went into the kitchen and turned on the light. He felt the pull of the uncovered window on the door, the dark beyond it, and felt as if he were being watched. An odd feeling of dread, or fear, slowed his steps.

He opened the kitchen door and peered out onto the screened porch. No one stood outside the door. She was probably on the step. Faith might have hooked the screen door before she went to bed, as she sometimes did.

He flicked the switch that should have turned on the porch light, but the porch remained dark. The bulb must have burned out.

"Who's there?" he asked, going in his socks out onto the cold boards of the porch, reaching the screen door and unlatching it.

"Magret?" He squinted into the darkness outside the door.

Then he saw her, standing at the bottom of the steps looking up at him.

She was perhaps five or six years old, and her body was a pale and ghostly blur of white in the darkness. In shock he saw she was naked. She stood looking up at him, her hands together in front of her, navel level, as if she were holding her thumbs, or holding something there against her stomach.

In the pale light that made a path behind him from the open kitchen door, he saw the mole on her shoulder.

He noticed her eyes then, and saw a reptilian coldness, and then a flash of something pure evil, or filled with utter hatred. The mouth opened. The rows of sharp teeth were not human, and he began to back away, the terror rising in him, paralyzing him, making him feel as if he were being sucked into a nightmare.

He was in his chair, he thought, and dreaming this, because that was its only explanation, the only way to understand what he was seeing.

In a moment he would choke awake, and the newspaper would fall off his lap.

This creature that looked like a child wasn't coming toward him, rising, coming up the steps, swift and sure and deadly. The thing in her hands wasn't a sharp knife, light glinting on the blade.

He tried to turn, to claw his way out of the nightmare, to lift his feet from the quicksand of his dreams.

FAITH LAY AWAKE. It was odd, she thought, the way the wind was howling tonight. Unusual for this time of year. Autumn was usually the quiet month, the month of chilly nights and mild days, of leaves falling and turning all those lovely reds and yellows, of wood smoke from the fireplaces, or in their case, the heavy cast iron stove in the den.

The bedroom was cool, almost cold, unheated, and her electric blanket warm, but she knew she wouldn't be able to go to sleep until Everett came to bed.

He had been acting very strange the last couple days. And for that matter, so had Peggy. She understood about Peggy, but she worried about Everett. With Peggy it was the child thing, which was a puzzle, and a little weird, as if she and the other girls had had a group hallucination about a child that might have been, if it had lived. A grave soon to be uncovered. Of course the second sighting was nothing short of group hysteria. Or in this case, a bit less than group, maybe, since there were only two. Two little girls with one big imagination.

She smiled into the dim light of the room.

But Everett worried her. Something was wrong with his heart, the doctor had said, and even though Everett assured her it was really nothing, still she worried. His father had died of a heart attack when he was in his fifties, and his sister had died while still in her forties.

The wind screamed, almost as if it were a living, wild creature, clawing at the house, trying to get into this human den where there was warmth and shelter.

She heard the moan of it through the pine tree boughs outside her bedroom window, a sound she had always thought of as the crying of lost souls in eternal agony.

Dimly, in the downstairs hallway, she heard the clock give one strike.

She sat up and looked at the alarm clock on the table at Everett's side of the bed.

One o'clock. And Everett still had not come to bed.

The feeling that something was terribly wrong with her husband washed over her and left in its wake the beginnings of panic. She could almost see him in his chair, asleep, yet not really asleep. His eyes open, staring sightlessly at the ceiling.

Was this a common fear among married middle-aged women, or was it uniquely her own? The thought of life without Everett came more and more often lately, tied her in knots inside, and caused spells of depression that hung over her for days, like terrible little clouds, or swarms of gnats around her head, slowing her movements, making her so tired that getting out of bed was an effort.

She put a robe on and tied it carelessly at her waist in a kind of knot designed just to keep the ends of the belt from dragging.

She went out into the uncarpeted upstairs hall, and felt the warmer air that rose from the rooms below. She could see over the banister that the den door stood open, at the rear of the hall, back near the kitchen door, and a soft light trailed out from it. She had closed the door when she left him resting in his chair, tipped far back, the newspaper on his flat belly, the light at the side of his chair outlining the round little bald spot in the top of his dark brown hair. She sometimes had teased him about it, calling it his silver dollar.

She lifted her robe so that she wouldn't stumble over it on the stairs. As clumsy as she could be sometimes, those stairs presented a hazard to her. In turn, Everett had often teased her, saying the level ground or floor was a hazard to her, since she could manage to stumble over nothing.

She felt as if a cold hand had tightened around her throat when she saw that Everett was not in his chair. She stood on the threshold for barely ten seconds, yet she saw every item in the room, from the vases on the shelf behind the black, iron stove, to the drawn draperies, to the chair still with its foot section raised, to the other chair, the couch, the soft, new, brown carpet.

The house was quiet. There was no movement anywhere, except for the rattle of the window pane as the wind pushed against it. But Everett had to be in the kitchen.

She opened the kitchen door, a few steps down the hall, and was relieved to see the light was on. Everett must be getting a snack. But at one o'clock in the morning? The man who went to bed every night at ten-thirty?

"Everett? Is something wrong?"

There was no answer. The kitchen cabinets, built out into an L shape at one end of the room, hid part of the kitchen, but then she saw as she paused near the table that the kitchen area was dark. The only light came from the fixture over the table.

The back door stood open.

Wind pushed it back against the end of a cabinet with a soft thud. The back porch was lighted only by a path of light from the open door, she saw, as she crossed the kitchen and stepped out.

She pushed the light switch, jiggled it, and the porch light came on.

Her heart, her whole being, came to a sudden suppression, as if the world itself had paused for that moment in which she saw him.

He was lying partly on the porch, his feet and legs on the floor of the porch, but his upper body out of sight on the sloping steps beyond the screen door. His body there, so twisted, so still, held the screen door open, and the door quivered in the wind, the tiny wires of the screen catching the light from the single bulb on the porch ceiling like spider webs catching the moonlight. Wind howled, rising and falling, and the door moved against him.

She cried out and rushed forward, stepping on the hem of her robe and almost falling. She went down onto her knees, the robe pulled tight beneath one leg, and reached for him.

She drew back, staring.

His head lay on the bottom step, twisted unnaturally away from shoulders that were face down. She could see the horrible wound in his neck gaping open and red, blood soaking into his shirt collar, his eyes open and staring at nothing.

For an interminable time she knelt beside him, the boards of the porch hard against her bony knees. She stared open-mouthed, unable to take in this horror, to see anything beyond the awful wounds in his neck.

Then she began to move, without conscious thought. She took his legs and started pulling him back up onto the porch where he could lie comfortably. He was not a heavy man, yet tonight his weight seemed like lead, frozen to the boards of the porch.

She pulled and pulled, and finally, inch by inch, he came up the steps and onto a flatter surface. She straightened him, placing his arms at his side. Then she stood up, and without wanting to, she saw the long smear of blood on the steps and the pooling of it on the bottom step.

And there, in the pool of blood, she saw something else.

It was a long, slender-bladed knife, a thin knife with a pearl handle, a kitchen knife. A sort of paring knife, she thought, as she carefully picked it up, staring at it. The kind of paring knife with an extra-long blade. Or perhaps it was a steak knife, with a smooth rather than serrated blade.

She had seen it before, but she couldn't remember where.

From her pocket she took a tissue and carefully wiped the blood away.

She put the knife into her pocket without thinking of what she was doing.

Then it occurred to her that she needed help. That Everett needed a doctor, and she hurried to the phone in the kitchen and dialed emergency.

CHAPTER 10

ISLAN COULDN'T SLEEP. She had come down with a cold and her nose was stopped up and her head ached and her throat tickled all the time. She hated to think it might be her own fault, for going into the chilly and damp evening with just a sweater on, just to show off to Sergeant Stoddard.

She got out of bed and went softly along the hall to the kitchen. There, she turned on the light and squinted against it, her eyes pained by its brilliance.

The cold medicine was in the kitchen cabinet, beside the sink. Neither of their two bathrooms had a medicine cabinet. Both of them had mirrors flat against the wall, with swag lights hanging from the ceiling. The aspirin and Tylenol and cold medicines were all kept in the kitchen.

She rummaged around and finally settled for a Co-Tylenol, then heated water for a cup of low-cal hot chocolate. She'd decided these last few days that she was far too fat. Friends told her she'd make a great Las Vegas show girl, and she'd taken it as an insult. They hadn't said model, they'd said show girl. Which, she thought, meant a far heavier figure than a model would have.

For a long time it had hurt her feelings that the boys, all of them shorter than herself, would try to hit her, pinch her, touch her. But then as they got older, and some of them grew taller than she, a few of them, the older and bolder, had begun asking her for dates. As if she would ever go out now with a guy who had yelled at her last year, "Hey, Islan, you're busting out all over!"

She'd been getting acquainted with college guys, though, as she hung out more and more around town, and had started getting really interested in various young men. Crushes, her mother called them. Islan thought the guys were handsome, usually, or cool. Sophisticated. It was a pleasure to be around guys that had a little sophistication, instead of the nerds she'd grown up with at school.

So she had dated a couple, without her mother's full approval.

But now they, too, seemed like runny-nosed nerds. In comparison to Collins, all the college guys seemed to lack something. Not only the college men, but all men.

She knew she had found the man she wanted to marry. It was as if she had spent her whole life just growing up, waiting for him to come along.

As if her thoughts of him were bringing him closer, she heard a police siren in the dark and windy night. At first it was so far away, so distant, that it seemed only a part of her vivid visualization of the tall, wide-shouldered, dark-haired, dark-eyed man. He looked so handsome in his uniform. She wondered how he would look in civilian clothes, without the gun in the holster, without the hat. Would more of his dark hair fall onto his forehead? She wondered what their children would look like, combining her pale blond genes with his. Blond with brunette. Would some of them be blond, like her, and some dark-haired and brown-eyed like him? Or would they all look like him?

The siren was real. She could hear it undulating in the wind, rising and falling, coming nearer on the curving road out of town. She went to the patio doors and opened them and stepped out where the only light came from the kitchen behind her and, in streaks that bypassed the patio and dwindled away on the back lawn, from the street lamp around the curve of the cul-de-sac.

She stood in her bare feet and thin pajamas and listened, and now she heard two sirens, one of them an ambulance.

They passed the street into the area where she lived and went on around the road toward the country, just beyond the trees, it seemed. And then, not far away, the sirens faded abruptly.

Peggy's.

They had gone to Peggy's house.

She heard a sound behind her, and whirled, her heart pumping. Her mother was standing just inside the open door, her arms hugging her flannel robe to her breasts.

"Why are you out there, Islan? I thought you were taking a cold? You'd better come back in."

"Did you hear the siren?" Islan asked.

"Yes, I heard it."

"It stopped at the Wasson place."

Lorna's eyes looked past Islan into the dark forest over their backyard fence, then she put a hand on Islan's arm and pulled her back into the kitchen.

THE BACKYARD of the Wasson place flickered with lights. Blue lights of the patrol cars swirled, and the red lights of the ambulance burned steadily into the dark night. Spotlights and floodlights shone on the area of bloody steps and on the figure lying so neatly arranged on the back porch.

Collins had left the body and the area around it to the homicide people from both the county Sheriff's Department and the State Police, and had gone on into the cooling room where the victim's wife sat huddled in one of the chairs. Others of the police were wandering back and forth from porch to hall to den. The little girl, Peggy, was clutched against her mother's side.

His had been the first of the police cars to arrive at the scene, even ahead of the ambulance. He had been up, listening, for some reason, to the scanner, and had picked up the call. With Chief roused and in the back seat of the patrol car, he had hurried out to the Wasson place. He had been planning to go early in the morning to talk to them a little. His information indicated the home had always belonged to the Wasson family, since the first settler had built the house. And the man living there, who might have had some vital information about the baby in the grave, had lived there all his life. And now, he lay dead on the back porch, his throat looking as if it had been chewed by a shark.

He had heard Peggy come downstairs screaming for her mother as he stood looking at the blood on the back steps, and he had carefully hefted himself onto the porch without stepping close to the blood or the body lying there. The back door stood open, and the single bulb in the porch ceiling glistened on the raw and open and ragged wound in the man's throat.

Though he obviously was dead, Collins had bent and touched the man's wrist. The coldness of death was already stealing over the body.

The ambulance arrived as Collins rose, and the screaming of the little girl stopped, somewhere in the lower part of the house.

He went through the open kitchen door and through another open door into a hall. Through the den door he saw the woman, sitting with the child tight in her arms. The pale faces had looked at him in silence.

He had seen murders, and survivors of those murders, but he had never seen anything like this.

A shotgun could tear a man's head half off, yet you knew exactly what had caused the death. And the family knew. And most of the time, it was one of the family, or another person present, who had done the killing.

But this time the feeling of something terrible being responsible, of something out of the dark, cold, windy night, had been with him from the moment he saw the horror of the man's throat. And the blood. He had never seen so much blood.

"Mrs. Wasson? Peggy? Do you remember me, Peggy?" The pale, round-faced child nodded, her soft brown eyes filled with terror. He wondered, would she forever-more be afraid of a man in uniform? Of a police siren in the middle of the night? Would she have nightmares about it?

"Are you related to the body on the porch, ma'am?" He knew, in his heart, that she was. But he had to ask. "Yes. My husband. Everett."

Her voice sounded a bit thin, but otherwise normal. He wondered if she was in shock.

"Would you like to see the doctor?"

She stared at him in silence, then she said, "You mean for myself? No, I'm all right. But Everett ..."

"I'm sorry, Mrs. Wasson," he said. "There's nothing anyone can do. Were you the one who moved him back up onto the porch?"

"Yes ... yes ... I couldn't let him lie there. Bleeding. Like that."

"Do you have someone near you'd like to call, Mrs. Wasson? A relative? A friend?"

"No. No ... yes. My husband's niece. She would need to know. Magret Treacle. Her number—"

"That's all right. Deputy Rawson will call her." He looked back at one of the other men who stood in the hall. Rawson nodded, and went in search of a phone.

"Mrs. Wasson, I hate to bother you about this, but we have to ask. Would you like to take your daughter upstairs first?"

"No," Mrs. Wasson's arms tightened around her daughter. "She'll have to know. I can't leave her alone."

"Maybe your niece could take her home with her and you could tell us afterwards?"

"No, Sergeant. It's all right. She's staying with me."

"We have to know what happened."

"I don't know what happened. I got worried because he hadn't come to bed at one o'clock, and I came downstairs. And I found him, out there, like that. I pulled him back onto the porch, and then I dialed 911. And I waited, and I sat here and then I started up the stairs to see about Peggy, because she was alone up there, and it just occurred to me that there was a killer—a terrible killer—somewhere around the house—in the yard, somewhere. It had been at our door, and Everett must have answered the door and all the doors were open, and it might have come on into the house. But then Peggy screamed—I guess it was the siren that scared her."

Collins had not used his siren, but had come out on the empty road with the blue lights flashing, to warn another motorist that might be out, and to warn of his own speed. The car behind him, and the ambulance, had come with sirens on.

He had been at the back steps of the Wasson home when he'd heard the screaming cry of the little girl. It had blended in with the dark forest behind him, the wind overhead in the trees, and the body on the porch, lying at the end of the trail of blood.

THE PHONE WOKE MAGRET, but Daniel answered it. As he turned on the bedside light, Magret covered her head. Her first burst of worry—a phone ringing in the middle of the night always scared her—was replaced by a kind of curious dread as she lay with her breath held. Leigh had been out on a date earlier, but had gotten home at eleven o'clock, which was her deadline on a weeknight. And she was allowed to go out only if she had done her homework, but Leigh was very mature and sensible for her age, and Magret had heard her come in and go to her room.

With all her kids at home safe in bed, and Daniel answering the phone, Magret allowed herself to hope it was a wrong number. She turned over in bed, with her back to Daniel and the light and the intrusion of the phone call.

"Magret," Daniel said. "It's a policeman calling from Everett's house. I think Faith needs you."

. . .

DANIEL WAS GOING WITH HER, he said, hushing her arguments. First, as soon as Magret was dressed, in warm, lined, gray wool slacks and a loose, thick sweater, she went to Leigh's room, woke her, and told her they were going out to Aunt Faith and Uncle Everett's, and that she was to help the younger kids get ready for school if they weren't back in time.

Sleepily, on one elbow, the pink blankets falling back from her, Leigh blinked in the light and asked, "What's wrong? What happened?"

"I'm not sure," Magret said. "Just go back to sleep."

She hadn't asked Daniel what had happened. She had quickly gotten out of bed and dressed. She hadn't even taken time to brush or comb her hair—she had just run her fingers through it with a quick glance in the mirror.

In the downstairs hall she put on her quilted jacket with the hood. Daniel was waiting.

For a few minutes they drove in silence.

"Are you all right?" he asked.

"Yes." She still couldn't bring herself to ask what had happened. She knew it was Uncle Everett. A heart attack? Her mother had died with one, and she knew Faith was worried about Everett. But if it had been that, would the police be there?

She was afraid ... afraid ... it had something to do with the grave ...

And she was afraid to ask Daniel what had happened. She wanted the drive to last forever, so she would never have to know.

Her mother's old home place was ablaze with lights. The front porch light was on, outlining the railing around it, throwing shadows out onto the brown grass of the front lawn that looked like the teeth of a monster, grinning at her—or opening its mouth to receive her.

In the driveway and backyard, lights from police cars swept against the tall side of the house and the dark trees, rotating like lights at an airport. The back porch light was on, and it was there the men seemed mostly to be gathered, moving toward and away from the back steps. Milling almost as aimlessly as a nest of disturbed ants. An ambulance was drawn up close beside the porch, its red lights sweeping the night and blending with the blue and red lights from the police cars.

Magret got out of the car and crossed the crisp, frosty grass to the old cracked cement steps up to the front porch. She had never before, in all her memory, gone up these steps. It was to the back door that family and visitors went, to see Gramma before she died, and then to see Uncle Everett after that.

It was to the back porch she had gone that night out of the woods, knowing in her heart he would help her.

... buried alive ...

No, no. It hadn't been like that. The baby had died in her hands.

Hadn't it? Dear Jesus, hadn't it?

Her throat was constricted with dread and memory. In her heart of hearts she feared it hadn't yet died when she left it. All these years her dreams had reminded her of that. She cringed now, remembering that the night she had left it there had been a much colder night than this.

No one would ever understand. And it wasn't fair. She shouldn't have to feel guilty. She wasn't guilty. She *wasn't.*

There was a policeman at the door.

"Mrs. Wasson is in the little room back by the kitchen," he said, moving aside in the cool hallway to make room for them to pass.

"The den," Magret supplied, and went on past him, noticing only that he was young and very neat in his uniform.

In the den, with the door open and the warm air from the stove escaping into the unheated portions of the old house, Magret saw Faith sitting in a big chair with Peggy hugged against her. A tall man in the brown uniform of the county Sheriff's Department stood near Uncle Everett's chair.

Magret hurried over to Faith, and felt the feverish hand clutch hers. It felt a little rough, as if the summer of gardening had not worn away yet. Faith looked up at her with blue eyes overlaid with tears.

Magret knew suddenly that Uncle Everett was dead.

"Mrs. Treacle?" the policeman said. "Mr. Treacle?"

Behind her Daniel gave the policeman their names, and asked what the problem was.

"Everett—your uncle, has been murdered."

Faith's hand tightened on Magret's until it seemed Magret would hear the bones crunch. She was too numb to care. Yet in some way the word "murder" did not surprise her.

"I'm Sergeant Stoddard, with the Sheriff's Department, county police," the man was saying, his voice soft and deep and very calm, as if he were trying to be gentle with them.

"When did it happen?" Daniel asked. "Who did it?"

Faith answered, her hand at last releasing Magret's. "I don't know who did it. I went upstairs to go to bed, and he stayed down here. He'd been reading the paper, and he was a little—ummm, bothered about something ..."

Bothered about something ...

Magret moved away from her aunt and niece, as if to find a chair, but she didn't sit down. She said instead, "Faith, would you like me to take Peggy home with me? Of course you'll have to come, too."

"Oh, no, no," Faith said, continuing, "... and I couldn't go to sleep. The wind was blowing so hard then. Finally, at one o'clock I got worried, and I came back downstairs to look for him. The kitchen light was on, and I turned on the back porch light, and I could see something lying on the back steps, holding the screen door open. It was Everett. Then I saw the blood ..."

Magret looked at Peggy, but the child's face didn't seem to have changed. It was pale, her eyes wandering about the room, her lower lip drooping, her white teeth faintly visible. It occurred to Magret she had heard this story before perhaps, at least in part. She seemed to be in a kind of daze.

"So I—so I pulled him back up onto the porch." She put her hand to her neck. "It was his throat. Just chopped to pieces."

"Chopped?" Daniel asked softly, puzzled.

"Yes. I don't know. Chewed, I first thought." She added suddenly, "Oh, yes. I had forgotten. I found this, Sergeant Stoddard."

She reached down into the deep pocket in her robe and pulled out a knife with a blade about seven inches long, a slender blade with a sharp point. The handle gleamed white and gray in the lamp light. Magret stared at it in shock and horror.

It was her knife, from her set of six, from her kitchen drawer. A set she had bought years ago on one of her shopping sprees. They were unusual; she had never seen others like it. The pearl handles had caught her eye, although the clerk at that time couldn't tell her if the knives were steak knives or paring knives. They were not serrated, as steak knives usually were, but smooth and sharp. She had occasionally used them to peel potatoes and other vegetables. Would Daniel recognize it?

She watched him as he looked at the knife. Sergeant Stoddard carefully took it from Faith.

Magret turned her gaze to Faith, and then to Peggy. They were all staring at the knife. Faith had been in Magret's kitchen many times, especially at Thanksgiving and Christmas, and had helped out in the kitchen. Would she remember seeing this knife there?

No, Magret could see that to Faith it was only an instrument of horror, of terror and death.

There was no blood on it, except in the crease between handle and blade.

"Did you wipe this knife, Mrs. Wasson?" the detective asked.

"Yes, I did. I wiped it as clean as I could, and put it in my pocket. I shouldn't have done that, should I? I shouldn't even have picked it up, should I?"

Two other men had come into the room, and one of them now spoke.

"Just where did you find it, Mrs. Wasson?"

From outside came the sound of doors slamming, then an engine starting, followed by tires crunching dead grass and gravel in the driveway.

"It was ... I don't remember exactly. It was just there, on the step, beneath him maybe. I pulled him back onto the porch. He looked so—so terribly uncomfortable there." Faith began to weep, and Magret moved closer to her again, putting her arm across her aunt's shoulders.

"I think I need to take her home with me," Magret said to the three policemen. "She doesn't know who did this."

Stoddard looked apologetic. "I'm sorry to have to ask you questions at a time like this, Mrs. Wasson, but in cases of murder, the faster we have the answers, the faster we get the killer. If you know of anyone who might have wanted to harm your husband—"

"Oh no, oh no, oh no." Faith shook her head with each word, a country woman with dark brown straggly hair, a permanent that had grown out and was left hanging. Her face was now red, blotched with white, from shock and tears. She clung to her little girl as if the child were her life.

"The knife," one of the other men said. "It looks like a kitchen knife. Do you know whose it is, where it came from?"

Faith started to say no, then pressing a tissue from her pocket to her eyes, she stared at the knife. To Magret, the ticking of the old clock in the hall was like the heartbeat of a giant. One of the men moved and the floor creaked.

And then Magret thought of something, and she, too, stared at the pearl-handled knife. *How had it gotten here? Who had taken this knife from her kitchen drawer?*

"No," Faith was saying, "it looks—familiar—no, I don't know where it came from."

. . .

Aunt Faith couldn't be moved away from the house, nor would she let Peggy go. "This—is our home. We'll stay—until we decide what to do."

The investigation continued on into the morning, and finally, with the sun high in the sky, Daniel took Magret home.

Magret was relieved to be alone, after Daniel went on to the hospital.

First, she bathed, the house quiet around her, the kids in school, the neighborhood quiet. But she couldn't rest in the tub, or think. Her eyes kept seeing, even when they were closed, the kitchen drawer where, among all the other knives, spatulas, strainers, graters, the pearl-handled paring or steak knives were in a container at the back of the drawer.

Dressed again, she went downstairs and pulled out the drawer. In the knife holder at the back lay the pearl-handled knives. She picked them up and spread them out on the cabinet.

Five. One missing.

She stood staring at the knives, at the white surface of the counter, at the tile behind it, at the kitchen window over the sink with the sheer blue and white curtains and the little pots of green plants. One was a ceramic chicken, and one a ceramic duck, greenery growing out of their backs. Two were ordinary little clay pots. The plants within them were unnamed, fernlike leaves ... ferns ...

Why had she bought ferns? Tiny ferns, large ferns, some of them in hanging baskets. Her house seemed filled with ferns, at this moment, when into all her fears came a new fear: madness. Insanity. She was going crazy.

She remembered other times, after dreams, nightmares of being in the woods, of seeing the infant rise from the grave, of going then to her closet off the utility room and finding soil on her walking shoes. As if she had been there, in reality, as if she had stood in the forest and seen the ground split and separate and rise with the head of the infant. Of something more than the infant she had left there.

That baby was dead. This baby ... this one she had seen, was something else, part of her dream, part of a strange and terrible reality.

She left the knives on the counter and went to the closet that opened off the utility room. She knelt and looked at the collection of boots and shoes. Her own walking shoes had dried crusts of dark soil.

She carried them to the sink in the utility room and rinsed the rubber soles and dried them carefully with a paper towel.

If she had been out at Uncle Everett's last night, if she had taken a knife from her drawer and gone there to kill him ...

If she had killed him ...

She put the cleaned shoes back into the closet and closed the door.

He was the only one who had known about the baby. He was the one who had buried it. Besides her, he was the only one who knew.

Had she killed him?

As she must have gone into the woods on nights she had felt lost in the nightmare, had she gone last night, while her family slept, to Uncle Everett's house and stabbed him?

Because he was the only one who knew her secret?

The only one ... unless he had told Faith.

Magret went back to the kitchen and picked up the knives. She looked around. Where could she hide them?

Yet it must not be obvious they were hidden.

If someone in the family heard of the knife that had killed Uncle Everett, and remembered the knife Magret held in her hand, it would be better if they were not hidden, if the police came ...

So she put them into the back of the drawer again, then once more she pulled them out and transferred them to a drawer of flat wear that was seldom used. She tucked them into the back, a small pile of knives. Five, now.

Had she killed Uncle Everett?

She must have.

CHAPTER 11

"CAN YOU IMAGINE?" Glorian said as she bustled around the kitchen getting Clyde's supper. "All of that going on around our old church? I haven't thought of that place in years."

Bustled, Clyde thought as he watched her. Glorian had changed over the years like he would never have believed. In the beginning she had been slender, almost too slender, losing what figure she had when the babies came and suckled the milk out of her breasts. He had watched her breasts shrinking and hadn't liked it, he remembered, as if the babies had taken something that had belonged to him.

Now, she was about fifty pounds heavier, maybe a hundred. She wouldn't tell him her weight anymore, though when it had started piling on, she had talked to him about it. In fact, she'd never stopped talking, it seemed then. All he heard about, as the kids were getting to be handsome teenagers, was how much she had gained, and why was she gaining it? He could have told her. He had watched her go from a nibbler to a shoveler, and once he did tell her something of the sort and she had gotten so mad at him that she didn't speak to him, or cook for him, for a week.

"Ain't it awful?" she cried, her face screwing up. "Can you imagine? We must have known the girl who left her baby in the woods, Clyde, do you know that? If it happened twenty to twenty-one years ago, that was back when we were going to that church every few days, several times a week. Why, Clyde, that was during the time we were having our own babies."

"Yeah."

He knew. He was sure. He hadn't thought of Magret Singer in years and years, but the moment he read in the newspaper about the infant's grave, he remembered. She had come to him telling him she was pregnant. And after that he had tried not to think about it. But he remembered wondering, as summer came again, as he and Glorian began going less and less to the church in the wildwood, as he'd called it to himself, he had wondered what happened to the baby. But then he had forgotten about it.

Glorian sat down at the table, her stomach pushing against the cloth. They were alone now, the other two chairs empty. Their son was down in Texas in college, and their daughter worked in California. Out seeing the world now, both of them, roaming around, having the time of their lives. He envied them. He would have been gone in a minute, if he could have. But Glorian seemed contented with her house, her yard, her church. And her gossip.

"And now this." She poked her fork at the front page news of the murder of Everett Wasson. "As I recall, that house where he was killed was once part of the very land the church was built on, right? And not far from the place where the grave of the dead baby was found, right?"

When Glorian said *right?* like that, it didn't mean she expected or wanted an answer. She was only confirming something in her own mind. He watched her eat eggs and bacon and biscuits dripping butter. Glorian had developed into a good cook over the years, that was one thing, but at times it seemed she hated him for staying lean while she got fatter. He knew he encouraged her in the cooking. During the years they'd had to eat Weight Watcher's menus, he'd hated every mouthful, and no one had been happier when she'd gone back to her old style of cooking.

"Yeah, right, right," he said.

"Is it a coincidence, or did opening that grave start something terrible? Do you think it might have a connection?"

He didn't have any idea. He knew only one thing—he wanted to see Magret, and satisfy himself as to whether she had buried that baby in the woods. Buried alive, some of the rumors went.

He wondered, frowning slightly as he remembered, as Glorian kept talking and eating, as the phone rang and she reached for it and changed from carrying on a one-sided conversation with him to one with the telephone.

He had seen Magret's picture in the society pages of the newspaper off and on over the years. He had seen it when she married Daniel Treacle, seventeen or eighteen years ago, and wouldn't have recognized her at all. She had changed from a soft-bodied, chubby, shy girl into a slender brunette with shining dark eyes and a white veil and gown. In three years. Something had happened to her to cause the change.

He got up, stretched, took a last sip from his cup of coffee, and with his fingers hooked in the belt loops of his jeans, went toward the kitchen door to the small backyard. There was a stack of boards in one corner back there that needed hauling away, old boards he had torn off the shed before it got the new siding put on. After all these years, with the kids costing less now, they were getting able to fix up the place. Next came the painting of the trim around the red brick house they had bought back when the kids were little more than toddlers.

But not today.

Today was like yesterday and the day before, only worse. He didn't have time to do any fixing up around the place.

His service truck was parked in the driveway, visible just over the line of shrubs between the corner of the garage and the yard next door, its metal frame high, the cables wound and hanging from the inside of the frame, and one TV antenna lying like a big spider in the bed. There wasn't much antenna work in the city anymore, what with cable and all, but he still kept busy repairing televisions, and the antenna in the truck right now was supposed to go up at a home out in the country where cable didn't yet reach. He had told them he'd be out Monday, probably, because he usually didn't work on Saturdays. But ... it would be a good excuse to cruise the neighborhood where Magret lived.

He thought he would talk to her. About what, he wasn't sure. But within himself was a growing certainty that the baby in the woods belonged to Magret, that it was she who had gone there for its birth and had buried it. He might have thought she'd had the baby at home, and her preacher dad had buried it, except he just couldn't see Reverend Singer doing such a thing. Clyde remembered him as being a very strict, very honorable and moral man.

Glorian yelled at him from the patio doors. "You're not going to work today! I thought you had the day off! What about the work that has to be done around here? What about that trash there?"

Load it yourself, he thought. The boards are short and easy to lift, and it won't hurt you to work off a little of that bulk. "Got an antenna to put up," he said aloud. "See you later."

"How much later?" she wailed. "You're not stopping at that beer joint, are you?"

"What beer joint?"

He went on, and whatever she said next just kind of blended with the neighborhood noises, the dogs and kids and cars and loud stereos and TVs and even a fight between a man and a woman somewhere in the big house across the street that had been turned into apartments a few years ago.

The roar of his truck was a comfort. It drowned out the rest of the racket.

"OH, MY GOD," Islan cried. She was at the end of the kitchen, in the family room section, dusting a table near the double windows that looked out over the driveway. She threw the dust cloth down and ran out of the room toward the bedrooms.

Lorna stood waiting, the dishrag in her hand. She had just finished wiping the table, where Wendy sat with her plastic carrier of crayons and a coloring book. The TV in the corner beside the fireplace had cartoon figures acting cute, but Wendy seemed to be listening more than watching. Lorna was aware of brilliant colors from the set, of pink and crimson and blue and green, a flash of rainbow-like movements. Islan had turned the volume low enough that it was soothing rather than irritating. The fireplace was cold, the screen in place, closed.

"Who ... ?" Lorna started to say, gathering that someone was coming to their house—someone Islan wanted to look good for.

Wendy said, coloring carefully, not looking up, "Sergeant Collins Stoddard - whenever Islan thinks she's going to see him, she goes ape. I think she's in love."

Lorna felt a cross-flashing of emotions. An odd, sharp thrill of excitement and a simultaneous dread.

She had enjoyed his company the other night when, after their fruitless search through the woods, he had sat in her kitchen and they had talked for over an hour. She had learned he was a bachelor, and was younger than she had thought. At thirty-three, he was two years younger than herself, but when he told her his age she had immediately compared it to Islan's. Was he too mature, too old for Islan? And the pain had started in her breast. He had asked her to go out with him for dinner, for coffee, anything, lunch or suppertime, and she had said no. He would never know how much she had wanted to say yes, but she would never be able to get close enough to him to tell him why she couldn't go with him. How could she, she had asked herself later as she lay in bed staring at the shadows in the room. How could she go out with a man Islan had a mad crush on?

She had hoped they wouldn't see him again, and Islan would forget him. That both of them wanted the same man was unthinkable.

But here he was, and so early on Saturday morning.

"Mama, can I go over to Peggy's?"

"It's too early, honey."

The doorbell rang. Lorna started toward the hall, but then she heard steps thudding softly in the house, hurrying, and then Islan's voice.

Her voice had a softer, breathier quality, and Lorna closed the door to the hall and went back to the sink. With her hands trembling slightly, she rinsed out the washrag and wrung the water out of it. She heard Wendy draw a long sigh, and from beyond the doors came the soft murmur of voices. They seemed to be drawing nearer. Her heart sped up and she began feeling oddly nervous. She wished they all would go away for a while and let her clean house, and maybe later she would calm down and accept what was to be. What man could ever want her, a drudge whose hands dug in the soil in the summer and scrubbed the floor, and whose fingernails never got far beyond the end of her fingers, when he could have a beautiful young woman such as Islan?

To think of Islan as a woman was like opening a box and having something jump out at her. Yet Islan was grown now, and had been for a couple of years, getting lovelier day by day. She had outgrown boyfriend after boyfriend, so that lately she wouldn't go out with anyone still in high school. Her little girl was no longer a little girl.

"Peggy's mother doesn't mind if Peggy plays mornings."

Lorna listened to Wendy, and gave a little prayer of thanks that she at least was still a child.

"We'll see. Later."

The door opened and they came into the kitchen. Before turning around, Lorna carefully hung the dishrag up to dry. Then she straightened and turned, and caught just in time an urge to reach up and touch her hair. She had brushed it, just as she always did when she got up each morning, but after that she had tied a scarf around it to keep it out of her face while she did the housework. That had been at six o'clock in the morning, and now, at nine, there was no telling what it looked like.

He wasn't in uniform, she saw. He was wearing a leather jacket with a band at the waist, and corduroy slacks. The colors ranged from dark brown in the jacket to tan slacks and a striped tan and brown shirt. The way he looked at her brought shivers up her spine and straight into her heart. She knew that look, that straight, warm stare into her eyes, and felt breathless. And exposed, as if Islan, who was looking from one of them to the other, could see right to the heart of her feelings. Lorna pulled her eyes away and looked at her kitchen. Over the years she had slowly decorated it with odds and ends she had found at flea markets and garage sales, so that now it had a warm, rich quality. Not rich in cost, but in color and texture. She went to the television and turned it off.

"Would you like coffee, Sergeant?" she asked, even before she turned. She paused to straighten magazines on the coffee table in front of the sofa.

"Mama," Islan said, with an odd, accusing tone in her voice, "the sergeant hasn't come on a social call."

Lorna straightened, her face turning warm, her eyes meeting for just a moment the cold, bright blue eyes of her daughter. The young woman was standing beside the sergeant, tall and slender and beautiful, but the man's height made her look almost petite. She was wearing flat slippers, and her head reached his ear. They looked good together.

"I hadn't—" Lorna started to say something, she wasn't sure what, that might excuse herself, what Islan had seen in her; but then as she hesitated, Collins spoke.

"I'm investigating a murder that occurred last night not far away."

A murder. Her first thought was of the tavern out on Highway E, just a mile or so away. There were brawls there now and then, and there was even a drug bust there not long ago. But that wasn't exactly in the neighborhood.

Collins said, "Everett Wasson."

"Peggy's daddy?" Wendy cried.

Lorna put her hands to her mouth, then dropped them away almost instantly. "I—the sirens I heard last night—about one-thirty or two? I heard the sirens on the road over there." She motioned toward the woods, and saw it in her mind, a black and winding strip that separated the woods and moved on toward both open valley land and the hills and mountains to the north and east.

"I know their house is quite a ways from here by car, almost a mile, but through the woods it's probably no more than a quarter of a mile, and I was wondering if you or your daughters might know anything that could open up the case."

"You don't know who killed him?" Lorna asked.

"No, we don't."

Wendy sat at the table, her face bleached pale with shock. She stared in silence at the sergeant. Islan still stood by the door, as silent as Wendy.

Lorna shook her head. "I'm sorry. We didn't know Peggy's parents well enough to know who their friends or enemies were, if they had enemies. I always just thought of them as being like any ordinary family, with a life like the rest of us."

When he left a couple of minutes later, she walked out to the car with him, drawn now by curiosity, by need to know about the murder, because it was closer to her than she had intimated in front of the girls.

"I didn't want to ask in front of Wendy, but can you tell me what happened?"

"He was found by his wife lying on the back steps, as if he had gone to answer the door or as if he were out looking for something. We would have thought he had been attacked by a wild animal, because his throat was chewed horribly, but then his wife produced a knife she said was under the body. So I guess the attack was made by a person with a knife."

The dog, Chief, sat in the back seat of the car as alert as any human, his head up, his ears perked. He sat dead center in the seat, it seemed to Lorna, watching and waiting.

"If it's all right with you, I'd like to leave my car here while Chief and I take another walk through the woods."

"Sure."

She watched as he snapped a leash onto the dog's collar. Chief got out of the car with his tail wagging, and came to put his muzzle into her hand in a friendly greeting. She smoothed the fur on the top of his head.

"Do you think," she asked as she walked with him to the open gate and through it into the yard, "Mr. Wasson's death has anything to do with the finding of the grave of the infant?"

For a moment he didn't answer. Chief was hurrying ahead of him, the leash tight, toward the back gate.

"I don't know. I'd been planning to talk to Everett and Faith Wasson today about the grave. I know Everett lived in that same house at the time the baby was born. But whatever he knew is gone now. Unless he told Faith."

"You haven't talked to her?"

"Not much. She was too upset last night—or this morning, I should say. It's only been six or seven hours now since I was at her house."

"You haven't had any sleep!"

He smiled at her just before he went through the back gate. "Not much. It doesn't matter. That's the least of my worries."

She stood at the gate as he and the dog entered the path into the woods. Just before the trees, underbrush, and twilight of the woods swallowed him, he turned back.

"Keep your doors locked, and be careful. Tell your daughters to stay in the house for a few days when they're home, just to be on the safe side."

She nodded, a tremor of fear and dread turning her cold. She hadn't thought of danger to her children, or herself. The grave in the woods had nothing to do with any of them—nor did the murder of Everett Wasson.

Except ...

Wendy had been instrumental in discovering the grave.

She had been one of the girls who had seen an unclothed infant in the woods. She had seen a small child, a girl, in the woods, and had taken clothing to it, and then was not able to find it again.

Lorna stood at the gate, her hands clutching the frosted metal, and wished Collins and his dog would not go into those dark woods that suddenly had taken on an aspect of mystery and ... horror.

CHAPTER 12

COLLINS RELEASED his tight hold on the leash, letting it slip through his fingers to the end loop of tough nylon, so that Chief could lead the way.

With his nose to the ground the dog ran, forcing Collins to run, too, pulling against him. At times Chief lifted his head, paused, and looked around. The leaves still fell, a few here and there, tinkling faintly like glass as they touched against tree trunks or limbs on their slow way to the ground, their surfaces frosted white. The air in the woods felt icy cold, damp, still. Nothing moved but the leaves. From back in the housing development came the sound of blackbirds, a flock of them moving into a tree.

Chief pulled him on, then cut across the woods, going straight for the grave again, Collins figured. They passed through underbrush and clumps of ferns, still green and tall and drooping. Leaves stirred under their feet.

Then the dog stopped suddenly and stood firm and still, looking deep into the woods, at a point that seemed to Collins to be between the ravine with the grave and the house where Everett Wasson was so brutally murdered just a few hours ago.

Collins saw the hair on the dog's back stiffen in a long line down his spine, and the muscles of his flanks quivered visibly. A deep growl emanated from his chest, so soft Collins wouldn't have heard it if he hadn't been standing within arm's reach. But it was a private growl, only for the dog's own benefit, not a warning. It was like a question the dog was asking himself. Something was there, but what was it?

Collins considered turning the dog loose, yet he hesitated. The leash between them now hung lax, and Chief didn't move. He kept staring, his head up, the hair on his back stiff, the growl so low it bordered on a breath expelled.

"What is it?" Collins urged softly.

Chief gave one single wag of his tail.

I don't know, the wag said.

He didn't seem eager to investigate.

Collins stared, and saw nothing, his eyes beginning to feel the strain of the search. He began to walk, going toward whatever it was that Chief thought he had seen. The dog didn't rush ahead now, but hung back, going at his side, or heeling.

Nothing moved, not even a squirrel or chipmunk.

Then Collins noticed that Chief was edging ahead again, and had his nose to the ground, sniffing. Whatever it was Chief had spotted was gone now.

Puzzled, still a little uncomfortable, Collins moved toward the ravine.

He stood where he could see the turned earth of the small, shallow grave. The ropes of the police had been taken down. It wasn't likely that anyone other than the children who played in the woods would come here, but even if they did, there was nothing to disturb now. All that could be gleaned from a grave that old had been removed. A tiny skeleton, with not even a shred of a blanket or wrap of any kind, no clothing, no identification.

In a way, although this had happened years ago, it was almost as bad, as fresh and horrible, as the murder of the man.

He moved away from the grave, his eyes searching the woods around him for movement. A bird fluttered through a tree, going up into the leaves that still clung brown and crisp to the upper limbs, and then was silent.

They came out onto the path again closer to the Wasson house.

The backyard opened up suddenly. There was no fence. A rusty swing set stood by a sandbox a few yards from the back porch. Not far away was a woodpile of neatly stacked, stove-length wood, a cord or more. Two police cars sat in the driveway. One man in uniform stood at the corner of the house. As Collins drew nearer, he saw the man was Deputy Rawson.

"Still here, huh?" Collins asked as he came up to the slender, tired-looking deputy.

"Yeah. Mornin', Chief."

The dog wagged his tail and licked Rawson's hand briefly.

"Any news?"

"None that I've heard of yet. A couple of the detectives from the State Police are upstairs looking around, but I don't think they'll get any ideas from the man's personal things. Whatever hit him came out of the woods."

"Yeah? What makes you think so?"

Rawson rubbed his nose. He shrugged. "Just a hunch. Standing here with nothing to do but look at those trees, and remembering that grave ... did you ever notice all the hiding places in a place like that?"

"Chief and I have been pretty much over the woods. Yesterday we went to the other side where we could see the farmland beyond the trees. It's about three miles through there. We didn't see a thing. No camps, no hunters, even."

"But that way," Rawson said, jutting his head toward the right, in the direction of the mountains, "that way it's a long sight more than three miles. The forest goes all the way to the mountains, doesn't it?"

"But there are houses spotted along the road. Do you know if Mrs. Wasson is up?"

"I don't think she ever went to bed."

"Do you mind holding Chief for a few minutes?" Rawson got his first pleasant look of the day. He squatted to communicate better with the dog. Nose to nose with the dog, Rawson said, "Hiya, Chief. Found any good rabbit tracks lately?"

Collins went up the porch steps, carefully avoiding the dark stains where the blood of Everett Wasson had spilled. It was too bad, he thought, that the Police Department didn't furnish someone to clean up for the loved ones, so they wouldn't have to see it. But the county police was usually on the verge of bankruptcy. There was never enough money to hire all the men that really were needed, or to provide the automobiles that so quickly wore out. His own cruiser was five years old now, and rattled badly from all the rocky, unpaved roads he had to travel in a year's time.

He found Faith Wasson in the same small room where she had been a few hours ago. She had stoked the fire and added wood, and the room was warm. The hall outside was even colder than it had been earlier, it seemed to Collins, as if it had captured some of the mists and fog from the woods.

She had gone up sometime during the morning and dressed. She now wore polyester slacks and a baggy sweater. She was, according to information he had taken earlier, forty-one years old, to Everett's fifty-five. The child, Peggy, age nine, was their only child. Faith had no relatives who lived close other than Everett's niece. Her own relatives, including some sisters and brothers, lived in Kansas, Iowa, and Missouri.

Her brown hair was frosted lightly with gray, but he didn't think it had been done by any beauty operator. She must not have been in the habit of putting makeup on, or she would have when she'd brushed her hair and dressed. He had noticed, in his investigations into murders, the members of the family closest to the victim went ahead and did what they were used to doing, on that first day after the death. In a kind of shock, they acted automatically. If they were in the habit of making up, they continued to, as if trying to bring back a semblance of normalcy to their lives.

Faith didn't smile when she saw him, but the flicker in her eyes told him she was glad he had come. She began to talk almost instantly.

"Peggy's upstairs in bed. I thought with the police looking around up there, she'd be safe. The poor baby doesn't know—doesn't—I mean it just hasn't—it's like she doesn't know what's going on. She didn't see her daddy, and I'm thankful for that. I didn't take her to him. I didn't call her or go to her. I didn't even think about it. Odd, the way a person reacts to something like that, isn't it?"

"Yes, it is." Collins sat down in the chair she motioned toward. It was a little too close to the stove, and the air was warmly stuffy.

"At the time, all I could think of was making him more comfortable. And calling the police and ambulance. Not until everyone was here, not until Peggy had come screaming downstairs, did I stop to think that maybe Everett's killer was in the house. The door was wide open." She leaned her head for a moment on her hand. "But the police have been all over the house, even up into the attic. So I guess now the killer never came in."

"I was wondering about the knife, Mrs. Wasson. It looks to me like it might be one of a set. A police woman in our department said she had some that were similar, with artificial pearl handles. This was imitation pearl also. It must have come from someone's kitchen, and you said you thought you had seen it somewhere. I was wondering if anything had come back to you."

She looked at him as if her mind had gone completely blank. After staring at him a moment she shook her head. "I just can't think," she said. "When will the police release the body?"

"It shouldn't be long. The body was sent to the State Medical Examiner because of the wounds. In a few days. We'll let you know."

"I have to arrange the funeral."

He sat with her a few more minutes, tolerating the heat from the stove. The room was furnished with an old couch that looked as if it might have belonged to Faith's mother-in-law. Above it on the wall was an arrangement of photographs, Faith and Everett when they were younger, and several of Peggy from babyhood on up to her present age. Among them were far older pictures, one an oval of a very sober man and woman. The frame was pearl, interestingly enough. It must have been taken back before the turn of the century.

"Grandma and Grandpa Wasson," Faith said, seeing his interest. "Or maybe great-grandparents, I'm not sure. I just kept it here because it had such a pretty frame. Now, I don't know if I can stand it. Seeing the pearl around it makes me think of the knife again. I shouldn't have cleaned it, should I?"

"It would have been better, of course, if you hadn't. But that can't be helped now."

Why tell her it would have been better if she had left the murdered man exactly as she found him, with the knife beneath him as she had said it was? It would just compound her problems.

He heard footsteps in the hall and met the two detectives from the State Police at the door. They hadn't found anything, they told him, that would help the county police. As Collins left the warm room, the other two went in.

He spent a couple of minutes talking to Rawson before he took Chief back through the woods along the path, and to his seat in the car. He didn't see Lorna or either of her daughters. He drove quietly away, back toward the Wasson home.

The road angled through the tall stands of trees, and the fog lay in patches over the road, like a ghost that swept ahead of the car to put up one more barrier in a futile attempt to stop the car.

There was no traffic at all. Collins drove slowly with his window down. Behind the heavy screen that separated the front from the back seats, Chief's nose puffed at the fresh air, just behind Collins's left shoulder.

When he glanced back he saw the black, round knob of Chief's nose pressed as far through the wire as he could get it.

The church was the next building past the Wassons', and beside it a one-story house that once had been white frame, but now had flaked and turned gray, the boards exposed to the weather. Who owned this place, he wondered. Did it belong to Everett Wasson? It was within an eighth of a mile from his house.

He drove into a driveway that had grown weedy over the years, beside a church that was similar in condition to the house. The whole scene had a very forlorn look. As he drove close to the cement slab of a porch at the rear, he saw an old picnic table beneath a tall, spreading oak tree in the backyard. The area around the church and house had once been cleared except for a few immense old trees, but now younger trees and brush had sprouted and made the area look ragged and unkempt.

He got out of the car and opened the back door without attaching Chief's leash. The dog leaped out, then looked around and back up at Collins.

"Just thought we'd take a look around," he told the dog. Chief began to explore, his nose to the ground part of the time, but watching always to see where Collins was going and staying close by.

Collins tried the back door of the church, but it was padlocked, and the lock, though rusty, looked secure. He walked around the church, which was a typical old country church, not large, the kind that usually was privately owned, and nondenominational. An old sign at the front had the remnants of a name, Holy something or other, a name Collins couldn't make out. Sunday school, it said, was at ten o'clock, and services were three times a week at 7 p.m. as well as Sunday morning.

A broken corner of a window gave him a view into the church. The pews were still there, two long rows, and the raised platform at the front with the lectern. Some candles in holders stood on a low table. There was no piano. At the front of the church where once a picture or statue had hung, there was just a bare spot now. The painters had not bothered to paint behind it and the spot was as gray as the exterior where the paint had peeled away.

He walked through the tall brown weeds and brush to the house next door. It had a porch across the front, almost obscured now by the growth in the front yard, and a screened porch at the back. Glimpses through windows grimy and cobwebby revealed empty rooms, with nothing left but curling linoleum in the kitchen. There were at least four or five bedrooms, though, small but adequate, as if there had been a large family or one that expected several guests sleeping over.

He was relieved to get back into the car.

The next house down the road was almost a mile away. He stopped in, and learned that the house had been built ten years ago by the couple who lived there now, the Gordons. They had three children, who stood to the side, listening to every word. The Gordons didn't know who owned the church and empty house, nor did they know the Wassons. He didn't tell them about the murder of their neighbor to the east. He left them staring curiously after him, and Chief in the back seat, as he backed out of their driveway and drove on west. The small town, a village more than a town, was almost within walking distance, if a person didn't mind walking a mile or so. He turned around in the parking lot of the village cafe and drove back toward the county seat.

He stopped in again at the Wasson home, and found that Rawson was still there, but the State Police had gone. In their place, though, was another car, a sleek Oldsmobile of dark and light blue with a tag that read 'maggie' instead of a license plate.

He grinned at Rawson as he got out of his car. "You still here?"

"Just getting ready to leave. Where'd you have that parked?"

"Over in Greenbrier Addition. You know—the other end of the path." At Lorna's, he thought.

"Oh, yeah."

"Who's here?" Collins asked, nodding toward the blue car. He had an idea.

"The Treacles. All of them, the way it looked. They brought something in dishes."

Collins pecked on the glass of the back seat where Chief sat and told him to stay. The dog visibly relaxed. By the time Collins had reached the porch, the dog had lain down, with only his chin resting on the car door so he could still see out.

Collins stepped over the police rope. The whole back porch was cordoned off. But by the time he came out again he knew the rope would be down. If Rawson had orders to leave now, there was no more reason for the county police to rope off the area. If Mrs. Wasson wanted to clean the porch steps, she could. Getting the blood out of the pitted cement of the steps would be impossible, though. They'd be dark and stained forever.

He saw figures through the glass of the kitchen door, and knocked. A young girl, sixteen or seventeen, opened the door. She was petite and pretty in a pale way, resembling the younger girl, Sheena. Collins guessed she was the older sister, Leigh. There was one boy, tall and thin, with intense dark eyes. Daniel Treacle stood at the end of the room with his hands in his pockets.

Faith sat at the big kitchen table, and Peggy had come down and stood in the hall with Sheena looking toward him.

The Treacles's offering sat on the kitchen table. Magret Treacle was at the refrigerator putting something in a casserole dish away. Her hand trembled, he saw, and the bowl chipped against another bowl. He wondered if it was his sudden arrival that had caused her nervousness. She quickly closed the refrigerator door, and then made a motion as if she were wiping her hands on the scarf that hung around her neck. It looked like a silk scarf, in autumn colors.

"I'm sorry to bother you again, Mrs. Wasson." Collins nodded silent greetings to Daniel and Magret. "But I'd like to know who owns the church next door, and the house and land. I'd heard it was once a part of this place."

"That land was given to Everett's sister," Daniel explained. "Magret can tell you more about it than I can."

"It now belongs to my oldest brother, as far as I know," Magret said, "and it was once part of this place. But when my grandfather died he left this house and a couple of acres to Everett for taking care of Grandma, and he gave my mother five acres of land. My father built the church and house. I have siblings, all older, who have moved to other states, for the most part, and some of them—two—have died. But they—or maybe their heirs now—own it."

Magret was moving about in the kitchen, keeping her hands busy, wiping the cabinet with a cloth, spreading the cloth over the divider in the old white double sink, dusting her hands together, straightening the plastic canisters on the cabinet, pulling the cover down on the toaster, so obviously nervous and ill at ease. Her husband hadn't changed his position, and the boy sat on a kitchen chair without moving. Faith sat near him, her chair pulled out from the table. The teenage girl moved about, too, but touched nothing.

Magret lifted and dropped her shoulders in a shrug. "I guess they just let the place sit. After my father left ... they were gone, too."

In the brief silence Collins heard Faith clicking her fingertips against the tablecloth.

"He passed away out west. California," Magret said. "He had left the church, you see, after my mother's death. My father kept the church another year, and then he left with another woman. This is something you would hear from anyone who had ever gone to church there, so you might as well hear it from me. I was seventeen when he left, so I stayed with an aunt in town, and a year later I married Daniel."

In his notebook Collins wrote dates and facts as fast as he could. He had a feeling he had to be very cautious about the question he wanted to ask.

"Twenty years ago you were about fifteen, sixteen, Mrs. Treacle?"

"Yes. Fifteen. That was the year before my mother died."

"Then the church was open at that time?"

Magret licked her lips. She had put on her makeup as she probably did every morning. Lipstick, mascara, even blush. Her skin otherwise was pale and looked slightly blotched. She was dressed in a dark brown knit suit, with brown pumps and dark stockings. The scarf around her neck was the only touch of color.

"Was in regular attendance," she said. "There were perhaps a hundred members, which was remarkable for a country church. Of course, most of them didn't show up most of the time. I grew up living in that house. I was used to—to going to church there."

She still wouldn't meet his eyes.

"Mrs. Wasson, that was before you knew your husband?"

Faith jumped slightly, and stopped clicking her nails against the table top. "Yes. That was before ... the church was already closed when I met Everett."

"Mrs. Treacle," Collins said suddenly, "do you know of any girl in your church, or young woman, who was pregnant at that time who might have buried her baby in the woods?"

Magret Treacle's eyes jerked toward Collins and stared without blinking or faltering.

"No!" she said quickly. "Of course not." Then, after a pause, in a less strident voice, she said, "There were babies born at that time, I suppose, but certainly none that—none of the other."

He asked a few more questions of the Treacle family and got the answers he expected. None of them had any idea who might have killed Everett Wasson. All of them had been at home last night. Leigh had been on a date, but had gotten home before eleven o'clock. Of course the girl was not suspected of anything anyway, but it was better, at least in his own notes, to know exactly what a family was doing on a night their uncle had been murdered.

His feeling that if he found the answers to the baby in the woods, he would begin to know the answer to Everett's death, did not leave him. He left the Wasson home with a sense of having left something important behind him, some bit of knowledge he hadn't been able to grasp.

CHAPTER 13

CLYDE JUDSON DROVE his truck along the street where Magret Treacle lived with her husband and children. He had gotten her address out of the phone book. The place was one of the better neighborhoods in town, the houses built in the hillier areas north of the city. The streets here weren't laid out in straight blocks, but curved and tree-lined. The lawns sloped, and he saw a variety of fences, and plantings, in some cases completely hiding the house beyond. The farther out on the street he drove, the more the places became estates.

The Treacle place sat on a slope of a hill above the street. It was a two-story house with large trees in the yard and at least one balcony on the second floor. The exterior was dark red brick, like his own house, but on this one it looked great. The trim was white, just as his was, but it didn't need painting. The neighboring houses weren't too close. The area was quiet and had a lot of privacy.

He felt more than a little inferior. He never liked going into these better neighborhoods. His opinion of himself lowered mightily, too damned mightily, when he saw what other men had done.

She must have married him for his money, for what he could give her, he thought as he slowly eased his truck past the driveway. By craning his neck, he could see a three-car garage, and one small car was parked in the wide, concrete driveway that curved up the slope of the hill to the house. It was a small older Bug. Probably belonged to one of the kids.

His own kids had had to earn their own cars, and his son had been proud as a king when he finally had saved enough money to pay one hundred and fifty dollars for his first pile of junk.

But the kids had fun with the car, fixing it up, making it run. It had puffed up and down the street in front of his house all summer, the year Jeffry was seventeen. Six years ago.

Jeffry had been two the year Shannon was born, the year he'd begun noticing Magret's eyes. He had seen something in them that spring, he remembered, when his wife was big as a cow with the baby before she was born. And then, while Glorian was in the hospital, he had gone to that church picnic with just one thing on his mind. Getting Magret into the woods.

He wondered if she ever thought of those days, that summer. Had she thought of it longer than he had? He had forgotten all about it, until the news came out in the paper about the grave found in the woods.

Infant skeleton, buried twenty years ago, give or take a year or so.

The way he had it figured, they were close to right. It would have been twenty-one years sometime this coming winter. She had come to him in the fall, when his daughter was a few months old. And Shannon had passed her twenty-first birthday last May.

He had to see Magret, maybe talk to her. The child was hers, he felt positive of that. Born in secret, buried in secret. Alive, some people said, but that was only their speculation. He wondered, was she the kind of girl to have killed her own baby? His baby, too.

He had to know.

KEEP BUSY.

She was feeling tiredness through her soul, it seemed, yet she couldn't stop moving. Keep busy, something within her warned, as if to stop would be to break down. She avoided the eyes of her family, especially the questioning eyes of Daniel. A glimpse upward at him showed her that he was feeling concern—or suspicion?

Yet how could he feel suspicion, when he knew nothing of her past, of that one year of her life that was a black hole in her being? How could he know ... unless Uncle Everett had told him.

Her breath caught. That had never entered her mind before. How many of her family actually knew more of that uncovered grave than she would ever have thought possible?

And the detective, Sergeant Stoddard. Now that he had been asking those questions of her, did he suspect her?

She had wanted to bite her tongue and lie, and say she had never lived in the rectory, knew nothing about those people who did. But it would have been too easy to trace, and Daniel, if not her children, knew she had lived there.

No one knew what it had taken for her to return today to the woods, to Uncle Everett's house. To hurry and get away was to leave a nightmare.

"There's nothing we can do, Faith," she said, seeing through the kitchen door the removal of the yellow ribbon that said '*Police, do not cross*'. Sergeant Stoddard stood for a while talking to the man in uniform, and then went to his car. She watched him get in and close the door. She saw him pick up a hand phone or mike and talk into it. What was he telling his superiors? Magret Treacle is the killer. She murdered her newborn twenty-one years ago, and her uncle knew, and she has killed him to keep the secret. I can't prove it yet, but ...

She had to get out of here.

Faith had been saying something, but Magret had missed it all. She began gathering up the bowls she had emptied and rinsed to take back home. Chicken and dumplings, a vegetable casserole, her special sour cream cake. There was enough cooked food in the refrigerator to last Faith and Peggy days. Part of it would spoil, probably, unless some of Faith's relatives came for the funeral.

She felt Daniel's arms go around her. "Let me do that, Maggie. You need to rest."

"No." She pushed him away. Daniel's arms around her sometimes made her feel smothered. She liked him better on his side of the bed, or an arm's length away in his chair, or across a desk. And yet something in her turned over painfully when she saw the shadow of hurt cross his face, and she reached out and patted his cheek. "I'm okay," she said. "Thanks, darling. I need to—keep busy."

He stepped back and stood in the middle of the room. There was still a downhearted look on his face that made her feel both sorry and annoyed. Why did he always have to act like an over-concerned parent?

Magret loaded Daniel with the sack of emptied bowls, gathered her children, and said good-bye to Faith and Peggy, saying to Daniel as they went out through the long front hall and across the seldom-used front porch, "One of her sisters will surely be here in a few days. I suppose it will be all right for them to stay here alone, if that's what they want."

"I could stay here, Mom," Ward offered.

"No, absolutely not." She looked at him, so serious, tall and thin as a switch. Barely eleven years old. What could he do against a vicious killer? But, of course, there would be no killer here, now. The killer had already been here and taken what it—she—wanted.

Magret felt a sob in her throat. Her son was not in danger, here or anywhere. She could never kill her son, never. Even though she knew that sometime in the night, in the darkness of that world she inhabited in the night, she had killed her own uncle.

EIGHT BLOCKS from the street on which he had located the Treacle residence, Clyde found a large Consumer's supermarket. This, he knew as surely as if her image remained indelibly in the parking lot, was where Magret did her shopping.

He pulled his truck into the lot and found a parking spot in the midst of cars and vans and motor homes. He got out, stretched his shoulders up from his body, carefully stuffed his shirt down into his pants, and looked around. He felt conspicuous just parking here, as if people walking and driving past would know he wasn't here to buy groceries.

Hell, he felt guilty, as if his wife might come along and see him, or one of her dozens of nosy friends or relatives. But his house was across town, in the southeast section, and the shopping center she used had a Piggly-Wiggly, or something like that. Maybe it was a Safeway.

He reached into the truck and pulled out the jacket he had taken off when he parked for a couple of minutes where he could see the Treacle house. If anyone had been at home he hadn't seen them. If they had any pets, it or they were hidden from view. He glimpsed only a backyard bird feeder.

He walked casually toward the grocery store. Women in a hurry passed him, and a man stood at the line of newspaper racks reading the headlines. As Clyde passed by, the man put coins in one of them and withdrew a newspaper.

He went back toward the parking lot reading the paper.

Clyde went into the unfamiliar store.

It was large, stretching off in three directions.

He crossed the sections of checkout stands, found an aisle, and wandered toward the back.

As he had hoped, it had a food bar. It was almost a small restaurant, with tables and booths, almost hidden from the shoppers.

He bought a cup of coffee and a cinnamon roll, and took them to the corner booth just as it emptied. He sat down with a sigh.

From there he had a good view of the wide aisle along which customers pushed their carts as they moved with the tide from east to west in the grocery store.

MAGRET CHANGED to slacks and sweater, a loose sweater that would hide the bulges that seemed to be growing around her midriff. Had she been eating more? Was her careful seven-hundred-calorie-a-day diet in jeopardy? She tried to remember if she had snacked yesterday. A few grapes from the fruit bowl, maybe, last night as she stood looking out through the window into the dark. A few grapes—high in sugar.

Grapes. Were they out of grapes? Oranges? Bananas?

She went downstairs and found Daniel and Ward in the family room. The TV was running a video the kids had picked out at the video store and Daniel was reading a newspaper. He looked up, Ward didn't. Ward was on the floor in front of the TV, the upper part of his body supported by two of the overlarge cushions that, when not in use, were stacked against the wall near the entertainment center.

"Where are Sheena and Leigh?"

"Upstairs in their rooms, probably," Daniel said, which meant that he didn't know. "Are you all right, Maggie?"

"Yes, of course." She wished he would stop asking her that. "I might have to go to the market, Daniel—"

"Want me to go for you?"

"No."

What she needed was to get out, be around people who wouldn't bother her or speak to her. *Keep busy*.

She checked the kitchen first, wiped the counter again, looked into the pantry to see what looked good to eat, and decided she would go to the market for pizza.

There was frozen pizza in the refrigerator, but she liked to keep extra on hand in case ... in case. It didn't matter. She didn't have to make excuses to herself or to anyone. If she wanted to drive down to the market, she would.

She pulled her heavy cardigan off the hook in the utility room and went out to the new blue Olds that Daniel had given her for their anniversary. She smiled, just a tremor really, pulling at the corner of her lips as she slid into the soft, smooth leather seat. He was so good to her. He had always been good to her.

When she went to work for him at age seventeen, that first year she was so completely on her own, he had treated her like a daughter, or perhaps a little sister. At first. She had seen the concern in his eyes then, and had drifted toward it like a cold animal just out of the winter winds.

Her memory of passion was the memory of darkness, and fear, and rejection, something she never wanted to think of. That she had never felt passion for Daniel was the least important thing in her life, and something he didn't know.

Passion. Sex. Her lips curled at the thought. She couldn't bear the reminder. She refused to watch an R-rated movie, because of the sex. It disgusted her. Why was it called making love? There was nothing of love in the act of copulation.

It should be private, just as private as going to the bathroom.

It was all centered in the same area.

She realized she was driving too fast, ten miles above the speed limit, her hands gripping the steering wheel tightly. She didn't need a ticket. Of all things, she didn't need to put herself before the eyes of the police any more than she already was.

She came to the four-lane street that passed in front of Consumer's, and stopped, waiting for the traffic to ease so she could pull out and turn right. An eighteen-wheeler roared by, exceeding the speed limit by far more than ten miles an hour. She watched it, wondering where it was going. Into her came a longing she had never felt so strongly. That she might go too ... far away ... away from her life that had suddenly turned into a nightmare, away from memories that had returned to haunt her, of an insanity that was growing like a fungus in her brain. Away from it all.

She pulled the car out onto the street and drove right, slowly, turning into the first entry to the Consumer's parking lot. She parked the car and walked with her head down against the misty wind toward the front of the store.

The warmth touched her as the doors opened to admit her, and she lifted her head. She glimpsed a reflection of herself in the mirror in the vestibule. She wondered if it had been put there to remind customers not to come to the store looking as if they had just gotten out of bed. Magret saw her hair mussed by wind and straightened by mist. Dark brown hair highlighted with blond streaks, professionally applied. She hadn't been blond even when she was a small child, but the highlights were as close as she dared come to bleaching her hair. Her makeup had worn off, so that she looked pale. She had an urge to take off her shoe and throw it at the mirror, but she only ducked her head again and went through the second set of doors and over to the carts.

She put her purse into the small seat in the shopping cart and pushed it into the beauty and drug section. She didn't need anything. She had a vanity full of makeup. Still, she chose a bright new lipstick and put it in the cart.

She left the drug section and pushed the cart through the fresh vegetable area, stopping for a few oranges, red Delicious apples, a couple of green Granny Smith apples—good for baking she told herself—bananas, more grapes.

From the vegetable bins she took broccoli. She would chop it and put a low-cal dressing on it. Lots of vitamins in the broccoli, and almost no calories.

The cart was filling, far more than she had anticipated when she came to the store, but the relief in her was enough to make her weep. It was almost like being herself again, as if she had turned the clock back to last month, last year, when life had been so good. Back beyond last year maybe, before the nightmares had started.

She pushed the cart toward the bakery section, where the smell of things baking overwhelmed her good intentions to keep on her continuous diet. Just this once, she told herself. A fresh doughnut, or a roll of some kind with icing and nuts. Maybe a cup of coffee, and a pause in the deli.

She saw an empty booth in the shadows of the restaurant, and then she saw the face, the eyes, staring at her.

She returned the stare. The man had a hatchet-sharp face, bony, with high cheekbones and a sharp chin. His hair was thinning almost to balding on top, a mousy gray-brown. He was wearing a worker's jacket and a shirt with a drooping, un-ironed collar. His undershirt, white, showed through the V of the open shirt, its ribbed top almost touching his sharp Adam's apple.

He was staring at her intently, and she saw recognition in his eyes. Even across the distance, through cigarette smoke from another table, past people who walked between them, she suddenly knew him.

His eyes ... brown ... rimmed in black.

Goodgod!

Clyde Judson.

He was staring at her in such a way that she knew he had come here to see her, perhaps to try to talk to her.

She jerked her own trapped stare away, jerked the cart left, and hurried down the stationery aisle. She didn't dare look back. He was following, she felt sure, right behind her, hurrying to catch up. His hand was out now, reaching to clamp down on her shoulder.

She left the cart and hurried on, almost running. Trying not to run and draw attention to herself.

She had to go around the long line of checkout counters. Only when she reached the end did she dare to look back.

He wasn't there. He wasn't there, thank God.

She hurried on out. In the parking lot she allowed herself to run to her car.

She slammed and locked the doors. As she drove away, she saw him. He was standing just outside the doors of the grocery store scanning the parking lot. She pulled the car sharply left and drove toward the street, trying to draw no attention to the blue Oldsmobile.

DARK FELL EARLY in the first days of November, and Faith stood at the window watching it creep inward from the forest behind the house. The doors were locked now. The windows, of course, had been locked and the storm windows secured back in October. Everett had been so careful about seeing that the house was prepared for winter.

She wondered if she dared turn up the heat. Now that Everett was gone, there would be less money than before. But surely, just for these few days, these most difficult days, they could have more heat? Yet did they really need the whole big house heated? The oven had warmed up the kitchen. She had baked the small loaf of bread dough Magret had brought, even though she wasn't hungry. Just the smell of baking bread seemed to make it more like home. She let herself believe that Everett would come out soon from the den, ready to eat with her and Peggy.

"Mama ..." Peggy said, as she'd been doing all day. Just "Mama" ... and nothing more, as if to reassure herself that she wasn't alone.

Peggy looked small, somehow shriveled, as she sat at the round kitchen table with the heel of the loaf of hot bread on a plate in front of her. The heel, her favorite part, was yellow with margarine, and had pink globs of apple jelly, but Peggy hadn't touched it.

Faith poured a glass of milk and set it by Peggy's plate, then went back to the door, where she stood looking out through the glass.

She saw the dark splotch of stain on the porch, trailing down the steps and pooling on the bottom step, and it struck her like an electric charge jolting through her brain.

"I haven't—" She stopped before it left her mouth. *Haven't cleaned the blood off the step.* In order to go out to the woodpile that Everett had so carefully cut and piled for the winter, she would have to go down those steps.

She had to clean up the blood.

From under the sink she took her mop bucket and ran it full of hot water from the faucet. She poured detergent in and watched it foam. From the pantry she took the broom.

"Where are you going, Mama?" Peggy asked when she opened the door.

"I'll be back in a minute," she said. "I have to bring in some wood. We can't turn up the heat. Papa cut all this wood, so we'll use it. You can take your bread and milk and go to the den and watch TV if you want to."

"All right!"

It was the first word Peggy had uttered all day that had life in it. Faith glanced back at her and saw that flush of pleasure that Peggy could get, and it pleased her.

The child would survive. She was young, and she might even forget most of it.

Faith turned on the porch light. Mists were moving out of the woods, making the trunks of the trees look like dark sentries to another world. As she looked at it, she felt a tremor of fear. For the first time since she had moved into this big old farm-like house, she felt afraid of the woods so close behind it, just across the yard. She was afraid even of the dark windows of the house, of the upper story, the corner out toward the driveway, those rooms never used.

She concentrated on cleaning the blood off the porch. It showed where she had dragged her husband's body, only hours ago, up onto the wooden floor of the porch. The color of the stain was brown there, but in the pits of the cement steps it was still wet and red.

She sloshed the hot water across the boards and down the steps. The water turned pink beneath the foam of the detergent. With the broom she began vigorously to scrub.

When she went back for more water, she could hear voices from the TV in the warmer den.

For an hour she scrubbed, feeling it in her hands as she gripped the handle of the broom, and in her aching back as she bent and swung back and forth. The mists of the forest became fog, yet she could still see the tree trunks, black and straight. Then she stopped, staring. There was something else out in the backyard. A dark skeletal thing, large, looming.

She stood bent over, listening.

Silence.

The skeletal thing, she realized, was the swing set. Distortions caused by the fog made it seem closer than it really was.

The light from the porch dwindled away in the fog, shining against its white frame flecked with rust several yards short of the woodpile.

She left the bucket and broom on the porch and went down the steps. She walked into the backyard, feeling the cold mist of the fog against her face. Icy fingers of fear trickled down her spine and across her shoulders and lifted the fine hair at the nape of her neck. Yet she didn't look back, nor pause.

The woodpile was suddenly a dark hill in front of her. She picked up the short, heavy sticks quickly, loading her arms, straining her back.

She tried to straighten and realized her load was too heavy. She'd have to leave one of the sticks.

From the top she rolled one off, and it fell with a thud into place on the large stack of wood. When she looked up she saw—*Peggy*...

Standing pale and naked at the end of the woodpile, a white ghostlike figure against the black background. She was like a wraith in the darkness, as if she were part of the fog.

"Peggy!" she exclaimed.

And then she was looking at darkness.

In the next moment she realized with cold shock that she had just seen the child Peggy and Wendy swore they had seen.

Faith swallowed something hard in her throat, then turned and hurried back to the house.

After laying the wood on the kitchen floor, she locked the door and turned out the kitchen light. She realized she had left the porch light on, but when she started to open the door again to turn out the light—the better to see the ghostly outlines of the child outside—she thought better of it and drew her hand back.

The door was locked with a simple little button lock, and the uncovered glass that came halfway down on the door made her feel unprotected.

Yet it was only a child out there. And now she knew the kids weren't making things up, or following the suggestion of Wendy, who was lively and imaginative, and pretending to see things they hadn't really seen. Now she knew it was there.

But it was only a child, she told herself as she went to the other windows in the kitchen and pulled the blinds. It was only a child, without clothing, or wearing something close-fitting and white, alone in the cold and the dark. It had come up to her, yet had not spoken.

She carried her wood into the den and pulled the door shut. At this moment she dreadfully missed their dog, a big old mutt who had grown old and died in the hot months of summer. And the cats that used to live in the barn, and who sat on the window-sills sometimes, and on the porch. Where had they gone?

The fog closed them in, she and Peggy, all alone, it seemed, except for the ... whatever she had seen by the woodpile.

The television was an intrusive noise to her thoughts. She wanted to shut it off so she could listen, alert as she was to every sound in and around the house.

She sat down in her chair without leaning back. Her fingers tapped against one another as she stared at the wall over Peggy's head.

She suddenly remembered the wood. Abruptly she stood up, opened the door on the heavy cast iron stove, and put into the low fire as much wood as the stove would hold. She turned the damper partway down to hold the burning low, to make the wood last all night.

Later they would go up to her room, if Peggy didn't want to sleep alone tonight, and stay warm under the electric blanket. Even if Peggy wanted to sleep in her own room, Faith didn't think she could let her. She was afraid to let the child out of her sight now.

Everett ...

His name, silent on her lips, was like a flash of hot pain through her heart. Lord, how they needed Everett.

She thought of calling Sergeant Stoddard and his dog. The clock on the shelf behind the stove told her it was after nine. She hadn't realized it was so late.

She should wait until morning, she told herself.

Her fingers entwined nervously, picked at one another as she leaned forward tensely in her chair. Above the sound of the TV she thought she heard something.

"Peggy!" she hissed. "Turn the TV down."

The child looked at her with sleepy eyes. She lay on her thick, fluffy rug right in front of the television, her chin supported by her hands. The light from the table beside Everett's empty chair made a pool that ended on Peggy's back.

"Turn it down!"

With alarm suddenly on her face, Peggy sat up and muted the sound on the television. "Mama, what's wrong?" she whispered.

Faith listened hard and heard nothing now, though a moment before she had heard a banging, like a window shutter slapping in the wind. Only tonight there was no wind. There was only silence, a silence so tangible it seemed she could hear the fog outside the window of the den, or the movement of blood in her own body.

For Peggy's sake she must remain calm.

"I guess I didn't hear anything," she said, and got up from her chair. She couldn't remember if she had locked the front door. She touched Peggy on the top of the head.

The child was staring up at her, mouth hanging open, skin almost as pale as the—whatever she had seen outside.

"Go ahead and watch the rest of your show. I'll just go check the doors and windows, and get the house ready for night."

"I thought you already did that," Peggy said, leaning forward and turning the volume up again.

"Well, so I'll check again to make sure."

As she went out into the hall, closing the den door behind her, Faith knew she and Peggy would not be able to stay here. Tomorrow they would pack what they needed and leave. They could go to Magret's for a few days, until the body was released and the funeral was over, then they would go back up north where she had grown up. She had sisters there, and a brother, and her father was there, too, remarried now since Mama passed away. Faith had never even met his wife.

She would be able to find a job there, she told herself as she went down the hall to the front door. Start fresh.

With a sudden sense of danger, Faith saw that the button of the lock on the front door was turned cross-ways, not perpendicular, as it should have been.

She was aware of the cold in the hall, of the dark of the night beyond the walls of the house, of the darkness in rooms not lighted, and felt the tremor of fear within her own body.

She had never been so afraid before.

This door should have been locked.

And then she remembered the policemen who had been in the house today and she almost collapsed with relief. Of course, she smiled as she firmly locked the door, half laughing at herself with no mirth, just a touch of contempt for her own ... foolishness? No, not foolishness. Her husband had been horribly, brutally murdered on the back steps, less than twenty-four hours ago, and she was in this house without him for the first time in her life, and she didn't know if she would be able to stand it.

She pushed the button that turned on the front porch light.

No one stood on the porch, or in the edge of darkness beyond the railing.

She went back down the hall toward the den.

She stopped, the iciness of terror paralyzing her.

The sound was at the back of the house, somewhere. A long series of scratches, as if a limb were being raked down over the wood walls, or the back door. Or claws ... or a knife.

As she listened, there was silence again, a fog-shrouded stillness in the world around the house. Faith hurried into the den and closed the door behind her.

Tomorrow morning, she promised herself.

CHAPTER 14

MAGRET HADN'T WANTED Leigh to go out tonight, and they had argued about it. Leigh thought about it as she sat in the car with Thad in the driveway.

"Not tonight, Leigh. It's not right. Think of your uncle Everett!"

"But Mom, I've had this date with Thad all week. You knew that. We're going to choir practice tonight just like always. Uncle Everett would understand."

The argument had gone on until it finally came to a compromise. She could go to choir practice if she didn't go anywhere else, and if she got home by ten-thirty. At first her mother had said ten, but she hadn't been thinking clearly, because choir seldom ended before ten.

Thad's hand clasped and unclasped on the back of Leigh's neck, a gentle to firm touch that usually thrilled her socks off. And sometimes more than that, if they were safely alone.

"What're you thinking about?" he asked.

"Nothing." She didn't want to tell him that she was thinking of an argument she'd had with her mother. She turned her face toward him, so that he could kiss her.

But she was aware of the yard lights along the driveway and the light on the side entry door. The car was in semi-shadow, but the balcony of her parents' bedroom was visible at the back corner of the house, and the French doors that opened onto it. She supposed her mother knew that she and Thad kissed, and petted, as Magret had called it once when she'd tried talking about sex to her, but she didn't want to be watched.

"Mama says we should cut our dates to a minimum until after Uncle Everett's funeral."

Thad sat back, his hand gently kneading the back of her neck again. She saw his profile against the paler light on the far side of the driveway. He was handsome, and she loved looking at him. He had blond hair, and a big-boned face, all skin and sharp angles. He wasn't much taller yet than she, but his dad and older brothers were tall, and she could almost see Thad growing, too, in the two years since they had started going steady when they were both just fourteen. This had been a great year. They had gone to drivers' school together, and gotten their driver's license at the same time. Then Leigh's dad had given her a VW for her efforts, on the promise that she would be a careful driver. Thad had borrowed money from his dad for his car, which was older, and bigger and clunkier, but it was a great car, because it had taken them into places alone that they otherwise never would have gotten to.

"What about Wednesday night?"

"Oh, gee." She looked out over the hood. "Yeah, you're right. We can't miss Wednesday night." It was a movie date, a movie she really wanted to see, but of course the main thing about the date was afterward.

He put his arm across her shoulder and pulled her against him. "We could skip school someday and go check that place out."

That place was a very private road by the lake. And on that night the moon should be full and the view would be fantastic. Besides, they'd had a date set, this special date, for two months now, when they would really be alone, really alone, for the first time. They wouldn't be parked in his driveway, or hers, or in the mall parking lot, or the school parking lot, or at the church in those few precious moments they dared park without being conspicuous. They would be alone.

"I'll talk to her," Leigh promised as she opened the door and started sliding out. I gotta go in now."

Their lips met briefly, and then parted. She ran up the steps to the side door, and turned and waved. Thad started the car, then pulled it around the circle drive near the garages and drove slowly back down the driveway.

She stood on the small porch until he was out of sight. Fog swirled over the hedges that separated the driveway from the property next door, and moved in large pockets along the street, obscuring the trees on the other side, and making the street light look as if it were wearing a bonnet of gauze.

The night was quiet. Fog always did that, she thought as she used her key to open the door. Fog silenced even the dogs' communications through the night, and slowed the cars, and sent the people indoors.

In the dim light of the hall she looked at her watch. It was past ten-thirty by at least ten minutes. But they had been sitting in the driveway for five minutes, and the fog had slowed them on the way home. She could tell her mother that if she was waiting up.

The interior of the house seemed as quiet as the exterior. She turned out lights as she moved through the house. Just outside the swinging door of the kitchen she heard Magret moving around within. It sounded like she was frantically cleaning, just as she had been doing all day. Leigh heard the rattle of metal things in a drawer, and the closing of a door, or drawer, the soft thud of wood against wood.

She drew a deep breath and pushed the kitchen doors open.

Then she stood blinking in the darkness, the only light behind her from the hall.

She saw movement of something pale, just the barest, quickest movement, as if the fog had entered somehow through the closed doors and windows. Then that, too, was gone in the darkness.

"Mama?"

There was no answer.

The house was so quiet. No one had stayed downstairs in the family room to watch TV, and Leigh couldn't hear anyone moving about on the second floor.

Puzzled, Leigh reached for the light switch on the wall.

The kitchen bloomed before her, from the round, cloth-covered eating table to the white cabinets, bright and clean. No one was there.

"Mama?" Frowning, she went toward the utility room, taking off her jacket.

The utility room, and washroom, and hall to the garages were empty, too. Leigh stood for a moment where one door went into the garage and another out into the backyard. Someone had been in the kitchen, she was sure, and now she was beginning to wonder if it had been a burglar, someone who had somehow known she was there, and slipped out before she entered, covered by darkness. It might have been done that way.

But the back door was locked, and so was the door into the garage.

Leigh hung her jacket in the closet, and turned off the row of lantern lights in the driveway, leaving on only the one at the far end, the way her dad liked it.

She went back through the house, turning off lights behind her. At the top of the stairs where the hall light above had been left on for her, someone stepped out from behind a corner in the hall.

Leigh almost screamed.

Then she felt a surge of anger brought on by the sharp sense of fear.

"Mama, why do you do things like that?"

Magret stood at the top of the stairs looking down, her arms clasping a blue velvet robe against her stomach. She suddenly looked dismayed. She had come to scold, and was forced into defending herself.

"Things like what?"

"Like jumping out at me."

Magret almost smiled. "I didn't jump out at you. I just wanted to see if that was you, that's all. Aren't you late?"

"Well, there was a terrible fog," Leigh explained as she climbed the stairs, "And choir lasted a little longer than usual. You know Clark, how he can be sometimes. He gets carried away with his leading. I think he's a frustrated orchestra conductor, or something."

"Anyway, you're home. Everyone else has been asleep for hours. We were all so tired tonight. The emotional strain, I suppose."

Leigh looked at her mother with sudden concern. Magret had lately been so high-strung, so nervous, so distant. And now her uncle had died, and died horribly. Leigh had heard about it at church, things she hadn't known. He had been stabbed so many times in his neck that it had looked chewed to pieces, like what a large, long-fanged wild animal might have done if it had been eating its prey. He had been caught on his back porch, Marian Soarks had told her, and Marian knew, because she had a cousin in the Sheriff's Department. She said Uncle Everett had been pulled head first down the steps. And they still weren't absolutely certain the damage had been done only with a knife. The coroner had thought the wounds might be teeth marks.

Leigh had shrugged off these gruesome details the best she could. She hadn't wanted to hear them in the first place. But Magret might not have been able to shrug them off.

"How about you, Mama, have you slept?"

"No, not yet. Now that you're home—"

Although she knew it was not possible, Leigh asked, "Mama, you weren't down in the kitchen just now, were you?"

On Magret's face then was such a sudden look of fear, a draining of color, that Leigh was afraid she would faint, or perhaps have a heart attack.

"No, why?" Magret said.

"Just wondered," she said, and went past Magret toward her room, pausing to kiss her mother's cheek. It even felt cold to her lips, as if there were no blood beneath Magret's skin. "Good night, Mama."

FOR A FEW MINUTES after Leigh went into her room and closed the door, Magret stood in the hall. The hall light wavered in front of her eyes, and the hall below looked like a dungeon. She told herself to go down, to check out the kitchen, the dining room, the pantry, all the places where someone might have been when Leigh came into the house. But she had taken a sleeping pill, and she could feel its effect now. All she really wanted was a deep and dreamless sleep.

She left the hall light burning and went back into her room, where Daniel was already asleep, and crawled into bed.

She let her eyes fall shut.

As she drifted away she heard a hymn she used to sing in the old church, as she had come to think of it. *Rocked in the cradle of the deep, I lay me down in peace to sleep.*

A child was singing it, a familiar voice from—from sometime in her past—

But the lovely peaceful words of the song were denied by the plaintive voice of the singer.

She struggled to remember where she had heard the voice, but then the swift darkness of sleep drew her in.

FAITH LAY stiff and tense in the soft bed, cold air in the bedroom around her cheeks like icy hands. In Everett's place Peggy slept, a warm little ball curled like a kitten, her face under the covers. Faith knew because she had just reached over and touched Peggy's head, and found that only her hair protruded above the blanket.

The room was dark. Faith was used to sleeping in the dark. But as she lay listening, unable to keep her eyes closed, she wished she had left a light on. Yet, a light in the house would draw to it whatever, or whoever was outside. All creatures sought light, did they not? Except those made of darkness. Hush, she told herself. Stop thinking nonsense.

There were sounds in the house, perhaps just outside of it, on the two porches, that she had never heard before. But this was the first night she had slept here without Everett, without the warm security he had given her. Were the sounds she was hearing something she might have ignored a few nights ago, or was someone deliberately trying to scare her?

She thought of Everett's murder, and it was like thinking of something foreign to her own life and experiences, as if she had viewed it on television. Then the shock of it would hit her, and it became her life, her husband's death. And she felt frightened and helpless.

She knew now she should have taken Peggy today, while it was still light, and gone to Magret's.

For Peggy's sake, if not her own.

Or they should have moved into a motel.

She knew now they would not spend another night in this house.

As soon as it became light enough to see, they would leave.

Thank God Peggy was able to sleep.

The sound on the porch below grated on her nerves like a fingernail on glass and became impossible to deny. It was not a limb moving against the house, this time, it was something at the door.

She sat up in bed, the blanket clutched against her throat. Terror sent cold shivers down her back as she sat tense as a board and listened to the scratch of fingernails, or perhaps a knife, first at the screen, and then a moment later at the glass of the door.

She knew now that Everett's murderer, that phantom that seemed not even actually to exist, was there. And it was coming for her and her child.

Should she call Sergeant Stoddard? But the only phone in the house was down in the kitchen.

The noises stopped and silence fell. But it was the silence of eyes outside her window peering in, watching her in all her fear and helplessness.

She had to leave the house. Now, before morning.

Somehow, she had to get Peggy into the car.

She got out of bed and moved as quietly as she could to the window. She peered out into a solid black of night, yet it seemed she could see the swirl of thick fog against the windowpane. The fog could work two ways, she decided. It could blind her, true, but it could also blind the murderer. Under cover of the heavy fog, she could get Peggy into the car, because she knew exactly where it sat, as it always had since she had come to live here. In the past she had asked Everett why he didn't clean the junk out of the one-car garage and use it for the car, but he never had, and now she was glad. His truck had always been parked at the side of the garage, but the car, which she used, had its grassless spot at the side of the driveway, just at the corner of the house.

She stood still in the dark room, the cold boards of the varnished floor icy beneath her bare feet, and visualized their walk to the car. Out the back door, down the cement steps still wet where she had washed them, to the path worn in the grass, straight across to the door of the car.

They could make it. They had to. Whoever it was that was trying to get into the house had left the back porch for the front. They had to hurry.

Once in town she would call the police.

She fumbled at the dresser in the dark, easing out a drawer that contained folded jeans and tops. She pulled the jeans on beneath her nightgown, the denim rough against her bare hips. There was no time for the niceties of dressing. She was hurrying so much her fingers fumbled and shook.

With the nightgown jerked over her head and dropped onto the floor, she pulled a heavy, warmly lined sweatshirt on over a bra-less bosom. She felt naked and oddly ashamed of that nakedness beneath her outer clothes. But she had to save herself and Peggy, especially Peggy, and it would make no difference to anyone whether she wore underwear.

She fumbled under the bed and found her house shoes. The rest of her things, the shoes she had worn during the day, clean underwear, stockings, were all in the bathroom. She didn't dare take the time to go after them.

Her daughter's soft breathing was the only sound in the room, in the whole house now, except the pounding of Faith's heart.

She went around the bed and bent to wake Peggy.

Peggy made a wordless sound, almost a cry of protest, and Faith lifted her and whispered her name. The sound seemed loud in the house, as if it might draw the attention of the murderer to them, and let him know where they were.

"Shhh, Peggy," Faith whispered, gathering the soft, limp, sleepy child up and wrapping her tightly in the blanket, making sure her feet were free and unhampered. Although she might be able to carry Peggy a few yards, they could never get down the stairs without falling or tripping, Faith was afraid. She had thought of just picking her up, but common sense had stopped her.

"Mama ... ?"

"Shh. Be very quiet, Peggy," she whispered as she pulled Peggy up onto the side of her bed and felt for her feet to push them into the fuzzy house shoes. "Listen to Mama. We're going out to the car. We have to be very quiet. Someone is on the front porch. You will need to walk. We'll hold the blanket around you."

As if Peggy understood immediately the urgency of getting out of the house and into the car, she became alert and cooperative. Faith felt the child's hand on her shoulder as she pushed the Donald Duck house shoes onto her feet. Then the hand pulled in and clutched the blanket to help hold it up as Faith pulled her off the bed and adjusted the blanket again.

Faith thought of the flashlight in the kitchen drawer downstairs—but no. It was better they moved in the dark.

She had never noticed the squeaking of the floor before. As they moved across it, they were followed by mouse-like squeaks that seemed to echo in the still, dark house. Faith's ankles, bare between denim jeans and house slippers, felt the cold air that swirled through the house in silent dark like the fog outdoors.

She murmured encouragement under her breath to Peggy as they started down the stairs, step by step. She held the blanket up so that Peggy would not trip on it.

A stair groaned beneath their weight, and Faith drew to a halt and waited, not breathing.

Something fell against the house or was thrown. But it was at the front of the house, over by the northwest corner now. It was like a mischievous child, she thought suddenly, out in the dark playing a game of threat and terrorization.

When they reached the bottom of the stairs, Faith began to hurry Peggy along, almost running. If the murderer was still at the front of the house, chances were good that they could be in the car and safely on their way before he realized what they were doing.

In the kitchen, Faith hesitated. There was no wall to touch for guidance. The back door of the house was across the room.

She could just make out the paler light of the glass on the door, dark, almost as dark as the blackness in the house, a ghostly rectangle.

She adjusted the blanket more securely at Peggy's shoulders, and bent to whisper in her ear, "As soon as we're through the kitchen door, run. Run as fast as you can to the car."

The keys were in the ignition, as they always were. There had never been any reason not to leave the keys in the car, here in the isolation of the edge of the woods, and now she saw the great advantage of that.

They crossed the kitchen, guided by the pale light of the door, and Faith unlocked the door and pulled it open. A damp coldness struck them head-on.

Faith grabbed Peggy off her feet and ran, the blanket falling away and trailing down the steps as if to cover Everett's blood.

Peggy's weight slowed her. She let the child slide to the ground, and the small arm trailed through her hand. She grasped Peggy's wrist and jerked her toward the car ... toward the place where the car should be.

She seemed for a moment to be lost in the thick moistness of the fog, with no object visible. It seemed she might have run out into the backyard instead of along the path toward the car. Peggy's wrist was clutched in her hand, the child almost dragging behind her. She paused to pick her up again and then she saw something ...

It was pale and ghostly, and suddenly in front of them.

A person, outlines lost in the dark of the fog.

A child, it seemed, about the size of Peggy, barely visible in the dark because it was wearing either a white, close-fitting suit ...

... or was naked.

... its skin unnaturally white and pale from a lifetime in the shadows and mists of the woods ... like some creature not quite human ... something not really alive ...

Someone screamed, and even through its distortions she recognized her child's cry.

"Mama ... *Mama* ...

There was more, something more, but Faith never knew what it was. She gave Peggy a shove away, as the naked, ghostlike child grew closer to her and became real, as it lunged in the dark and became suddenly, clearly visible. A hand rose above the small head, an arm as white as the underbelly of a snake, and in the hand as it came toward her with the glint of something in the damp fog ...

... a knife ...

And she remembered, in that moment, where she had seen those knives.

"Magret."

. . .

PEGGY HEARD the single word in the still, dark night as she stood paralyzed.

"Mama?"

Who was it in the dark? Someone was here besides her and her mother, and now her mother had disappeared.

Fear overcame her caution and she cried out, "Mama, where are you? Mama, where is the car? *Mama?"*

She heard sounds now. A kind of gurgling, as if someone were in a bathroom gargling salt water, as her daddy used to do when he had a sore throat. Thoughts entered and left her mind, as swiftly as arrows. Of her daddy and mama, and the warmth of the den. Of the coldness and darkness tonight in the halls as they had come downstairs, and the damp of the air in the outdoors.

And a glimpse of something, like a ghost, so pale, so fleeting. There was something here, keeping her mother from answering her. Keeping her away.

It was the child, she saw, grown a lot bigger now. Much larger, taller.

As the sight of the child came, it was gone, swallowed by darkness.

"Mama!" Peggy screamed.

The night was all around her, and in the complete dark she had lost even the sight of the strange, white girl. Then, as if the fog moved, as if a door within it opened, she saw her mother on the ground, and the girl bending over her. The door closed again and there was nothing but darkness.

Yet out of the dark she heard a command.

"Run, Peggy ... '

"Mama," she screamed again, hearing her voice strange and shrill and filled with fear. "Mama, where are you?"

Tears choked her, and her skin was wet with the heavy fog and the tears. With her hands out she felt for her mother, yet she knew in her heart the girl was killing her, and the girl would kill her next.

Run, Peggy.

The door in the blackness of the fog opened once more and Peggy saw the girl standing an arm's length away. She saw the vague outlines of the face and the shoulders, bare and white. It had seen her, too, and was now looking at her.

Instinct sent Peggy running toward the path to Wendy's house. No longer crying out, her tears drying in her consuming terror, Peggy ran. She had found that path so many times during her life she came again to it now in the complete dark, her hands out, brushing against the trunks of the trees that lined the path.

She ran, and ran until her breath burned in her throat. Her feet caught on something at the side of the path, and she fell, headlong.

The air for a long moment was knocked out of her and she lay gasping, unable to rise. In those few moments of stillness she heard a steady sound in the woods far behind her, the running of bare feet, a sound as soft as the beating of a calm heart.

It was coming after her—the girl—the child that had grown now to her size. It was coming for her, for Peggy.

She pulled herself up, but fell again as she tried to stand, pain shooting white-hot through her left ankle.

She reached down and felt it swelling, and with terror pounding in her ears, she began stumbling onward.

But now she had forgotten ...

Where was she? Where was she going?

Who was she?

She knew only one thing. There was a girl in the woods, a little girl not much larger than herself, that she had to hide from.

CHAPTER 15

Lord, I sometimes feel like a stranger here, as I travel down life's road, and nobody knows the ...

She was in the church, sitting on the front bench, as she'd always called the pews, where her father wanted her to sit, and her voice was lifted with the others in the hymn.

Yet the singer was singing alone, she realized, a fine, flutelike child's voice that was, oddly, hers. Though she was not now singing, she could hear it clearly, coming from some other source.

... and my burdens are so heavy, Lord ...

The church was empty, and she sat alone in it, and as she rose, the outlines of the windows, the dark rows of pews, the pulpit, the picture of Jesus on the wall at the front, all of it misted and faded, and there was nothing but the child singing a hymn.

... disappointments hover 'round, and the way seems long and dark ...

Magret woke, and widened her eyes in the light of her bedroom. She was alone. Daniel was not on his side of the bed, nor in the room, and there was a stillness in the house that made her feel her isolation. The dream receded as she woke, becoming misty and almost lost, but the hymn carried on, and she sat up in bed, chills moving over her like waves on a seashore.

... for this world of sin and night is an unfriendly world...

The voice of the child drifted away, and the house was silent, but Magret sat in cold and terrible fear.

The voice had been her own. The hymn was one she had sung often when she was a child in her father's church.

Yet the voice in the house had been real. Her own voice, somewhere in the house. As real as the voices of her own children. The stuff of madness. What was happening to her?

Her children.

She threw back her covers and ran without her robe or slippers to the door, into the hall, and breathless, frightened speechless, flung open the first door she came to.

Leigh's bed was neatly made, the quilted satin spread in a floral arrangement of colors from lavender to deep rose, touching the carpet precisely evenly all around. Leigh had put her last doll, a lovely pink-cheeked baby doll wearing bonnet, dress, and ruffly underwear, on her pillows, as she always did when she tidied her room.

Magret turned back to the hall and toward the other bedrooms crying out in a haunting fear, "Sheena! Ward! Where are you?"

She saw to her horror that each bedroom was empty. Ward's bedspread had been flung over the bed, leaving lumpy blankets beneath. Sheena's bedroom was as neat as Leigh's.

Magret turned and ran downstairs.

In the entry hall she noticed the sounds of cars on the street, and the slant of sunlight across the stoop outside for just a flashing moment, before the shadows of a cloudy day returned. And then she looked at the big grandfather's clock against the wall of the entry.

Quarter of ten.

Good God.

She became so weak with relief suddenly that she sat down on the bottom steps and rested her face in her hands. How could she have slept through the noise of the kids getting up and getting ready for school? And Daniel—she could almost see him tiptoeing around trying not to wake her. And probably he had gone to the room of each of the children and cautioned them to be quiet.

And maybe it wouldn't have mattered how noisy they were. The sleeping pill had really knocked her out. If she had dreamed at all, it was the fuzzy, misty dream of being in church as a child ...

... and then waking to the sound of her own voice singing a hymn she hadn't heard since she was sixteen years old.

It was all part of the dream, the sleeping pill, the disorientation of waking from one world to another.

She stood up and went down the hall to the kitchen, and there on the table, which had been left very tidy and clean, was a note propped against the sugar bowl.

Mama, we have let you sleep this morning. We love you.
Ward. Sheena. Leigh. Daniel.

Tears came to Magret's eyes. She stood with the note in her hands looking out the windows to the backyard. Someone had filled the bird feeders, and the one visible from where she stood had a few birds still breakfasting. Cardinals, crowned sparrows, a blue jay that swooped into their midst and scattered them to the nearby trio of lilac bushes.

Magret folded the note and went back upstairs. She slipped the note into the cedar chest at the end of the bed, along with all the other notes and cards and keepsakes she had gathered over the years.

She made the bed, and went to take a shower and dress.

As the water poured down upon her shoulders, she thought she heard the singing again, the voice so strangely her own, yet separated from her, as if it came from another room in the back of the house.

... there is a fountain filled with blood ...

Magret turned off the water and stood with it dripping from her body, but the house was quiet. She turned the water back on to finish her bath. And the song returned.

... and sinners plunged beneath that flood ...

But now she knew her mind was only playing tricks on her. The rushing water, the memory of the dream, worked somehow to create sounds that weren't there.

When she stepped out of the shower to the silence of the house, she turned the radio on. With its noise behind her, she quickly dressed.

She couldn't stay alone in the house. The silence, as she turned off the radio, seemed to have mixed with it voices from her past, layered one upon another maddeningly.

She had to go back to the woods. She felt drawn, as if by an immense and invisible magnet. She had never wanted to go back, but now she had to.

As she drove out toward her old home, slowly, leaving traffic behind her as she turned off the main highway out of town, she let the car get slower and slower. She wanted to turn around and go home, yet she kept driving.

Had she killed Uncle Everett?

She couldn't decipher the mixed messages in her heart. They were as confusing as the dreams and the singing. She was going mad, she felt, and she needed desperately to talk to someone. Someone who would tell her, no, you're not crazy, you're simply overwrought. She tried to tell herself that, but the fact remained that her uncle had been killed with a knife from her own drawer, and she was the only one who could have done it.

She thought of going to the police and telling them, "I am the mother of the infant buried in the woods. But it—she—was not buried alive. She was dead already when I left her there. She—I didn't even know it was a girl. I never knew. I'll never know. My uncle Everett went back and buried the baby when I went to his door for help. And now I've killed him, because he was the only person who knew my secret."

Except ... there were others who might know. Faith, for one.

And Clyde?

He had come to the supermarket looking for her, she felt surely. As she drove the shadowed and curving road into the beginnings of the forest, she knew he had come out into her part of town looking for her. She had checked his address in the telephone directory later, when she got home, and saw he lived miles away in the southeast part of town. So she knew he had come to see her. What did he want? She wanted never to speak to him again, as she had wanted never to return to the woods.

She should have left town when she was seventeen, instead of staying. She had wanted to leave, to go to Saint Louis, or Chicago, or even farther away, to Los Angeles, or New York, or New Orleans. But the timidity that had been growing in her was too firmly entrenched. It was adventurous and daring enough that she simply move to town, to lose herself among the forty or fifty thousand people who lived there.

She saw ahead of her a small place to park along the edge of the woods. She pulled into it and turned off the ignition. The silence of the woods seemed complete.

Around the next corner would be Uncle Everett's house, where Faith and Peggy now lived alone. It seemed she could see the white corner of the front porch through the trees.

She got out of the car and stood beside it listening. Somewhere far over the trees a crow cawed, and then came silence again.

She pulled her quilted jacket close and zipped it. Fog left over from the night drifted in silence among the trees like ghosts rising. In the sky above, heavy clouds drifted, sometimes thinning to let through a single splash of sunshine before they closed again.

Magret crossed the road, her sneakers making soft padding sounds. She entered the woods on the other side and moved straight ahead and then swerved northwest. She paused. The trees seemed larger now, but there was the old hickory tree she had gathered nuts from when she was a child, and there, farther on, its bark ghostly in the twilight of the woods, was the sycamore tree.

She stood transfixed, staring, the present dropping away.

It was dark again, ice on the fern cracking beneath her feet as she tried to run. She was scared, so scared. The awful pain was fire in her body, the foreign weight in her belly dragging her down. She slumped against the base of the ghostly old tree, feeling the sudden expulsion of the baby, the wet stickiness between her legs, the pain that doubled her over from that foreign warmth passing from her. She heard the hooting of an owl, the screech of a lost soul. And her own harsh breath in the cold winter air.

She turned now, her hands to her face, trembling against her cheeks.

She had choked back all emotion, through all these years, but now she was shaking as if she had returned to that terrible night.

It had seemed so long then, the birth, her hours in the darkness, her hours at her uncle's house. But it had all taken place within the span of one night. One night in which she had left her bed at home, and in which, a lifetime later, she had returned to it.

As dawn grew sickly gray in the east, she had gotten into her bed again, her body hovering around her pain and her chilled soul. In another bedroom she could hear the snoring of her two older brothers. In her parents' bedroom, safe behind closed doors, her mother and father slept.

And no one knew.

Except her uncle.

She tried not to think about what had happened. She tried not to think at all. That part of her mind, her memory, was closed off from that day forward. The next day when she was alone, she went back to her uncle's for her pajamas, and no one ever knew. He had given her the bundle in silence, and they never talked of that night.

Now, as she stared at the white-barked tree that rose so majestically among the other, darker trees, her memories seemed to belong to someone else. When she moved away from the rectory, she had left in spirit as well, and started a new life for herself.

But the nightmare had forced itself upon her, and now she had no choice but to return. There was something she had to do—see—know—something she didn't yet understand. She had known from the moment she heard that Sheena and her friends had seen the baby in the woods.

She began to walk and came to a path that crossed the woods in front of her, the path Peggy and Wendy Parker used. Sheena had told her about it months ago. "Wendy and Peggy don't really live as far apart as you think, Mama," Sheena had said in her excited, bell-like voice. "They don't go around the road. They go through the woods. They've got a path that runs from Peggy's backyard to Wendy's. Why can't we live out there so I can use the path through the woods?"

"How do you know about the path? You didn't go into the woods, did you?"

Maybe it had started then, with that conversation. Those nightmares that had begun to haunt her life and draw her back to the grave of her firstborn—no, not firstborn. Leigh was her firstborn. But no, that was wrong. She had tried hard and long to shut out the truth, to forget.

"No, Mama, really I didn't. But I saw the path. It's not far, really, through the woods. And nothing is there to be scared of."

It seemed now that it had been inevitable that she return. Inevitable that her uncle would marry again and have a daughter the same age as her own youngest. Inevitable that the grave would be discovered.

She crossed the path and walked through fallen leaves that crackled softly beneath her feet, "The colors now seemed all to have fallen from the trees and blended together to a uniform brown. The limbs above pointed toward a sky, searching for a sun that was hidden beyond the clouds, naked limbs in a silent cry searching for warmth.

She came to the tree and stood with her hand on its bark and looked at the open grave at the edge of the ravine. A tree root snaked through it on one side. It was that, she saw, that had exposed the tiny skeleton, that and the rain that washed away the soil from the bank. Twenty-one years ago the ravine had been much smaller, much shallower, and at least ten feet from the trunk of the tree. Now the white tree roots reached out like the bones of a huge creature, themselves exposed.

If she had thought returning would answer something for her, she had been wrong.

With a long sigh, a feeling of terrible, deep sadness, her mind drifted back to the dark woods on a cold and icy January night, and the pain, and blood that was black in the night, and the tiny, warm thing that had lived its short life out in her hands ...

Dear God, it had, it had. It couldn't have been alive when she left it there.

All these years she had pushed aside the pain that struck her again, now, wrenching her belly as if she were giving birth again, alone, in the dark and cold of the woods, in the winter death.

She couldn't have left it to die, on the cold ground, a tiny creature too weak to cry. She couldn't have. She didn't.

And yet she knew now the fear had lived hidden within her all these years, that she had left it to die. And now, somehow within her, that infant was living again. In her nightmares it had risen.

Magret found herself shivering, not from cold. Nervous tremors came up into her face and she drew her chin down into the collar of her coat.

As she turned away from the grave, it occurred to her that the police might yet have an interest in this spot, and what would it look like if they found her here? Sergeant Stoddard had questioned her more extensively than he had anyone else. Why? Did he suspect her?

She hurried away from the grave. She should never have come back.

She was startled by a sound behind her, a falling limb, or a limb being stepped on. The tree trunks rose dark and confining around her—just like in her nightmares.

She began to run. Breathless, the cold air stinging her lungs, she crossed the blacktop to her car. Inside she sat gripping the steering wheel.

There was no place to turn around. She would have to go on down to Uncle Everett's house. Perhaps she would visit with Faith and Peggy for a while, and try again to persuade them to come to her house.

She drove alongside the house and parked behind the gray sedan.

The place seemed unnaturally quiet. She could see the tracks of the many automobiles that had parked in the backyard, muddy tracks that cut through the browning grass.

She got out of the car and started around the house.

Something was on the ground a few feet from the front of the gray sedan. A sprawl of clothing, a ... hand flung out.

Magret ran a few steps around the car and stopped, staring.

Faith lay on the ground, her arms out, fingers curled into the grass and mud of an empty track as if she had been trying to crawl for help.

Although her head was turned facing away, Magret could see the raw, red open wounds on her neck.

"Oh, Jesus, no."

It was a low cry that might have come out of the air. She fell to her knees beside Faith and touched her hand, but it was cold and damp as if it had lain there a long time.

Magret got up. The browning grass in the yard between the step and the woodpile was rutted where the ambulance and police cars had parked. The trees that lined the backyard, with their few remaining leaves, were dark mixtures of black and brown. Nothing stirred. No bird. Not even a chipmunk in the woodpile.

Peggy ... where was Peggy?

Magret stumbled around Faith, to get to the porch, and then she stopped abruptly, staring at the ground.

The knife lay partly under Faith's twisted body, the handle protruding, a small strip of white on the muddy soil beneath Faith.

Magret bent and pulled the knife away. Blood from its blade and handle wiped partly off on the grass beneath Faith.

Magret stared at the knife pinched between her fingers.

The pearl handle ... the slender, sharp blade.

She turned, trapped, searching for a hiding place. Yet even as she turned, she pulled a tissue from her pocket and wrapped the knife, rolling it over and over in the thin, pink paper, rolling it until it was hidden.

She thrust it under the seat of her car.

CHAPTER 16

COLLINS LEFT Chief sitting alert in the car, with his nose to the heavy mesh that divided front from back. Two other police cars had arrived just ahead of him. Magret Treacle's blue Olds sat in the driveway nosed in toward the house, just behind the old gray sedan that had been parked in its same spot the last time Collins was here.

One of the deputies stood beside his car, door open, using his radio to call headquarters. Collins walked past him and paused to look down at the body. A brief look sent a chill along his backbone and shoulders. That was all it took to see that whoever had killed Everett had now killed his wife.

Magret Treacle was over near the woodpile, her arms clasped against herself. Even as Collins walked toward her, another car pulled into the driveway.

"Mrs. Treacle?"

She nodded. Her dark, highlighted hair had droplets of moisture from the heavy fog that still coated the countryside in spots, especially back in the trees. Her eyes moved past him and her face crumpled as if she were going to cry, but tears didn't fall. She held out her arms.

Daniel Treacle, dressed in a dark suit and pale blue shirt and tie, went to her and took her into his arms. His eyes found the body on the ground.

"Oh, no. Oh, you shouldn't have come here, Maggie."

She said nothing. Collins waited a moment. He could hear sirens on the road drawing nearer. More police. Probably the coroner following closely behind.

"I called my husband, too," Magret said to Collins.

"I need to get her home," Daniel said. "Could one of you bring her car in later?"

"No, no," Magret said quickly. "I can drive, Dan. Really. But first, before I leave, we have to find Peggy."

Collins said, "I need to get the basic information from you, ma'am. What time did you discover the body?"

"I don't know what time it was. I woke late. After ten. An hour ago, maybe. Then I found Faith."

That would have put the discovery about noon.

"After you woke, you drove out to see your aunt?"

"I—yes, I did."

"You didn't call first."

"No."

"Can this wait?" Daniel asked. "I'd like to get my wife home."

Collins nodded. "Yes, there's no reason for you to stay here."

Magret said, "But Peggy ..."

Daniel urged her to walk, giving the body on the ground a wide berth, going around toward the driveway. "They'll let you know when they find her. You don't need to stay here, Magret."

Collins let them go. He watched as the deputy who had been at the radio went over and talked to them, followed by a couple of plain clothes men. The detectives.

Collins returned to the body on the ground. He stooped to touch a cold hand. She had been dead many long hours. The coroner, his face set in a permanent grimace, rounded the corner of the house.

"Another one," he said as he squatted. "What's going on out here in what I always thought was a peaceful neck of the woods? Nothing like this has ever happened here before, even when I was a little kid. There was a bad car wreck once, about twelve years ago, about a mile on down the road. A couple of teenagers who couldn't control their car. We had to get blow torches to extricate them. But this?" He shook his head, and his jowls wiggled, but there was nothing comical about him. "Frankly, Stoddard, I don't know what's going on. Look at that neck, those wounds. Whoever wielded that knife was doing more than killing, he was mutilating."

One of the detectives had come up unnoticed behind Collins, and now said, "I'm surprised he stopped at the neck. Usually a killer with a knife stabs the body. This is more like something one of the big, wild cats would do if he just wanted to chew off the head."

The coroner shook his head. "No animal. I'd say another knife, like the one found in the first killing."

The detective stooped and, with the coroner's help, turned the body so they could see beneath it. Collins paused only enough longer to see there was no knife beneath this body, and none in the grass near it.

"There's a child missing," he told them. "I'm here to find her."

He went into the house and through it, walking quickly, checking in case the little kid was hiding somewhere in fright. He opened closets and even the wide doors of the buffet in the dining room. Upstairs he checked out the bedrooms. One of them, obviously a child's, looked as if it hadn't been slept in for a couple of nights. A child's pair of jeans and a shirt lay crumpled on the floor, with a pair of socks scattered, one by the bed and the other by a chest of drawers. The room was cold.

Down the hall he found what must have been the master bedroom. This bed was unmade, covers flung carelessly back, falling onto the floor. There on the floor again was a small pair of jeans and a shirt and socks, as if Peggy had slept part of last night with her mother.

The scene suggested a hurried departure, the dragging of the covers off onto the carpet, trailing toward the open door. The end of an electric blanket cord stretched like a long, thin finger pointing toward the door, the blanket gone, pulled away.

The picture was hauntingly clear in Collins's eyes. Something had happened to cause mother and child to hurry from the room, as if they were trying to reach the safety of the car.

The mother hadn't made it.

But what had happened to the child?

Collins ran back downstairs. In the kitchen he found the electric blanket hanging over a kitchen chair.

He hurried outside, opened the back seat of his cruiser, and snapped Chief's leash in place. "We got a kid to find, Chief," he muttered.

The crowd was gathering. Men and women from the county rescue team mingled now with police. Collins left them to organize and start searches of their own. With Chief pulling against the leash, his ears alert, his body strong and straight, Collins took from his pocket a single sock he had taken from Peggy's bedroom. It had five little dirty spots where her toes had fit. He held it down for Chief to smell.

"I know you're not a bloodhound, but let's find Peggy. You remember Peggy."

Chief wagged his tail and put his nose to the ground.

Collins followed him in a jagged line over the backyard, from the door of the gray car to the step, and then close to the body that was still being examined by the coroner squatting beside it. The dog jerked away, his nose going to an invisible trail, toward the woodpile, as if the child on her way to the car had pulled away, or had been sent away, and had run at first at random. Then Chief was running straight for the path, that almost invisible spot in the trees.

For perhaps a hundred yards, Chief stayed with the path, and then he began to zigzag back and forth, ten feet or more on each side of the path, as if the trail of the child had disappeared.

ISLAN HAD HEARD the sirens even through the roaring in her ears, the horrible cold in her head. Why had she gotten a cold now of all times? She had been planning to go with a girlfriend to the cafeteria near the courthouse this afternoon and hang out a while, in hopes she would see Collins, but her mother wouldn't let her out of the house this morning.

"You've got a cold, and you want to go to school? Really, Islan, you're at your most contagious now. Stay in bed, at least for today. Don't spread the cold among all your friends."

"Well, one of them must have spread it to me! And besides, cold germs are all over school all the time anyway. I don't think you care about how I feel."

"Of course I do. Why do you think I want you to stay in bed?"

She had felt Islan's forehead.

Islan wasn't in the mood to be babied. But she had to admit she was miserable. Her head felt as if it were stuffed with rags, and her nose had grown overnight to three times its original size and was turning red from being blown so much. Maybe it was just as well Collins wouldn't see her like this.

The last time she had seen Collins she'd had a funny feeling that he hardly knew she was around. He'd talked mostly to her mother. Her *mother*. As if he liked her mother better than he liked her. Islan loved her mom, but couldn't imagine any man being attracted to her. She guessed she was nice-looking, but she was, after all, just her mom.

Or so Islan had thought.

She wondered now if she should revise her opinion.

Sometimes she had a notion to go live with her dad. She didn't mind her grandparents at all, or her stepmother. In a way she felt at home with them as she never had with Mom and Wendy. Mom and Wendy were alike in so many ways. They enjoyed the same kinds of TV programs, mostly travelogue and nature and animal shows, so long as they didn't see animals eating one another. They enjoyed going out for drives on strange little narrow country roads, and they liked picnics in out-of-the-way places. A boiled egg, a cheese sandwich, a can of soda. All the boring things that Islan didn't understand. It was as if she stood alone against them.

She remembered the years on the farm up north. She had been eight years old when her mother left, and there had been a question for a while, she recalled, as to whom she would live with. She had wanted to stay with her dad and grandparents, and yet she had wanted to be with her mother, too. Wendy, barely a few months old then, never felt the same way about their dad as she did. Wendy wouldn't even go visit him, and in the deepest part of her heart, she didn't think her dad cared. He had four other kids now, Karen, Frankie and Fran, the seven-year-old twins, and the baby, Josh, who was just a little over a year old.

Josh was a doll, round-faced and white-haired, with blue eyes like jewels in his happy face.

Karen was Wendy's age.

It was the atmosphere, she decided, as she stood at the window looking into the backyard, her arms folded across her stomach. The atmosphere of the big farms, the cattle pens, the faraway horizon, the people who worked on the land. The sense of activities and busyness.

She thought of Collins and herself, in that setting, and a terrible sadness came over her.

She belonged there, but not Collins. Never Collins.

The sirens seemed to be heading toward her own street, though she knew they were on the highway out of town, just beyond the woods. She went out onto the patio and stood there, listening.

The sirens suddenly stopped. A long shiver went over her body as she realized they were at the Wasson place again.

The air on the patio was getting cold, the dampness in the air almost as if she stood in the mist rising among the trees. She turned back toward the sliding glass doors and the warm kitchen.

She was stirring a cup of hot chocolate at the sink when she caught a glimpse of movement beyond the fence. An animal ...

She frowned.

There were small animals living in the woods, chipmunks, squirrels, maybe even some nocturnal animals that Wendy could have named and identified, but which Islan wouldn't know about. But this flash of brown that she had seen was too large. Then he came in view again, this time clearly as he approached the gate. Islan's heart thrilled with expectation. Right behind the dog, within eight feet, was Collins.

Good grief. She had wanted to go to the cafeteria to see him. And here he was, coming through her back gate.

She ran out onto the patio, making sure she slowed before he saw her, so that she wouldn't look too eager.

"Hi," she called, and waited as man and dog crossed the yard. The dog's nose was to the ground as he moved somewhat erratically. Collins pulled on the leash and said something, and the dog heeled.

"Hello, Islan," Collins said as he stopped at the edge of the patio. The smile seemed too brief, his eyes wandering across the yard to the houses around the cul-de-sac. "Have you seen Peggy?"

"Peggy? No. Why?" The chill air settled into her. Her voice sounded husky to her own ears, and hollow, as if it were closed into a drum. "What happened? Has something else happened?"

Collins looked at her again, as if for the first time. "You've got a cold," he said. "You'd better not stand out in this air. I'm looking for Peggy. She's missing. Her mother's been murdered."

Islan put both hands to her mouth. For the first time she realized there was a real danger in the neighborhood. Not far from her own backyard fence two people had now been murdered.

"ARE YOU ALONE?" Collins asked. He saw the girl's hands come down from her mouth. She nodded mutely. He told her, "Go back into the house and lock your doors. Don't open them. What time do you expect your mother?"

It took two tries for Islan's voice to work. "She—she usually gets home ab—about five-thirty."

"Is Wendy in school?"

"Yes."

"When she gets home, call me. The dispatcher will contact me. If I'm not available at that time, I'll be back around six. Is that all right?"

"Sure." She nodded.

He waited for her to go back into the house, but she didn't move. Then she asked, "Would you like hot chocolate? I've just made some."

He shook his head. "We've got work to do. I want to see you go back into the house. We don't know how safe you people are."

She went back into the kitchen, and locked the door.

"Let's go," he said to Chief. Halfway back on the path he met one of the searchers, and paused to talk to him.

"Where does the path go?" the man asked. His name was Larry something or other, Collins couldn't remember. He was young, no more than twenty, one of the volunteer rescue workers.

"To a housing development called Greenbrier. The two little girls, Peggy Wasson and Wendy Parker, seem to have made the path themselves, from the backyard gate of Wendy's house to the backyard of Peggy's. The path ends there, and doesn't involve any of the other houses."

"Who lives in the other places?"

"I'd have to look in my notebook to give you names, but couples on both sides of the Parker residence work, no children. Some smaller children live on around the street, but both parents work in town. I don't think Peggy would have gone to any of the houses there except Wendy's, and she isn't there. Why don't you cover the areas between here and the road, and I'll take Chief over deeper into the woods."

"Do you think it's going to do any good?" Larry asked as Collins and Chief moved away. "What I think is that she was kidnapped. Whoever killed the dad hung around in the woods, or maybe in that old church or house next door, the empty ones, and then when night came and the woman and kid were alone again, he came back and he took the kid. He had a powerful hatred for the parents. Could it be the kid is a stepchild, and her real parent came after her?"

"No," Collins said. "Nothing like that at all."

"Then why ... ?"

The man was talking mostly to himself, it seemed to Collins, asking that question that had been in the back of Collins's mind since he had seen the body of Everett, and multiplied tenfold since he had seen Faith. Two people who never bothered anyone, who worked at their jobs and reared their child quietly, people who had no enemies. Who would want to do this to them? And the child. What would anyone want with the child?

"Let's go, Chief. We're going to cover every square inch of these woods before we give up."

. . .

"WHERE'S MAMA?" Sheena asked as they went into the house. It was the first words she had spoken to her dad since he had come to school to get her. She couldn't have described to him the terrible feeling of having the school principal come to her room, talk in private with her teacher, both of them standing halfway between the teacher's desk and the door to the hall, and then to have both of them look at her.

She knew something terrible had happened. Something even worsethan the murder of Uncle Everett. Behind her Wendy leaned forward and whispered, "I wonder what happened?" Sheena couldn't answer. The desk in front of her that belonged to Peggy was empty. And as she watched the teacher come toward her, while the principal, Miss Arlo, waited at the door, she thought of the emptiness Peggy's place had left in her, too, and the emptiness was growing, and she was mute with it.

"Your daddy has come to take you home, Sheena," Mrs. Harlong said in a whisper to her. "You may get your things and go with Miss Arlo to the office now."

Sheena rose, gathered up her books, and carried them away. She didn't —couldn't—look back at Wendy. Wendy, who sat now with two empty seats in front of her, her two best friends gone.

Her daddy was waiting in the office. He put his hand on her shoulder as they went out to the car. She couldn't bring herself to ask him anything yet, and he hadn't spoken either. On the clock in the car she saw the time was two-fifteen. The day was shadowed and dark, and sometimes a little rain fell, just enough for the wipers to swipe once, and stop again, only to rouse and swipe again at rain on the windshield when the car reached the end of the next block.

When they got home, the house felt empty, as if no one lived there anymore. Sheena was terribly afraid something bad had happened to her mother, and that was why her father had brought her home.

He took her hand and drew her into the family room. There was a small fire burning on the hearth, and the screen was set up in front of it. The clock on the mantle above ticked loudly, and at the big window looking out into the backyard a few errant drops of rain made little rivulets, crooked and wavy, down the glass. Sheena drew a deep breath as her daddy pulled her against his knees.

"Sheena, your mother is all right. She's upstairs in bed, sleeping, resting, and I don't want you to bother her, but I wanted you here at home with her. Something terrible has happened, and—" He drew a long breath, and Sheena could see that his skin looked different, as if the color had drained, leaving it all soggy and white. "Well, Sheena, I just felt safer with you here at home."

She waited. She felt the wide-open stare of her eyes as she watched him, and that awful emptiness that she had started feeling at school this morning when Peggy's desk stayed empty.

"Your aunt Faith is dead, baby. And—your mother found her today. And I brought your mother home and made her go to bed, and then went after you. But there's something else. Peggy is missing. We don't know where she is."

Sheena stared at him. She felt no surprise. It was as if she knew, in her heart, the minute she saw Peggy's empty desk, that Peggy was lost.

He said, "A lot of people are looking for Peggy, and they will find her. But for now, I want you to stay here in the house with your mother, while I go back out and see if I can help. All right? Leigh and Ward should be getting home in another hour or so. Will you be all right?"

Sheena nodded.

He gave her a little push toward the door to the inner halls, and said, "Why don't you go up to your room? Ward will be here, you'll hear him, and Leigh. You'll be all right. Your mother is here."

Sheena obeyed.

On the landing she paused, listening. Her mother's door, the door at the back of the wide hall, was closed. She turned right and went around toward the smaller bedrooms, walking close to the railing. She could see down into the entry, and it looked very deep today, as if she stood on the brink of a long fall.

She went into her room and closed the door.

Her room seemed dark, the rain sliding down the windowpane now like water over a fall, and as she stretched out across her bed, she thought of the tiny naked baby she had seen in the woods. And then, the next day when Wendy and Peggy had gone without her, they had seen it again, only it had grown and was standing. A naked baby, its white body clean. It was like the story of the water babies. Was Peggy going to become a water baby now, too, and live forever in the woods with the other children? And Wendy ... Wendy lived out there, just over a fence from the woods. Would something happen and make her a water baby, too, and would she disappear into the woods forever?

Was that why Mama had warned her never to go into the woods? Because she knew what happened to children who spent too much time in the woods?

Sheena leaned her cheek on her folded hands, stretched on her stomach across her bed, and stared at the water flowing down the window. She could hear the rain on the roof, a steady drone that stopped all other sounds in the world. If there were cars on the street, she didn't hear them. They were silenced under the rain.

Would Peggy mind the rain now that she had become a water baby? Did they play games, she and the other children, and the tiny baby?

No, no, no.

The rain was cold, and the woods were dark and wet. It was not like the water babies story. This one was dark and scary, in which Peggy's cries were lost beneath the pouring of the rain.

Another sound, which seemed at first only in her thoughts, finally separated from her and became real. Sheena sat up, gladness in her heart.

Footsteps in the hall, quick and light, somewhere, passing, or already running away, reached out to her.

Mama? Not Mama. Her steps weren't like that. But it might be Leigh, or Ward.

Yes, Leigh or Ward had come home from school and had passed her door on their way to their own rooms. But it hadn't really sounded like Ward's heavy sneakers, nor Leigh's slower steps. It was more as if Wendy was going down the hall looking for her. Or Peggy.

Peggy—

Sheena opened her door. The hall was empty. The door to her mother's room was still closed, and the door to Ward's room was still half-open as it had been.

She went tentatively along the hall and looked into Ward's room. She saw his collection of cars and balls and mitts and helmets and things on the shelves around the head of his bed, and the wild posters on his walls. Some of them were of neat-looking old cars, but others were as gross as Halloween masks.

She pushed the door wide open to make sure he wasn't behind it. Then she went on to Leigh's room.

The door was closed, but Sheena opened it. Leigh's room was as still and empty-feeling as Ward's. She left the door open and stood, puzzled, in the hall.

She wished her mother would wake up.

Suddenly she heard something from behind the closed door to the attic. A footstep on a squeaky board, a creaking step. Someone was going up to the attic!

It must be Mama, Sheena thought.

It must have been Mama who had run past her door like a child, and was now climbing the attic stairs.

Sheena went to the attic door and opened it.

The splintery stairs rose up before her, leading into darkness. She flipped the light switch. Why had Mama gone up into the dark?

"Mama ... ?"

An answering voice began to sing, only the voice sounded oddly fine and distant.

Sleep, ba-by, sleep, thy father watches his sheep, thy father watches his sheep, thy mother is shaking the dreamland tree...

Sheena stood transfixed. Fear made her unable to move either up or down the stairs. Air slipping silently down out of the attic was colder than any Sheena had ever felt. The singing was not pretty or soothing, but part of the cold and the dark.

The song was cut off suddenly and another began, the words almost lost in the drifting, eerie tune.

Broad is the road that leads to death ... with here and there a traveler...

"Sheena!"

The cry behind her was loud and demanding, almost frantic. Sheena recognized her mother's voice at once. She whirled, her heart racing wild in terror.

"Sheena, what are you doing?"

The footsteps of her mother were in the hall below her, and Sheena felt as if she had been caught doing something terrible and forbidden. She acted instinctively, running back down the attic steps, going out into the hall and slamming the door behind her.

Then she stood in the hall against the closed attic door and stared at her mother.

She had heard Magret singing in the attic, in a strange, childlike voice. She had earlier heard her running past the bedroom door like a child. Yet her mother was not in the attic. She was standing halfway between Sheena and the end of the hall, her hair all in a mess, her eyes looking kind of wild and scared, her mouth hanging open, a frown on her face.

"What were you doing in the attic, Sheena?"

But I thought you were ... Sheena's mouth felt dry inside, as if she had turned to dust.

"I—I was just—just looking."

Her mother was calming down, becoming more like the mother she knew. For a few moments she had seemed a stranger. A frightening stranger. It was as if Sheena were surrounded by parts of her mother. And all of them scared her.

Magret ran her fingers through her hair. Her face looked pale and older than it did yesterday. She was wearing her pink robe, the one she sometimes dressed in to relax in the evening to watch TV and read. It zipped up the front and had a little white tassel on the zipper. White piping trimmed the collar and sleeves.

"When did you get home?" she asked. "Is school out? Have I slept all afternoon, for goodness' sake? Where are Leigh and Ward?"

"Daddy brought me home," Sheena said. "He—he said he didn't want you to be alone. He said he wanted me to be safe at home. Peggy's missing, he said, and Aunt Faith is murdered, too."

Had he said *murdered* or just—*dead?*

Both were terrible, and frightened Sheena, although she didn't understand exactly what it all meant.

"Where did your father go?"

"I think he went out to Aunt Faith's. To help look for Peggy."

"Leigh and Ward are still in school?"

"Yes."

Magret touched her cheek gently for a moment. Sheena felt herself recoil inside. It was the first time in her life she had pulled back from her mother's touch. But ... it had been so scary this afternoon. The footsteps. The voice in the attic.

"Baby," Magret said, "you run on downstairs and watch the Disney channel. I'm going to get dressed. I'll be down later."

Sheena obeyed, glad to go downstairs and into the family room, where the fire was burning low in the fireplace. She moved the screen and put two of the small logs from the holder into the fire. Then she replaced the screen and turned on the television.

Rain still made a shimmering light on the window-pane, but she could no longer hear it falling.

MAGRET CHANGED CLOTHES QUICKLY, hanging the deep pink robe in the closet in the bathroom. She put on the first things she found. Gray slacks and a long-sleeved cotton shirt.

What had awakened her earlier was the sound of the rain, and the child's voice singing the old songs she had sung when she was a child. There were footsteps, too, light and airy, overhead, it seemed.

Still half asleep and half dreaming, she wondered if the sounds were real, and slowly awakening, she got out of bed and went into the hall. Her pink robe was wrinkled from having been slept in. Her feelings were almost crushing her.

Fear. Anger.

She could hear the voice clearly, yet so far away. And the words of the old hymn ... *Broad is the road that leads to death ... with here and there a traveler* ... a song she had forgotten.

Then she had seen the attic door was standing open. And as anger throbbed through her feelings of fear, she realized Sheena was upstairs, singing the song.

How did she know that old hymn?

Was it—had it been Sheena she had heard the other night?

When she called out, Sheena had come out of the attic as if she'd been doing something sinful. She had slammed the door and stood against it, her guilt as clear as the blue of her eyes.

Magret left her bedroom and stood in the hall looking at the closed attic door.

What had the child been doing in the attic?

There was nothing up there but old clothes, big boxes holding old tablecloths, bedspreads, curtains, the kind of thing she hadn't wanted to give away, yet hadn't really had a use for at the time. Someday, she had thought each time she added to the boxes upstairs, someday, she would hang these curtains again, use this tablecloth, even this dress. And meantime they stayed in their boxes.

Magret opened the attic door. Sheena had forgotten to turn out the light. On sudden impulse, she climbed the steep steps to the unpainted floor of the attic.

At first she noticed nothing out of place in the dim light. Then she saw something trailing out of the old trunk. A ghostly, limp arm, hanging down the dark front of the trunk and crawling along the floor a few inches.

She went closer.

It was the sleeve of a white dress. The dress had belonged to her mother, and had lace overlay, coming to a point at the wrist. Now it lay in the years' accumulation of dust on the attic floor.

Magret muttered beneath her voice and bent down, lifting the convex lid of the old trunk, and picking up the long, white dress, yellowed over the years. Magret remembered her mother wearing it, that one very special Easter when Magret was nine years old. Her mother had looked so pretty in her white dress and the white straw hat with the floppy wide brim and the velvet flowers.

Her own dress that Easter had been pink, matching the flowers on her mother's hat. She had folded the pink dress away with the white dress. A pink dress with ruffles and lace and a full gathered skirt with underskirts of white mesh that made it stand out.

As Magret carefully folded the white dress, it dawned on her that the pink one was missing.

Putting her mother's dress aside, she began to dig frantically through the dresses and other items in the trunk. There was a beaded evening bag that had belonged to her great-grandmother, and a tortoiseshell hand mirror that belonged to another of the women in her grandmother's family, her sister or someone. She couldn't remember at the moment. It didn't matter. Nothing mattered but the pink dress. It was the only good memory she had left from her childhood. That Easter—it was the best time in her life.

She stood up, shaking all over, unable to control the trembling in her cheeks, her hands. She moved around boxes in the attic, looking between them, on top of them, sometimes within. They were in disarray, not neatly placed now; but the pink dress was not there.

Sheena must have taken it out of the attic, or hidden it somewhere.

Magret ran down the attic stairs, one hand on the wall for support, the trembling in her body making her feel almost sick to her stomach.

She hurried along the carpeted upper hall, and ran down the stairs to the lower hall. From the family room in the back came the murmur of voices and the rhythm of background music as cartoons played.

She found Sheena lying on the floor, half supported by a cushion from the pile against the wall, and the sight of her, so absorbed in the figures on the screen, so relaxed on the cushion, brought a fury into Magret she had never known before.

Sheena's small arm, supporting her head, had its elbow buried in the cushion. Magret grabbed the forearm and jerked it out from beneath Sheena's head. She saw the terror in the girl's face as she looked up, eyes as round and bright as full moons, in a face drained white.

She jerked Sheena to her feet, feeling the helplessness of the child in her hands.

"What did you do with the pink dress?"

Sheena started to cry, her rounded eyes overflowing with tears that ran down her cheeks like the rain on the windowpane. She seemed to be making no effort to speak beyond a gargled sound in her throat. Magret began shaking her.

"I said, what did you do with the pink dress? The Easter dress? What did you do with it?"

Sheena shook her head and the tears overflowed. Magret could see the horror and the fear in those eyes, but she was too angry to care. She drew her hand back and slapped Sheena, hard. *'Don't lie to me!"* she shouted.

Sheena crumpled, limp, hanging by her arm as Magret gripped her by the wrist. She was sobbing helplessly now, unable to speak.

Magret felt as if she, too, had been struck. All her energies suddenly dissipated. She sank down onto the cushion and pulled Sheena into her arms.

Dear God, what was happening to her? What was happening to them all?

CHAPTER 17

Sheena felt her mother's arms, yet was afraid of her. She wished Leigh would come home, or Ward, or Daddy. She didn't want to be alone with her mother. Magret's arms held her as if she were a baby, rocking her, one of her cold hands holding Sheena's cheek against her throat. Sheena could feel the movement of Magret's throat as she talked.

I'm so sorry, baby. I've never hit you before, have I? We will forget this, forget all about this, won't we? We won't talk about it. Mama will never do it again, I promise ..."

But Sheena didn't believe her. The sound of her voice, so silky and so filled with apologies, sounded false to her ears. Sheena tried to control her sobs, tried to stay limp against her mother while she wanted to pull away and run, out into the rain, into the shrubbery, anywhere.

"Sheena," Magret said in her soft voice of apology, "I have to know, dear, about the pink dress. The one you took out of the old trunk upstairs, in the attic."

Sheena tightened. Every muscle in her body grew into a little knot of its own, and her sobs became smaller. She listened.

"You see, Sheena, that pink dress is a very important dress to me."

Sheena didn't know what she was talking about, but she couldn't make her voice work to tell her mother.

"Maybe I never showed it to you? I know I showed it to Leigh. I should have told you, maybe, that it wasn't to dress up in, to play in, or anything like that. You see, it was my Easter dress when I was your age."

Sheena sat, unable to move or speak, even to lift a hand and wipe her runny nose. The sobs were almost silent now, jerking her stomach into one big knot of fear.

"Sheena, don't you understand? I have to know what you did with my pink Easter dress. If you want one like it, we'll go buy one. Have you ever been denied anything? Do you know what it's like, do you have any idea what it's like, to have owned only one very pretty dress in your life? While you were still small and slim and could look something like the other girls? Do you have any idea of how important one little dress can be?"

Her mother was sounding so strange that Sheena knew she was going to have to answer. She pulled back from Magret, and Magret let her go, so that they were both sitting on the big cushion, their bodies inches apart, Magret's face above hers, the dark of her eyes intimidating, her dark hair with the lighter streaks all mussed and wild. Sheena's head began to shake back and forth, back and forth.

"I don't know—I don't have the dress—I don't—I don't—" She was crying again, beaten down under her mother's disbelieving eyes. "I—I heard someone go up into the attic. I thought it was Leigh—"

Magret lifted a hand as if she were going to slap Sheena again, and her lips pulled in. She said in a hard, angry voice, "Don't blame Leigh when you know as well as I that she isn't even here. Sheena, I don't know what's gotten into you."

Sheena, weeping again, said, "I thought it was you. I heard you singing."

Magret opened her mouth as if ready to speak again, but her gaze was drifting beyond Sheena, drifting idly, as if she were remembering something.

She got up from the cushion and smoothed her blouse down. Then she smiled faintly and reached down and touched Sheena's cheek in a gentle brushing motion, almost the way she used to.

"Let's just forget all about it, all right? You stay here and watch cartoons."

Sheena watched her leave the room, then she went to the sofa and pulled the afghan off and took it with her to the cushion, the end dragging along the floor. When she lay down again, she covered herself with the soft, knitted afghan and pulled it beneath her chin the way she used to pull up her buffy, the old tattered baby blanket she had hung on to until she was five years old.

She watched the movement of the cartoon figures, but she didn't know what they were doing. She watched the water run down the windowpane, and thought about Leigh and Ward, and wished they'd come home. She wondered where her daddy was. Out in the rain in the woods? And she thought about Peggy. But she couldn't see her face. It was as if Peggy had gone away, forever, like Uncle Everett and Aunt Faith.

And she thought about her mother and she pulled the afghan closer around her head. The place where her mother had hit her felt tight and hot and hurting, and the dull pain reached up into the top of her head, and deep into her, rushing into her heart.

COLLINS LET Chief walk where he chose now, and the dog stayed closely against his right leg, his soggy coat rubbing into the damp material of Collins's pants.

They went through the back gate and toward the house. A kitchen light was on, and a light on the wall outside. Darkness hadn't quite taken over, but it would soon. The rain was relentless. Good for the soil, but hard on the creatures who had to move about in it.

Collins and Chief moved up onto the patio and beneath the wide overhang of the roof. Rain poured down the drain spouts at the corners of the house, but for the first time in hours, they were out of it for a few minutes.

Chief humped his back and shook as hard as he could, just as Islan was opening the sliding glass doors. She laughed and put up a hand for protection. Behind her stood Lorna, looking at Collins with a direct, brown-eyed stare that was so solemn and so worried he wanted to take her into his arms and kiss her and hold her forever. He thought of her, and her daughters, living this close to a place of such vicious murders, and the uneasiness that had been growing in him lately was for a moment almost overwhelming. He felt a little sick that Lorna didn't know him well enough to allow him to take her away from this place.

He was vaguely aware of Islan's eyes moving from him to her mother and back again.

Collins pulled his stare away from Lorna.The kitchen and family room, one big combination room with cabinet dividers, seemed to stretch across most of the rear of the house. He could see a fireplace, and a fire glowing. The atmosphere was warm and bright and comfortable-looking. He longed to go in. It was at the round oak table that he had sat with Lorna a few nights ago and talked until almost dawn, drinking cup after cup of coffee or hot chocolate, or something. It could have been muddy water and he wouldn't have minded.

"Come on in, both of you." Lorna said. "Lord, you're wet."

Collins had earlier gone back to his car for a raincoat, a flimsy little plastic thing he kept among his other necessities, and a big flashlight, but the dog didn't have a coat, and Collins's plastic hadn't helped a lot. All it had taken was one good tear on a broken limb.

"Afraid we'd mess up your floor."

"A little water won't hurt us."

Collins looked down at Chief. The dog was about as bedraggled as he had ever been in his life. They had been out all afternoon in the rain, until every last scent was washed away. Still, with Chief right at his side, they had kept looking, shining the light ahead of them in the darkening forest over drenched leaves fallen to the ground, soggy vines and ferns, and the darkly wet trunks of trees.

"Bring Chief in, too." Lorna insisted.

"You're sure?"

"I'm sure." She smiled. He thought he had never seen a gentler, sweeter smile. It had a Madonna quality that made him want to kneel at her feet. Yet she could be fun, too. He had found that out the other night. They had laughed about a lot of little things.

"If you have an old rug that Chief could stand on ...

Lorna put her hand on Collins's arm and pulled. "Get in here!"

Collins and Chief stepped through the door, and just as he had feared, Chief prepared to shake again. Collins dropped his hand hastily to Chief's back to stop him, and the dog settled down.

Collins saw the younger girl, Wendy, was on the floor beside the raised stone hearth. She had a notebook or workbook of some kind spread open on the hearth and was half working on it. With her pencil poised in her hand, she looked from Collins to Chief and back again.

"Coffee?" Lorna asked.

"No thanks, Lorna. I need to talk to Wendy most of all. You know we're looking for Peggy?"

Lorna nodded.

"I need to find out if Wendy knows anything about where Peggy could have gone." He turned his attention entirely to the little girl. She had a forlorn and lost look in her eyes, though her face was composed. Her almost-white blond hair gleamed in the fire light. Shadows danced on the curves of her face. She was almost as pretty as her big sister. Collins saw the vacant stare as she looked at him, and then the drifting of it away. Her lips parted. He could almost see her thinking.

Lorna said, after a long silence, “She said Peggy wasn’t in school, and that was all she knew, I’m sure. She said Sheena’s father came and got Sheena before classes ended and took her home.” Lorna went over to stand beside Wendy. She leaned down, her hand on Wendy’s shoulder. “Wendy, how about some of the places you and Peggy played in the woods? Is it possible that she could have hidden there? Did you have a hiding place?”

Wendy stood up. “Yes,” she said. “I’d almost forgotten. Last year, when we were still smaller. There was a tree, growing right beside two other trees, across the ravine. It had a big hole in it. It had leaves and acorns, like some animals lived in it. And we pretended it was a house in *The Wind in the Willows.* Maybe she went there.” She started briskly across the room toward a closed door. “I'll show you.”

“No.” Collins held out his hand. “Give me directions to it. We’ll look first. If we can’t find it, we’ll come back for you.”

She hesitated. “Mama won’t mind if I go. I want to go.”

“Wendy,” Lorna said. “It’s better if you just try to tell Sergeant Collins.”

“All right. It’s across the ravine. It’s ...” She motioned vaguely and shrugged her shoulders. “It’s three trees growing together. That’s all I can tell you. It’s just in the woods, that’s all.”

Collins questioned, trying to pinpoint the area, and realized it was a vague memory to Wendy. The little girls, playing together, had found it, and had found it twice more, but had not been there in over a year.

But it was a chance.

He left the house again and felt Chief holding back slightly as they passed from beneath the overhang into the downpour. The rain hadn’t slacked, although once they reached the trees they didn’t get the full force of it on their heads, and in Chief’s case, all along his body. The dog stayed against him, moving along the narrow path with darkness pushing in from each side.

As closely as he could figure, the girls had met about halfway between the houses, and the trio of trees was as far across the ravine as it was to the ravine from the path. Collins had walked the path enough now to have a rough idea of when he was halfway. He pulled Chief off the path and into the soggy leaves.

Chief hesitated once more, almost as fastidious as a cat, it seemed to

Collins on this cold, dark, and rainy night. Or as if he were timid, perhaps growing afraid of something in the woods.

Chief, afraid? The dog who would leap at a man with a gun in his hands and bring him down with one wrench?

The dog stayed against him, as seemingly blinded and senseless in this wet, dark world as Collins himself.

"No smells left, huh, Chief, but the smell of a wet world," Collins said. His voice sounded too loud to his own ears.

The main body of the County Rescue Team had left at twilight. He had last seen them gathered in the backyard of the empty Wasson home. They had combed the woods between the path and the road and had started working back from the path to the ravine. Tomorrow, if nothing came up, they would try again.

People in the neighborhood had been questioned but nobody had seen anything out of the ordinary. No strange cars on the road. No child wandering. Nothing at all. Surrounding towns had not seen Peggy Wasson, whose picture had been circulated by mid-afternoon. If she had been taken from the area in a car, she had been carefully hidden. For a hundred miles in all directions, no one had seen a little girl who looked like Peggy Wasson.

She was in the woods, Collins was sure. Yet the woods seemed to have swallowed her up, just as it had the infant baby girl twenty years ago.

They reached the ravine and crossed it and walked straight southwest, making a path of their own, horizontal to the path that connected the Wasson house to the Parker house.

He could only guess at the distance. He stopped, sending the beam of his flashlight into what looked like a thicker growth of trees, of black boles whose limbs were high above.

Suddenly he noticed the change in Chief. The dog was standing with his head high, the ridge of his backbone stiffened. A low growl, almost inaudible, made the dog's body tremble against Collins's leg.

Collins said, "Go, boy."

Chief leaped forward, going toward darkness, away from the beam of the light. He strained against his leash, and Collins heard the growl again. The dog came to a sudden stop, his head turning as if he was following something through the dark trees. For just an instant, Collins caught a glimpse of something light. Chief had come to a stop again, and when Collins reached him, he found the dog shivering hard, though his head was still up and his nose out, and the hair on his backbone standing stiff.

But someone was out there. Collins had seen just enough of it to know that it was not large. It was small, the size of a small child, and pale.

Peggy, he prayed. She would be afraid, that was to be expected. Afraid of everyone now.

"Peggy!" he called, standing still, moving the light in an arc through the woods ahead, seeing nothing but the black, wet trunks of tall trees. "Peggy! We're here to help you, Peggy."

He waited, searching with his light, watching Chief, seeing the dog's head steady, pointing in one direction. He shined the light where the dog was looking.

The woods around them held the soft drips of raindrops falling in gathered globs from the limbs and leaves still clinging above.

There was no answering voice, no movement in the leaves.

Then his light fell upon a tree that seemed divided into three trunks, with the center trunk larger than the other two.

This was it, the hollow tree Wendy had told him about. The place where the two little girls had played.

As he moved toward the trio of trees, Chief turned his head and lifted his nose into the air, sniffing. Suddenly he was lunging forward, pulling against the leash. Behind him Collins began to run.

Chief's tail was wagging furiously several feet short of the large central tree, before the flashlight touched on the edge of the open wound in the base of the tree, the large hole into which a small child could climb.

Chief began whining, his tail fanning drops of water into Collins's face, and Collins knew they had found Peggy.

The child's white face was almost owl-like as she pressed back into the dark hole of the tree. Collins felt as if a large hand had squeezed his heart. The terrified child cringed farther and deeper into the hole of the large tree, her face turning so that it was against the decaying wood, yet her wide eyes never leaving the light in his hand.

He turned the light on his own face.

"It's Sergeant Collins, Peggy, do you remember me?"

At his knees, squeezed between him and the tree, Chief stood with his nose in the hole of the tree, his tail beating a rhapsody against Collins's leg. Under the misty edge of the light that still illuminated the dark and rotted interior of the tree, Collins saw Peggy's eyes settle on Chief, and her fear seemed to lessen. When Collins turned the light back, he kept it low, out of the child's face. He reached toward her. She didn't seem to be hurt. There was no blood that he could see. She was soaked and shivering, dressed only in a pair of pajamas. But so far as he could tell, the murderer had not reached her.

"Come with me, Peggy. I'll take you ..." Not home, as he had almost said. He changed it to, "I'll take care of you."

She did not move, or lessen her hold on the rotted wood. Only her eyes moved, as they lifted from Chief back to Collins.

She had seen the murder of her mother. She knew the danger out there better than he. What could he say to her?

"I'll take you where it's warm and dry, Peggy. Where you won't have to be afraid anymore."

She did not answer, nor make a move to leave her place in the tree. He would have to lean in to reach her, to bring her out.

"Peggy? Don't you remember me? I came out with you and Wendy, remember? To search for the baby in the woods?"

As he looked at the little girl, and the way her eyes swung slowly and in a dreamy way appeared to examine the interior of her tree, he began at last to realize there was something terribly wrong with this child.

DINNER WAS HALF COOKED when Magret came downstairs. Leigh had opened cans and boxes and put frozen vegetables into water to cook, and Magret had not criticized her random choices of food. Another time Magret might have been annoyed at her or amused at her; tonight it didn't matter.

Magret had unsuccessfully looked all through Sheena's room for the pink dress. She had even gone into her own closet and searched briefly, wondering if in a forgotten moment of madness she herself had taken the dress from the attic.

"Mama ..."

"Hmmm?"

"Mama, where are the knives?"

Magret's attention focused sharply on her daughter. Leigh was at the drawer where the knives were ordinarily kept and had it pulled so far out it looked on the verge of falling. The clink of utensils as she rummaged through it grated on Magret's nerves. In Leigh's left hand was a large tomato, ready for slicing. She shut that drawer and pulled open the next. Magret held her breath as Leigh found the knives.

Leigh looked down at them curiously.

"Hey, what happened to all the knives? Didn't we have six of these?"

She took one of the pearl-handled knives from the drawer. "I thought these were always kept in the box in the other drawer, and there were six of them. Now there are only three."

"Three!" For just a moment Magret's surprise dominated her feelings. There should have been four, not three. The one she had taken from beside Faith this morning was still under the seat of the car, where she had forgotten about it until now. "I suppose they're in the dishwasher, Leigh, where things usually are after dinner has been prepared."

Magret took the tomato out of Leigh's hand and closed the knife drawer. Leigh looked at her in surprise.

"We have salad already made," Magret pointed out. She put the tomato back into the crisper in the refrigerator.

But when she looked back at Leigh, her daughter's clear, sky blue eyes met Magret's only for an instant, and then turned quickly away. Without another word, Leigh left the kitchen and went into the family room.

Magret's heart raced with fear. Was Leigh remembering the knife that had killed Uncle Everett? Surely she would never suspect her own mother ...

Maybe she ought to bury the knives. She could do it tonight, while the family was asleep. But where could the third missing knife be?

The phone rang, and Leigh answered it. Her voice was high and excited as she held the telephone receiver away from her face. She looked from Magret to the others in the family room.

"Peggy has been found!"

In the face of everyone else's relief and excitement, Magret realized she had always felt sure that Peggy was safe.

It was as if she had ***known*** that Peggy had escaped the murderer of her parents.

But how could she have known it?

CHAPTER 18

"THANK YOU, God, for finding Peggy. Thank you for Sergeant Stoddard and for Chief. And thank you for everything else, too." Sheena cast a glance from beneath her folded hands at her mother. She saw only Magret's blouse, but she could hear her mother breathing. She wanted to be done with her prayer so her mother would leave, but she couldn't think of what to say.

"And thanks for your family," Magret urged softly.

It was like the afternoon had never happened, Sheena thought. As if her mother didn't remember any of it. This mother who had always been so nice and so—so just right had shown Sheena something of herself that Sheena was afraid of now. She still felt the terrible slap on her cheek. After dinner Leigh had asked, "Sheena, what's wrong with your face? Your left cheek is red and raw-looking, as if it were frost bitten."

And Magret had answered immediately, "She's been sleeping this afternoon with her face against the afghan."

Sheena said nothing, even though she hadn't been sleeping. She hadn't even really watched TV. She had only lain there, hurting, afraid, waiting.

"And thank you for Leigh, and Ward, and Daddy, and ..." Sheena knew her hesitation was too long. "And ... for Mama. And uh—thank you for saving Peggy." Her mother waited until Sheena climbed into bed, then kissed her cheek. The left one.

"Good night, dear."

Sheena watched her mother go to the lamp on the dresser and turn it out. The only light in the room came now from the hall, spilling shadows and a narrow shaft of light through the half-open door. Magret pulled the door shut without looking back at her daughter.

Sheena drew a long breath and closed her eyes. The warm darkness in her room was welcome. No one could see her now. But even with her eyes closed, Sheena could still see her room, and the way it had looked when she came up to bed.

Two of the dresser drawers were open just a little, and a white pair of panties stuck out just a tiny bit. And the closet door stood open, and Sheena had seen that her dresses had been pushed back.

Her mother had been in her room that afternoon, going through all the drawers and clothes, to see if she could find the pink dress. She had left Sheena's room in a state that she would have scolded Sheena for.

But the worst thing was that Mama hadn't believed her when she said she didn't take the dress.

Sheena had never lied to her mother, nor anyone.

The lost and abandoned feeling in her heart was as dark as her room. It felt as if a part of her had died, too, like Uncle Everett and Aunt Faith.

MAGRET STARED out the French doors onto the balcony. The rain had stopped, but the small panes of the French doors were still blurred with dampness. A street light beyond the house and trees next door filtered a few streams of light into the backyard, and Magret could see the outlines of tops of trees and a few shrubs. Three of the white posts on the railing around the small balcony stood out like thin little ghosts.

She waited.

Waited for Daniel to go to sleep so she could go downstairs and bury the knives somewhere in the muddy soil of the backyard. After that she would see to it that Leigh did not help with the kitchen work. Magret also planned to call the cleaning lady tomorrow and tell her not to come anymore.

"Aren't you coming to bed?" Daniel asked sleepily, putting his book aside. He turned out the reading lamp on the head of the bed. Now the only light in the bedroom came from the bathroom, where a light had been left on and the door only partly closed.

With her robe still on, Magret eased beneath the covers on her side of the bed.

She lay still, her mind drifting.

Peggy was safe. Daniel had called the hospital and was advised to wait until morning to see the child. She was warm and safely in bed, he had been told, and Daniel had passed the information on to the rest of the family.

There had been so much happening that Magret felt sick with it. Faith's family had been notified, and all arrangements made for the funerals when the bodies were released from the state medical examiner. All of it handled by Daniel, yet involving her, too.

Daniel, who had taken care of her since she was seventeen years old, in ways he was never aware of, still took care of her. When she had gone to work for him, her old life as she had known it gone entirely, he had become the central figure in her life. The father, the big brother, even perhaps the mother.

That he had never really become her lover, not in her heart, was a secret she had kept from him always.

He had never known about Clyde Judson.

Daniel, I have something to tell you. I'm the mother of the dead baby. I was fifteen, and I was scared. Do you understand? Do you forgive me?

She heard a soft snore, deep breathing, and knew Daniel was at lastasleep. She slipped out of bed and went downstairs in the dark, her hand out for guidance along the wall, the banister, the furniture. In the kitchen she did not dare turn on a light. From the bedroom upstairs, Leigh, or any of the others who happened at this moment to be awake, might notice the light on the lawn below.

Magret felt her way to the drawer and slid it open. The sound it made was as soft as a sigh, but it caused her heart to flutter nervously. She could smell the odors in the kitchen. The cleanser used on the sink. The vague food smells. The mustiness of a drawer that needed cleaning.

She felt in the dark for the knives. Long, slender blades, kept as sharp as razors. The cool, smooth handles, slightly curved at the tip.

Three.

With them tight in her hand, she opened the back door and went out across the patio. She stood in the backyard, the grass dew-wet and cool on her bare feet, and with a quiet terror closing over her heart, she realized she had almost forgotten the knife in the car.

She went to the garage through the small door at the back and opened the door of her new Olds. Daniel was so good to her. The car had been a complete surprise. She had admired another like it one day, and a month later here it was, with his pet name for her written in script on a special plate on the front bumper. *Maggie.*

She found the knife, still rolled in the tissue, tucked beneath the driver's seat.

In the backyard, streaks of light from the street lamps pierced the black of the night. She avoided them, keeping to the shadows at the perimeter of the yard.

She went to the small garden at the rear, where in the summer Daniel grew a few tomatoes and other vegetables. Here the soil was soft, and she could dig into it with her hands. She went to the far corner, where the garden plow wouldn't dig too deeply, and beside a dead rhubarb plant, she used the point of a knife to dig the tiny grave.

She buried the knives, smoothing the soil back over them and adding a layer of leaves from the corner of the yard.

She stood up and looked back at the house.

Her eyes had adjusted now to the dark, and she could see outlines of things. The shrubs, the fountain in the middle of the lawn. The bird feeders scattered about like very slender men wearing large hats.

And just for a moment she saw something pale, half hidden by a shrub. Something that looked like a human figure—a small figure—a child—as if Sheena, or Ward, had followed her and was watching. No, not Ward. Smaller than Ward.

She frowned and narrowed her eyes, but whatever it was no longer stood there.

She hurried across the lawn and slipped back into the house. She locked the door, then wiped her muddy fingerprints with the hem of her robe.

In the utility room she washed her hands. Then she made her way back upstairs, and dropped her robe at the side of the bed.

As she lay down she heard Daniel give a snort. He turned over, and his breathing settled. She lay listening to a silent house.

I didn't know what I was doing, Daniel. I really loved him, and I thought he loved me. He said he did. I knew he was married, but ... it was like his marriage was something separate from us. Not real. It was wrong, I know. I knew it then. How could I not know? I had heard of adultery and fornication all my life. Yet somehow it didn't apply to what I felt, to my pleasure in his body, his lips, his eyes. The woodland was our bed, you see, our private place. So it was only natural that it become our baby's grave. Do you understand? Do you forgive me, Daniel?

. . .

CLYDE LISTENED to the night sounds, still as wide awake as he had been the whole damned evening. He had wanted to stay up, but it seemed to him that Glorian was already suspicious. At the supper table she held demanded, "What's the matter with you? Here I spend four dollars a pound for your favorite cut of steak, and all you're doing is letting it get cold."

That had jolted him out of his reverie for just a few minutes while they went over the price of steak. "A goddamned dead cow worth four dollars a pound? You have got to be out of your mind, woman."

Then he saw she was smiling. She was like that. If she couldn't get his attention one way, she'd try another. There were certain behaviors that he had to keep up with Glorian, or she'd start nagging him to tell her what was wrong.

So after dinner they had done their usual thing and sat with coffee and dessert in the living room and watched television and discussed the events of the day. Glorian had gone shopping with her sister, and had bought the special cut of steak for him because she had felt he was down about something. She had no idea what it had cost him to choke down a portion of that steak, nor that he had hidden most of it in a napkin between his legs until he got up from the table. He had slipped it outside and fed it to the dog, who was chained to his house in the corner of the backyard. The big, black lab hadn't had any trouble getting it down.

Clyde lay with his arms up and bent, his hands clasped under his head. Glorian, so close against him in the queen-sized bed that he could feel her warm rump against his hip, slept soundly. Not even thunder would wake her. He had thought about getting up and going back to the living room, where he could turn on a light and try to read a newspaper or something while he thought, and thought. Or where he could just sit quietly and think.

He wanted to call Magret, to talk to her. He wanted to tell her, 'Keep quiet, don't worry about me. I'll never say a word.' Christ, all hell would break loose if Glorian ever found out. He'd lose his pants, and all his money still in the pockets. She'd run him off, more than likely. She probably wouldn't even let him have Joe, his dog.

He might even get close to Magret again. She had turned out to be pretty darned gorgeous. Thinner, elegant, looking like money. It made his own wife look dowdier than ever. Back then, it had been just the opposite. Magret had had clear, bright eyes and dark lashes, but her eyebrows were too thick and untrimmed. Her cheeks were too round. Now, those eyebrows were neatly plucked and flying away on her white forehead, and her cheeks sunken just right, maybe rouged a little, he didn't know. Certainly she now wore lipstick, which she hadn't back then.

He thought about the weird murders of her aunt and uncle. The second murder had been on tonight's news.

He had a very uncomfortable feeling that the murders had something to do with the finding of the grave, but he was blind to the reason. He could feel the wrinkling of his brow, the strain of his brain, as his mind kept picking up on those murders along with the grave of the infant and the little bunch of bones found there.

Joe lunged suddenly into a barking fit, as if something had sneaked up on him, something far worse than the unleashed neighborhood dogs, or the neighbor's cats. It seemed to be an angry bark, or maybe a frightened bark. Clyde had heard him bark that way only once before, and he had gone out to find a rattlesnake crawling into Joe's bed.

Clyde lay still a moment. The night was cold and damp, a dark November night, and he didn't want much to go out. Whatever it was would probably drift on out of the yard before long. If it was someone with an idea to burglarizing, they'd probably already skipped out when Joe burst into song.

The dog kept barking, and it seemed that Clyde could hear him lunging against his chain, angry maybe because of his lack of freedom. He'd have to build that fence around the backyard someday, the way Glorian had been after him to do, so Joe could run free. Being on a chain for five years hadn't done much for his disposition, Clyde guessed, but he just hadn't gotten around to a fence.

Clyde sat up. If Joe didn't shut his mouth, he'd wake the whole goddamned neighborhood. He began to listen more carefully. The bark was furious, and he could definitely hear the lunging against the chain that was connected by means of a heavy bolt to the front of the doghouse. The dog was lunging repeatedly at something.

A bobcat, maybe, down out of the hills? Or even a black bear, out of his territory. Yet even as ideas came to him, Clyde dismissed them. Any wild animal would have had to come through too many miles of heavily populated area. Coons came in, and skunks, sometimes. Not bears. He bent and pulled his shoes on, leaving the laces dangling. He stood up. Glorian was still asleep. He could hear her soft snores.

Before he got to the bedroom door, Joe's bark was suddenly shut off with a cry. He paused, listening. In the moment of silence there was nothing, then all the neighborhood dogs began to bark, a frightened, curious response to Joe. But Joe was now silent.

Then it seemed to Clyde he heard a whine, and a soft, terrible howl.

Clyde hurried into the hall and through the kitchen into the backyard.

He paused on the step outside the door. Light lay in unrevealing paths across the yard, narrow and unwavering, and the darkness between was all the darker because of it. Black and yellow, and within it nothing moved. A narrow streak of light lay across the top of Joe's doghouse, coming from a yard light two houses beyond the trees and shrubs that separated yard from yard, but Joe was invisible in the black shadows beneath it.

"Joe? Hey, what's wrong?"

The neighborhood dogs paused in their barking, as if to listen.

There was no answer from Joe, no whine, no slap of the tail against the walls of the doghouse. Clyde suddenly felt the hair rising along the length of his spine and the back of his neck and head. Something was out there. He could sense it, almost smell it.

He stepped back into the kitchen, grabbed the flashlight off the counter, and went back outside. The long beam from the light pierced the darkness of the yard in spots, broken by the piles of junk that he had dumped here and there to be picked up another time and gotten rid of. He moved out toward the doghouse, and his light fell on black fur, stretched on the ground, back toward the house.

Something had gotten to Joe.

The dog was stretched full length on the ground, his head back, his legs straight out from his body, as if he had struggled at the last to resist something he was helpless against.

Clyde went forward, sweeping the light around, thinking once he saw eyes glittering, round and red, then noticed it was a cat that disappeared in a blink.

Clyde shined the light down on Joe and stared in horror.

The dog's black fur was red with blood on his neck and belly in a dozen places, it seemed. Joe's eyes stared at nothing. He was dead.

Clyde bent only briefly to see what kind of wounds had been inflicted, feeling that something was watching him.

The wound on his chest was small, oozing blood still soaking the fur. A knife wound?

Clyde straightened, shining the light all around the backyard, wishing there weren't so many hiding places. The old pile of tires could conceal two men, if they bent over. Same with the old lumber that had come off the shed and had never been hauled away.

Clyde wasn't looking for an animal now. Animals didn't carry knives.

He started back toward the house and the telephone, his light circling the yard in the rear, around the piles of junk, as he moved backward toward the house. When he was within ten feet of the door, where the grass had been trod almost to nothing, he swung around, the sweep of the flashlight beam going ahead of him.

He stopped abruptly.

The little girl was standing on the porch steps.

In his first flush of surprise, as his light barely grazed her, he thought of the danger she was in. A madman was loose in the area, carrying a knife. And then the *wrongness* of her, being where she was, and the way she was dressed, hit him. No more than eight or nine years old, she was standing in the misty, cold night wearing a pink, frilly dress with short puffed sleeves.

And then he saw what was in her hand, and the blood in his body congealed.

It was hanging down, and blood dripped from the point of the knife to the step. It was soundless, yet it seemed to Clyde in that moment that covered a hundred years and took him all the way to eternity, that he could hear the drip, drip of the blood against the cement step.

He saw her face. It seemed oddly familiar. She was round-cheeked, and her eyes were bright and fringed with dark lashes. She was a pretty child ... familiar ... where had he seen her before?

Then her mouth spread, opened, at first he thought the beginning of a smile, but then he knew better. The teeth revealed were razor sharp, pointed, and seemed to fill the widening mouth. The eyes had become as cold and deadly as the eyes of a viper. The whole demeanor of the face, the body, the movement of the arm that lifted, said this was not a living child. This was something God had not made.

Suddenly it leaped at him, in an arc off the porch, almost like flight. He dropped the flashlight as he tried to run, to fight for his life, but he went down, full-length, the thing heavy on his back. He felt something sink through his neck from the back, heard the horrible cutting of gristle, and then his face was pushed into the hard mud of the ground.

THE WORLD WAS BLACK, and her movements within it were helpless, as if she were swimming through a terrible, endless, lightless abyss. She was dreaming again, Magret knew, and tried to wake herself up. She put out her hands and felt something cool and hard and sharply defined.

Then she blinked in the darkness and the vague outlines of things began coming to her. The corner of a cabinet, the edge of a counter grew ghostlike in front of her eyes.

Magret turned, confused, frightened. Light came in from a source beyond a wide window, and she saw she was standing in her kitchen, at the end of the cabinet. She could see beyond the divider into the family room. The dim and distant light was coming through the picture window.

Magret felt on the wall for the light switch, and for the first instant after turning on the light she was blinded by its glare.

What am I doing hen?

She looked at the clock on the wall and saw it was past four, the night dark and heavy with silence.

She looked down and was relieved to see she was wearing the heavy flannel pajamas she had put on when she went back to bed after burying the knives at midnight, because she had felt chilled throughout her body. But she was now wearing old sneakers she must have taken from the closet in the utility room.

As she took them off, with hands that shook so hard they threatened to lose their hold, she saw the soles of the shoes were coated lightly with mud.

Where had she been?

Or was the mud there from her walk into the woods yesterday morning? When she held found Faith. The mud crumbled as she touched it, as if it had been there awhile.

Of course she hadn't been out tonight, she told herself as she carried the shoes back to the utility room. She rinsed the soles in the sink, and washed the flakes of mud down the drain. Of course the mud was left over, not drying in the closet. She, who never put away muddy shoes, had done so this time.

After putting the shoes in the closet, she went upstairs to check on each of the kids and found them safe and sleeping in their beds.

Daniel, too, was asleep, as if he had hardly moved since he went to bed.

Magret crawled in beside him and closed her eyes, her hands clinched on her breast. She felt very tired, as if she hadn't slept. As if she had walked a long, long way.

No, no. She had only gone downstairs, and had put on the shoes. That was all she had done. She had to believe that.

She couldn't sleep. When she heard the clock strike four-thirty, she got up and took one tranquilizer, just enough to help her relax and make her drowsy.

As she drifted into the soft warmth of sleep, she heard the young voice singing, far away in her memory, as if she were listening to herself.

I once was lost, but now am found, was blind, but now I see ...

Distant, fine, clear.

Cold, unfeeling, bringing terror to her heart, the singing separated itself from her and took on a voice of its own.

Abide with me! Fast falls the eventide, the darkness deepens ...

Swift to its close ebbs out life's little day ...

Magret tried to get out of bed, to go find the child who sang her terrible songs, hymns, snatches of hymns she had long forgotten, but she couldn't move. Her body felt weighted, and blackness was moving almost visibly into her brain, and she wondered if she had made a mistake and taken one of the strong sleeping pills instead.

The hymns drifted with her as she fell back onto the bed and into the darkness of undreaming sleep.

CHAPTER 19

SERGEANT COLLINS STODDARD told Chief to relax as he left the car, and the dog leaned back against the seat, disappointment clear on his face. Collins stood for a moment beside the car, looking over the neighborhood. A car from the city police was still parked in the driveway, although the body was already down in the morgue. Collins had gone to see it as soon as the news of the murder weapon reached him. A knife that could have been a steak knife without serrated edges, or a long-bladed paring knife. With a pearl handle.

He had seen that the wounds on Clyde Judson were very similar to the wounds on Everett and Faith Wasson, although Clyde had been attacked at the back of his neck and shoulders, as well as in front, in the soft part of the neck, as if he had tried to run.

Collins had gone to see the dog, too, which the police had picked up, and had found stab wounds over the vulnerable parts of the body.

Collins went around the house. The driveway was narrow, made originally of concrete probably when the house was built, but had long since cracked in a number of places and now had dead weeds in the cracks. A pickup, with racks and coils of wire and tools, was parked just off the driveway and on a bare spot at the side of the detached garage. The houses next door weren't far away, but a stand of trees and shrubs separated the yards in most places. Most of the other houses had fences, some of them privacy fences eight feet high. No one in the neighborhood, he'd been told by the city police, had heard a thing except for the barking of the dogs.

The spot on the ground where the body had lain was outlined in white.

The policeman on duty pointed from the white outline by the small back porch to the doghouse about fifty feet away.

"Looks like he was on his way out to see about the dog, and whoever it was jumped him from the back. He must have walked right past him. Sure was a brutal sight, let me tell you. That man's throat looked like something had tried to eat it."

Collins listened a few more minutes, his eyes covering the yard as he stood without moving. Near the door were a multitude of footsteps, just as there had been out in the Wasson house, but he knew it didn't matter. There had been no footprints of the killer anyway. He had been one of the first at the scene of Everett Wasson's death. And the ground behind the house carried no footprints other than Everett's, Faith's, and one print of Peggy's in the rain-softened soil.

At this house there probably were people running in and out all day, all kinds of neighbors, relatives. There were enough cars parked along the street out front that for a while Collins had thought he wasn't going to find a spot for his car.

He said good-bye to the man on duty and went around to the front of the house. Just as he reached the covered front porch, a man and a woman came out the door. They smiled and nodded and went on by, their eyes lingering on the sheriff's car at the curb with the mesh between the front and back seats and the big, silver-gray German shepherd sitting up and taking in the action in the neighborhood.

Collins knocked at the door.

An elderly man opened it. When he saw Collins's uniform and badge, he pulled the door wider.

"I need to talk to Mrs. Judson for a couple of minutes, if I may. I'm sorry to come at this time, but in a case like this, we have to talk to survivors at the worst of times."

"Certainly, we understand. My daughter's in the bedroom. I'll tell her you're here."

Collins waited in the living room, where a young guy in his mid-twenties or so sat on the couch, thumbing through a magazine. He looked up just long enough to nod at Collins. He was long-legged and uneasy-acting, and Collins wondered if he was the son. Down at the police station he'd learned Clyde Judson had a son twenty-three years old, and a daughter twenty-one.

But the son couldn't help him. The questions Collins had in mind had their basis twenty years ago.

A plump woman entered the room, with her father and two other women—one older and one much younger. The plump woman Collins gathered was Glorian since her eyes were red and swollen from crying.

"Mrs. Judson, I'm Sergeant Stoddard from the Sheriff's Department. I wonder if you would talk to me for a few minutes? There are some things we need to know."

"Okay," she said, and let herself fall into an arm chair that had a footstool almost as big as the chair. Glorian put one leg up on the footstool and sat sideways. She hardly paused to take a breath. "I heard all the neighborhood dogs barking, and I got up and went to look for Clyde. I knew something was wrong right away because Joe was quiet. Just all the other dogs. They'd bark awhile and then they'd hush, and then they'd start in again."

Someone told Collins to sit down, and he finally did, on the edge of the couch where the young man was leafing through the magazine. Glorian kept talking, her head leaning into her hand, her elbow propped on the arm of the chair. She had found her husband, and called 911. The police had come, followed by ambulances. The police had even taken the dog away, she said, to be examined.

The telephone rang twice while she talked, but the calls were taken by other members of the family.

Finally Collins interrupted her. "Mrs. Judson, I need to know if you knew Everett or Faith Wasson. They lived out northwest of town, toward the hills."

She had looked up at the first sound of his voice and was staring at him. She blinked in surprise, tears drying.

"Oh. Yes. They were murdered, too, weren't they? I had forgotten ... for a moment. Our own troubles, you know ..."

"Yes, of course. The thing is, Mrs. Judson, the knife that killed your husband is the same kind of knife that killed Everett Wasson, and could be the murder weapon that killed Mrs. Wasson. We haven't found one, but the wounds are similar. I need to know if you or your husband knew the Wassons."

Glorian frowned. "Do you think there's a connection?" she cried.

Collins nodded. "Either that, or we have a killer who picked your husband at random, maybe because he just stepped out into the yard at the wrong time."

A call to the back door, in the middle of the night, just as it had seemed to be in Everett Wasson's case, and maybe even in Faith's, although it had looked more as if Faith had been in the process of leaving her house. Perhaps Peggy could tell him when he went to see her.

He had checked at the hospital before he came to see Mrs. Judson, and the doctor had told him Peggy was slowly coming out of her state of shock.

"Everett occasionally went to the same church we belonged to back when our babies were small," Glorian said. "But I never knew the woman he married."

"Is that the church that's now closed? The one next door to the Wasson place?"

"Yes. I started going there with my folks when I was a young teenager. We lived in Clifton, a small town on the other side." Collins knew the town she spoke of. It was in the county, and under his jurisdiction.

"Clyde began going there," Glorian went on. "Not with his folks, but just going, like kids do. He and I were married there. And our babies were baptized there." Her face had softened in memory and looked almost pretty.

"But the church, I understand, closed about eighteen years ago."

The pleasant look left her face, as if his words had dropped her harshly back to the realities of life and death.

"Yes, it did. Everything seemed to collapse at the same time." She hesitated, then asked, "But what does all this have to do with Everett Wasson and my Clyde? We haven't seen Everett in—oh—a dozen years or more."

"I don't know what it has to do, ma'am. That's what I'm trying to find out."

She shrugged. Her face sagged in lines of deep exhaustion and grief. "If I thought I could help, Sergeant, I certainly would."

"I'd like to know ... your youngest child is twenty-one years old, right?"

"Yes. She's on her way. We're to meet her at the airport at four-thirty."

"I was wondering if you remember seeing a girl at the church, or in the neighborhood, who might have been pregnant at that same time? Someone who never had the baby with her after its birth?"

Glorian looked at him as if she were refocusing her eyes. Collins knew this was one question she wouldn't have been asked before by the city police. He was the only one that had a feeling the burial of the baby twenty years ago, and the deaths now, were in some way connected. The serial murders had seemed to begin with the discovery of the baby's grave and the tiny skeleton it had yielded.

But Glorian was shaking her head. "Not in church, Sergeant. I'm sure I would have known. There weren't so many of us. Seventy-five people, maybe, and that only on Easter or Christmas. No, there weren't any pregnant girls. My baby girl was the last baby born, or baptized there, before Reverend Singer seemed to lose interest. We stopped going, and then a few months later we heard he'd left and closed the church. We'd bought our house here, and going all the way out there was inconvenient. So we joined a church here, just three blocks away. We've been going there ever since." She leaned her head into her hands again and the tears began to fall. "We walked, Clyde and me, except in the worst weather. We walked in snow last winter, and it was beautiful. And we've walked in rain, with our umbrellas. Now I ..."

The rest of their conversation yielded no further useful information. Collins made his apologies and left. When Chief saw him, he stood up and started wagging his tail.

He drove back toward the hospital where Peggy Wasson had been taken yesterday, crossing a network of railroad tracks that weren't very busy anymore, many of them looking rusted and brown in the thin light of a cloud-filtered sun. The big old buildings that had been part of the railway system forty years ago now seemed to be warehouse buildings or empty places that the homeless leaned against, and perhaps lived in. If he had jurisdiction here he'd check them out, but the city had first responsibility.

He drove on past, and saw men spaced along the south side of the building like animals seeking warmth from the sun. Their heads turned as he drove past. The sheriff's emblem on the side of the car, he thought, and perhaps the dog in the back seat, had caught their attention. Some of them might have had occasion in their past to be afraid of an emblem such as was on the car, and a dog like the one in the back seat.

The city police had probably questioned all the transients in town, including these men. Before Collins got entirely past the railroad tracks, he saw a woman bundled in an old coat and tattered scarves and cap come out from between two buildings. At each hand were two small children, as crudely clothed as she. Collins shook his head in remorse, but drove on.

"Something's not right, Chief," he said. "This world. If you really look around, from the slaughterhouses, the cattle pens, the chicken houses, to the rich and powerful, who feel they have a right to everything, and then to the homeless, who have children even though they can't take care of them, if you really look at this world, Chief, you'll see we're all living a horror story. Did you know that?" He looked over his shoulder at the dog, and saw an answering grin and a wagging tail. He reached a hand back and stuck three fingers through the mesh. Chief carefully licked the fingers.

If it weren't for things like his dog, and the beauty of the hills and mountains and valleys, and for people like Lorna, Collins had a feeling he'd sink, too, in the hopelessness that seemed to be the main component of the men and women who wandered without purpose.

"Chief, what do you think of a world that is crawling with living creatures, none of which can escape alive, and in order to live you have to eat one of the other creatures? Eh?"

Chief wagged his tail against the door.

"How do you think it happened that two people who once belonged to the same church, but who haven't seen each other in twelve years or so, were both killed the same way, probably by the same person? And the one man's wife. Was she killed because of what she knew? Or did she just get in the way? Is Glorian going to be next? And then Peggy, in case she ever remembers what happened?" He paused. He had reached the old downtown now, where stores still lined the main street, but which had lost most of their trade to the shopping centers farther out.

"What's going to happen to Peggy, Chief? She's an orphan now."

The Alice Manswell General Hospital was in the green rolling country northeast of town. In his research of the past few days into the background of everyone even remotely connected to the Wassons, the old abandoned church, and possibly, the grave in the woods, he had learned that the Manswell General, as it was locally called, had been named for Daniel Treacle's mother, who had been the daughter of the original founder. It was a big concrete and brick structure that had grown in several directions, part of it old and part new. The grounds were like a park, with carefully spaced trees and closely mown grass, with beds of azaleas blooming in all colors in the spring, and beds of roses and summer flowers, now covered with mulching of some kind.

Collins found a parking place. "At ease," he told Chief, and followed the walk uphill to the main entrance. In the lobby, he went unnoticed through the people milling about.

On the third floor, at the door of Room 546, he found Magret Treacle, Daniel, their teenage daughter Leigh, a man in a brown suit who was talking to them, and a man in uniform. Magret Treacle smiled a brief, quick greeting that didn't reach her sad eyes, and Daniel put out his hand.

The doctor was one whom Collins had seen earlier, and he now nodded.

"She's still very quiet, Sergeant, but she seems to remember at least enough to know her mother is dead. I think it would be all right if you talked to her."

Peggy sat in a bed that was raised to the maximum. On her lap was an arrangement of coloring books and crayons. Other books littered the sheet on each side of her, and there was a new doll, a lovely thing with frilly, lacy clothes. But it was sitting unnoticed beside her, just as the books lay untouched. Peggy's eyes, dark and round, were on the door.

He thought of the night he had found her and carried her unresisting back to his car, which was parked at her home. All evidence of her mother's murder was gone, but the old gray car was still at the side of the house. He had debated in his mind whether to take her to Lorna, but had decided that he was closer to his car, where he could more quickly call for an ambulance. He had put his hand against the side of her face, to shield her eyes from the place where her mother had lain, but the child seemed not to notice where she was. She had continued to lean against him, her head on his shoulder. And when he had put her down in the front seat of his car, she had leaned her cheek against the upholstery as if she were no longer aware of anything outside that inner world into which she had drawn.

But now her eyes seemed to have come more alive. They moved with him as he came toward the bed. He reached into his pocket and pulled out the lollipop he had bought for her at a convenience store.

"Do you like chocolate?" he asked. "Do you like Tootsie Pops?"

She took the sucker and held it without attempting to unwrap it. Her eyes came back to his.

"Would you like me to unwrap it for you?"

She nodded, and he tore off the brown paper. Still she held it without tasting.

"Do you remember me, Peggy? I'm Sergeant Collins."

After a moment of hesitation, she nodded.

"Do you think you can talk to me a little while?"

She nodded again, and her gaze flicked toward the chocolate sucker, and back again to stare steadily and unnervingly into his eyes. He hated this part of his job, where he had to drag something unpleasant, and sometimes horrible, out of the memory of a child. A child ought to be able to live his or her few years in a happy world, where violent deaths did not occur. He took a deep breath.

"Peggy, do you remember leaving your house the other night?"

She looked at the sucker again. It was so close to her face her eyes looked slightly crossed. He saw they were a light, soft brown, with dark brown pupils and a dark, almost black line around the edge of the iris. After a long time, she nodded.

"I need you to tell me about it, Peggy. Did you go out with your mother?"

She nodded, and still looking at the sucker she said, "Yes. She put a blanket around me. She walked with me downstairs. And I lost the blanket."

Collins waited. He could almost see the heavy fog of the night, the fear at being taken from her bed with only a blanket wrapped around her.

"She told me to run," Peggy finally whispered.

She lowered the sucker and her gaze drifted toward the door, the windows, the television high on the wall. A nurse came in and stood on the other side of the bed from Collins, smiled at him, then watched Peggy for a moment before she backed away to watch.

"Where were you when she told you to run?" Collins asked.

"Outside."

"Did you see the person who was there, Peggy? The one who hurt your mother?"

Peggy's mouth twisted and began working as if she were trying to speak and couldn't. The nurse stepped forward instantly and took Peggy's wrist.

Then Peggy was saying, "It was the girl. I saw her. The girl in the woods. The one who was a tiny baby, and then grew to a little kid who could walk. It was her, only she was bigger. A lot bigger, as big as me or Wendy or Sheena. She was there, she didn't have any clothes on, and I could barely see her in the fog. And when I ran away, I heard her running behind me." She wriggled on the bed, twisting, as if trying to escape something. The frown of bewilderment on Collins's face deepened as he watched her. The nurse continued holding her wrist in silence, but when Collins glanced at her, the nurse shook her head.

"I could hear her footsteps in the woods behind me when I ran away."

Collins looked back at the child, feeling remorse that almost sickened him. She was confusing reality with the truth, whatever that was.

The nurse said softly, "I don't think Peggy is quite up to talking about this."

"Yes, I am." Peggy said clearly and startlingly, almost angrily. "It was the naked girl in the woods who hurt my mother. I saw her. She was there, as tall as me, and when she opened her mouth, she had a million teeth, as sharp as knives, and she bit my mother on the neck. And in her hand she had a knife."

Peggy sank back on the pillow behind her, and her voice weakened as her eyes closed. "Mama told me to run, and I did."

The doctor came into the room and stopped at the foot of the bed. After a moment, Collins drew the doctor aside.

"Is she all right, Doctor?"

"Little children in a good environment have a remarkable resilience. It will take time."

Collins went to the door. He felt sorry, puzzled, confused. It sounded as if Peggy's imagination had taken over when she couldn't accept the reality of what had happened.

It chilled him, though, the way these kids kept talking about a naked child in the woods.

The Treacles were still in the hall outside the door. Collins asked if Peggy would be staying with them.

"No," Daniel replied. "Peggy's Aunt Glenda is on her way. To take her home. She told me on the phone that she's never had a child, and she'll be happy to take care of Peggy."

Magret said, "It's the best arrangement that could ever be made for Peggy. Faith has told me a lot about her sisters. Glenda will be like a mother to Peggy."

"Mrs. Treacle," Collins said, "the morning you found Faith, did you pick up an electric blanket somewhere and put it over the chair in the kitchen."

"Yes, I did. Did I do wrong?"

"Well, Peggy remembers coming downstairs with her mother, wrapped in the blanket. Then she says she dropped it when her mother told her to run. I'd like to know exactly where the blanket was."

"It was outside. On the porch and steps actually, between the two doors."

Daniel asked, "Did Peggy see the killer?"

"I don't think she did," Collins said.

"Thank God for that," Daniel said. "She'd be in danger if she had, wouldn't she?"

"Probably," Collins said, suddenly cautious. For the first time he looked at Daniel and Magret, and even their daughter, Leigh, as possible suspects. "But I'm sure she saw no one. It was very foggy. Were any of you out that night?"

Of course they weren't, he told himself as all three of them shook their heads. Magret's report, given to the city police, had stated simply that she had gone out to see her aunt and niece, and had found Faith dead and Peggy missing. He believed her.

Collins was about to leave when the doctor looked out the door and beckoned to him.

Collins went back into Peggy's room. The little girl was leaning forward in bed, her eyes watching the door expectantly.

"Will you get her, you and Chief?" she asked. "She's there, in the woods. That's where she lives."

Collins clasped the small, dimply hand between his, wishing he knew what to do to help her.

Peggy said, "Her hair is short and curly and dark brown like mine. And she's *growing*.

CHAPTER 20

MAGRET WANDERED ALONE through the house, pausing to look through windows at a world of sunshine and shadows. The evergreen stood in dark green sculptured beauty against trees whose limbs suddenly had become bare when she wasn't noticing.

She thought about taking a walk or going for a drive, but it was almost time for dinner, and the children would start coming home soon. After leaving the hospital she had dropped each of them off at school, and had come on home alone. Then Daniel had come home, for coffee, for a talk, perhaps.

She recalled the puzzled look on his face as he stared at the wall and recounted what he had heard from the coroner. And then the shock of what he was telling her closed her into her own world of fear, and she had sat nodding her head and pretending to be listening. She had hardly been aware when he left again to go back to the office.

The knife ... the knife ...

"The same kind of knife," Daniel had said, and his words went through her mind again and again, like a terrible song repeating itself. "Used again last night to kill a man over on the other side of town. Same kind of knife as was used to kill Everett. A man named Clyde."

Clyde. *Clyde.* There was only one Clyde.

She realized Daniel was talking to her, no longer staring at the wall, but at her.

"Wh-what?" she asked.

"I said, what connection do you suppose there would be? The coroner said the police think there's a connection. Did you ever hear of Clyde Judson?"

"No," she said. "But I'm sure Uncle Everett knew a lot of people ..."

She didn't remember if she'd said any more.

The knife found embedded in the butchered throat of Clyde Judson was exactly like the knife found at Everett's death. Now the police knew it was one of a set.

And now she knew where the third knife had gone.

One for Everett. One for Faith. And one for Clyde.

"I wonder," Daniel had mused as she walked with him out toward the car, "what connection there might have been between a general worker in the TV business, and Everett, who lived miles away and worked for the gas company."

Magret felt a hysterical weeping building within her. She held on to it successfully. She walked beside her husband in quiet dignity and kissed him good-bye, with murmurs that she would see him at dinnertime.

She was glad to be alone, to walk the floor as she needed. To wash her face in cold water, and try to stop thinking about Clyde.

Once she had loved him ... oh God, so much.

And now ... had she killed him?

She wandered the house from room to room. Dust was gathering, but she dared not call Carrie in to help clean.

She went to the kitchen to start dinner, and turned on all the lights so she was bathed in brightness. But then she stood looking out the window at a sunshine that was turning pale and finally gave up to shadows as clouds gathered again in the west.

DANIEL, sometimes I wake, and I'm not in my bed, and I'm afraid I'm the one who killed them all.

I'm the connection, Daniel. The knives are from our own kitchen, don't you remember when I bought them and showed them to you? Years ago?

NO, Jesus, let him not remember.

She couldn't bear for him to know this about her.

She had been killing all the people who knew about the baby she had left to die. Yes, left to die. Now she was terrified, and sick inside, to think that it might have been that way.

She was the connection. Uncle Everett had known, of course, and he might have told Faith. And Clyde would have remembered, too, the day she went to him long ago, as if he would help her.

Clyde had to die.

And now ... had Peggy seen her?

Peggy had told Sergeant Collins something, but what? She didn't know.

A door opened with a soft whisper of sound, and then a moment later it closed again. Magret grew tense, her hands gripping the edge of the cabinet. Footsteps, soft and hesitant, came closer.

Magret turned, and sagged inwardly with relief when she saw it was Sheena. The little girl acted odd, her eyes watchful. She hesitated by the door.

"I'm going up to my room," she said in a questioning tone, as if asking permission.

Magret nodded. Then she saw the clock and the time. Sheena was over thirty minutes late.

"Where have you been, Sheena? You're late."

"I was just—walking," she said. "I was kind of waiting for Ward, but he didn't come."

She sidled toward the door to the inner halls, still watching Magret, and Magret longed to run to her and take the child into her arms and hug her and hug her, and tell her it didn't matter about the pink dress. But then Sheena was going away, and it was too late. Magret called after her, "How was school?"

"Okay," the voice came back, timid and distant. "Wendy was there."

Ward came in a few minutes later, his jacket unzipped and almost falling off his shoulders, his hair mussed and curling over his forehead. Magret would have liked to push his hair back and kiss that smooth forehead, as she would have done a month ago, but she couldn't move toward him any more than she had been able to move toward Sheena.

He threw his coat down in the hall to the utility room just as Leigh came through the door.

"Hang up your coat, Ward," Leigh ordered. "Why'd you throw it down?"

Ward whirled back and grabbed his coat off the floor. Out of the corner of her vision Magret saw them, and was comforted by them, as she prepared a haphazard dinner. She was following her own daughter's path, she thought as she looked in the freezer for something different.

She gave up. Frozen food was too much bother. She went to the pantry instead. Daniel would be coming in within the next thirty minutes, and dinner should be ready. It was always a relief to her to just get the whole affair over with. Eating was no longer the comfort or the pleasure it had been before she had started worrying about her weight.

She managed to have the table partly set by the time Daniel came through the door. After his usual greetings, he went on to join Ward in the family room.

Magret checked on the food heating in the microwave and on the stove.

"Mama," Leigh said in a curiously sharp voice, "what on earth happened to these knives?"

Magret turned and stared, cold shock keeping her voice silent.

Leigh was at the knife drawer. The drawer was pulled out, and Leigh held in her hands two mud-coated knives. The third, still tissue-wrapped, the pink tissue stained dark brown with soil and dried blood, lay in the back of the drawer in the original box.

Magret felt as if she were being executed, the cold ripping away of her scalp and skin, the severing of her inner self from the shell that was left. She waited for Leigh to unwrap the bloodstained tissue, waited without breathing, staring at the change that had come over Leigh.

Then suddenly Leigh returned the knives to the drawer and closed it.

Magret got a glimpse of Leigh's face as she left the kitchen. It was almost as white as her blouse. Even her lips had a dry, bleached lack of color.

After dinner Magret sent them all away. "Watch TV, read, do your homework. I'll take care of the dishes."

It had been such a strain, the sitting through the meal. Daniel and Ward had done most of the talking, but Leigh had sat in the silence in which Magret was enclosed. Sheena had been subdued to the point that Daniel had asked her once if she was okay, and Sheena had said yes.

Magret, alone in the kitchen, pulled out the knife drawer again and looked at the muddied knives. Specks of dark soil clung to the handles and blades. Leigh, though, thank God, either had not seen the knife wrapped in the tissue, the knife that was dark with blood, or had chosen not to touch it.

Who had dug them up, brought them back in?

Who could have, but herself?

Magret ran hot water into the sink and poured in enough liquid soap to build bubbles to the top of the sink, then she dropped the knives into it. She threw the bloodstained tissue into the trash can beneath the sink, wadded into a small, wet ball.

She washed the knives, the counter, the stove, the table. She worked until Daniel called from the family room wanting to know if she was going to join them.

She carefully dried the knives and put them away. This was twice Leigh had shown she was aware of them. And Magret knew ... she desperately feared ... Leigh knew her mother was the killer.

THE WEATHER TURNED warm and lovely for the funerals of Everett and Faith, and Leigh stood with the large crowd that had gathered at the cemetery. Flowers made mounds behind the two caskets, and groups of people stood talking together after the graveside services. Both coffins had remained closed.

Leigh felt a hand slip into hers, glove against glove. She felt Sheena touch her. She looked down. Sheena didn't smile anymore, it seemed to Leigh, nor did their mother. Leigh wanted to help them, more than she had ever wanted anything in her life, but felt so helpless.

"Leigh," Sheena said, "where's Peggy? Why didn't Peggy come to the funeral?"

"Because her doctor and her aunt felt it would be better if she didn't."

"But how's she going to know ... they're dead now?" Leigh squeezed Sheena's hand. She tried to remember how she had felt about life and death when she was only nine, but couldn't.

"She'll be all right, Sheena. Her aunt and uncle are taking her away with them soon."

"I won't get to see her anymore?"

"You can write to her." Leigh said after a hesitation. It was sad, she thought, how life changed, when people you loved were no longer there.

She saw their mother standing at the foot of the two coffins, beneath the overhang of the green tent the funeral home had erected over the graves. Her head was down, her eyes closed, as if she were praying in silence. Leigh's heart ached for her.

She looked around for her dad, and saw him talking to a couple of men several yards away. He seemed unaware of Magret's need.

Leigh patted Sheena's hand then dropped it. "I'm going over to Mama for a minute, Sheena. Do you want to go wait in the car?"

"Will you be there soon?"

"Sure. Soon."

Leigh wove through the drifting crowd and came to Magret. She put her arm around her mother's waist and hugged.

Magret looked up in surprise, and her eyes met Leigh's for just a moment.

Leigh saw with shock the lines on her mother's face. Overnight, it seemed, she had started looking old and haggard.

Leigh wanted to say something comforting, but could think of nothing. Finally she said simply, "Why don't we go to the car, Mama? The services are over now."

The ride home seemed to take forever, though it was only a few miles. Leigh watched the houses slip past the car window, saw the trees, most of them leafless now, and looked for familiar areas. She had gone with her mother and dad to the cemetery north of town a few times on Decoration Day, and she had gone to the other, bigger, cemetery east of town where her father's people were buried. It was there, she knew, her mother and dad owned enough cemetery plots for all of them, but it made her shudder to think about it.

They were turning into the driveway when Ward suddenly asked, "I wonder where they're burying that other guy, the one that was murdered like Aunt Faith and Uncle Everett? Isn't his funeral today, too?"

Leigh reached over Sheena's head and poked Ward in warning, but it was too late, he had already said it. When he looked at her with puzzled eyes, though, he got the message. Shut up. If you can't talk about something pleasant, don't say anything at all.

Daniel answered something, but Leigh didn't listen. They had reached the garage, and everyone was getting out.

The afternoon stretched ahead. All her friends were in school, and there was no one to call or talk to or anything. She would have gone on back to school, if it had been acceptable. But of course the funeral was at two o'clock, and it was now past three, and by the time she got her jeans on, it was almost time for school to be out anyway.

She would like to go to the mall and hang out awhile, and she looked in her purse to see if she had any allowance left. Three dollars? Well, she couldn't buy anything except a Coke maybe, but ...

She went out into the hall and started toward the stairs.

The little girl was standing just around the corner toward the master bedroom.

Leigh stopped, half smiling, surprised. Sheena was having company today?

She must be a new friend of Sheena's. Leigh had never seen her before. She was dressed as if she were going to a party, in a pink frilly dress that stood out over many lacy petticoats. Leigh had almost run into her.

"Oh, excuse me," she said, and walked around the little girl and down the stairs.

After she was in the lower hall, she looked back up, thinking of how rude she must have seemed. But the girl was not visible from where she stood. She went on down the hall, bewilderment growing in her mind. There had been something wrong with the picture the girl presented. Her lovely dress had seemed to have several dark spots on the front, and ... she hadn't been wearing socks or shoes ... had she?

She must be wrong about that.

Leigh went on into the family room, and found her mother sitting alone, a magazine in her hands. She hadn't even changed clothes. She had removed her suit coat and her gloves and hat, but was still wearing the black shoes, skirt, and blouse.

"Where is everybody?" Leigh asked.

Magret looked up. "Daniel and Ward went out to the garage to look at something, and Sheena's in her room, I guess."

"Who's the little girl?"

"What little girl?"

"The little girl in pink."

Magret stared up at her. She laid aside the magazine. "Girl in pink," she repeated. "Was it Sheena?"

"Sheena? No. It was—I thought it was a new friend of Sheena's. Didn't you see her come in?"

"No."

"Well, I almost ran into her in the hall upstairs. I guess Sheena let her in, but she looks like she just came from a party." The soiled places on the front of the pink dress suddenly explained themselves. "From a party where she had chocolate ice cream. She'd spilled some on her pretty dress. Mom, is it okay if I go down to the mall for a while?"

Leigh was already on her way to the door, expecting her mother to say it was all right so long as she was home for dinner. She saw her mother get up and stand in front of her chair. Leigh reached for the denim jacket she had left on the hook inside the hall to the utility room.

"Describe the dress to me," Magret. said.

Leigh stood in the doorway, her jacket half on. "It was pink and frilly, with ribbons and lace. I don't know, it was just a party dress."

"Did it have a scalloped hem, with lace edging?"

"It might have. Why?"

"What did the girl look like?"

"Gee, I don't know, just a kid. Darkish hair, short and curly. I've never seen her before." But then, as the picture of the girl returned to her thoughts, Leigh realized something. "But she did look familiar. I've seen her somewhere, I guess."

Magret was going toward the hall to the upstairs, but paused briefly, to say, "I'd rather you didn't go anywhere alone. I feel safer knowing you're—not alone."

"Oh, it's okay, Mom, really. I'm perfectly safe. Who'd want to hurt me?" She laughed, sort of, to try to settle her mother's worries. What was going to happen now? Was her mother going to be so afraid that she would try to make hermits out of her kids?

"Take Ward with you," Magret said.

Leigh almost objected, then decided it was better than not going at all.

"Okay, Mom. Thanks."

She pulled her jacket on and adjusted her shoulder bag strap on her shoulder and went in search of Ward. Was he going to have to go along on her dates, too? Sheesh!

MAGRET WENT UPSTAIRS. Shadows filled the halls, the doorways, and lingered behind furniture even after she had turned on the lights. She stood in the hall listening for voices, for Sheena and the friend who might have entered unseen by her. She wanted to hear voices. But there was nothing but silence.

She was gripped in a shroud of coldness and fear, as if she were a part of the world that Faith and Everett, and Clyde, too, now inhabited. As if death were in her, not just of her hands, but an integral part of her.

Leigh had described the pink dress that had disappeared from the trunk upstairs, but she had said the girl wearing it was not Sheena. The girl was a stranger. No, perhaps not quite a stranger. A girl familiar, yet not remembered.

Who was she?

Magret found Sheena's door closed, and she knocked softly.

"Sheena? Are you in there?"

A moment later she heard Sheena answer quietly, "Yes."

"May I come in?" She opened the door as she spoke. Sheena was lying across her bed with a book open in front of her. Magret went to the bed and sat down.

The book was *The Wizard of Oz,* a story Sheena had read many times before. The room was neat and quiet, and Sheena had changed from the trim little black and white suit she had worn to the funeral to a pair of loose blue jeans, faded and bleached as she liked them, and a sweater. Her fair hair had been held back by barrettes and was now coming loose. Magret removed a barrette and replaced it more firmly in the soft, silky hair.

"Leigh told me you had company," she said.

Sheena's face brightened visibly, and she sat up. "Who?" she asked, sliding off the bed, getting ready to run downstairs to greet her guest, ready to play again in nine-year-old exuberance.

Magret said, "But Leigh said the girl was up here, in the hall. I thought you knew. I wondered who she is, and where she is."

Sheena slumped, her face changed again, as visibly as it had before, going through the stages of bewilderment and disappointment. She shook her head and shrugged a shoulder.

"There's no one here."

She slid off the bed and went to the hallway.

"There's no one here, Mama."

She tilted her head suddenly, listening. She looked out into the hallway again, and up, listening to something overhead, in the attic.

Now Magret could hear it, one of the old hymns she used to sing in church, the words lost in the distance, the tune floating in the air and disappearing like motes in moonlight.

It sounded as if it were coming from the attic, but Magret had a terrible feeling that if she went into the attic she would find nothing. As the hymn drifted to silence, she moved past Sheena as if she had heard nothing.

CHAPTER 21

"YOU'RE the only native who lives in the neighborhood, did you know that?" Collins asked.

Lorna stood with the door open, looking at her unexpected visitor on the front stoop. He was dressed in a leather jacket, blue jeans, and a cream-colored knit shirt with brown stripes across the chest. His thumbs were hooked in the pockets of his jeans and she could see he wasn't wearing his usual holster and gun. The car parked in her driveway was an ordinary cherry red, with no mesh between the front and back seat, and no dog.

"Where's Chief?" Lorna asked, stepping back to allow him room to enter.

"Chief is off duty. He kind of wanted to come along, but I told him he might have to sit in the car a long time by himself. That is, if I could talk you into going to a movie or something."

Lorna glanced back and saw that Islan had come out of her room down the hall and was standing in the shadows. Islan had been turning down dates like mad lately, and she hadn't gone out at all. One explanation might be that she was just getting over her cold, but the other Lorna suspected, was Collins, although Islan had stopped talking about him.

"Oh, I—" Lorna wanted to go, more than she had wanted anything for a long time, but tried to think of a polite way to decline. An excuse.

Excuses were always the best. How could she even think of going out with a man her own daughter had such a crush on?

"You—?" Collins said, smiling, brushing against her as he entered, looking down into her face.

"I just can't. It's late."

"They still have second shows."

"I can't leave the girls here alone."

She felt he knew instantly what she meant. The smile left his face. He said hello to Islan, and to Wendy, who had come from the living room.

They went through the hall back to the family room at the end of the kitchen, where Wendy had her coloring books, her dolls, and a menagerie of animals spread on a soft rug in front of the TV. Islan, Lorna saw, had withdrawn into her room again. She heard the phone ring once, and knew Islan had picked up an extension. Most of the calls were for Islan, a few more for Wendy, and almost none for Lorna. That was all right. When Lorna got home from work, she didn't want to spend time talking on the telephone.

Wendy went back to her play until Lorna told her it was bedtime, and grumbling, she went to change pajamas, then back again to kiss Lorna good night. Islan came in and drank a cup of chocolate at the table with Lorna and Collins, and then she, too, said good night.

At the door she paused, looked back, and said, "If you two want to go out, we'll be okay, Mom. I'm not afraid to stay here with just Wendy."

Lorna shook her head. It was ten o'clock now, and she didn't feel right about it. Islan had as much as given her permission to date the man she herself had been raving about, but Lorna couldn't accept it.

"I suppose I should leave," Collins said after both girls were gone, and silence had fallen between them.

Lorna started to say no, but then closed her lips. She wanted to keep him awhile longer, yet couldn't voice something that might be an encouragement.

"You said when I opened the door that I am the only native living here. What was that leading up to? You must have had business on your mind."

"Some. In a case like the murders of Faith and Everett Wasson, and then Clyde Judson, on top of the sightings the girls saw in the woods behind your house, between your house and the Wassons', and the finding of the baby's grave, you kind of live with it until you get all the pieces together. In questioning the other people who live here in Greenbrier, you're the only one who was born in the area, who grew up here, and who now lives here."

Lorna smiled faintly. "Am I a suspect?"

Collins gave her such a sudden, unexpected stare that she laughed. He relaxed and laughed with her.

"I hadn't even thought of that," he admitted.

"Really, I hadn't either until just now."

"Did I ever ask you how long you've known the Wassons?"

"I don't think you did. The truth is, I've known Everett all my life, I guess. Certainly not well, just to speak to. I even went to Reverend Singer's church for a few months when I was a kid. My folks had moved to a house on the other side of town, a small farm, for a few years. I rode the school bus with Magret until I was about twelve, then we moved to the city on the east side, and I finished my growing up there. I didn't meet Faith Wasson until I bought this house three years ago, and our daughters became friends. How is Peggy, anyway?"

Peggy, he told her, had left town as soon as she was dismissed from the hospital, with her aunt and uncle, and Lorna felt a large weight she hadn't realized she carried lifted from her shoulders.

"She's safe then," she said.

"Yes, she is, but why do you say that?"

"I don't know." Lorna stared at the black night outside the kitchen window over the sink. She hadn't pulled the blind there. As she looked at it, she had a creepy feeling that eyes were beyond the window, in the darkness, looking in at them. She wished Collins had brought Chief and left him on guard in the backyard. She got up and went to pull the kitchen blind, closing out the night and the invisible eyes.

"You felt she was in danger," Collins said, and Lorna realized he was questioning her, in a subtle way, as if she knew something she didn't realize she knew and in getting her to talk on a level of friendship he would uncover the mystery.

"I don't think you came out here on a social visit at all," she said smiling, only half teasing. "You're all cop. You want information."

"My intentions were originally honorable, honest. But ..."

"I know. It's okay. About Peggy," she said as she sat down again, "I hadn't thought of her as being in danger, not consciously. But now I know it must have been somewhere in my mind, because I'm relieved she's safely away. Do you think she saw the murderer? And just doesn't remember?"

"What makes you think she doesn't remember?"

Lorna shrugged. "Just rumors, I guess, around town, around the office where I work anyway."

"Actually, and this is just between you and me, Lorna, she did remember the murderer. But she said it was the little girl in the woods."

Lorna stared into Collins's dark eyes.

"You're not serious," she said.

He nodded. "Peggy believed that was what she saw. She said the girl is growing."

Lorna felt a long chill go over her body. "That's weird, Collins."

"I know it is. The police psychiatrist feels it's a form of denial. That perhaps she only wanted to see the person who killed her parents, and didn't. Or that in the heavy fog of that night, she saw something pale, and her mind created the image of the girl. At any rate, she's no help as a witness. So she's been taken away to what we all hope is a better place where she'll learn to be happy again."

They talked of other things for the next hour, but Lorna's thoughts kept going back to what she felt was the beginning. The baby in the woods. And then the baby who was larger, who was walking about. A baby that, according to the girls who saw it, had grown overnight.

At the door, as Collins was leaving, Lorna asked, "Collins, is it possible that a family actually lives in the woods? A baby, a toddler, another larger child? And, of course, adults?"

"Who for some unknown reason came to the Wasson house and killed? And then went across town and killed Clyde Judson? With two pearl-handled kitchen knives? It just doesn't fit together. Also, I was all over those woods with Chief the day I looked for Peggy, and over part of it earlier when we were searching for the baby the girls swore they saw. Besides that, the County Rescue team were all through the woods. Believe me, there was no family living there. Nor anyone else."

"What about the other side?"

"Out toward the valley? Farms. Small towns. Nothing. And on the other side? More trees, more housing developments like Greenbrier, and then the hills and mountains and old hermits like Harry."

He had entered through the front door, but was leaving through the sliding doors at the back. The porch light was on, and the light threw fingers across the yard with the shrubs and trees and fence at the sides and rear, like fading moonlight. The forest beyond the fence was black. The sky overhead rolled with dark gray clouds, and the air felt cold.

"You'd better go back in," Collins said gently, and bent toward her, touching his lips to hers briefly and unexpectedly.

He was walking away, going toward the gate into the front yard. Just before he went out of sight, he waved good night.

Lorna was left standing in the light on the porch, feeling a mixture of thrill and love and foolishness. She hadn't expected the kiss. It had come and gone before she had a chance to realize what was happening.

She stepped back into the kitchen-family room and closed and locked the door and pulled the drapery.

It was almost as if she'd never been kissed before in her life, she thought as she stood just inside the curtain.

DANIEL MASSAGED the back of Magret's neck and shoulders as she sat with her elbows on the vanity top in the bathroom. Lights around the mirror revealed gray in the top of her hair, mixed with the highlighting done at the beauty parlor, but Daniel said nothing about it. He loved her dark hair, and she had been lucky about the gray. She had reached thirty-five with very little gray showing up, while in his own fringe of dark brown hair the white had started when he was still in his twenties. It had never seemed to get much worse though, he thought as he looked at his own image in the brightly lit mirror. What little hair he had left was still salt and pepper.

But he hardly looked at himself. It was Maggie he looked at, was concerned about. Since the deaths of her uncle and aunt, she was deteriorating before his eyes, it seemed.

"You don't have to do that," she said, her forehead down and resting on two white-knuckled fists.

"I want to do that," he said. "Unless you really don't want me to."

The phone rang, and Magret lifted her head.

Daniel went to the phone on the bedside table, on his side of the bed, where he could take calls without disturbing Magret any more than was necessary. The hospital didn't often call after 9 p.m., but when it did, there was no reason for Maggie to be bothered.

"Treacle speaking."

"Dad?" Leigh's voice, sounding young and light, and making his heart glad. "Dad, we've got car trouble. Something went wrong, and it just died, and we had to push it off the street."

"Where are you? I'll come and get you. We won't be able to do much tonight besides having it towed somewhere."

"No, it's okay. We don't want you to come after us. We'll just walk home. It's not far. I just wanted you to know we'll be a little later than Mom might like."

"Just you and Ward?"

"No, Thad's with us, and a couple of others. Jennie and Vincent, you know, we're just a couple of blocks from Jennie's house. We pushed the car into Brock's driveway. He said it would be okay there. We can get it tomorrow."

"I'd better come and get you."

"No, Dad, really, it's great out. Sometimes the moon comes out. It's almost like Halloween all over again."

"Well ..." Brock's house was only four blocks away, and it wouldn't take the kids long to get on home. Thad lived on down the street about three houses, and they had been in and out of each other's houses since he and Leigh were in kindergarten, maybe even before, when they had played together as toddlers in the sandbox. Besides, he didn't want to leave Maggie. Although Sheena was in her own bedroom, she was asleep, and Maggie would be alone here if he left her.

"We're having a ball, Dad. The car is okay in the driveway. We pushed it in, all of us."

"Well, don't dawdle."

Ward was with her, too, he thought as he hung up. And that group of kids, and others in the neighborhood, had been wandering the streets between their houses and the mall down on Bishop since they were big enough to be allowed out of the house. They'd be all right.

"Not the hospital," Magret said when he went back to the bathroom.

"No," he said. "It was Leigh. Seems her car stalled, and she and the rest of the kids are walking home." Magret looked up, her face drawn with alarm and worry.

"Oh, Daniel, no, they can't. Go get them."

"They don't want me to. She's with Thad, and a couple more. Ward's there. There'll be at least three walking together by the time they get here. They'll be okay, Maggie. Why don't you come to bed now?"

"I wouldn't be able to sleep."

"Try. Want something to take?"

He looked through the medicine cabinet. There were a couple of bottles of tranquilizers, and one bottle of sleeping pills. It was a fairly mild dosage, but he knew that any of these medications, any medication at all that brought about relaxation, could also cause an insidious depression. A sort of tit for tat, as one old doctor who had access to the hospital used to say. You pay for your tranquilities, he'd say. You pay for every ounce of peacefulness you get out of a drug. Was it worth it? Maggie seemed depressed to him, too much so. She had loved her uncle, he supposed, though she had seen him only on holidays and an occasional picnic in the summertime. But of course she talked often on the phone to Faith because Sheena and Peggy had become good friends. Yet Maggie's depression seemed to be getting worse, not better.

He ached to take her into his arms, to carry her to bed and hold her. He wanted to make love to her, praying it would comfort her the way it always comforted him. Would this be one of the nights when she would let him hold her? Make love to her? Or would she plead exhaustion, and retreat from him?

He moved nearer to her, leaned down and slid his hands around her flat stomach, then whispered against her hair, "Let me carry you to bed, Maggie."

She twisted, and he knew this was not the night. The loneliness her movement gave him was for a moment a pain as sharp as an arrow. "Not now, Daniel, please," she said, her voice soft and low and sad.

He straightened. "Do you think a sleeping pill might help?"

"No," she said, and then started to say something else, but stopped. She got up and went toward the shower stall.

Usually she liked to take long soaks in the tub.

He watched her. She let the robe drop to the floor. Her body looked white and too thin. He could see her hip bones protruding against the colorless skin. He wished again that she would see a doctor, yet he said nothing. Later, in bed, he would try to talk to her, he assured himself. Later, she might let him hold her.

"I'm going to take a shower," she said, stepping into the shower stall and closing the door. Her voice became muffled behind the glass door. "Go on to bed, Daniel."

He put the small vial of sleeping capsules back into the medicine cabinet and went into the bedroom. He sat on the bed in his robe, leaning back against the head of the bed.

Maggie had been the center of his life since she came to work for him when she was seventeen years old. She'd had lovely, perfect skin, a kind of fine, silky texture to her dark hair. It fell past her shoulders, with curls that looked natural.

At first she had worked only afternoons, on one of the programs from high school, an on-the-job training. He had watched the change in her, as he grew to love her in all ways. She at first had been very quiet and shy, and seemed to have almost no friends. Then as she lost some weight she had blossomed, and made friends among the others in the training program and had begun to go out with them. Yet she had seemed too elegant, too dignified, as if she were older than they, and didn't know how to giggle with the girls or flirt with the boys.

At times he felt, as he saw the faraway sadness in her eyes, that she had lived through tragedies others her age had no concept of. He knew her mother had died unexpectedly from a heart attack when Magret was sixteen, and a few months later she had moved to town to live with an elderly great-aunt. Her father had left the area, as had her brothers, but there was more to it than that. He felt it, but he never knew what it was.

She had turned to him, perhaps finding in him something that was important to her. He never questioned it. It was as if in his heart he was afraid to know.

He was no great bargain, he knew. He was not handsome, or rich. He had a good background, a good income, and he wasn't poor. But he was pudgy and bald, except for a fringe, and he was twenty years older than she.

As every year of their marriage passed, he felt more blessed. She was a marvelous wife, although a bit modest perhaps, and very proper. He might have enjoyed a burst of passion from her but he didn't dwell on it. In fact, he made a point of pushing it out of his mind.

A fantasy, now and then. Once a young whore had approached him when he was at a conference, and he was tempted by her graphic promises, lewd and forbidden, and then he was ashamed that he had even been tempted. Would he jeopardize what he and Maggie had for one wild sexual romp? He'd have to be crazy, and he wasn't.

Besides, he didn't want wildness from any other woman. He just wanted a bit now and then from Maggie.

But at this moment, though he waited for her to come to bed, as his arms ached to hold her, he wanted only that. To hold her. To comfort her. As he had tried to comfort her during her bad times in all the years she had been part of him.

I love you, Maggie.

. . .

THEY HAD LEFT Jennie in her driveway, and Leigh and Thad had dropped behind after that. Vincent, who'd been one of Ward's best friends all their lives, poked Ward's arm as they looked back and saw a two-headed shadow lagging along against the hedge that lined the front yard of Mrs. Rogean's place. He snickered. "They're going to sneak a little kiss or two." And he made a smacking sound and pretended he was going to hug Thad.

"Cut it out! I'm no pervert, man." Ward shoved at Vincent and Vincent shoved at Ward, and they dodged back and forth across the wide sidewalk.

Behind them, getting slower and slower, it seemed, when at the corner of the block Ward glanced back again, Leigh and Thad for a moment were just part of the black shadows hidden beneath the trees that lined the street. Then they moved out into the street light again.

"Hey, Leigh," Ward called. "Come on."

"Gotta go," Vincent said, and angled across the street to his own driveway. Ward could see the lights of his house beyond the fences and trees. Instead of being uphill from the street as Ward's house was, Vincent's was downhill, so that his wide driveway had a great slope to it and made a good place to sled after a snow.

"See you," Ward answered, and went slowly along, half waiting for Leigh to get the lead out of her pants and catch up with him.

It had been a neat evening. It seemed like months since he had gotten away from the sadness that had come into their house, and the need to show respect, as his dad had called it. "I know it would be better for us psychologically to pretend it didn't happen, Ward, that no one has died, that Peggy isn't alone now. It would be easier to go play ball, to be with friends. But you have to remember your mother, at least, and show respect."

For days, weeks, it seemed, he had gone around as quietly as he could. Then tonight had come, and Leigh had invited him along. She was going to the mall, she said, and did he want to go, too? You bet your sweet booties, he'd told her, and his dad, who'd had his eye on him ever since Uncle Everett was killed, to make sure he behaved in a respectful way, had given a nod. He was free to go. More than that. He was free. Now life would get back to normal for him.

Not that he wasn't sorry about Peggy. She was just a little kid who came to the house now and then to play with Sheena, and sometimes during the course of a year they had gone out to Uncle Everett's house.

But, like his dad had understood, it was easier to just go on and play ball and hang out with friends.

At the mall, Leigh had told him to meet her at the main hall entrance at closing time, and by that she meant the closing of the stores, not the doors. He knew, because a few times before she had let him come along.

He had sat on the edge of the seat, trying not to complain about Leigh's driving. She whipped her VW bug around the corners as if it had no brakes. But he'd put up with her driving just to get to go to the game room at the mall. He knew a bunch of his friends would be there. They always were. And sure enough, there was not only Vincent, but several others from school, some he knew well, and some he didn't.

He had spent most of his money on the machines, playing a video baseball and a space wars game, and driving a car under terrible conditions along a road that made sudden and unexpected turns. He had a feeling, when he finished that game a winner, that he could drive Leigh's car better thanshe could. Not that he'd ever get a chance. Once when he had begged her to let him try, she had snorted, "Are you out of your ever lovin' mind? I wouldn't let you drive my tricycle."

"Whaddaya mean! I'll bet you my next two months' allowance that I can drive better'n you and I've never even driven a car before!"

He hadn't meant to say so much. She had grounded him, made him walk for the next month. Then she'd started feeling sorry for him again. So he was more careful now about criticizing her driving. They both knew if he wanted to ride with her, he'd better keep his mouth shut.

Then, on the way home, she'd killed the thing right in the middle of the street. She had put on the brake, finally, after it had rolled half a block, and had tried to start it. From his cramped position in the back seat Ward could smell gas, and knew she had flooded the hell out of it. Vincent smelled the gas, too, and he wasn't as smart as Ward about keeping his mouth shut. He'd leaned over Leigh's shoulder and told her, "Stop goosing the damned thing, Leigh. It's flooded."

The really interesting thing was, Thad had sat there in the passenger's seat in front and hadn't said a word. Thad's own car was in the garage. Maybe he didn't know too much either. Ward had satisfied himself by muttering under his breath, and Jennie, who sat squeezed between him and the window, had said she'd get out and walk. She was only a couple of blocks from home anyway.

So they had all gotten out. After they, and some more kids who were walking home from a church meeting, had pushed the car into Brock's driveway and out of the way of his mom and dad's car, they'd started walking.

At first it had been fun, but now Ward was alone, and the air seemed colder. His ears felt as if they had been frosted on.

He walked backward a dozen steps, his hands in his pockets, trying to locate Leigh and Thad among the shadows along the street. And it began to seem as if Ward were alone. The houses were closed now, and most of them without lights. No traffic moved on the winding two-lane street, and the trees drooped naked limbs that made the widely spaced street lights look like huge prison windows, all bars and shadows and distant, pale lights. Ward shivered.

For two cents he'd run on home, and let Leigh come on in when she got ready. But he had started out with her, and maybe he'd ought to wait for her.

They moved into the light again at the corner, two figures walking so closely together they looked like a two-headed freak, with one head that turned to look one way and the other head turning to look the other way. Ward could hear the sound of their laughter as they ran together from one curb to the other and once more faded into shadows.

Ward turned and walked on, his hands deep in his pockets, his chin down into the collar of his jacket.

The chill seemed to start over his body even before he heard the terrible cry, that hoarse scream that was at first like something from the dark woods, like an owl maybe, or an animal that had been caught in a trap. A cry that seemed neither human nor animal nor owl, but a cry of need, of pain, and terrible, horrible fear. Ward could almost see the rusted, cruel trap snapping shut on the animal's leg.

And then the scream rose to a crescendo and Ward turned, himself and the world around him moving in slow motion, and he saw Thad stumbling out into the middle of the street where the light flowed like a pale river, and stumbling along half bent, that awful scream rising and blending with sobs in his throat. Then he fell to his knees, and as Ward watched, unable to make himself move faster than the slow motion that ruled existence now, he saw Thad twist himself about and get to his feet and run back the way he had come, his voice now hoarse and low and crying, but still sounding unreal.

Ward's feet were moving. Without realizing that he was running or exactly where he was going, Ward was running through the shadows of the sidewalk, back the way he had come. He could see from the corner of his eyes that Thad too was coming back, angling across the street toward the sidewalk. But he was half a block now behind Ward.

He almost fell over her. She was lying at the edge of the sidewalk, her head in the dark shadows of a hedge, the light coming through the tree on the corner putting those prison bars across her.

Ward saw her face, and it looked as if it were separated from her body by a wide, red gash.

"Leigh," Ward cried as he fell to his knees beside her. "My God, Leigh. Leigh!"

She didn't answer. Her body was twisted, her arms out as if she had just fallen back from her attacker, her head almost detached. Even in the dim and filtered light from the lamp across on the other corner, Ward could see the blood.

Then he felt something under his hands, and he picked it up.

He stared at it.

The thin, sharp blade was dark and wet, and he saw the blood dripping from it onto his hand. He turned it, the handle in his palm, and his heart stopped.

A pearl handle, white and almost luminous in the dark shadows and striped light. He recognized it immediately. Like a flash of lightning, several things came through to him. The knife that had killed Uncle Everett. The missing weapon that had killed Aunt Faith. The pearl-handled knife that had killed that guy across town. And now this one.

He recognized it, and the horror of his sister's death was only a part of his feelings. He had peeled apples with this knife, or one just like it.

Yet not once before had he made the connection.

He heard footsteps running along the street. More than one person was coming now. Voices began to call out, and lights came on in houses surrounding him. Thad was coming back, and Ward could see him over his shoulder, twenty feet away.

Ward wiped the knife on the grass within inches of Leigh's head, of her eyes staring wide at his actions, and then, with a grimace of horror and distaste and sorrow and frozen tears and screams smothered inside him, he slipped the knife into his jacket and zipped it up.

CHAPTER 22

"My baby! My baby! Oh God, no, not my baby! Not Leigh, not my baby! Daniel, no, no!"

Daniel held her, though his body shook so hard he could hear and feel the chatter of his teeth. The scene of his daughter, his firstborn, lying dead in the shadows of the hedge, would live with him forever. But he had to think of Maggie, he told himself sternly. He had to think of Maggie.

"Maggie sweetheart, please." He wanted to comfort her, but he didn't know how. He had wanted to comfort her when Everett and Faith were killed, but he hadn't known how then either. Now he felt as if he were coming apart, unable to stand up under his own strength. Yet he had to control himself. Maggie needed him. Ward and Sheena needed him.

He pulled Magret closer into his arms, clinging as much as being clung to. She was still wearing her nightgown and robe. She had run down the street barefoot, as had he, to the terrible scene of their daughter's death. He had brought her back, forcibly, and was using all his strength to restrain her on the bed.

He wished the doctor would hurry and come. He wished for an ambulance. His wishes turned to weeping curses, jumbled and contradictory words. *God help us, why the goddamned hell doesn't the ambulance get here, where is that cocksucker doctor, oh, God, help us.*

"No, no," Magret screamed, and reared up, her eyes wild and glistening with tears. Her hands like claws clutched his arms, and her voice lowered from its scream of anguish to a conspiratorial whisper. "Daniel, I've got to tell you—Daniel—I killed her. I, Daniel. I, my own baby, my own child. I've been wanting to tell you—I've got to tell you—Daniel—I walk in my sleep—I killed her—"

"That's crazy, Maggie," he cried, before he thought of the words he was using. He shook her. Was he going to lose her, too? "Maggie, you weren't even asleep." He shook her again, harder, and her teeth clicked together, chattering as if from an intense coldness. "Maggie, you were right here with me. You weren't even asleep! *Maggie, don't leave me."*

She was staring at him. "I don't understand," she said in a soft and bewildered voice. "I don't understand."

"Where's that goddamned doctor?"

At that moment their family doctor stepped through the door, his gray hair as disheveled as if he had come through a strong wind. He was tall and slightly stooped, and didn't have a very pleasant look on his face. An odd, stray thought drifted through Daniel's mind. This was the first time in the seventeen years Dr. Roust had been their family physician that he'd had to make a house call for them. Daniel knew him well, and occasionally had lunch with him.

"She needs to be in the hospital," Dr. Roust said as he picked up Magret's hand. "Haven't you been eating lately, Magret? What's the matter with you women that you starve yourselves to such thinness that when you do run into a problem you don't have anything for your body to feed on? Have you called an ambulance, Daniel?"

"She doesn't want to go to the hospital."

"Oh, no, no, no," Magret wept, collapsing back onto the pillow. "Please just let me stay in my home. Please. Oh, God, my baby, my baby ..."

WARD HAD LET the doctor in and had followed him back up the stairs. He stood in the hall, around the corner from the master bedroom. His mother's screams seemed to still thunder at him from every wall, every corner of the house although now he could barely hear her. The crying was terrible, and the pleading of his dad for help was even worse. What were they going to do, take her away?

He could see a reflection of the blue and red lights from the police cars down the street, coming against the window at the front of the stairs. Or maybe it was just his eyes, remembering, seeing them go on and on and on.

He heard a door open and saw Sheena was up again, her face looking like a mask, she was so scared. He went to her.

"Come back to bed, Sheena. Try to go to sleep."

"Are they going to take Mama to the hospital?"

"I don't know. But if they do, I'll be here. I'll be here with you. Go back to bed."

"I'm afraid, Ward."

"I'll sit with you. You go back to bed. It's real late, Sheena."

"What happened to Leigh, Ward?"

"Shhh. Go to sleep. Do you want your teddy bear?"

"Yes."

He picked it up off the floor where it had fallen when she got out of bed again. She had been getting out of bed and coming to him ever since he got home, and he hadn't known what to tell her. Tomorrow she'd have to know Leigh was dead, but tonight she must sleep.

"Don't leave me, Ward."

"Okay, I won't."

He sat on the side of her bed, leaning forward, his elbows on his knees, and stared at the open bedroom door. He could hear the sounds in the front bedroom, voices that now didn't include his mother's, but they were too subdued for him to grasp the words. Not that he was trying. The other thing was going through his mind as if it were a car on a circular track, just going around and around. He could feel the knife beneath his jacket, its handle poking into his stomach just above his belt, and it seemed he could feel the sharp blade against his chest.

He wanted to go to his dad and tell him, this is Mom's knife, Dad. She killed Leigh.

He remembered the words Thad had told the policemen who first arrived on the scene, hearing them over and over again as his thoughts went around in the endless circle.

"I thought it was an animal at first. It jumped out of the hedge right at Leigh's throat. Then I saw in a streak of light from the street lamp the knife and a hand. That's all I could see."

"What kind of hand—did you notice?"

"Small. A little kid's hand."

"Female? Small? Could it have been a small man's hand? Are you sure it couldn't have been a man?"

"It was dark. Except for that little streak of light. And pink—" Thad added, as if he had forgotten until now the color. "Pink, just a flash."

And Ward, remembering standing there, about ten feet away, understood that it was like a black hole on that part of the sidewalk. If the police lights hadn't been illuminating Leigh's body, still twisted as he had found her, he wouldn't have been able to see her at all.

It was then his mother came running up the sidewalk, her pink robe undulating behind her, flapping in a way like wings, loose from her shoulders down. She'd come silently, with Dad behind her, running, too, wearing only his pajamas. He didn't understand what they were doing here. Had a policeman already gone to the house? Ward had told them he was Leigh's brother and that the girl definitely was Leigh. But the death scene was too close to his house.

He wanted to call his dad to him and tell him about the knife.

It was Mama, wasn't it, Dad? A small hand. A flash of pink. Pink robe. Could have been my mother's hand, had to have been. Why?

Who else would have used the knives from the kitchen?

He saw that Sheena was asleep, and he slipped quietly from the room and went to the top of the stairs. The doctor was gone now, he thought. The room behind the closed door was quiet. Maybe the doctor had given his mother something to make her sleep.

He went downstairs. Just as he passed the big grandfather clock in the hall, it began a low-toned strike that caused his heart to leap and almost burst in his chest. Moving in the shadows of the unlighted foyer, he went to the front door and put his face against the glass strip at the side of the door. He could still see the lights of the police cars. Were they still there, long after the ambulance and the medical examiner had left?

He unlocked the door and opened it and looked out, but all he saw was the slant of the light beam from across the street, from the lamp on the corner. Fog made a kind of diaphanous sack around the lamp, and the air felt damp against his face.

He stepped back into the house and closed and bolted the door.

The only light came from the upstairs hall, and he waited only a moment before he turned on the downstairs hall light. The house was so quiet now, yet he felt as if it were alive around him, as if something terrible had come into this safe place, and it was no longer safe. Eyes looked at him from photographs as he went down the hall. Open doors into dark rooms had monsters in the darkness, and long arms with terrible claws reached silently out at him after he had passed by.

In the kitchen he turned on all the lights, even the one over the sink where he had watched his mother using the pearl-handled knives to chop salads and other vegetables. Where he himself had stood to peel apples.

He pulled open the drawer where the knives had always been kept, and stood several minutes staring at the place where the knife box once was, the box with red felt interior, and slots in it for six knives.

Now the box was gone, and other tools and knives and things had been pushed back to cover the empty place.

The knife that had killed Uncle Everett, the knife under his jacket, and the knife that had killed the man on the other side of town, they were all part of the set. Where were the other three?

He heard movement behind him, and whirled. A footstep, soft, as if on the rug of the eating area, between the kitchen and the family room, was like a scream in the back of his head, warning him, run, *run*.

But he was trapped. In one movement he slid the drawer shut and turned and stood with his hands behind him on the edge of the cabinet.

His dad stepped into view.

"Ward? What are you doing down here? I went to your room to see how you were."

"I—came down for—for a drink."

Daniel looked at him strangely for a moment, and Ward knew why. If he had wanted a drink, why didn't he do as he usually did at night and get it from the bathroom? It was the same water, after all, from the same source.

But Daniel went to the cabinet across the room and took out a glass, then went to the refrigerator.

"Milk," he said. "It comforts me, always has, since I was a little kid and my mother gave me warm milk when I was sick. Do you want some?"

"No."

Ward edged away from the knife drawer and stood in the middle of the room watching his dad pour half a glass of milk and put it into the microwave to heat.

"I don't think it's as good this way," Daniel said. "It should be heated on the stove, the way my mother did."

"Dad ... "

"Ummm?"

I HAVE TO TELL YOU, Dad, my mother is the killer. She must have slipped out of the house tonight and waited by the hedge down the street. She dropped the knife ... I think she's the one. Who else could it be?

DANIEL LOOKED AT WARD, waiting, and Ward opened his mouth again to tell him all his deepest and worst fears.

Who else had access to the knives?

Dad.

Dad did.

His dad could have done it.

The thought struck him like a kick in the stomach. The knife handle had warmed against his skin, and he was as conscious of it as if it had burned him.

Dad had access to the knives.

And Sheena. But of course that was ridiculous. It wouldn't have been Sheena.

He felt now as if the circle his thoughts had been running in was spinning him off into the dark reaches of space. He couldn't think. He felt dizzy and sick.

"What is it, son?"

"Nothing, Dad. I think I'll go up to bed."

Daniel nodded. "Sleep, if you can. Sleep helps. It puts distance between you and the day before and everything that happened then."

"They took her body away, didn't they, Dad?"

"Yes."

Daniel stood with his head down, a rim of milk white on his upper lip, and Ward sensed he wanted to be alone now.

"Is Mama asleep?"

Daniel nodded, and squeezed his eyes tightly shut. Ward saw teardrops edge out from beneath his short, fine lashes and rest on the pouches beneath his eyes. He wanted to reach out, but his dad was closed into his own world now.

Ward went quietly upstairs and into the bathroom. He unzipped his jacket and took out the knife. His velour pullover was stained where the knife had touched it, but the stain wasn't red, it was brown now, dried against his skin.

Ward held the knife in the sink, a few inches away from the running water. He was going to do something that he knew was wrong. He should leave it the way it was, and hand it over to the police just as it was, and tell them he had picked it up, just as Aunt Faith had picked up the knife that killed Uncle Everett. But he couldn't. Someone in his house had used the knife to kill his sister.

He washed it carefully, and then dried it and threw the towel into the hamper. He pulled off his sweater and rinsed the stain under cold, running water until it was no longer there. He left the knife lying on the cabinet a few inches from the edge of the sink. Its blade caught the light, and its handle gleamed white and gray, and the pearl looked real, luminous and jewel-like.

When he went to his room he took the knife with him, and slid it beneath his mattress.

COLLINS FED small hunks of cheese to Chief as he talked. Chief sat with his front feet between his master's feet. On the kitchen table at Collins's elbow was a plate of cheese and crackers. It was his breakfast, his lunch, and maybe his dinner. The night had been another long one, without sleep. And the day had moved on toward afternoon with nothing accomplished.

He had come home to eat and take a nap, but found he wasn't sleepy.

"Let's start at the beginning, Chief." He fed the dog another small chunk of cheese. "First, we get this call about a baby in the woods out west of town, on Highway 12, right? So we go out, and we meet Lorna and her two daughters, and Peggy Wasson and Sheena Treacle. Note especially Peggy Wasson and Sheena Treacle. So far, Wendy Parker and Lorna and Islan have escaped the—uh—" He fed the dog another bite of cheese and saw without really noticing the eager waiting of the dog.

"So," he said after a moment, "we look over the woods where the girls swore they saw the baby. It's our job—at that point, nobody else is in on it. Not even the County Rescue Team. Just you and me, Chief, and the girls. And we found nothing, right? So we figured if they had seen a baby, and we weren't sure if they had or not, its mother wasn't too far away and had taken it away."

Chief ate another bite of cheese, chewing with his mouth open.

"And then, the next day we get another call. The girls, Peggy and Wendy, have seen the baby again, only this time it's growing, has grown overnight to the size of a toddler. Right? Doesn't make sense, does it, only the girls are sure of what they saw. They even took clothes out to it. So we, you and I, go looking again. Nothing. The only answer could be that a family of homeless people had decided to make the woods their home. They had a baby and a two-year-old. The girls say it's the same child, but that's not possible, so we don't even put it in our report, right?"

Collins put a hunk of cheese on a cracker with a couple of dill pickle slices and ate it himself. Chief watched him closely.

"You and I feel a little uneasy about these people who have kids in those woods and no clothing. It sounds farfetched, this time of year, for even the most negligent parents not to dress their kids in something. But we have no doubt something is going on, right? So we look, and you find the grave."

Chief chewed cheese, and then Collins gave him a cracker. He took it. Collins offered him a dill slice, and Chief took it, then daintily dropped it on the floor.

"Anybody ever tell you you've got messy manners, boy?" Collins asked as he picked up the slice of pickle. "Anyway, back to the find. It seems that somebody buried a newborn infant there in the woods, without clothes ... without even a blanket ... there would have been a scrap of it left, a few threads, something. So it had to have been buried without. Twenty years, the coroner tells us, it's been in that grave. And that, you remember, was the end of the sightings of the small child. As if its only purpose was to guide us to the grave." Collins frowned and looked out the kitchen window into his backyard. Bare tree limbs hung down, and the top of a cedar tree had a bright red cardinal singing toward the sky.

"But that's not something to put in a report either, Chief. It doesn't make sense, so we write down that probably a family camped out there a few days and moved on. But do we really believe it? We don't know what to believe."

"And then, a few days later, we're called to a death scene. Everett Wasson has been murdered on his back step. His wife has picked up the murder weapon. It's a pearl-handled knife. Now, you and I, we look through the woods some, because we remember all the earlier stuff too well. There's a funny thing about the wounds on Everett's neck. Like if the knife hadn't been found, the coroner might have concluded that some kind of animal with long fangs had tried to rip out his jugular vein."

He fed Chief a cookie from the bag on the table. Chief's eyes gleamed, and he edged closer to Collins. He liked cheese, but cookies were a special treat. Born with a sweet tooth, like every creature, man, mouse, dog, or honeybee.

"There are animals that only eat the head, you know, Chief. Several of the predators, like the badger, will eat the head of a chicken and leave the body, if it gets into a chicken house. He'd eat the heads of a dozen chicks before he's stopped. Remember, we've been called to a few scenes out in the country."

Chief was almost between Collins's knees now. Collins gave him half of a chocolate chip cookie.

"And then, the very next night, Faith Wasson is killed just before she reaches her car, and Peggy is missing. We finally find her. And do you know what she told me? It was the child, the little girl, she said, only bigger. She's growing, Peggy said."

Collins pushed the cookies away.

"That's enough of that," he said. "It's cheese or nothing. That's all I've got on the table that's good for you."

Chief took the cheese. But it took him longer to chew and swallow. The last cookie half had gone down in one gulp.

"There was no murder weapon, but the wounds are the same as those of her husband. Then, the city police have a murder. Just like the others. A man fifteen miles away, and his only connection to the Wassons was a long time ago, through the church. That dates back about twenty years, Chief. Did you know that?"

Chief watched him solemnly.

"There's a murder weapon this time, and it's another of the pearl-handled knives."

Chief looked into Collins's eyes, and Collins looked back at the gentle brown eyes of the dog. The eyes that could turn almost red with fury and anger when he rushed to an attack.

"And then, Chief, last night the older Treacle daughter is murdered. Same kind of wounds, although not so many. This time a knife wound to her heart, too. Oh, yes, did I tell you that Clyde Judson had a knife wound in his back? As if he were running from something. But the girl was attacked from someone jumping out of the shrubbery. Her boyfriend got a glimpse of a knife, and a brief glimpse of pink, and a small hand, about the only things he remembers seeing. He ran, lucky for him, maybe. But the killer evidently took the knife away, again, as he did from the Faith Wasson death scene."

Chief waited, and finally Collins gave him another bite of cheese.

"What's the connection, Chief?"

Chief chewed.

"Who's doing these things?"

Chief watched his master.

"And why?"

Chief licked his lips.

"It's a good thing we don't have to write reports on everything, eh? They'd read like a story out of a crazy man's brain."

LORNA SAT in her most comfortable recliner with the television droning an afternoon soap opera. She had a blanket pulled up to her chin, but still she shivered now and then. Her head ached, her nose ran, and her throat hurt. This was the first day in three years she had taken advantage of sick leave.

She uncovered her hand enough to get hold of the remote control and change the channel to UHF and she hoped a nature show; but found a woodworking show instead. She had no interest in woodworking, and began to feel cranky and bored, and realized she was getting too warm. She pushed the blanket back. Her fever was breaking, she supposed, and good health was on its way again. At least to tell herself so made her feel the future wasn't as gloomy as it had seemed for a while.

She heard a car spin into the driveway and stop. A door slammed. It sounded like Islan's car, but the clock on the mantel claimed it was only twelve-thirty. Had it stopped again? No, it was Islan, home from school early. A feeling of dread came with the shadow of her daughter across the patio. What had happened to bring Islan home from school early? Had she gotten sick again?

"Hi, Mom," Islan said as she came into the family end of the kitchen and dropped into a chair, her arms hanging down on each side, her legs stretched. They looked long, encased closely in jeans as they were. "You feeling any better?"

"Are you sick?" Lorna asked in return.

"No." Islan sat up, drawing her long legs in, putting her elbows on her knees. "The most awful thing happened. School closed this afternoon."

Lorna waited, watching Islan's face go through stages of emotions as she talked.

"Do you know Leigh Treacle? Sheena's sister? I don't know if you ever saw her. Well, she was murdered last night. She and her boyfriend were walking home, just two blocks from her house, and someone jumped out at her through a hedge. Can you imagine? They didn't get the boy, just her."

Lorna listened, part of the time staring at the silent woodworker on the TV screen, part of the time looking at her daughter's pale face. School was going to be closed this afternoon in honor of the student who had been murdered, and it would open again tomorrow as usual. Lorna heard the speculations that were being passed around among the school students who had known Leigh, and among those who hadn't known her very well at all.

"It wasn't a rapist, she wasn't raped. The guy she was with, Thad Wilson, said it was a small person, wearing pink. That was all he could see. Of course, that's just hearsay, too. He certainly wasn't in school this morning."

Islan got up and left the room, and Lorna stared at the TV screen. She had seen Leigh a few times, and didn't know her as well as she knew Sheena, but it was almost like losing a relative. Her heart went out to Magret, and to Daniel.

The woodworking show changed to something for children, and Lorna let it keep running, its figures moving in silence, the sound muted.

Islan came back into the room and sat on the couch where Lorna would have had to turn to see her face.

"Mom, I want to talk to you about something very important to me."

Lorna nodded. "Sure. What?" She longed to reach over and touch Islan to assure herself that she was really there. She felt almost guilty for the good fortune of having her daughter healthy and alive.

"I'm leaving, Mom."

At first Lorna couldn't absorb the words. Leaving? Going to the store, to the mall? On a date? Leaving? Yet she knew in her heart, as a strange and lonely coldness settled in her, that it meant far more than that. "What did you say, Islan?"

"I'm leaving. I've already talked to Dad and to Grandma and Grandpa, and they want me to come up. Dad's wife said I was welcome, but I think I'd live with Grandma and Grandpa. I want to go up there to finish school."

"Islan!" Lorna twisted sideways in her chair and reached toward her daughter, but Islan was just far enough away to avoid her touch. Islan's eyes didn't meet hers.

"Mom, I've really been thinking about this for a long time. Since I was there two years ago, remember? And spent two months during the summer? Well, I had a great time, and met some kids I like and everything. And I love those distant horizons and the long grain fields, I really do. It's sort of in my blood, Mom. After all, I lived there until I was eight, remember? Didn't you sort of know that I'd want to go back someday?"

"But Islan, this is your senior year. You don't want to leave until you graduate. What about your friends here?"

Islan kept her eyes down. Her hands picked at her fingernails. "That's not important."

"Has this—this death of Leigh scared you?"

"For myself? No."

Lorna leaned back in her chair and stared again at the TV. A deep sadness had control of her now, as if she had been sucked into a black hole from which all light had gone. She had known that someday Islan wouldn't be living with her, but she hadn't thought she'd move permanently back to North Dakota.

"Maybe I should sell the house and move, too, take both of you away from these woods, from whatever is happening here. It seems to be spreading, like a horrible plague of some kind."

"No, of course you shouldn't move. I mean, you don't want to leave this area. You like it here, and so does Wendy."

"But you don't."

"It's not that. I'll always come back to see you, Mom." She suddenly was on her knees beside Lorna's chair, her head in Lorna's lap. Tears ran from under her long, golden-brown lashes and across the arch of the high cheekbone. Lorna wiped them away with her fingers and left her hand on the cheek, her heart aching with love for this first child, and with the loss that was coming.

"Islan, please reconsider. I know you're almost eighteen, and you certainly have the right to choose. And you do get to see your dad whenever you have time away from school. You can go up for Thanksgiving, if you want, and again for Christmas, but please finish your senior year here."

"Mom, no. I've already told them I'm coming." Silence reigned for a few minutes. The wind made a soft crying sound in the pine tree in the backyard, and Lorna saw the limbs moving with the force of a sudden wind.

"When are you going then," Lorna finally asked.

"As soon as I can."

"You're not yet eighteen, Islan," Lorna said, not wishing to take this route, but feeling that she had to. "That's six weeks away. Why don't you at least compromise with me and stay until the end of school term?" Islan said nothing for a moment. Her tears had stopped flowing, although she hadn't moved. One of her hands held Lorna's against her cheek.

"I'll tell you what, Mom. I'll stay until semester end. Would that do?"

Lorna started to say no. Nothing would do. She didn't want her child moving a thousand miles away. But then she thought of Magret Treacle, and her daughter, Leigh, and suddenly the thousand miles seemed as nothing.

She patted Islan's cheek.

"That will do," she said softly.

ISLAN STOOD in her bedroom looking out the window. She had thought of trying to pack a few things, some of the trinkets she would like to take, but when she picked up the little bell her mother had given her as a surprise gift once, or the ceramic kitten that was a birthday present from Wendy, she put them down again in their little spots.

Places from which she could never move them.

Most of the stuff she had told her mother was not true. She hadn't been planning to leave, not until just recently. And although the long grain fields were beautiful in their featureless way, they weren't as close to her heart as the hills and trees of Missouri. This was her home. Yet she had enjoyed her two-month vacation on the farm, and she had met kids she liked, and with whom she still corresponded. And she had talked to her dad and stepmother and grandparents, and they had told her she could come and stay anytime she wanted to. But she didn't want to go live with her dad and stepmother and the four younger kids that seemed more like cousins than brothers and sister. All of them ranged from Wendy's age on down to the baby, and she had wondered about that. Was there more to the divorce than Mom had told her? How was it her dad had two daughters Wendy's age, if something hadn't been going on before Mom divorced him? But Mom had never offered any disparaging remarks about her dad, and she appreciated that. She had grown up thinking him a kind of Norse God, and hadn't noticed that his and her stepmother's oldest daughter, who looked so much like Thornton that she couldn't possibly be anyone else's daughter, was only two months younger than Wendy.

But that had nothing to do with her decision to leave.

She had seen the way Collins looked at Lorna, and the half-embarrassed way Lorna tried to avoid noticing. And she knew as long as she stayed here, Lorna would not even go out with Collins.

Mom needed someone other than herself and Wendy. Even Wendy would grow up and leave to live her own life. Mom needed to be forced into accepting other people into her life, and especially someone like Collins, who so obviously wanted to be in her life.

And there were other factors. A change that Islan felt she needed. A response to this growing restlessness that was in her. The boys she had dated until recently now looked so immature. And she had fallen too fast for Collins, and that was something she had to move away from.

She had learned over her few weeks of knowing him that he wasn't for her, he was for her mom. But Mom would never accept him as long as she was around because she had opened her big mouth too soon.

It was all so confusing.

Sometimes she was afraid of leaving them here, alone, so close to the place where two murders had occurred, but then she told herself it had nothing to do with them. Whatever it was, it was not part of their lives. And yet, she wasn't sure.

The security she had felt in her life here a month ago was now gone.

CHAPTER 23

Ward walked about in the backyard. The day was warmer than yesterday or the day before, for a week of days maybe, he couldn't remember. He felt the sun warm on his head and on his shoulders as he walked aimlessly in the backyard, going from the fountain that was now dry to the bird feeder where birds flew away at his approach. He walked with his thumbs in his back pockets.

Some people had come earlier and left things to eat. People from church. But his mother hadn't come out of her room, not today, or yesterday. And Sheena had come out only to eat part of a bowl of cereal at breakfast time, looked over by their dad. Later on, relatives would be coming, Dad had told him. Daniel had asked him if he wanted to go in and say something to his mother, but Ward held back. And finally Daniel patted his shoulder and said, "Well, maybe tomorrow. She's very—umm—sedated. The doctor wanted her to go to the hospital for a day or two, but she didn't want to. Right now she's in denial. It didn't happen, she says."

Ward walked alone, the thoughts that had kept him awake most of the past nights going through his mind like the endless circle.

It kept going back to the woods, no matter how hard he tried to dismiss that part. There was something about the woods. He could feel it. First, the kids had seen something out there. A baby. It had been kind of a joke when the other two kids, without Sheena, had seen a bigger baby, who still needed clothes. He and his friends had had a good time with that one. For a while. Then there was something really dampening about the little grave. The fun had ended.

His mother.

It all had something to do with his mother.

It was like it was coming straight toward her.

First Uncle Everett was murdered, then Aunt Faith. Then a stranger, a man he'd never heard of, but who was connected because he'd been killed with a knife that belonged to Ward's mother. Then Leigh. And Thad said it was a small hand holding the knife, and he'd caught a flash of pink. So, whoever it was must have been wearing pink.

His mother wore pink a lot. And her hands were small.

And the knife belonged to her.

He found himself standing beside the bicycle rack. Leigh's bike was there, and Sheena's, and Mom's and Dad's, and his own.

It was about three miles out to Uncle Everett's house.

Nobody would miss him.

He pulled the bike out of the rack and pushed it to the gate. He closed and latched the gate behind him and got onto the bike.

He coasted down the driveway almost to the end before he began to pump.

The air was sharp and cool in his face, sweeping his hair back. He rode hard, keeping to the far right side of the street, moving into traffic and then out of it again as the road, past the woods and toward the hills, lost its traffic to the downtown streets and westward highways.

He came alone into the shadowed trees that leaned over the two-lane road northwest out of town. In the shade the day seemed like winter, the sun left behind in another world, another season.

When he reached the driveway to Uncle Everett's house, he got off his bike and stood looking at the desolate, two-story farmhouse tucked back into the cleared spot in the tall trees. It looked darker and more isolated than it ever had before, as if death had brought the trees closer to the house.

He left his bike at the side of the driveway, hidden from the road by the ditch and tall weeds that leaned above it.

He heard no sound but his own steps through the drifts of brown leaves. He stopped, listened, and looked at the windows of the house.

It had started here. The murders.

Why?

He walked around the house and tried both the back door and the front. Tried them, even though he knew they would be locked. This house belonged to Peggy now, but he had a feeling she would never be back.

On the back steps and porch he saw the dark stains where his uncle had been killed, and in the brown grass at the corner of the house, where the car had stood, where no grass grew, and where there were permanent tire tracks, he thought he could still see a darker soil where Aunt Faith's blood had soaked in.

He went over to the woodpile, and stood a moment with his hand on the cold and rusting metal of the swing set. He heard a weird squeak, and realized the swing had moved. He jerked his hand away.

Then he saw the path into the woods.

It was almost invisible, narrow and bare, like a deer path to a watering hole.

He went toward it.

This was the path the girls had walked every day for two or three years. Sheena had told him about it. Wendy and Peggy, going back and forth to each other's house. He had envied them these woods. How much fun, he'd thought when he heard about it. All these big acres of woods to play in. Trees to climb, squirrels and things to watch. Games to play. How much fun he and his friends would have had in here.

But now there was a spooky feeling as he entered the path. He hesitated and looked ahead, and saw the little path meandering, turning, disappearing. The trees looked big, like giants. The silence was overwhelming.

But in here, somewhere, was a grave.

In here, somewhere, was the answer.

He could feel it.

He walked softly along the path, seeing that at times it was hard to follow. The grave had been away from the path, and in the edge of a small ravine. He had heard that. Maybe he had even read it in the paper, because he had read about the baby skeleton. It had fascinated him. He had wondered about it for days, and had talked about it until his mother made him stop. Who would take their little tiny baby out in the woods and bury it, he had wondered aloud. What kind of monsters did a thing like that? And a girl baby, too, they thought, by its skeleton, though he wondered how they could tell. Somehow, it seemed even worse to bury a girl baby like that, because girls were weaker. But he guessed tiny boy babies were, too. They all needed protection. The weakest of the animals, he had learned in Biology. Very few other animals were as weak at birth as human babies, and none needed care longer.

Of course all little furry creatures were born helpless and with their eyes closed. Some were born without fur even. You couldn't get much more helpless than that.

But humans ... humans were the only ones who would bury a baby alive.

He turned right off the path and went through a leafy floor, pausing at the sound of his own movements through the leaves, feeling as if someone were watching him.

He walked on, trying to pick ground less cluttered with leaves, less obstructed by vines and ferns still green, looking for a ditch in the woods down which water ran when it rained. The ditch would be fairly wide and not very deep, he had heard, and the grave was there, on its edge, uncovered by past rainstorms.

He stopped.

Behind him leaves rustled, stopping a moment later, as if someone stalked him.

He could feel the stare of the eyes on the back of his head.

He turned slowly, almost afraid to move, every nerve in his body changing to ice.

It was a little girl, standing about twenty feet away.

She was Sheena's age, with short, curly dark brown hair.

And she was wearing a pink party dress.

It was her eyes that turned his soul to terror.

They were cold and flat and filled with the reflection of the woods, the trunks of the trees like black sentries, and even with the distance he could see himself there, tiny and helpless—her prey.

She was coming toward him.

THE HOUSE WAS TOO QUIET. The television only made a racket and annoyed Lorna more than it entertained her, and with a sigh she turned it off. She should have gone to work today, she told herself as she got up from her chair and went toward the patio doors. But her head still ached, and her nose needed too much attention, and she was beginning to cough. Also, she didn't feel like seeing anyone. She needed time to herself now to get used to the idea of losing Islan. Islan had assured her she wasn't losing anyone, that she'd be back to see her. Yes, Lorna understood that. Once a year, maybe, for a few days. And Islan didn't think that was losing her?

Of course she knew she'd have to let Islan go on to her own life. She had always known that. But couldn't Islan live her own life in the same town with her mother and sister?

There was no way to make herself feel better. Her firstborn would be leaving at the end of the semester, and she had to adjust to living without her.

She just wanted to be alone, away from her coworkers, to feel the creeping loneliness in her heart and let it take its toll so that it would leave her in less pain. By and by. It was grieving, a necessary condition of losing someone.

And then again she thought of Magret Treacle.

Night before last she had lost her firstborn daughter forever. She wasn't just going away to live in another state. She would not be able to come home once a year, a healthy, normal young woman who would one day bring her babies down for Grandma to see and to love.

Lorna opened the patio doors and went outside. Birds around the feeder at the edge of the patio flew at her approach. They had scattered seed all over the cement floor of the patio and into the lawn. The feeder was empty.

Lorna went back to the kitchen for the bag of bird seed and refilled the feeder.

"It's not even winter yet," she said, "and you're eating me out of house and home and birdseed. Go eat some blue cedar berries."

Most of them seemed to be sparrows, but what the heck, the sparrows needed to eat, too. A few were crowned sparrows, with the black and white striped heads. Two cardinals brightened the top of a shrub a few yards away.

A bluejay flew into the big tree in the backyard.

It was so quiet, and the weather cloudy but mild, so that Lorna didn't feel uncomfortable in her sweater. The air had a soft touch against her face, slightly damp.

She was going back into the house when she stopped, listening.

There had been a sound from the woods behind the house, but she wasn't sure what it was. The cry of a bird? An animal?

For just a moment she had thought it was a scream.

. . .

WARD PULLED HIMSELF UP, breath like fire in his lungs. He had fallen, and he had cried out when he fell, without meaning to. The girl might have heard him, and would now know where he was. He had been running from her for so long he trembled in every muscle in his body. He couldn't run much farther.

He held on to the bark of the big tree, pressed against it, feeling bits of it crumble damply against his cheek. He was afraid to look around it, for fear he would see her.

He had been trying to find the road, to find his bicycle so he could escape whatever she was. But the forest seemed endless, and he didn't know where he was.

He listened.

He heard the sound of leaves, moving against one another, a soft sound almost felt, rather than heard. And he heard the harshness of his breath, and in his ears the pounding of his heart. Overhead the heavy limbs of the trees intertwined like something in a nightmare, and the huge trunks of big trees, and slender saplings of younger ones went on forever, as if there were no end to this dark world.

And somewhere here was a girl dressed in a pink party dress that was stained dark in front, a swift and almost silent girl, like an apparition, like something from hell.

... and her face ...

... looked familiar ...

But Ward could not think, not think of anything but escape—finding the road and running away.

He knew he couldn't stay here. He had to move, to take a chance. He tried to remember his Boy Scout training. North side of trees ... moss ... but not here, not this far south. Moss sometimes grew on all sides. He tried to remember other training. The only one he could remember—*don't panic*—was the one he was unable to control.

But he couldn't just stay here, or she would find him.

He moved, and heard the rattle of leaves beneath his feet, and shuddered at the sound. He took another step.

She was standing just a few feet away, those strange, mirroring eyes finding him.

He screamed, all the terror in his soul pouring out.

LORNA HAD STARTED to close the patio doors behind her when she heard the cry. It shattered the stillness and wavered in the air, its echo in her heart. The cry of death. She had heard it before from a dog that was dying of bullet wounds. He had lifted his head and howled in terror and pain and something else—that cry to infinity. *Why? Why?*

She was running. The cry in the woods might have been from an animal, but it didn't matter, it was in mortal danger, and she would help if she could. She went with nothing but her hands, not thinking of anything but answering the scream.

She fumbled at the back gate, trying to get it open. Beyond her was a furious scrambling in the woods, something running through brush and leaves, and then falling. She heard the rolling and scuffling sound of bodies, just out of sight somewhere beyond the short growth of vegetation that grew at the edge of the forest. Then came the running again.

At first, as she finally burst through the gate, the running was toward her, then it swerved and was going away.

She called out, just a cry of her own, with no spoken syllable as she ran along the path into the woods.

She heard the scream again, lower, hoarser, and recognized it as human.

Through the shadows of the trees she saw movement, off to her right, in an area of heavy growth, of vines reaching thick trunks of their own up into the limbs of the trees, of ferns growing waist high. She saw a head bobbing there, lifting and falling, and she saw something pink, a brilliant spot of color in the drab darkness of the woods.

She cried out again and whoever it was turned and came toward her. She saw him fall again, and the one dressed in pink went down upon him. The scream that came then was gurgled and low.

Lorna pushed her way through vines and ferns, and found herself facing an area less cluttered. On the ground was a boy, blood running down the front of his shirt where his jacket opened. He was crawling, lifting himself up, reaching one hand out toward her. His neck looked as if it had been slashed.

There was a darting movement of pink, and then for just a moment, for one indelible passage of a few seconds, the girl stood facing Lorna.

They stared at each other, the girl in pink, and Lorna.

Then Lorna ran forward, going to the boy. She knelt at his side, and felt his arms go around her neck. He was sobbing against her, and she held him, a boy no more than ten or eleven years old, no older than the girl in pink who had been attacking him.

When Lorna looked up again, the girl was gone.

Lorna picked up the boy, and hardly feeling his weight at all, half carried him back to her house, through a gate she had left open, and a door she had left open.

She put him down on the sofa in the family room and went back to close the doors. Her hands shook as if she had no control, and her legs felt weak and useless.

The boy was silent now though he, too, trembled. She knew he was alive only by the violent trembling of his body.

She quickly telephoned 911, gave brief instructions, then she went to see about the boy.

He opened his eyes when she looked at his neck, and suddenly she knew who he was.

"Ward Treacle? Sheena's brother?"

He barely nodded, wincing at the movement. Fresh blood oozed from the wounds on his neck.

He looked as if claws had raked his jaw and neck, but the wounds were hardly more than skin deep, not as bad as she had feared. She reached for a tissue and dabbed lightly at the blood that had run down onto his collar. It was clotting on the wounds now.

"It's going to be sore, but you're all right. What—who—?"

Then suddenly she knew, and the shock of that recognition threw a wall of blackness between her and the real world. It couldn't be, and yet it was, it had been. Magret—Magret Treacle—as a young girl—the Magret she had known years ago.

The pink dress—the Easter dress—everything as it had been then—as Magret had been then—except for the eyes.

That terrible change in the eyes, those reflecting eyes.

Magret.

It was, yet how could it be?

Magret. This boy's mother.

The next thing she was aware of was the sound of a siren as the ambulance drew near.

She heard the boy trying to talk. He cleared his throat, as if the pain were deeper, far deeper than the actual wounds.

"Don't tell," he pleaded, his brown eyes asking even more than his words.

Lorna understood.

CHAPTER 24

"I'M SORRY," Dr. Roust said, his face drawn and tired and bewildered. He stood at the door to the room where Ward had been taken, guarding Ward from his own family. "He just doesn't want to see anyone but Sheena. I think at this point we'd better let him have his way."

Magret was quiet. It was as if she had lost all contact with the world, Daniel thought. No, it was deeper than that. It was as if her grief at Leigh's death had hurt her so much there was no room for any more hurt. When he had gone to tell her about Ward, she had only stared at him. Yet she had wanted to come, to be here, to be with him.

"It's his mother's right," Daniel tried to explain, trying to control the fury that was growing in him. What in the goddamned hell was going on? What was happening to his family?

Dr. Roust shook his head. "Just take my word for it that he's all right. The wounds were not terribly serious. But he does not want to see anyone but his sister."

Daniel had left Sheena downstairs, as always. The hospital policy was always in effect in his mind. No one under the age of twelve to be allowed beyond the first floor.

Daniel wiped his hand across his nose and cheek, and felt the looseness of his jaw.

"Well, what happened to him?"

"He says he fell and scratched his neck on some limbs in the woods."

"Well, what the frigging hell was he doing out in the woods?"

Daniel saw a nurse look at him as she went by and knew he had raised his voice too much. But the anger boiled in him, seeking release. He was lucky he hadn't used the words that had bubbled in his throat. The anger was borne of fear, he was realizing, and the awful helplessness he was beginning to feel lately. But what had his son been doing out at the house where Everett and Faith had so recently been murdered? What?

The doctor said, "I suggest that we humor him, at least for now. Why don't you bring Sheena up and let her be with him for a while?"

LORNA CALLED the Sheriff's Department for the third time. This time she was determined to get in touch with Collins. The other two times she had simply asked if he was there, and had received no for an answer. She had been reluctant to leave her name.

The boy's request was not to tell, she reminded herself each time, feeling guilty that she was going to tell after all. And she had hung up the phone because of her promise to him. Yet it hadn't really been a promise. She hadn't said she'd never tell, she had only nodded her head. Perhaps in time he would understand that she had to tell.

For his sake.

For ...

Lord, she didn't know. What was it out there? It was in the woods, just beyond her open gate, and it knew where she lived. It knew where she had taken the boy.

It?

She.

The same female voice answered the call to the Sheriff's Department, and this time Lorna said, "Would you please have Sergeant Stoddard get in touch with Lorna Parker as soon as he can? It's urgent."

"I can try to contact him."

"I wish you would, please. Tell him—" She had started to say tell him it has to do with the child in the woods, but changed her mind and repeated, "Tell him it's urgent. I'm at home."

"Yes, ma'am. I'll do what I can."

SHEENA JUMPED at the touch on her shoulder. She had been sitting in the plastic chair in the big lounge for so long that she had put her chin on the back of the chair and drawn her knees up into the seat, trying to get more comfortable. She had been staring out the glass front of the hospital, watching people going up and down the wide series of steps, and counting steps as they climbed or descended. She knew there were twenty steps in all, and five steps between each flat landing area that took ten steps to cross. Counting had kept her mind off everything else.

She turned to look up at her mother and dad.

Daniel leaned over her, but her mother sat down in another of the plastic chairs across from Sheena. It was her mother's turn to count, Sheena thought, as she straightened her legs and stood up.

"Ward wants to see you," Daniel said softly, close to her ear.

Sheena tried not to feel the jolt of fear. It had been better to feel as if she were surrounded by an ice wall, and everything was happening on the other side of the wall.

"Is he going to die, too?" she cried before she remembered that her dad had told her to say nothing about death in front of her mother.

"No, he's—almost fine. Almost. He just wants to see you."

She walked beside her daddy, her hand in his. They went into a wide corridor and stopped in front of the elevator doors. Some people went past while others gathered with them to go into the elevator. Sheena wanted to ask what had happened to Ward, but there were too many people around. All she knew was her dad had called her out of her room and had brought her to the hospital because her brother had been hurt. She had ridden in the back seat of the car as her dad drove faster than she had ever ridden before, with her parents in the front saying nothing.

They got out of the elevator, but still there were too many people around. Daniel's hand felt slick and sweaty, and once her own hand almost slid away, then he changed his grasp and took hold of her wrist.

Then they were at a wide door where a smiling nurse stopped her dad from entering as she came out and let Sheena go in.

Sheena stared at the bed. It was raised at the end, and Ward sat in it leaning back against pillows. His neck was bandaged on one side, but he looked almost like he always did. Relief burst in her, melting for a moment the ice wall around her. She ran to him.

"Ward—what happened?"

He didn't look as if he was really glad to see her. He didn't smile. He took hold of her hands and leaned toward her, but his eyes looked toward the door in a furtive manner, as if he was afraid someone there would hear him. Or someone he was afraid of would enter.

"Sheena, listen. I went out to the woods—"

"What woods?" she cried, wanting to hear faster than he could talk, wanting desperately to help him, because each time he uttered a word, he acted as if it hurt him. "The woods where—where—?" She thought of the little naked baby she had seen in the woods, lying beneath the ferns, and she remembered the feeling of horror at seeing it open its mouth—and the teeth—those horrible teeth—like shark's teeth, like razors, like needles, rows and rows, and suddenly she understood, and as she felt her eyes grow wide, she listened, unable to say any more.

"Listen—Sheena—you've got—to get out—don't stay alone—with Mama. Do you understand?"

She stared at him, mouth open, tongue drying and thickening. She had understood part of it, the part about the scratches on his neck—

"She—she—it was the teeth—" she whispered.

He nodded.

But she didn't understand the other part. The part about Mama.

"Hear me," he pleaded. "Sheena—make Dad—take you away from Mama. It's Mama—somehow—I don't know how—"

Sheena stared at him, not understanding the part about their mother.

Ward leaned closer to her.

"Don't—be alone—with—Mama."

The door opened. It gave a soft swish, and the air pulled at Sheena. She turned her face toward the door and saw the nurse, and in front of her Dad was coming smiling toward the bed.

Ward leaned back onto the pillows. The nurse touched Sheena's shoulder and Sheena followed her out of the room.

"Is it my turn now?" Daniel asked, feeling the back of Ward's hand, finding comfort in the warmth, the being of his son. He wished there were a way to gather these two remaining children up into his skin and hold them forever, where they would be safe.

Ward nodded. He swallowed.

"Does your neck hurt much?" Daniel asked, touching a finger to the undamaged skin at the edge of the big bandage.

"No, not much now. Just—inside."

Daniel licked his dry lips and tried to smile again, but gave it up. "I guess it wasn't such a bad wound, eh? What happened?"

"Dad—" Ward said, looking up at him with pleading in his eyes. Daniel had never been able to turn away from those brown eyes when they looked at him that way. Even when the boy had needed a bit of punishment or at least discipline, he hadn't been able to resist those eyes.

"I'm here, son."

"Dad—take Sheena somewhere—else. Please."

His voice was so low Daniel had to lean closer. But he stiffened in surprise and looked over his shoulder at the door. Sheena was no longer in the room.

"What do you mean?"

"Out—of the house—Dad. Please. She's—not safe there."

Daniel frowned. In one part of his mind he named off relatives where Sheena might be taken, a swift rundown of names and faces, uncles, aunts, even a few friends, but it was only a list discarded the moment it was thought of. Sheena taken away from home?

"Of course she's safe at home, Ward. I'll see to it that she is. I'll make sure all the windows and doors are locked. I'll have a security system put in, today. She'll be safe."

"No, no." Ward's fingers dug into his wrist. "You—don't understand, Dad. It's Mama. *Mama.*" He whispered the name, tears in his eyes.

"Don't worry, don't worry," Daniel assured him, glancing quickly to see if the nurse were near. His son wasn't as well as they had claimed. "Don't you worry, I'll see that Mama is safe, too."

"No." Ward reared up and clutched Daniel's arm. "It's her—she'll hurt Sheena, don't you see?" He fell back, his head turned away.

Delirious, that's what he was. The poor kid. Too much for him. How did a person ever know how a child was going to be affected? He had seen Leigh after her death, and it had been too much.

Daniel touched Ward's turned cheek, and looked again for signs of doctor or nurse.

"It's going to be all right, Ward, I promise."

But as Daniel moved toward the door to find help, he had a feeling of black hopelessness, of despair such as he had never known.

SHEENA SAT in the back seat of the car listening to the low voice of her dad. The car changed lanes, passing other cars. Shop windows beyond the sidewalk passed so quickly it was like the movie game she and Ward had played, making their own pictures and drawing them through a square cut in a cardboard, and sometimes drawing them too fast to see. She and

Leigh had never played games, but the house, the whole world, seemed strangely lost and empty without Leigh in it.

"They gave him something," her daddy was saying to her mother. "The poor boy must have had some fever. He was ranting crazy things."

Her mother didn't ask what kind of crazy things.

Sheena looked at the back of her mother's head, at the dark hair curled and hanging just to her collar. And she remembered Ward's last words to her.

Don't be alone with Mama.

She was afraid to go home, to the house that looked big and dark on its hill as the car slowed and climbed the driveway. She sat still, until her dad had parked in the driveway near the side door and went around to open Magret's door.

Sheena got out and followed. Her dad was going into the house with them.

It would be all right because her dad was here, too.

LORNA WAS STANDING at the double windows in the family room, facing the driveway, when the sheriff's car came unexpectedly into sight and parked. With a low cry of thanksgiving she ran to the patio doors and around the corner of the house to the gate. She hadn't known Collins was coming, that he had even been reached.

He was in uniform, and Chief sat in the back seat, alert, watching her, and watching his master.

She took his arm, pulling him toward the house. "I have to talk to you. I know you're going to think—I don't want to know what you're going to think. It's that—it's impossible."

"You're all right?"

"I'm fine, except for a cold. I took a couple of days of sick leave. That was why I happened to be home when I heard the boy screaming—but you don't know about that, do you?"

"No. What boy?"

"The police weren't called. The boy, Ward Treacle, asked me not to call the police or even to tell. But I have to break my word to him, Collins, for his sake, for Sheena's sake, and maybe for many others. Even my own children and myself. I don't pretend to understand what's going on, but I saw this with my own eyes, and I was not hallucinating as it's been said the little girls were when they saw the baby in the woods."

"I think we'd better go in and talk about this," Collins said, so calm she felt amazed at his control. His hand was firm against her back. "Coffee, or tea, or milk first, to calm you. I think you've had a harrowing day. Why didn't you call me earlier?"

She almost laughed, a hysterical bleating that she stopped as soon as it began. "You think I haven't tried? Twice, three times maybe. It seemed like a dozen times."

"I'm sorry. I came as soon as I got the message."

He presented an odd figure in her kitchen, looking for things in the cupboards, and then making coffee while she sat at the bar between the kitchen and small dining room.

"I have a picture," she told him, and laid it on the counter facing him. "First, let me give you the bare background of this morning. I heard the screaming, and I ran into the woods. I saw the boy, and he was being attacked by this girl. I fully believe she would have killed him if I hadn't interfered."

She put her finger on the picture of one little girl out of a group of twenty or thirty, all young people from the ages of a baby sitting on the ground to a tall young man about twenty at the back of the group. They were dressed in their best, from white gloves, in some cases, to cute little Easter hats.

"Magret Treacle," Lorna told him as he looked closely at the girl in the pink dress. She had short, curly dark brown hair, and her face was round and unsmiling.

Collins stared at the picture, saying nothing.

"That's an Easter grouping, the young people at the church. That was the year I went there, and that's how I happen to have this picture. It was taken by a photographer. I'm standing right beside Magret. It was this girl, in the woods."

Collins had leaned his elbows on each side of the five-by-seven photograph. He stared at the photo for several long moments. Without speaking he slowly raised his head and looked at Lorna.

Sheena wandered about in her room. Her lights were on, all of them, the ceiling light, the light by the bed, the one on the dresser, and the one on the desk, but still it seemed dark in her room.

It felt cold, too, and she hadn't taken off her coat. Usually she left her coat in the closet downstairs when she came into the house, but today she kept it on, and no one noticed.

She felt her isolation. She could feel that Leigh's room, across the hall, was closed and empty. And Ward's room, by Leigh's, was empty. The upstairs was so quiet.

She got two of her Barbie dolls and sat on the floor, and undressed one and looked through her wardrobe for something different to dress up in, but then she sat, her hands limp, the doll between her knees, undressed.

She thought of the baby in the woods, and then the growing child Wendy and Peggy had seen the next day. They told her about it, both of them talking at the same time, the next day at school.

"It was the same baby, I know it was," Wendy said, with Peggy saying almost the same thing. "It was just bigger, and its hair was thicker and darker, but it had the same mole on its shoulder, and it was like we could almost see it growing right there, wasn't it, Peggy?" And they had all been afraid then, all three of them.

Mama had a mole on her shoulder.

Peggy and Wendy didn't know that, but Sheena had seen it, at the beach, in the pool, when Mama wore her bathing suit.

Don't be alone with Mama ...

Ward's voice came again to her, as if he had whispered into her ear.

But it's all right, she thought. Daddy is here.

She dressed the doll. She didn't like seeing it without clothes. It kept reminding her of the person growing in the woods.

Then a sound in the driveway took her mind from the doll.

She jumped up and ran to the window, her hands gripping the window sill as she pressed her face to the glass.

Her daddy ... was driving away ... turning the car around in the wide place in the driveway by the garages and never once looking up at her.

MAGRET WEARILY CLIMBED THE STAIRS. On the landing she paused and listened. On the street below was a soft murmur of a car driving by, the sound deadened by the distance from the street. It didn't stop the feeling of isolation, of a world made of silence. A silence that might never again be broken. Would the sound of happy children's voices ever fill these halls again?

She looked down the hall toward the children's rooms. Sheena was such a quiet little girl, even more so lately. Magret started toward her room, but stopped again.

She was so tired. The medication, she supposed, kept her feeling a little numb, and too weary. But she would have gone insane without it. She would never, as long as she lived, be able to shut out the sight of her Leigh on the cold sidewalk, head thrown back, the bloody tissue of her throat exposed.

But she hadn't killed Leigh. Daniel had made her believe that. She hadn't killed Leigh, and she hadn't hurt Ward. She wouldn't have been able to stand knowing she had, and Daniel had saved her again, just as he always had.

She was innocent. She was not a murderer.

She was not the one who had brutally murdered Uncle Everett, or Aunt Faith, or Clyde. She had been afraid, but now she knew, it was not she who had killed.

Who?

The question was a whisper in the depths of her mind.

The knives, the whisper said, its breath cold and bitter in her brain. The knives. Only you knew where they were buried.

Only you.

Magret turned away.

She was so tired. So weary.

She went into her room and took off her jacket and dropped it on the low blanket chest at the foot of the bed. The door to her dressing room stood open, and its full-length mirror reflected her as she moved toward it.

She stopped, and put her hand to her hair, staring at her face, thinner, older. So much older in just a few days. The white in her hair around her ears had not been put there artificially.

At first she was almost unaware that someone else had entered the room and stood behind her, halfway between the mirror and the bedroom door.

Pink. The color pink.

Her eyes focused on the other figure and her heart stood still.

A child, wearing the pink dress. Her Easter dress. Stained now on the front.

Not Sheena, not any of Sheena's friends. It was a girl larger than they, the dress almost too small, as if the girl was growing too fast for it.

She saw the face then, and the cry of shock and surprise burst in silence in her chest. It was herself, her own face, the way it had been once, round and solemn, but the innocence eaten away by something horrible.

Magret whirled.

The girl was standing just inside the bedroom door, the hallway visible behind her, and around her, but not through her. She was not an illusion, a specter, a ghost of the past, a fantasy. She was real, and her face carried such evil that Magret felt herself being destroyed by it. The evil embodiment of herself? Was this what stood before her?

Then she saw what the girl had in her hand.

A pearl-handled knife, edges of the pearl white in the dim light of the bedroom, the blade sharp and long and pointed.

The girl's lips parted, as if she were going to smile, but it was a grimace, a sneer, and as her lips drew back the teeth were revealed.

Magret screamed once, a short, shrill cry. The girl moved, not toward her, but backward, stepping over the threshold into the deeper shadows of the hall.

Magret slammed the door shut.

She leaned against it, her forehead wearily to the cool wood.

SHEENA HEARD THE CRY. She listened, turning her head slowly from the window where she still stood, the damp of the pane cool on her skin.

She crossed the room to the bedroom door, opened it, and went out into the hall. Someone had screamed once, a short, high-pitched cry that even in echo sent long, slow chills over Sheena's body.

Someone was on the landing.

Sheena went forward.

She wasn't alone in the house with her mother, someone else was there.

Sheena moved in silence, hesitantly, wanting to be with the other person, seeking company, protection.

She stopped at the corner.

A girl was standing in the deeper shadows, halfway between the corner and the master bedroom door. She was facing Sheena.

Sheena started to speak, but stopped, her throat feeling tight and strange.

The girl was wearing a pink dress, all ruffly and lacy, a pretty dress, though the front had dark stains. She instantly thought of her mother's pink dress, the one she hadn't seen, the one Magret had slapped her for lying about. The girl was bigger than Sheena, and the dress looked too small. The puffed sleeves were tight on muscular arms. The skirt with the lace and the petticoats came only halfway down on strong legs to the bony knees. She seemed to be growing even as Sheena looked at her.

Fear leaped in Sheena, a sudden and terrible warning that paralyzed her within feet of the girl in the pink dress.

The lips parted, and Sheena saw the needle points of white teeth.

The eyes stared at her like two reflecting marbles, cold and without depth.

She had come here to the house, from the woods.

The master bedroom door jerked open suddenly, behind the girl in pink, and Sheena caught a glimpse of her mother's face, white and ghostly.

"Sheena! Get back! For God's sake, run!"

Sheena was running suddenly, as if her mother's orders had torn the paralysis from her.

She started back toward her room, then realized there was no way out, and swerved around toward the stairs. She felt the cold grip of a hand, and heard the swish of the knife close to her face. She dodged instinctively and kept running, jerking her arm free.

Without looking back she grabbed the newel post at the top of the stairway and swung herself down the stairs. She stumbled on the first step and fell, rolling several steps before her flailing hands once again caught and held to a post and stopped her fall.

Above her was a flurry of movements and colors, of pink and dark blue and white, of her mother's skirt and blouse and the pink dress. She caught a glimpse of light on metal as a knife moved swiftly, darting, snakelike. She saw the pearl handle of the knife as it poised for a moment in the air.

The girl was going to kill her mother.

Ward had been wrong.

Her mother ...

... needed her.

She pulled herself to her feet and ran up the stairs again.

Magret saw Sheena coming back toward her. For just an instant, as her little girl had fallen down the stairs, she had felt relief, that she was out of reach of the horror that Magret was now forced to confront. She hadn't thought of broken bones caused by the fall. It was nothing compared to this horror that she didn't know how to eliminate.

Then Sheena was coming back. Coming back to help her, she realized. With tears and a terrible fear, she screamed again at her child, "Go, Sheena, run, Sheena!"

But the child kept coming, her eyes on the girl in pink.

Magret gave the body of the girl in pink a shove, putting all her strength behind it, and felt the solidity under her hands, and recoiled inwardly from it. The body had a cold, cold feeling, not warm and alive, but cold and horrible. She saw it falling back, its face twisted, the knife coming free from the hand and falling, bouncing across the carpet and through the banister and falling to the foyer below.

Magret whirled away, caught Sheena up into her arms, and ran down the stairs and to the closet with the lock on the door.

She unlocked the door with one hand and literally threw the little girl into the dark closet.

She slammed the door between them and locked it again, hearing on the other side the cries of Sheena as she pounded on the locked door.

Magret turned to face the girl in pink.

Memories of nightmares returned. Of deep, dark forest, tree trunks black and tall, of forest floor and the soil splitting at her feet and rising. A dead infant born again.

She had thought it was her dead baby, buried so long ago. But she was wrong. It was herself, buried there that cold night, the evil that was herself, rising, living in a separate entity.

A girl in pink.

She had reached the bottom of the stairs, and paused there just for a moment.

The knife lay on the floor halfway between them, and Magret made a lunge for it.

She fell to her knees, her palm flat on the floor inches from the knife. The girl leaped, seeming to fly through the air, lifting herself in a kind of horrible slow-motion effortlessness, her arms out, her fingers clawed, her lips spreading back.

Magret felt the weight of her on her back, a heaviness that was too real, that belied her feelings of unreality, of illusion happening.

Magret's fingers grasped the knife, and she twisted and reared up, throwing the girl off.

She brought the knife down, feeling in her own arm a strength she didn't know she possessed. She saw the knife rip through the flesh of the girl's cheek, and felt the cold spray of blood as it hit her own face.

The pounding on the locked closet door, and Sheena's screams, were only a small part of the other sounds that thundered in Magret's head. The roll of her body against the other, on the floor, as Magret fought with her down the hall, as at last it seemed as if the girl were trying to escape.

The voice in Magret's head screamed, *"You can't have her. You can't have my baby."*

Magret pulled herself up from the floor and ran three steps after the girl in pink and clasped her shoulder and felt the pink dress tear. They fell through the swinging door and into the kitchen as Magret slashed with the knife at the girl's face, at her chest, her stomach. The dress came away in shreds from the body that was turning dark red with its own blood.

The girl fell, and Magret went down beside her, feeling the slipperiness of spreading blood, of bright red blood, dark blood, everywhere, it seemed.

She was growing faint. The dizziness ... the fading of her eyes ...

the pain ...

COLLINS HAD DRIVEN without his siren toward the Treacle house, all the time wondering if he should turn it on and try to get there faster. Yet what did he have?

Nothing. Just some weird happenings that defied common sense.

He checked the street signs and turned left. The area was hillier here, homes built on slopes that in summer would be green and lush and well landscaped with shrubs and flowers and trees cared for by professional gardeners. But now the grass was touched with brown, and the trees mostly bare. There was little traffic, and he pressed the accelerator closer to the floor.

He found the number on the post of a fancy mailbox, at the beginning of a wide driveway.

He slowed enough to make the turn.

There was no sign of life anywhere in the area. He drove up a driveway that had lights on brick posts along one side.

When he turned off the engine and got out of the car, he paused, looking around.

The sound of someone screaming reached him, accompanied by a distant pounding.

Muffled sounds, coming from somewhere inside the house.

Collins left his car in a run and crossed the crisp grass of the lawn to the small porch at the front of the house. He tried the door and found it locked. Inside, the screams continued, interspersed with silences, with the continued pounding. It was a child's voice, and she seemed to be screaming the word *mama,* but it was hard to distinguish.

The door was heavy, solid wood, the kind that would probably take an ax to open, and Collins ran down the steps and around the house, drawing his gun from his holster as he ran.

He came to the back, and to sliding glass doors.

They, too, were locked, and through the glass he saw a tile floor, and the furniture of a casual dining or eating area, table, and chairs, with a wall behind that was decorated with odds and ends, copper molds, a clock, other things that to Collins were only the background of an area that contained no visible sign of life.

He left the glass doors. They could be more difficult to enter forcibly than wood doors. He skirted shrubbery, and a flower bed with flowers dead and brown, and came to another set of steps, another door.

He tried the knob and found it locked, too. He pounded on the door, calling out, expecting no answer. The screams of the child were barely audible now.

He tried kicking the door, ready to shoot the lock off if necessary.

The lock gave, the door flew open, and he stumbled into a back hall.

The house was suddenly silent, with only the sound of his footsteps accompanying him along the hall.

He came to the kitchen and stopped.

Magret Treacle lay on the kitchen floor, in a spreading pool of her own blood, her sightless eyes staring up at the ceiling.

Her skirt had been slashed away, and her abdomen hacked to a bloody pulp with the knife she held in her right hand.

The blade was still embedded in her stomach.

Somewhere in the front of the house, the child's voice cried out again, "Mama, help me."

EPILOGUE

"I THOUGHT you might like to take a ride with me to see about an old guy I have to check on once in a while, not only for his good, but for the good of the hikers in Mark Twain Forest." Collins smiled at Lorna, sitting against the door on the passenger side. At first glance it would seem she was trying to get as far away from him as she could, but on second she just looked very relaxed, her elbow on the arm rest, her shoulder against the door.

She nodded, smiling.

It was the first time he had managed to get her to go with him anywhere, but it was a start.

"There's this old guy, see, who thinks the world should be the way it was a hundred years ago. He doesn't own this land, but he thinks no one else has a right on it. Once, he shot over the heads of a group of hikers, and he said he'd never do it again, but I haven't heard from him in a while—"

Actually, it was just an excuse. He was off duty. The car he drove was his own, and Chief, in the back seat, had no mesh between him and the front.

He hadn't really talked to Lorna since the day she had shown him the picture, not enough to explain what little he knew, or to talk about all he didn't know, but wondered about.

"You knew Magret Treacle's case was closed, didn't you?"

"I thought it might be. But ..."

"I see you have your place up for sale, and I'm glad. I don't think there's anything left in those woods, but I'll feel better when you don't live there."

She had told him Islan was leaving soon, and she and Wendy didn't need such a large house. But he knew, in his heart, she must have the same feeling about those woods that he had, a lingering dread. He was glad to know she'd be closer in town.

"The paper said Magret committed suicide. That she killed the others. What do you think?" Lorna asked.

"Daniel Treacle swears she couldn't have killed Leigh, yet he admits he fell asleep and doesn't really know where Magret was. The call woke him. The police at his door. Magret was there, then. With him."

"The pink dress, I read, was on the kitchen floor. The little Easter dress."

"Yes, beneath her. And it was her knives that were the murder weapons. She had put her daughter into the closet, evidently to protect the child. No one could trace any little girl, such as Sheena said was there. There was blood trailing from near the closet door to the kitchen, but it was Magret's own blood." He paused. "We think, we're pretty sure, it was Magret's baby buried in the woods near the church. And it's my idea that the baby belonged to Clyde Judson."

"Sheena said there was a little girl there?"

"Yes." Collins shifted slightly in his seat. "On a happier note now—the Treacles have all gone south for the winter. I think they plan to lose themselves on an island somewhere for a year or so. I hope it works. They've all had a bad time."

They rode in silence.

Lorna said, "But it wasn't the adult Magret, Collins, who did the killing. Sheena saw a girl. And so did I. I was there, with Ward, and I saw the... *girl.* Sheena was right. Peggy was right. There was a growing girl. Magret, nine, ten, eleven years old again. Something—that looked like Magret used to. Peggy saw her, Wendy saw her, Ward saw her. And Sheena. And so did I. Maybe you find it unbelievable. I think I would too."

Collins said nothing. On the record the killer was Magret Treacle, thirty-five years old, and the motive was the infant buried so many years ago. A kind of story had been pieced together. The murdered uncle and Clyde Judson both had connections to Magret's baby. The aunt was too closely connected with the uncle. She must have known something about it.

The daughter? Leigh?

On the official level, in the various reports, it was dismissed as something only the killer understood.

And in truth it was something nobody understood.

OTHER NOVELS BY RUBY JEAN

1974 The House that Samael Built
1974 Seventh All Hallows' Eve
1974 House at River's Bend
1975 The Girl Who Didn't Die
1978 Child of Satan's House
1978 Satan's Sister
1978 Dark Angel
1982 Hear the Children Cry
1982 Such a Good Baby
1983 The Lake
1983 MaMa
1985 Home Sweet Home
1985 Best Friends
1986 Wait and See
1987 Annabelle
1987 Chain Letter
1988 Smoke
1988 House of Illusions
1988 Jump Rope
1989 Pendulum
1989 Death Stone

OTHER NOVELS BY RUBY JEAN

1990 Vampire Child
1990 Lost and Found
1990 Victoria
1991 Celia
1991 Baby Dolly
1992 The Reckoning
1993 The Living Evil
1994 The Haunting
1995 Night Thunder
Pending Bear Hollow Charlie
Pending Cry of the Soul
Pending Pride of Bella Terra
Pending Animal Backtalk

www.ingramcontent.com/pod-product-compliance
Lightning Source LLC
Chambersburg PA
CBHW020609310726
48979CB00008B/1410/J
* 9 7 8 1 9 5 1 5 8 0 6 5 0 *